Daniel Cole (@DanielColeBooks) is the *Sunday Times* bestselling author of the *Ragdoll* trilogy, which has now been published in over thirty countries and is currently being adapted for TV. He has worked as a paramedic, an animal protection officer and with the RNLI lifeguards, but for the past five years has been describing himself on paperwork as a 'full-time writer'. *Mimic* is his fourth novel.

He lives on the south coast of England and divides his time between the beach and the forest.

Also by Daniel Cole

Ragdoll
Hangman
Endgame

MIMIC

DANIEL COLE

ORION

First published in Great Britain in 2021 by Orion Fiction
an imprint of The Orion Publishing Group Ltd
Carmelite House, 50 Victoria Embankment
London EC4Y 0DZ

An Hachette UK Company

1 3 5 7 9 10 8 6 4 2

Text and illustrations copyright © Daniel Cole 2021
Illustrations by Alexandra Limon

A CIP catalogue record for this book is
available from the British Library.

ISBN (Hardback) 978 1 4091 9800 0
ISBN (Export Trade Paperback) 978 1 4091 9801 7
ISBN (eBook) 978 1 4091 9803 1
ISBN (Audio) 978 1 4091 9804 8

Printed in Great Britain by Clays Ltd, Elcograf S.p.A

www.orionbooks.co.uk

The Day
Death Came Visiting

And so, the old man returned home to find Death slumbering in his chair, having come for him at last. But, thought the old man, is Death not merely another foe? A foe both weary and alone?

So, stepping lightly over the robes that spilled across his floor like rivers of tar, he searched his little house for a blade and then, with the stealth of Death himself, crept back over to his sleeping guest. Drunk on the desire to live forever, the old man raised his hands high and then drove them down hard, sinking the knife deep into the ashen insides. But he had done little more than awoken Death, who rose up to tower over the whimpering man, more vengeful and cruel than ever and unconcerned by the blade still embedded in the chair.

'You mean to evade me?' laughed Death. 'You need but ask. Rest assured, you shall *never* feel my mercy. For only the living can suffer as you will.'

And with that, Death showed himself out.

He had much to do.

Almost seven years to the day, Death returned to the tiny cottage to find the old man slumbering in his chair, a familiar knife resting in his lap.

So, stepping lightly over the blood that spilled across his

floor like crimson ribbons, *D*eath took hold of his wrinkled arms. On feeling the chill of his grasp, the old man stirred, eyes flooding with tears as he regarded his healed wounds.

'Please!' he cried. 'Have you not already taken everything from me? Have I not suffered enough?'

Amused, his visitor leaned over to whisper in his ear:

'No, my old friend . . . Not yet.'

And with that, *D*eath showed himself out.

For he still had much to do.

Thursday 2 February

1989

CHAPTER 1

The indicators clicked loudly, shapes illuminating and then being reclaimed by shadow, as though an unseen audience were sparking matches in the darkness. When a lanky silhouette waved him down, Detective Sergeant Benjamin Chambers turned the wheel into Hyde Park. The figure hurried over to open the gate, the dark green of the *Parks Department* jacket catching in the headlights as he struggled with the lock. Tackling the frozen metal barehanded, his guide gestured for him to follow as he jogged ahead on foot.

Chambers stifled a yawn, put the car in gear and set off along the untreated service road, hearing the change in pitch as wet concrete gave way to compacted ice.

'Don't run him over . . . Don't run him over,' he muttered under his breath, not at all confident the car would stop should his escort decide to, the wheels spinning more and more regularly, the deeper they ventured into the sprawling London park.

Suddenly, the man in front lost his footing, disappearing somewhere beneath the bonnet in time to a concerning thud. The brakes juddered underfoot as the car slid to a leisurely stop.

Chambers winced, leaning forward in his seat and watching the end of the bonnet anxiously . . .

But then a cheerful face popped up between the headlights, an illuminated name badge proudly declaring its owner: *Deano*.

'Sorry!' the man waved, getting back to his feet.

'*You're* sorry?!' Chambers called back incredulously, shaking his head.

'It's just up past those trees!' shouted Deano, not learning his lesson as he assumed his position three precarious steps ahead of the car.

Reluctantly, Chambers started the vehicle rolling again. Keeping his distance, he eventually parked up beside a patrol car, two uni-formed officers inside sheltering from the cold wind that rushed in the moment he pulled on the handle. He gritted his teeth and climbed out, bundling his coat up around his neck as his Parks Department guide regarded him with surprise.

'Never met a black detective before,' he informed Chambers, who took the inane comment in his stride.

'First time for everything. Although, if you ask me, I am in fact a very, very, *very* dark brown,' he replied sarcastically, already scan-ning the vicinity for a body.

Deano chuckled: 'So you are. Guess that's why you're the detective.'

'Guess so,' replied Chambers, frowning now, seeing only an assemblage of footprints encircling the stone base of a statue. 'It's *all* in the details . . . details like: where's this dead body I'm meant to be looking at?'

At that moment, a car door slammed: one of the uniformed officers finally working up the nerve to head back outside. With dirty-blond slicked-back hair, he was a good decade younger than Chambers: twenty-one years old at most. Pocketing the remainder of a chocolate bar, he made his way over to shake the detective's hand.

'DS Chambers?' he asked with a South London twang. 'Adam Winter. And that . . .' he gestured to his partner, a Viking-like tree trunk of a woman who had begrudgingly followed him out, 'is Reilly.' The other officer nodded curtly and then returned to the matter of not freezing to death. 'We've actually met before,' Winter told him, 'on that jumper job.'

Chambers nodded: 'With the . . .'

'Thing.'

'And the . . .'

'Thing.'

'I remember.'

The conversation paused when a bitter gust of wind blew through the trees, both men needing a moment to compose themselves.

'*Jesus Christ*,' complained Winter, shaking off the chill.

'So, I was told you'd found a body under a statue,' said Chambers casually, pretty sure he'd had a wasted drive. 'It's like Chinese whispers that control room,' he joked, in no way pointing blame at the young constable – *he had enough enemies as it was.*

'No kidding,' replied Winter, directing him over to add his footprints to the dozens already stamped into the grass. '*Errrm* . . . The body isn't *under* the statue . . . The body *is* the statue.'

Chambers raised his eyebrows sceptically and then looked up to the ice-coated figure perched ten feet above them atop a stone pedestal.

'First noticed by a jogger at about eleven-thirty.'

Chambers glanced down at his watch.

'. . . a.m,' Winter clarified. 'Eleven-thirty *a.m.*'

Now even more confused, Chambers took a few steps back to better appreciate the scene. He squinted up at what he was still reasonably confident was a weather-worn piece of art: completely naked upon a rough stone slab, a muscular male figure sat with his chin resting on his right knuckle, as if deep in thought. In the exposed areas, windswept icicles covered the skin like fur; in the more sheltered, it was an inhuman blueish hue.

Chambers looked unconvinced as Winter continued:

'Said she'd passed these statues a hundred times without really noticing them, but this time something felt different. She let it play on her mind all day until coming back this evening and realising that, *yeah*, something wasn't right: first and foremost – it was a frozen corpse.'

'It's meant to have been here *all day*?' asked Chambers, moving around the base to find a better position. 'And *no one* else noticed?'

'Would you?'

'. . . Still haven't,' he conceded, squinting up at it.

'I'm thinking,' piped up Winter's intimidating colleague, whose name he'd already forgotten, 'we can put this down as "bizarre way of committing suicide" number seven million and one. It's pretty common in the parks. But then, what do *I* know? That's for *you* to decide in your infinite wisdom.'

The woman clearly had an issue with him, but Chambers was both too cold and too tired to rise to it.

'Sorry about her,' said Winter, shaking his head at his partner. 'She's a delight when you get to know her though, aren't you, Kim?' he called, receiving a middle finger back in response.

'Have you been up there?' Chambers asked him.

'Wouldn't want to contaminate the scene,' Winter smiled back, playing his *get out of jail free* card impeccably. 'Plus, you know, we figured he wasn't going anywhere.'

Chambers let out a frozen sigh: 'Can't do a lot without a lad—'

'There's one built into the base,' an eavesdropping Deano informed him helpfully. 'Round the back.'

Winter made no effort to conceal the smirk on his face. Chambers, meanwhile, looked as though he might cry.

'. . . Great.'

The fifteen-rung ascension had felt far longer, the biting wind building strength with every inch he climbed as Chambers scrambled onto the pedestal's flat summit, his pocket torch clamped between his teeth.

With its broad back facing him, the figure appeared as inanimate and perfect as it had from the ground. Carefully crawling across the ice to reach it, he removed the flashlight from his mouth, tracing the beam along the form's opaque glaze, still uncertain as to what he was looking at . . . until he came across the crease in the statue's elbow: a wrinkled area of blue skin – but unquestionably skin. Even though a part of him had been expecting it, Chambers was startled and dropped the torch, which rolled off the podium and twisted through the air like a falling star.

'Shit,' he whispered, a little embarrassed.

'Everything OK up there?' Winter shouted up.

'Fine!' he called back, tentatively getting up onto his knees to look at the frozen face by the light of the moon:

He was handsome – movie-star handsome – flawless. *Perhaps he was an actor*, thought Chambers. It would certainly align with the attention-craving mindset required to climb up naked onto a podium and strike a pose until one went solid.

Growing more confident in his footing, Chambers stood upright, leaning in close to see whether there were any identifying marks or features, his face mere inches from the statue's, his misting breath reflecting off the shiny skin.

Something wasn't right . . . Something he couldn't quite put his finger on . . . *Something about the eyes perhaps?* Icy blue . . . Intense . . . Piercing . . . Not the glassy gaze of a vacant vessel.

He stared into them, transfixed . . . when a hand grasped out at him.

Instinctively staggering backwards, Chambers tore his arm from its grip and felt himself fall, the sharp intake of breath he took on the way down robbed from him the moment he hit the ground.

'Detective!' shouted Winter, the first to rush over.

'He . . .' Chambers wheezed, looking up at the night sky. 'He . . .'

'What? I can't understand you. Just stay still!' Winter turned to his partner: 'Call an ambulance!' Chambers attempted to sit up. 'Please, sir. Stay still!'

'He's . . . He's still . . . alive!' gasped Chambers, lying back down and struggling to breathe as the others' horrified expressions manifested into a frenzy of activity.

And all the while, he just lay there, unable to do anything more than stare up at the twinkling stars and the tragic, yet surreally beautiful, figure above him.

Winter had draped his jacket over the immovable man's shoulders, an act of kindness akin to hurling a sponge at a tsunami. They'd attempted to move him but found the majority of his joints locked in place, the awkward positioning thwarting any aspiration of lifting him down unaided. And so, Winter had remained up there beside him, a muttered monologue of reassurances and insincere promises filling the time until a procession of blue lights followed Deano through the trees.

Chambers was back on his feet just in time to move out of the way. Using a cherry picker, two firefighters covered the frozen man in blankets before lifting him off his slab and onto a wheelchair, their patient's pose barely altering. The moment they'd rattled back to earth, they handed him over to the paramedics, who rushed him straight into the ambulance.

'Hope you weren't planning on sleeping for the next six months,' quipped Winter, joining Chambers to watch as the ambulance crew struggled to attach their equipment. 'Think I *royally* screwed up tonight.'

Chambers didn't respond. He actually quite liked the over-talkative officer, but it was difficult to argue with his accurate self-evaluation.

'I mean, we were here a good hour before you,' continued Winter. 'I should've gone up there . . . shouldn't I?'

Chambers turned to him. Being both older and wiser, it felt one of those perfect moments to bestow an invaluable pearl of wisdom for the young man to carry for years to come: '. . . Yep.'

Winter was clearly beating himself up over it but moved the conversation on nonetheless: 'No sign of a struggle?'

'Not that I could see.'

'Who'd do something like that to themselves?'

Chambers opened his mouth to answer, when there was a commotion from the back of the ambulance:

'Paddles!'

A monotonic tone rang out over the clearing as the crowd of emergency-service personnel watched helplessly.

'Clear!'

'Shocking!'

The body barely flinched, despite the surge of electricity coursing through it.

'No pulse!'

'Charging!'

While the others watched the inevitable events unfold, Chambers turned his back on the futile resuscitation efforts and returned to the empty podium.

'So, what are you thinking?' asked Winter, following him down, '. . . Detective Chambers?'

'Who'd do something like that to themselves?' he mumbled in reply, still lost in thought as he stalked the footprints around the large stone base. 'It's extreme. No doubt. And yet, feels a little . . .' he struggled to find the correct word while the man they were discussing was dying just twenty metres away, '. . . non-committal.'

'Non-committal?' asked Winter, sounding only moderately appalled.

'That jogger could've called it in twelve hours ago,' reasoned Chambers, looking into the dark trees as if there might have been someone there. 'Things could've been very different.'

'True.'

'And why here?' he continued. 'It's on show, but it's also shielded by trees on most sides and ten feet up in the air. If the idea was to go out in a blaze of glory, why not climb Nelson's Column or do it somewhere a little more public at least?'

'. . . Non-committal,' said Winter, watching the detective in fascination.

'Non-committal,' Chambers nodded, finally tearing himself away from the trees.

As the final token chest compressions slowed to a stop, Winter sighed: 'Guess he got what he wanted regardless.'

'Actually,' said Chambers, kneeling down to more closely examine a set of footprints, 'I'm not so sure he did.'

Friday

CHAPTER 2

'Detective? . . . Detective?' Chambers awoke with a start, grasping a fistful of the woman's lab coat and staring up at her wild-eyed. '*Woah! Woah!*' said Dr Sykes, New Scotland Yard's Head Medical Examiner.

After taking a moment to absorb his insipid surroundings, he let go of the doctor and rubbed his face: 'Sorry.'

'No harm done,' smiled Sykes, who was probably only a year or two from retirement and could do without being assaulted first thing in the morning. 'Long night?'

'You could say that,' Chambers replied, habitually economical with his words.

'Are you finishing soon?'

He glanced at his watch: '. . . Two hours ago.'

Sykes raised her eyebrows: 'How about we get you some coffee?'

Having officially assumed responsibility of the patient, the ambulance crew had followed protocol and transported the thawing body back to St Mary's Hospital, meaning that Chambers had wasted the remainder of his shift trying to get it moved to the forensic lab for testing. Eventually successful, he had fallen asleep in one of the plastic chairs out in the corridor until being woken by the very person he'd been waiting to see.

'I've got a backlog already,' said Sykes between sips of her coffee.

'London's been especially kill-y this past week.'

'Take a look at the file. That's all I ask.'

'Detective, I—'

'Just take a look.'

Clearly exasperated, the medical examiner placed her cup down to pick up the photocopied incident report and corresponding ambulance form, brow furrowing as she scanned the first page.

'It's a strange one. I'll give you that,' the doctor conceded after reading it in its entirety. 'And you suspect foul play?'

'Just a hunch.'

'I can't prioritise a hunch,' Sykes told him, placing the documents in her lap while she awaited an explanation.

'I . . .' Chambers hesitated. He hadn't fully organised his own thoughts yet. 'There were dozens of footprints at the scene, not one of which was barefooted. I've had officers scouring the area all night and searching nearby rubbish bins. No shoes or clothing have been recovered.'

'According to your report, he'd been there at least twelve hours. That's plenty of time for footprints to be disturbed or fade entirely, including the warmest part of the day. Did it get above freezing at any point yesterday?'

'Barely.'

The doctor shrugged as if to say: Well, there you go then.

'I can't see him walking naked *that* far into a London park unnoticed.'

'Stranger things have happened,' said Sykes, who seemed to be rather enjoying her role as Devil's advocate.

'OK. It's possible.'

'Could he have buried his clothing somewhere?'

Chambers was about to dismiss the theory but then decided it was actually a very good point. He leaned back in his chair and rubbed his weary face again, feeling as though he were fighting a losing battle.

'OK. OK,' said Sykes. 'I'll take a look at him this morning. Go home.

Get some rest. Give me a call around lunchtime.'

Chambers gave her an exhausted smile: 'I owe you one.'

Foolishly, Chambers had thought it a good idea to stop by his desk on his way out of the building, having failed to reach it all shift. He walked into the office to discover that someone had put the department's tired Christmas decorations to good use by placing a five-foot snowman on his chair before covering his computer in a blanket of cotton wool. Expectant faces broke into communal laughter as he opened his top drawer to find it too overflowing with fake snow. Fixing a smile in place, he nodded along like a good sport, despite the extent of the mess feeling borderline malicious.

'*Duck. Duck. Duck*,' warned DI Graham Lewis, once his softly-spoken training officer, now one of the few friends he had left. 'Boss's looking for you.'

Chambers crouched behind the tatty snowman while Lewis smiled pleasantly:

'Morning, Boss.'

'Don't be such a kiss-arse, Lewis.'

'Very good, sir . . . OK. He's gone.'

Stepping back out, Chambers gestured to his desk: 'I take it you heard?'

Lewis nodded: 'You know this place: word travels fast.' He hesitated, it seemingly always falling to him to be the bearer of bad news, experience pre-empting the bureaucratic shitstorm about to rain down on his friend. 'You went up to check the body the *moment* you deemed it safe to do so. Whatever you do, don't say "you thought he was dead" or "he looked dead" or anything along those lines. Heads are going to roll for this and Hamm will be swinging for yours. Now get out of here before he—'

'Chambers!'

'Shit,' whispered Lewis.

'Yes, Boss?' Chambers called across the room, his colleagues wearing the same smirks of anticipation they had as he'd approached his workstation wonderland.

'My office! Now!'

'The *moment* you deemed it safe to do so,' Lewis reminded him quietly.

DCI Hamm had only been in the role for eighteen months, a short enough time to still be considered 'one of the boys' by his employ of close friends and former contemporaries, past loyalties deterring any criticism of his blatant favouritism and questionable promotion criteria. Hamm had, however, had the sense to ease up on his vocal dislike and offensive behaviour towards Chambers since assuming the position, which had only served to make his attacks less predictable.

'Sit.' Chambers did as he was told. 'So . . . What the *fuck*?'

'It's all in the report, *sir*.' Chambers winced, he hadn't meant it to come out so sarcastic. 'I arrived on scene, where the situation was explained to me. The moment I deemed it safe to do so, I climbed up to reach the victim.'

'Victim?' scoffed Hamm, chomping on the gum that seemed to perpetually reside inside his mouth. '"No sign of trauma" and just sitting there like that; he *clearly* did this to himself. That's like me calling my fat arse a "victim" of my love of KFC.'

'The "deceased" then,' said Chambers. 'I ascertained that he was still alive at that point and immediately requested an ambulance.'

'*Uh-huh*,' said Hamm, eyes bulging as he watched his subordinate for any sign of weakness or doubt.

'With all due respect, *sir*,' Chambers winced again: he had to stop adding that, 'I clocked off two-and-a-half hours ago. I'm spent.'

After a childish attempt to stare him down, Hamm waved him away dismissively: 'Go on then.'

Getting up, Chambers reached for the door handle.

'One last thing,' blurted Hamm, stopping him in his tracks. 'What was your opinion of this Constable Winter?'

Chambers' face dropped. Clearly the management wanted their pound of flesh.

He forced an impassive expression and then turned back to his boss: 'Who?'

'Adam Winter. He's named in your report as the first officer on scene,' said Hamm, lifting the file off the desk.

'*Ah*. Joint first,' said Chambers. 'He had his partner with him.'

'Irrelevant. It was Winter's job . . . So?'

Chambers quickly considered his limited options:

'Incompetent,' he replied harshly. 'I've a good mind to submit my own complaint about him. Typical wannabe detective – unable to get past his own ego long enough to even manage the basics. I strongly suggest you see he loses his job over this mess.'

Hamm appeared a little surprised by his impassioned reaction: 'Do you now?'

'I do . . . *sir*.' That one was intentional.

'Well, I'll certainly take your advice on board. You may leave now.'

Chambers nodded and closed the door behind him, hoping that his damning opinion of a fellow officer might convince his chief to make the right call.

At 10.35 a.m. Chambers stumbled through the door of his Camden loft apartment. An unfortunate but conveniently timed inheritance, providing him a helpful leg-up on the inflated London property ladder. He made his way into the kitchen, disorientated stomach rumbling with hunger, to find a note stuck to the fridge door:

Had to go.
Sleep well.
E X

He smiled and took the note down, pausing when he went to drop it in the bin, feeling irrationally guilty for destroying anything that Eve had given him, no matter how inconsequential. Opening a drawer, he tucked it beneath the instruction booklets for the microwave and answering machine, where she would hopefully never find it.

'What's happening to you?' he chastised himself, raiding the fridge for leftovers before heading into the bedroom.

He had only just removed his shirt and finished brushing his teeth when the phone started to ring. In his exhausted state, he'd forgotten to unplug it from the wall. Looking longingly at his bed, he walked back through to the hallway and picked up the receiver:

'Yes?'

'Detective? This is Charlotte Sykes . . . from work.'

'Oh. Hi,' said Chambers, wondering how the medical examiner had managed to get hold of his number.

'I'm sorry to disturb you at home. We can talk later if you'd prefer?'

'No. It's fine,' he yawned, stretching his free arm up to grasp the wooden beam above his head.

'I just thought you'd want to know sooner rather than later that you were absolutely right.'

'Right?'

'Your hunch. Because there's physically no *possible* way that this man could have killed himself . . . Someone did this *to* him.'

Chambers rubbed his stinging eyes. He was so tired: 'I'll be there as soon as I can.'

CHAPTER 3

Chambers had dozed off on the Tube and missed his stop. Frustrated with himself, he got off at Victoria and made his way on foot through the frozen city – streets sullied with dirty grit, the wind – river-chilled and lost amid a maze of grey buildings. After passing through security at New Scotland Yard, he was met with an enquiring look from Lewis, who rushed across the lobby to intercept him.

'What are you doing back here again?' he asked in exasperation. 'Get out! Boss's looking for you.'

'Again?' complained Chambers.

'Yes. *Again.* Go home.'

'Can't. I'll stay out of his way though.'

Shaking his head, Lewis stepped aside to allow his friend past.

In a tactical but energy-sapping move, Chambers had taken the stairs. It wasn't only DCI Hamm he needed to avoid but his entire network of tattletale subordinates. Checking the coast was clear, he hurried down the forensic corridor and knocked on the door at the far end, his face dropping the moment he crossed the threshold.

'Shit.'

'Shit indeed,' Hamm concurred, abandoning his conversation with Dr Sykes to square up to Chambers. 'Got an overtime query through after you left. *Apparently*, two technicians were instructed to transport a *non-urgent* body across the city minutes before the end of their shift.' Chambers opened his mouth, but Hamm cut him off: 'At which point, I said: "That can't be right. None of *my* detectives would be *stupid* or *disrespectful* enough to do something like that without my approval." Right, Chambers?'

'I didn't design their rota . . . *sir*,' he replied, lack of sleep shortening his fuse. 'They have a job to do. I asked them to do it.'

In a demonstration of his unsuitability for the position, Hamm gave Chambers a sharp shove. He then moved in uncomfortably close despite being half-a-foot shorter than the tall detective: 'Do you want to get yourself suspended right here, right now?'

'. . . No, sir.'

'Boys! Boys! Boys!' snapped Sykes, the matriarchal woman quite terrifying when she wanted to be.

Still glaring at Chambers, Hamm stepped back: 'Then, I find out you've got our head medical examiner working on your bullshit suicide case rather than the *four* murder investigations we picked up yesterday alone!'

Chambers calmly wiped the spittle from his face: '. . . Five.'

'What was that?'

'Five murder investigations,' Chambers corrected him, glancing over at Sykes.

'He's right,' the doctor backed him up. 'And due to the . . . *state* of the body, we had to move quickly. Every degree it thaws, the more evidence we risk losing.'

Hamm's furious expression endured, but it was clear that the doctor's assessment had smothered some of his fire. He turned to Chambers: 'Go behind my back again, *boy*, and I'll *fucking* end you . . . Understood?'

'Yes, sir.'

On that note, Hamm stormed out, leaving Chambers and Sykes alone with the body. They moved either side of the metal table, the man's icy glaze now replaced with mottled freeze burns, two fingers on the left hand blackened from the joint up.

'Frostbite,' Sykes explained when she noticed Chambers looking. 'I suppose it goes without saying that he was suffering with critical hypothermia by the time you reached him, his organs barely functioning sufficiently to sustain life. Then the ambulance crew got involved, warmed him up *far* too quickly and his system couldn't handle it.' She huffed. 'Probably wouldn't have made a difference anyway. I need to show you something. Help me roll him over.'

Donning disposable gloves, they struggled to lift the heavy corpse enough to reveal the red dot at the nape of its neck.

'See the puncture mark?' asked Sykes rhetorically, as she'd already given up supporting her share of the weight. 'He'd been injected with something . . . a bit of an unpleasant cocktail from the looks of it. I'm still trying to sort out what's what. What could be attributed to diet pills, protein supplements or steroid abuse. An admittedly judgemental but educated guess based on the sheer size of him.'

'Makes sense,' agreed Chambers.

'One thing that most certainly *shouldn't* have been in his system, however, was significant levels of pancuronium bromide.'

Chambers looked understandably blank.

'It's used in surgeries where they require the patient alert but can't risk the smallest chance of movement. It's impossible to even estimate how much he was given without a definitive time frame and considering the extreme temperatures involved.'

'He definitely couldn't have administered it himself?' asked Chambers.

'There's no mention of a needle or vial being found at the scene, and I don't think he'd realistically have had the control of his limbs required to throw it any distance. It's my impression that the victim would have been in an almost dreamlike state – awake but completely malleable, maintaining just enough residual muscle tone to hold whatever position his killer decided to put him in.'

'Then walk away and leave him to freeze to death. That's twisted.'

'We don't tend to get many happy stories down here,' shrugged Sykes. 'Know who he is yet?'

'Not yet. Gyms and leisure centres seemed like a good place to start though.' Noticing something, Chambers crouched down to more closely inspect the corpse's right knuckle: the raw wound unlike the others adorning the frost-damaged skin.

'Glue,' Sykes told him, pre-empting the question. 'Similar marks beneath the chin, on the left forearm, knee and both buttocks. Crude but . . .' She trailed off. 'So, first impressions?'

'Suspect's male . . . probably. Strong enough to move two-hundred-and-fifty pounds of this guy around anyway. Feels personal: shaming him, stripping him naked, placing him on display like that, the cruelty of leaving him there to suffer. It was premeditated . . . organised . . . and yet impassioned.'

Sykes nodded in agreement: 'Guess we can only hope he doesn't have any other enemies out there.' When Chambers turned to the doctor with a troubled expression, she smiled back awkwardly: 'Just saying.'

'The next station is High Barnet, where this train will terminate. All change, please. All change.'

Chambers peered vacantly to his left and then quizzically to his right along the length of the deserted carriage: 'Oh, cock.'

Eventually emerging from the lift at Camden Town, Chambers looked down at his watch, dismayed to discover that he had only four hours and ten minutes before his alarm would be getting him up for work again. Feeling painfully hungry, he made a beeline for KFC; for some reason, he'd been having cravings ever since talking to the boss that morning.

Armed with a Bargain Bucket, he found a park bench to dine on so that Eve wouldn't smell it in the flat and lecture him again about his ever-increasing waistline. Halfway through his feast, he realised he'd been staring out over the frozen pond while his food went cold, mind still on the job, his thoughts in the company of thawing corpses and empty podiums. He glanced over his shoulder at the phone box, shook his head, and shoved some more chips into his mouth, resolute on not giving in . . .

'I hate myself,' he muttered, dropping a half-eaten leg back into the bucket as he walked over to squeeze into the cramped red booth. One-handed, he picked up the receiver, clumsily dialling the number for the department: 'It's Chambers. Put me through to whoever's working on my iceman case today,' he said, filling the ensuing pause with another mouthful of chips. 'Yeah, where are we at with IDing our vic? . . . *Uh-huh*. Well, stick with it. Have we still got anyone at the park? . . . Good. Tell them to restart the search, this time looking for needles, vials, anything medical . . . I know. You can blame me. We also need to find anywhere that supplies a drug named pancuronium bromide . . . No, pancu— I'll spell it.'

With the phone in one hand, his Bargain Bucket in the other, he attempted to retrieve the notebook from his pocket, throwing the remainder of his chicken extremities all over the floor.

'Bastard! . . . Not you. I dropped my breakfast . . . dinner? I don't even know any more. It's P.A.N.C.U.R.O.N.I.U.M. Got that? . . . Last thing, I need you to find out who looks after the statues in that park. Why was that base empty? Have they got the sculpture? Did the killer make off with it? We need to know . . . That's it for now . . . Yeah, seven o'clock. OK. Bye.'

Crouching down to scoop the Kontaminated Floor Chicken back into the bucket, he couldn't help glancing at his watch again – three hours, forty-five minutes now.

At 6.37 p.m. Chambers stepped off the Tube at Embankment as intended and set off on the short walk to New Scotland Yard. Having successfully negotiated the underground network this time, he was feeling particularly smug with himself but no more rested than when he'd left earlier in the day. Between forgetting to unplug the phone again, a fire alarm going off in the building opposite, and a pair of Jehovah's Witnesses, who came a hell of a lot closer to witnessing Jehovah than they'd probably realised, the impracticalities of resting through the daytime had got the better of him. Giving up, he'd sprinkled a few salad leaves across the top of the bin and, before leaving, written Eve a note which he stuck to the fridge – these scrawled clusters of words their only form of communication when he hit a run of nightshifts like this.

'Henry John Dolan,' a young detective constable announced as Chambers removed Frosty the Snowman from his chair. 'Our victim. Fitness instructor, backing dancer, and minor celebrity. No doubt you'll remember his turn as "Muscle Man Five" in that episode of *Minder*?'

'Oh, *that* Henry John Dolan!' replied Chambers, tongue-in-cheek.

'I'm interviewing the girlfriend tomorrow. No luck on the needles or vials though.'

'What about the statues?' Chambers asked her, swearing under his breath as he stuffed a drawer-full of cotton wool into the bin.

'Complicated. This one seems to come under Royal Parks *and* the City Council, who outsource the work to private firms.' The constable handed him a scrap of paper. 'Someone'll be there until eleven, should you fancy paying them a visit.'

Looking down at the address, Chambers nodded: 'I might just do that.'

From the outside, Sleepe & Co. Restoration and Conservation Solutions didn't look the most fitting establishment to be housing some of the country's most prized works of art – just an anonymous roller door built into the old railway arches off Hackney high street. Picking an arbitrary spot, Chambers knocked loudly to make himself heard over the radio blaring inside. He looked up at the obvious camera above the door and then noticed two others nearby as the music went quiet.

'Who is it, please?' a voice called.

'Detective Sergeant Benjamin Chambers with the Metropolitan Police.'

'Have you got identification?'

'Yes.'

'Hold it up to the camera, please.'

Rolling his eyes, Chambers produced his ID card and held it above his head.

'Closer, please.'

Muttering, he stretched his arm out further, standing on tiptoes, when suddenly the metal door rattled open to reveal the strange little man behind. He must have been in his fifties and had the appearance of a cyclops – one eye enlarged by the magnifying glass suspended from a leather headband. He had a monk's hairline and was wearing an oily apron that was almost as grubby as his hands and face.

'Sorry. Can't be too careful,' said the man, peering anxiously up and down the street before gesturing for him to enter. He then closed and relocked the door behind them. 'Tobias Sleepe,' he introduced himself, regarding Chambers with interest.

Inside, the industrial unit was moodily lit. Four grand statues stood upon wooden plinths, spotlights positioned above each of them as if displayed in a gallery, their size intimidating within such an intimate setting. Chambers strolled between them, taking in the subtle details: the intricate creases adding movement to bronze clothing, the all-too familiar lines etched into world-weary faces, and looked forward to getting home to tell Eve that he finally 'got art . . . or whatever'.

'You work here alone?' Chambers asked while casually walking a lap of the space, noticing the assorted tools laid out across a work-station, a discoloured pill pot covered in red warnings, and the simple pulley system erected in the centre of the room, its empty rope hanging like an expectant noose.

'The past thirty-two years.'

'Heavy work, I bet,' he commented conversationally.

'Not if you've got the right tools,' replied the man without taking his eyes off his wandering guest.

'And you live here?'

'Sometimes . . . That will be enough personal questions, thank you.'

Chambers smiled, walking back over to join him: 'Sorry, always did want to do something creative. I digress. The Hyde Park statue: which one is it?'

The man turned his back on him and the four illuminated sculptures, heading instead for a darkened corner of the room. Chambers tensed up as he watched Sleepe pass the workstation covered in tools. But then, pulling an old cloth to the floor, he revealed a statue of a man riding a horse, whose right arm looked to have been smashed off. Both the rider and the horse's eyes had been scratched out, and one of the animal's legs lay broken in a box beside it.

'Vandalism,' Sleepe announced. 'It's a strange thing that the very worst aspects of the human condition are what keeps me in a job . . . Well,' he chuckled, 'just look who I'm talking to. I'm interested: I suppose, like me, you think of what you do as a calling . . . your purpose in life?'

Chambers remained silent.

'So, let's say one day all your hard work pays off,' Sleepe continued regardless. 'The world miraculously turns into a nice place, that fabled utopia we've all been striving for . . . What would your purpose be then, Detective? . . . Huh? Here's hoping we continue our collective fall from grace for all time . . . for both our sakes.'

The two men stood in silence for a moment, the statues' blind eyes watching everything.

Clearing his throat, Chambers asked: 'You retrieved the statue yourself?'

'I did.'

'When?'

'Monday . . . Morning.'

'And . . . who is it?'

'The sculpture? I believe it's a lesser known depiction of The Duke of Wellington.'

'Do they routinely remove statues from the parks for repair?'

'Almost never, and only as a last resort. But when they realised the horse's leg was missing, it was deemed unsafe and they requested I remove it immediately.'

'Was the arm recovered? I'm only seeing a leg.'

'No. Nor the sword.'

Chambers looked confused.

'It was holding a sword,' explained Sleepe.

'And is anyone currently looking into who did this?'

'I expect it will be dismissed as "petty vandalism" as per usual . . . It's not like it's a dead body, is it?'

Chambers frowned and watched the man for a moment – watched the peculiar little grin that he'd fixed upon his face:

'Don't touch this again. I'll have forensics round first thing to dust for prints.'

Now it was Sleepe's turn to watch Chambers closely:

'It would appear the Metropolitan Police are taking vandalism rather more seriously these days.'

Chambers met his eye, giving nothing away: 'On this occasion, yes. Yes, we are.'

Tuesday

CHAPTER 4

The Tower of London seldom managed to sneak up on anybody, but Chambers was a little surprised to see it through the driver's-side window as he realised he was in the wrong lane. He'd been rolling through the city on autopilot, his mind too preoccupied with their stalling investigation to worry about the angry honks as he cut someone up.

They'd learned that the work order for the statue had been submitted four days before its eventual removal, a strip of yellow tape, which had promptly blown away in the wind, holding the fort until then. Working off the assumption that the killer was responsible for the damage, it also seemed fair to assume he'd been returning to the park on a regular basis in the hope of finding his chosen spot now vacant. Officers had spoken with all the local homeless, the Park's Department staff and every dog walker they'd come across. They had also retrieved the tapes from every security camera providing a view of the park – all to no avail.

The same could be said for the victim, Henry John Dolan, who'd attended his regular gym session on the evening before his murder. A creature of habit, he'd also made it to his nearby Applegood Health Food Market on the way home, according to a receipt found in his rubbish. This still left them with a fourteen-hour time frame to work with between leaving the store, arriving home and first being spotted by the jogger.

None of the hospitals they'd contacted thus far had reported any unusual shortfalls in their stocks of pancuronium bromide when accounting for breakage and general misplacement. And when the search widened to include veterinary practices and a number of specialist dental surgeries, the undertaking had become more of an 'ongoing' concern. Forensics, meanwhile, had discovered a staggering number of prints on the statue considering the thing had been ten feet up in the air.

To top it all off, Chambers had picked up another murder and serious assault to add to his already crippling workload, and Eve had found the stash of his mother's home-made 'Fatty' biltong he'd ingeniously hidden in an empty butter tub at the back of the fridge.

Overall, it hadn't been a good few days, the only ray of light being the revelation that the killer needn't be a well-built man as originally suspected after seeing the makeshift pulley system which would no doubt make shifting a cumbersome corpse considerably easier; that coupled with the fact that Chambers had now encountered just such a shifty, not well-built man, who had already made just such a makeshift pulley system and, therefore, could now consider himself a suspect.

Chambers slammed his foot on the brake, having just driven straight through a red light. Once the seemingly endless queue of vehicles had finished hurling abuse at him, he decided he was in desperate need of caffeine.

Parking up, he was just about to climb out when the radio went off: 'All units. All units. Have we got anybody in the vicinity of Bethnal Green? I *think* we might have a body.'

'*Think* we *might* have?' a gruff Glaswegian voice chimed in, before playing up for the sake of his eavesdropping audience. 'Tell them if it's either peach or brown, got arms and legs, and doesn't get up when they ask "are you a body?" . . . it's probably a body.'

'Thank you, Detective,' said the dispatcher, struggling not to laugh. 'The caller doesn't speak any English.'

A drawn-out sigh filled the speakers: 'All right. Allocate to me.'

There was a pause. 'Did you get that? You can allocate it to me.'

'Sorry,' the dispatcher came back to him, turning abruptly professional. 'Additional details: it now sounds like there could be *two* bodies.' Her voice became muffled and distant as she spoke to someone at her end. 'They're saying something about glue . . . or that they've been glued together maybe?'

Snatching the handset from its cradle, Chambers responded before anyone else blocked the channel: 'DS Chambers,' he identified himself, switching the engine on, hitting the sirens and pulling out into traffic. 'Allocate to me. I'm on my way.'

'You sure, Ben?' the Scotsman asked over the air.

'I'm sure. Pass details.'

Just then, a fourth voice joined the conversation, one that Chambers was a little surprised to hear: 'This is Constable Winter. We'll be backing him up.'

'Received.'

In no mood for the inevitable argument to come, Chambers accelerated northwards through the city.

'Pietà! Pietà!' a dark-haired woman cried in anguish as Chambers pulled up outside a run of terrace houses that suggested neglect was contagious. She spotted him the moment he shut the engine off and came rushing over, her face wet with tears, a look of terror in her eyes. She grabbed a handful of his overcoat: 'Pietà!'

'I'm going to check on him,' he promised, taking a step towards the open doorway. But when her grip failed to loosen, he had to forcibly remove her hands.

'No. No. No. Pietà!'

'You need to let me go to him,' he told the woman firmly, passing her back to her teenage relatives and heading into the property.

The smell hit him instantly: dirty litter trays, body odour and putrefaction. The bedroom to his left stood empty, so he proceeded down the hall, where Winter intercepted him:

'Sergeant,' he greeted Chambers curtly.

'Constable.'

'As you might be able to smell,' he started, trying not to gag, 'we've got two dead bodies.'

'Are you absolutely sure this time?' deadpanned Chambers, not because he particularly wanted to provoke the young man, just because he'd handed it to him on a platter.

Winter didn't seem impressed: 'Looks like it's been a couple of days, at least. And . . .'

'. . . And?'

'Like control said: they've been glued together.' Cupping his hand over his nose and mouth, he gestured for Chambers to follow him.

They entered the gloomy living room. Rubbish blew around their feet on a cold wind, the French doors propped open while Winter's partner stepped outside for a minute. Careful to keep the bizarre shape in the corner of his eye, Chambers braced himself . . .

He turned to face it.

In the centre of the threadbare sofa, a woman in her early thirties was sitting upright, a flowing cloth hooding her head before cascading down to the carpet. Across her lap lay the body of a teenage boy, head tilted back in her arms, ribs teasing the skin, naked but for a narrow strip of material around his waist. Despite the delay in finding them, and the smell to the contrary, both looked to have a healthy colour.

'In all seriousness. You *did* check they were both dead, right?' Chambers asked him.

'Yes!' Winter replied, affronted. 'No pulse. No signs of breathing. No eye reflex.'

Chambers nodded, satisfied, and then pulled his jumper up around his face just to breathe. 'Glued?' he asked.

'Her hand under his armpit, his hand, legs and head . . . and the back of her head to the wall.'

'*Je-sus*,' said Chambers, sliding his hands into a pair of disposable gloves. Stepping lightly over the robes that spilled across the floor, he inspected the back of the boy's neck.

'Looking for something?' Winter asked him.

'Clues,' he replied.

'. . . In particular?'

Finding no puncture wound, Chambers didn't respond. But then he frowned on noticing the beige-brown powder coating the fingers of his gloves. Next, he attempted to gently manoeuvre the woman's head, but gave up on realising that the material had been stuck onto her scalp to hold her in position.

'Know who they are?' asked Chambers. At which point, Winter's perpetually aggravated colleague stomped back inside, notebook in hand.

'Take it you met the neighbour on your way in?' she asked. He nodded. 'She's calling one of them Peter or Peeta, but as far as I can tell, they're Nicolette and Alphonse Cotillard. Mother and son. And *this* is their house.' Reilly flipped the notebook shut as though she'd just solved the case. 'On the plus side, she's gonna shit a brick when she finds out this Peter's OK.'

Both Chambers and Winter shot her disapproving looks.

'Found methadone in the bathroom cabinet,' she continued, oblivious. 'Look at how skinny they both are. It doesn't take a genius to work out . . . scumbag junkies,' she concluded in a way that implied they'd had it coming.

Chambers scratched his head and looked at her: 'The envelope in the hallway stamped *Cambridge University Admissions*, framed medal on the bedroom wall awarded at the under-eighteen's British Championships, and the fact that there's a nose clip beneath your great *bloody* hoof would suggest otherwise . . . He was a swimmer. A damned good one from the looks of it.'

Winter had to fight a smile as he watched his idiot partner lift her foot to reveal the bent piece of plastic she'd stamped into the carpet. Insulted, embarrassed, impressed and bemused, she stood there on one leg regarding the detective as though he'd just per-formed witchcraft.

'Get forensics down here,' Chambers told them, taking note of the paler areas of skin where he'd touched the male victim. 'I'm going to get my camera.'

He made his way out of the house and across the front garden.

'Detective! . . . Detective!'

With a hefty sigh, he turned to face Winter: 'Now's not the time.'

'Pietà! . . . Pietà!'

'For Christ's sake,' he muttered, unable to catch a break as he watched the middle-aged woman come running over to them. 'Go back to your house,' he told her pointlessly. 'Could somebody take her, please?' he asked of their growing audience.

Still inconsolable, she was shown away by an accommodating couple.

Chambers shook his head and looked to Winter: 'Before you say anythi—'

'What's your problem?'

'OK. Before you say anything *else* . . . I don't have a problem,' he told Winter while buttoning up his coat.

'Bullshit. I saw what you said to your chief about me. I almost got suspended thanks to you!'

'Well, I'm glad you didn't,' smiled Chambers, turning to walk away, the young constable ill-advisedly grabbing his arm. 'Don't . . . touch me,' he spat in a cloud of warm breath.

Winter let go but continued with what he'd come out to say regardless: 'You were there that night. You know the conditions we were working in. Anyone would've thought that guy was dead. You could've had my back. You could've—'

'I saved your arse,' Chambers cut him off.

'What do you . . .?' he started, trying but failing to remain indignant.

'You said it yourself: they showed you something I told my chief in confidence. So, whose side do you think they were on?' Winter looked confused. 'They couldn't pin this one on me, so started looking for someone else to blame. If I had fought your corner, they'd have screwed you over just to spite me. Instead, you got off with a slap on the wrist for a sackable mistake. You're welcome.'

'So, you *don't* think I'm an "incompetent wannabe, who can't get past his own ego to even manage the basics"?'

'Oh, *that* bit I meant,' joked Chambers, slapping a relieved

Winter on the back, when the vocal woman came rushing back out of one of the houses.

'Pietà?' Chambers guessed.

'Pietà,' nodded Winter.

'Pietà!' shouted the woman, thrusting a book into Chambers' hands, the page open at a photograph of Michelangelo's renaissance masterpiece: a youthful Mary holding her son across her lap in the wake of his crucifixion, the positioning eerily familiar, the statue a five-hundred-year-old recreation of the crime scene twenty feet away.

'Oh, shit,' Chambers muttered.

'What?' asked Winter urgently.

Chambers turned the book around to show him, the constable's face dropping to mirror his own: '. . . Pietà.'

CHAPTER 5

'Ben? . . . Ben? . . . Ben!'

'*Huh?*'

'Are you even listening to me?'

Chambers stared at her with a blank expression on his face. It was 'Treat Night' and they were sitting in a booth at their favourite restaurant. A coconut and lime chicken had appeared in front of him, while Eve's dish already looked half-eaten.

'Yeah, sorry,' he apologised. 'I'm just tired. So, was Paul all right?'

'I was telling you about that ten minutes ago!'

'Oh . . . But was he?'

'I'm not telling you,' she said, folding her arms. As usual, her Jamaican accent had returned with her temper.

'Putting *this*,' he gestured between them, 'aside, it sounded quite serious. I like Paul.'

'Dead . . . Alive. You won't know now until we see him at his birthday.' Chambers looked relieved. '. . . Or funeral,' she added, turning her attention back to her dinner. 'Is something going on at work?'

'*There's always something going on at work*,' they chimed together, reciting Chambers' go-to answer every time she asked the question.

She scowled at him: 'I can handle it.'

'Oh, I don't doubt that,' laughed Chambers.

'Then tell me.'

He smiled and then shook his head.

Dropping her cutlery onto the plate, Eve looked at him impatiently.

'Look,' started Chambers evenly, 'I chose this life. I could've been a postman or something.'

'Veronica's husband is a postman . . .'

'That's nice.'

'. . . He was mauled by a dog.'

'Oh.'

'And now he can't pee standing up. Can *you* still pee standing up?' she asked him rather loudly, several other diners staring in their direction. '. . . *Huh*?'

'. . . Yes,' Chambers answered in a whisper. 'I can still pee standing up.'

'Then how about you get over yourself, tough guy?'

He laughed, wondering why he'd even bothered putting up a fight at all. 'All I meant is that I *chose* to invite all this darkness and cruelty and hatred—'

'Jumbees,' she interjected, her Caribbean superstitions actually summing it up quite succinctly.

'Yeah, *demons*,' he nodded. 'I spend my time in the company of demons, and I can't risk bringing even *one* of them back home to you.'

Eve's expression didn't even flicker. Chambers knew he was defeated.

He huffed: 'OK . . .'

'. . . So, I stopped by the library on my way back and found this . . .' Chambers had been talking for over eight minutes when he produced the crumpled photocopy from his pocket: the frozen man rendered in weathered bronze. '*The Thinker* by Auguste Rodin,' he announced. 'Meaning that at *both* crime scenes, the bodies were positioned to resemble famous sculptures.'

'But,' started Eve, swallowing her mouthful, 'neither of the bodies today had puncture marks in their necks.'

'True,' conceded Chambers. 'Or any trace of the paralytic drug used in the first murder. But the mother's arms were already covered in track marks and all signs are pointing towards a heroin overdose.'

'But what about the boy? He was hit on the head.'

'I don't know. Maybe something went wrong,' suggested Chambers. 'Maybe he fought back. Either way, the killer covered up the damage he'd done with make-up, made them both look perfect again. Twisted, right?' he smiled, the thrill of sharing a demon's company again causing him to forget himself. When Eve looked at him in concern, he cleared his throat and sat up. 'I'm taking it to the chief tomorrow.'

'Who you got backing you up?' Eve asked him.

'*Huh?*'

'You know, who's looking out for you? Who you working with on this?'

'A new guy . . . A constable.' Her face dropped. 'He's good,' Chambers assured her. 'You'd like him.'

'*Hmmm,*' she replied, playing with her braided hair as she finished the last morsels of her meal.

'What's wrong?'

Pushing her plate away from her, Eve met his eye: 'Know what every path leads to if you follow it long enough?'

Chambers looked blank.

'It leads to what you're looking for.'

'O-K?'

'And you're looking for a demon in human form. You already knew that he was intelligent. Now you know he can also be violent. You sit there and smile like it's a game, but it's not. It's your life, and today it became entwined with his – with a serial killer's.'

Reaching across the table, Chambers took her hand. 'One: I won't take any risks, I swear to you. And two: technically, he's not even a serial killer. And we're going to catch him long before anyone starts throwing terms like that around.'

*

'I'm hunting a serial killer!' shouted Winter, slopping half his pint over the floor.

'What?!' the woman yelled over the music.

'I'm . . . hunting . . . a . . . serial killer!' he nodded excitedly, making a stabbing motion with his arm.

'What?!'

'Serial killer!'

She heard him that time and promptly excused herself to visit the bathroom.

'Toilets are that way!' he advised helpfully, pointing in the opposite direction as she made her way up the stairs and then out through the exit. '. . . Yeah, she's not coming back.'

Undeterred, having been 'throwing down' some of the best 'shapes' of his life, Winter headed back out onto the dance floor as the synthesiser intro to 'When Will I be Famous?' blasted through the speakers. Flawlessly substituting the word *famous* for *hunting a serial killer* every time the chorus came round, he cleared himself a sizeable space from the rest of the crowd, feeling invincible, feeling like the luckiest man alive – a hero among mere mortals and utterly immune to the effects of alcohol.

'That's *a* . . . *lot* of vomit,' sighed the cleaner at the Cyber Rooms on being faced with the career-best challenge that Winter had set for him. '. . . I hate my life.'

At 8.55 a.m. the next morning, Chambers cursed on seeing the state of his visitor. Partially dressed with his hair frizzed forward over his eyes and a large dark stain still spreading across his uniform, Winter held an empty mug in his hand, having fallen asleep in a chair.

'Hey!' barked Chambers, snapping his fingers next to the sleeping man's ear. 'Winter! . . . Winter!'

He awoke with a start and then winced in pain, smacking himself in the temple when he raised his hands to his head: '*Ahhhh*. What?'

'Meeting's in *five* minutes.'

Exhaling deeply, he peered down at himself: 'You made me spill my coffee.'

'Stand up!'

Rising unsteadily to his feet, he allowed Chambers to tuck him in and tidy him up a little.

'Are you *drunk?*' Chambers asked him, doing up his top button.

'Sick . . . Food poisoning.'

'Oh,' he said, softening a little. 'What did you have?'

'Eleven beers,' belched Winter.

Chambers regarded him, thoroughly unimpressed: 'Know what? Forget it. You're useless to me.'

'Hey!' Winter shouted after him as he walked away. 'Hey! Wait up!'

'Go home!' Chambers called back. 'You're off the case.'

'I was under the impression Constable Winter would be joining us,' said Hamm, making no effort to disguise his displeasure at Chambers scheduling the meeting. He closed the door to his office.

'He couldn't—'

There was an urgent knock at the window.

'*Ah.* He made it. Better luck next time,' Hamm told him, waving Winter in.

Face still wet, hair now at least pointing in the right direction, the young constable appeared almost presentable as he took a seat.

'OK. I've got a lot on today. What's all this about?' Hamm asked them, the phone on his desk ringing the moment he'd said it. 'Hang on.'

'I told you to go home,' hissed Chambers while his DCI was otherwise engaged.

'I'm a part of this too,' Winter whispered back.

'Part of nothing if we can't sell this to Hamm.'

'I'm here, aren't I?'

'Fine. Remember, make him believe you hate me.'

'Shouldn't be too hard,' muttered Winter just as Hamm finished his call.

'Right then,' he said, finally giving them his attention. 'What have you got?'

The two of them presented their case faultlessly, Chambers coming across as confident in his theory, proactive in his course of action. And, as planned, Winter had contradicted him at every opportunity, using their apparent animosity to gain favour with Hamm while feeding him exactly what they needed him to hear. As the detective chief inspector compared crime-scene photographs from the previous day to pictures of the famous sculpture, Chambers and Winter shared a smile, knowing that it couldn't have gone any better.

Eventually, Hamm looked back up at them. 'What an *utter* load of steaming shit,' he concluded, tossing the photos at them.

'Boss, I—'

'Shut it!' he snapped, cutting Chambers off. 'You've been talking bollocks at me for the last *fifteen* minutes. It's your turn to listen now. You've come in here with two murder scenes miles apart, three different M.O.s, *no* link between the snowman in the park and *either* of the junkies, and only your *word* that he was positioned anything like this sculpture when you found him. It's a statue of a bloke sat on his arse! *I'm* sat on my arse right now – think I look like it too?'

'To be fair, the physique is a little different to yours,' Winter interjected, evidently still a little tipsy. 'You're a bit softer around the . . . everything.'

Hamm glared at him.

'Probably stop talking now,' whispered Chambers.

'Yep.'

'Is there a connection between these two statues, at least?' Hamm asked them. 'Who made the sitting guy?'

'Rodin,' answered Chambers. 'He's French.'

'Never heard of him. And the Jesus and Mary one?'

'Michelangelo.'

'You've probably heard of him,' said Winter.

Hamm held up his hands in exasperation. 'I know what this is about, by the way,' he told Chambers, pointing an accusing finger across the desk at him. 'Your lot. Always out to prove something, aren't you? The very *last* thing we need at the moment is some token hire spouting his half-baked ideas, getting the press all riled up over nothing.'

Appalled, Winter opened his mouth to say something but noticed Chambers give him a subtle shake of the head.

'My orders,' Hamm continued, 'investigate these as two completely separate incidents. One more word about statues or serial killers and I'll have you reassigned. Do I make myself clear?'

'Perfectly, sir,' replied Chambers, taking his cue to get up.

'Sir,' said Winter, also getting to his feet. 'I'd like to request to stay on and work these two cases under DS Chambers. I was the first unit on scene at both and feel it could be an invaluable learning opportunity.'

Hamm looked bored: '. . . I'll speak with your chief.'

'Thank you, sir.'

With that, the two men promptly showed themselves out and moved a safe distance from the door.

'I take it I'm to disregard every word that came out of his mouth?' asked Winter.

Chambers nodded.

'So, where to?'

'The Forensics lab . . .' Chambers told him decisively.

Performance over, Winter was starting to look as though he might die again.

'. . . Via the coffee machine,' he added.

'Oh, thank God.'

CHAPTER 6

'Think next time you come down to see me, you could bring something straightforward?' asked Dr Sykes as she stood over the body of Alphonse Cotillard, the teenager found in his mother's arms. 'For example: a guy without a head. And then you'll say "what was the cause of death, doc?", to which I'll reply: "Well . . . he's got no head, so there's that."'

She seemed a little stressed.

After taking another hit of her coffee, she asked: 'How's the sculpture angle panning out?'

'Dead in the water,' replied Chambers, figuring the less people who knew they were still pursuing it, the better.

'How very apt,' nodded Sykes, without elaborating. 'So, do either of you want to hazard a guess at cause of death? I'll give you a clue: it begins with a *B*.'

Chambers and Winter shared a look. Under the harsh fluorescent lighting, and in the absence of any make-up, the indent to the young man's skull was obvious, the deep wound running through the middle glued together with precision.

'Blunt force trauma,' shrugged Chambers.

The doctor turned to Winter.

'Blunt force trauma,' he agreed.

Sykes shook her head manically: '*Bloody* drowning!'

'On his *sofa*?' asked Winter.

'No doubt as a result of the head trauma, but the volume of liquid in his lungs suggests he was still alive after being struck with something solid and round, six to eight inches in diameter. I also found numerous bruises on his arms and neck indicative of a struggle. But what I still *haven't* found is a puncture wound anywhere on the body.'

The three of them stared down at the cadaver in silence.

'. . . What sort of liquid?' asked Chambers.

'I'm sorry?'

'In his lungs.'

'Just boring old water, I'm afraid.'

'Was it chlorinated?'

Winter glanced across the table at Chambers, realising where he was heading with this.

'No. Why?' asked Sykes.

'How about on his skin?' Winter asked urgently, shooting Chambers a significant look.

'I can certainly take a sample and—'

'No need,' Winter told her, leaning over to sniff the corpse's arm.

'*Umm.* Excuse me. What do you think you're doing?' Sykes asked in alarm.

'That's revolting,' remarked Chambers, pulling a face.

'Yeah,' gagged Winter. 'Regret it already.' Standing back up, he took a deep breath, needing a moment. He looked to Chambers and nodded.

'Chlorine on his skin, fresh water in his lungs,' the experienced detective pondered aloud.

'. . . The showers at the swimming club?' suggested Winter.

'What swimming club?' asked Sykes, feeling rather left out of the conversation.

'Let's go,' said Chambers.

Without another word, the two detectives showed themselves out, leaving the doctor to her windowless existence and entourage of dead bodies.

'OK . . . Bye, bye then!' she called after them, receiving only the slam of a door in response.

*

'What is it with old men and changing rooms?' asked Winter, looking traumatised. 'I mean, I go swimming from time to time. And
yeah, at some point the trunks need to come off, but—'

'But you wrap a towel around you!' Chambers concurred, clearly
feeling as strongly as Winter when it came to the subject.

'Or do that thing where you hold the towel in your teeth so it
hangs down like some sort of crotch curtain.' Chambers' lack of
agreement suggested he might have shared a little too much. 'Either
way, what you *don't* do is stand there straightening up your tie with
your bits swinging about in the wind.'

Chambers nodded in agreement as they stepped into the shower
block. 'Our murder scene . . . Maybe,' he announced.

'Perfect place to wash away the blood.'

'Perfect place to sneak up on someone,' countered Chambers,
doubting that the killer's intention had been to damage his
'artwork'.

'Cracked tile behind you,' Winter pointed out.

'Could you see if they've got a Phillips head screwdriver handy?'

He looked to Chambers inquisitively, who gestured to the three
metal drain covers set into the floor. 'Sure.'

He had only been out of the room twenty seconds before
Chambers heard him calling his name. Hurrying to the top of the
stairs that descended to the pool area, he looked down at Winter – a
gloved hand holding one of the weights used in underwater exer-
cises high above his head. Bar the small handle, it was completely
round and clearly quite heavy.

'Our murder weapon?! . . . Maybe!' he called up triumphantly, before noticing the concerned faces of the people taking lessons. Lowering the weight, he gave them an awkward wave: 'Don't mind me.'

Much to the displeasure of the leisure centre manager and horde of
old men keen to drop their pants, Chambers and Winter had closed
off the shower room, confidence growing that they had found where
the teenager's murder had taken place.

Accessing the drainage system, however, had taken more than the proposed screwdriver, the caretaker having to shut off the water supply in order to remove the plastic filtration system concealed beneath the metal grate. The first two drains had taken over half an hour to disassemble and had produced little more than a twenty-pence piece, a lost locker key and, inexplicably, a soggy Ritz video rental card.

But as the final cover was removed, Chambers edged forward in anticipation, abandoning his spot beside the broken wall tile.

Several grunts and groans later, the caretaker pulled the plastic box from the floor, carefully unscrewing it to inspect the contents within. He looked surprised: 'Is that . . .?'

'A needle,' Chambers finished on his behalf.

'And broken glass,' Winter added excitedly. 'Don't move a muscle,' he told the man, kneeling beside him with an evidence bag at the ready. A smile broke across his face: 'We've got blood.'

Chambers nodded. Sure enough, a handful of the shards were speckled with crimson.

'Bag it,' he instructed Winter. 'I'll get someone over to pick it up.'

'Why? Where are we going?'

'To pay Mr Sleepe another visit. See if we can't persuade him to part with some fingerprints and a sample of his blood.'

At 3.15 p.m. Chambers and Winter were sitting in the pie and mash shop on Tower Bridge Road, the day's excitement combined with their frequent trips to and from New Scotland Yard causing them to forget about lunch entirely. By pure coincidence, the establishment's floor-to-ceiling tiles were fittingly reminiscent of their shower-room discovery.

They had been eating in silence for over five minutes when Winter felt he needed to get something off his chest:

'I'm sorry about this morning.'

Chambers took a moment to realise what he was referring to; so much had happened since then.

'A friend's birthday and the excitement of working an *actual* serial killer case got the better of me,' he continued. 'It won't happen again. And I really do appreciate you letting me tag along.'

The protracted silence that followed started to feel a little uncomfortable while Chambers finished the last of his jellied eels. He dabbed his mouth with a serviette and then looked across at Winter.

'You did OK today,' he said rather anticlimactically, getting up from the table. 'Got a phone I can use?' he asked the woman behind the counter, flashing his ID.

'In the back,' she replied distractedly, her conversation with one of the regulars taking precedent.

Heading through the door, he took out his address book to find the number for the Forensic lab.

'Doctor Sykes,' a voice answered.

'It's Chambers.'

'Ah, Detective! Do you want the good news or the bad news?'

'Good.'

'There were trace amounts of Alphonse Cotillard's blood on one of the weights you brought in. You found the murder weapon.'

'Prints?'

'Wiped clean.'

The door swung open, smacking Chambers in the shoulder.

'Sorry, darlin',' a woman apologised as she squeezed past with a stack of dirty dishes.

'And the needle?' Chambers asked once she was out of earshot.

'It's the right diameter. Not much else to say about it. But the glass, although shattered, is curved and covered in tiny black marks. It's a syringe; I'd stake my career on it. I know what you're going to ask next, but the answer's *no* – any trace of pancuronium bromide, if there ever was any, has been washed away. But the needle and syringe prove that your two investigations are almost certainly connected.'

'So, what's the bad news?'

'The blood on the glass: it's not Sleepe's.'

Chambers punched the wall in frustration: 'Doesn't mean he

didn't do it.'

'It doesn't. But I'll run it through the computer all the same. See if anything comes up.'

'Let me know,' said Chambers, hanging up the phone and heading back out to the table to update Winter.

'So . . . we head straight to Hamm's office and tell him he was wrong, right?' asked Winter, now up to speed. '. . . Right?'

Chambers looked unsure: 'He'll take it off us.'

'But . . .?'

'It won't be enough without the drug, and there was no trace.'

Winter sighed: 'OK. So, what do we do now?'

'Split up. You head back to the leisure centre. See what you can find . . . And check whether Henry John Dolan was ever a member there.'

'And you?'

Chambers hesitated: 'I'm sure I'll find something to do.'

CHAPTER 7

Jason Donovan's 'Too Many Broken Hearts' was providing an unwelcome backing track to the meeting, made worse by the fact that nobody was talking. Fighting every fibre of his being not to join in for the final chorus, Winter tried yet again to extract blood from a stone:

'Anyone you might've seen him talking to? Perhaps someone you hadn't seen around before?'

On arriving back at the leisure centre, he had asked the duty manager to gather everyone who had been working the night Alphonse Cotillard died. The result: six gormless teenagers, one of whom he was pretty sure had fallen asleep.

'Anything at all?' he tried, looking hopeful when a hand shot up in the air, only to realise it was just a yawn. '. . . Thank you. You've been most helpful.'

As his languid audience shuffled back to work, he went to speak with the manager.

'Teenagers, *huh*?' the young man scoffed.

The guy looked like a child wearing two thirds of a fake moustache.

Nodding politely, Winter pulled an evidence bag from his pocket containing the locker key retrieved from the shower-room drains.

'Would you or anyone else know when one of the lockers is missing its key?' he asked, knowing he was grasping at straws.

'Detective, we didn't even know when someone was getting murdered up there. So . . . No,' he answered flippantly, but abruptly changing his tone on noticing Winter's expression. 'Unless someone reports losing their key, we wouldn't routinely check.'

'And is there any way of knowing which locker this belongs to?'

'If the tag's gone . . .' the young man shrugged unhelpfully. 'The only way's to try them all.'

Winter sighed: 'Thought you might say that.'

Just one of the numerous drawbacks to whiling away one's time beneath disused railway arches is their open invitation for the purpose of public urination, a drawback that Chambers suspected he'd trodden in as he sheltered from the rain. Across the street, an illuminated window threw a welcoming glow over the cobbles. Teeth chattering, he tucked his hands under his armpits and stepped out of the puddle, eyes fixed on the familiar roller door.

Able to disregard any locker with a key already protruding from it, it had only actually taken Winter fifteen minutes to locate the correct one. A satisfying click later, he heard the ransomed twenty-pence piece drop and was pleasantly surprised to discover the locker still full. He reached in and removed the jeans, retrieving the wallet stuffed into the back pocket as a set of keys dropped to the floor. Excitement building, he unfolded a paper driving licence belonging to Alphonse Cotillard.

Pulling the rucksack out, he took a seat on the bench and started to unpack it: a screwed-up jumper . . . a lunch box . . . a water bottle . . . a selection of textbooks . . . a diary. He opened it up and flicked through to find the most recent entries:

. . . don't know why Jordan is being such a jealous bitch about it.

He turned the page:

. . . feeling so torn, like it's a choice between my future and my mum not killing herself.

Next page:

Hopefully I'll see Robert again tonight. He gets me, especially as he went to Cambridge himself. 'Prosperous Paupers' – that's what we call ourselves. Sometimes we talk for hours after training. He's such an inspiration and has taught me so much. His passion for his work and his art is . . .

His art. Winter had read enough and needed to share this latest development with Chambers. He tucked the diary into his coat pocket and shut the locker back up, holding on to the key as he rushed out of the changing rooms and straight into one of the teenagers he recognised from the unproductive meeting.

'Sorry,' he apologised, stepping around her, when she stopped him:

'Actually. I was waiting for you,' she told him, looking anxiously down the corridor. 'Can we talk?'

'Sure,' he said, following her through the nearest exit and out into the night.

The heavens had opened while he'd been inside, so they didn't stray beyond the boundaries of the covered entranceway. When she offered him a cigarette, he accepted, lighting up as they stood watching the rain for a moment.

'I didn't want to say anything in front of the others,' she started, closing her eyes as she inhaled a blissful breath of smoke. 'Long story short: I complained about this guy before and he lost his job over it, but none of them in there believed me. You won't tell them, right?'

Winter could barely hear her over the sound of the downpour.

'Not unless I really, really have to,' he answered honestly.

The girl nodded, apparently satisfied.

'What's your name?'

'Jordan.'

'Well, cheers, Jordan,' he said, gesturing to the cigarette in his hand while trying desperately not to choke on it. He didn't smoke, but knew that finding common ground was the best way to get a teenager to open up.

'I liked Alfie,' she said sadly. 'Alphonse. You know . . . *really* liked him.'

'Cool,' wheezed Winter, aware that he was overcompensating.

'It was like . . . the two of us against the world, if that makes any sense? I tended to notice where he was going . . . who he was going there with.' She took a steadying breath. 'There was this man . . . like a really creepy sort. Not anything wrong with him in particular, but you know how you just get a feeling sometimes? Anyway, he kept coming in to see Alfie. I'm talking about *every* night. Kept touching his arm and stuff when they were talking. He was there the night . . . *That* night. He was there, and he hasn't been back since.'

She dropped her cigarette to the ground and stamped on it as though it were a particularly repellent spider, so Winter followed suit, glad to be rid of the horrible thing.

She gave him a strange look: 'You still had like half left.'

'Yeah, but I had the best half,' he told her wisely, taking out his notebook. 'Any idea what this man's name is?'

'Robert.' She shook her head: 'No idea about a surname though.'

'Can you describe him?'

'Your age, maybe,' she shrugged. 'Weird hair – like a bowl cut – always in his eyes. He was thin. Athletic . . . Tall.'

'That's all really helpful,' said Winter, jotting it down.

'Oh, that's nothing,' she told him. 'By the third time he'd shown up, I had a go at getting him to sign up for membership to get some details out of him. But he wasn't having any of it, so I followed him out to his car.'

Winter kept his expression neutral but could feel his heart beating faster: 'Happen to get a colour or make?'

'Vauxhall Cavalier. One-point-six litre. Maroon. Tax disc stamped in Wandsworth. Got his number plate too,' she said, handing him a folded piece of paper.

Winter looked simultaneously stunned, grateful and rather ill: 'You'd make a hell of a detective one day.'

She smiled bashfully. 'Like I said, he creeped me right out . . . You don't smoke, do you?'

'No,' he admitted, opening the door and hurrying her inside. 'So, I'm going to go throw up for a bit and then I'll get right on this,' he promised, already making a beeline for the toilets to implement step one of his two-step plan.

The lights went out.

Keeping to the shadows, Chambers watched Tobias Sleepe lock up for the evening, his suspect not noticing him in the archway when he jogged past through the lashing rain, nor when he turned his van around, two bright beams sweeping the perimeter like a searchlight.

Watching the darkness swallow the rusty vehicle, Chambers darted over to the roller door and then up the fire escape to the vulnerable office window. Checking the coast was clear, he jabbed his elbow through one of the ill-fitting panes, the crack of the glass lost in the building storm. He reached through and loosened the catch, opening it just enough to clamber across the desk and land ungracefully on the other side.

Switching his torch on, he shut what was left of the window and placed a branch he'd found outside amongst the broken glass to make it appear as though a flying piece of debris, rather than a desperate detective, had caused the damage.

He began by flicking through the paperwork on the desk, searching for any mention of *The Thinker*, Rodin, *Pietà*, Michelangelo, swimming pools, hospitals – anything that could link Sleepe to the murders. Moving on to the drawers, he soon grew frustrated, finding nothing bar invoices, tax returns and photographs of restoration projects at various stages.

Giving up, and conscious that every minute he spent in there was a minute gambling with his career, he opened the door to the main room. The statues below cut unnerving silhouettes in the gloom – like four sentinels lying in wait.

Making his way down to ground level, he froze when his foot knocked something heavy off the final step. Sounding like a thunderclap in the silence, it hit the hard floor before rolling into a metal tool chest.

Everything went quiet once more.

Bracing himself, Chambers shone the torch over the damage.

'Shit,' he muttered on seeing the incriminating trail of liquid leading across the room and still flowing copiously from a metal can.

Deciding there was little he could do about it, he moved on to the pulley system. He traced his light the length of the thick rope, from the excess coiled around the winch all the way to the noose-like end, his eyes growing wide as he spotted something.

He quickly moved round to better see the inner edge, where coarse threads sprouted from the main weave, the colour darkened through years of usage and grime. But he'd definitely seen it: dried blood and what looked like human hair.

His breathing quickening, he pulled a pair of disposable gloves from his pocket and had just found an evidence bag to collect some samples when the sound of wet tyres approached . . . the hum of an engine . . . a vehicle pulling up directly outside. Switching off the torch, he stood motionless, listening but hearing only the pelting rain.

Suddenly, the metal door slid open.

Taking cover behind the closest of the statues, he flinched when the spotlights above buzzed to life and then heard unhurried footsteps approaching.

'There you are!' announced Sleepe victoriously.

Chambers held his breath, expecting to be confronted, but then heard the jangle of keys, followed by the sound of footsteps leaving . . . but then they paused. He risked a glance round the statue but was only able to see Sleepe's shadow as it crouched down to pick something up off the floor. Chambers winced, already knowing what it was.

'Hello?' Sleepe called out. 'Is there someone there?' Chambers watched the shadow arm itself with a large tool. 'If there's somebody there, come out now!'

The footsteps drew nearer.

He was trapped in the middle of the room with nowhere to go and nowhere to hide. Edging around the statue in time to the footfalls, Chambers knew he was only delaying the inevitable, that he would be discovered at any moment, the open shutter tantalisingly close and yet so far from reach. But then, a gust of wind slammed the office door violently, attracting Sleepe's attention.

'Somebody up there?!'

Chambers watched him take one last look around the room before slowly making his way up the steps. He dashed across to the next statue, making sure he hadn't been heard before going for the next one. Crouching behind a bronze saint, he could feel the wind on his face, the rain splashing the back of his hand. He'd made it out.

'*Shit. Shit. Shit*,' he whispered, looking back at his evidence hanging in the centre of the room. He couldn't leave it, not when he was so close.

Sleepe entered the office.

Seizing his opportunity, Chambers sprinted out into the open. With time for neither gloves nor evidence bags, he grasped a handful of bloody rope fibres, hoping he had some hair in there as well as he tore out through the open door.

Holding the branch in his hand, Sleepe heard someone run past his broken window. He hurried back out onto the walkway and looked down over the main room, where the suspended rope was swinging wildly like a snare that had failed to go off. But from his elevated position, the wet footprints were as clear as day – weaving between his statues before returning for something, and then escaping into the storm.

Thursday

CHAPTER 8

Chambers and Winter weren't speaking to each other.

The frosty silence had endured the length of Wandsworth High Street while they negotiated the morning traffic. The next red light blurred across the windscreen as the 'drizzle' turned into something between 'spitting' and a 'light shower', the British having about a dozen different terms for essentially the same thing: yet another miserable day.

Chambers huffed: 'Are you planning to sulk the whole way there?'

'I just don't feel you're giving him a chance.'

'I agreed to meet him, didn't I?'

'Reluctantly,' scoffed Winter.

'I'm just not sure he's "the one",' said Chambers, pulling them one place forward in the queue.

'And your guy *is*, I suppose? My guy couldn't *be* more perfect,' argued Winter. 'He's tall. He's athletic.'

'He lives at home with his mum,' Chambers pointed out.

'At least he's not old.'

'My guy's *experienced*. Plus, he's smart.'

'So is mine!' snapped Winter. 'He's a lecturer at a university!'

'My guy works alone because he owns his own business.'

'Oh yeah? Well, *my* guy . . .' Winter trailed off, realising that perhaps the conversation was starting to sound a little odd. 'All I'm asking is that you keep an open mind until Sykes gets back to us with the test results.'

'Of course I will,' said Chambers, finally making it through the lights and turning into the residential roads. 'Look, we're here,' he announced, pulling up outside a charming terraced cottage where an army of ceramic gnomes fished, wheelbarrowed and climbed around the immaculate front garden. 'Not exactly Scaramanga's lair, is it?'

'Shut up,' Winter bit back, climbing out.

He gestured towards the maroon Vauxhall Cavalier, then led the way through the picket gate and up to the front door. They both reached for the doorbell at the same time.

'You want to?' Winter asked impatiently.

'No. No. All yours,' Chambers smiled, taking his hand back.

He looked around at the cheerful ornaments while the musical bell played its tune: there was a tiny rock pool complete with trickling water feature, a couple of well-chewed dog toys, and just about every newspaper in circulation waiting on the step.

A distorted shape approached the glass. Three sets of locks later, it finally opened the door to them.

Winter went to introduce himself, but then completely forgot what he was going to say, both detectives just staring at the bizarre-looking man. As the teenager had described, he was tall, hair poker-straight and mousy brown, cut into layers that seemed to move independently of one another and, as stereotypes of his profession dictated, he wore defecation-brown trousers with a tweed blazer. What she'd neglected to tell them about, however, was his almost insect-like characteristics – his beady little eyes darting about from behind thick round glasses, a toothy pursed mouth that looked primed to take a bite at them.

'Detective Constable Adam Winter from Shepherd's Bush Green Police Station, I presume?' he said, breaking the silence.

'*Umm*. Yeah,' replied Winter, a little surprised he'd remembered their brief phone call with such accuracy. 'And this is—'

'Chambers,' Chambers interrupted his colleague. '. . . Just Chambers.'

The man regarded them, almost seemed to study them, for a moment.

Feeling uncomfortable, Winter smiled nervously: 'Thank you for seeing us.'

'I informed my employer of my unavoidable tardiness in good time. They should have been able to make suitable arrangements.'

Neither Winter nor Chambers knew quite how to respond, so didn't.

'May we come in?' asked Winter, half-hoping he'd say *no*. But when he stepped aside to allow them past, they unenthusiastically made their way down the gloomy hallway, hearing the locks click back into place behind them.

They went through to the living room, where a mismatched selection of armchairs were pointed towards an open fireplace, the net curtains yellowed with nicotine.

'I'm a bit scared,' whispered Winter.

'Yeah, me too,' admitted Chambers, both smiling pleasantly when their host entered the room.

'Please, have a seat,' he said.

The indecision on their faces wasn't subtle as they each tried to determine which of the threadbare chairs looked the least haunted. Realising that they were both going for the same one, Winter practically dived across the room, looking smug as he sank his buttocks into the prize.

'Tea?' the man offered. 'Coffee? Custard Creams?'

'No. Thank you,' replied Chambers.

'I've literally just had a coffee,' lied Winter, '. . . and some Custard Creams.'

Chambers shook his head at his partner.

The man walked over to take a seat, both detectives noting his distinct limp. He then perched on the very edge of the cushion as if ready to strike, his dark eyes watching their every move.

Winter took out his notebook and flipped it open: 'So, Mr Robert Douglas Coates . . .'

'Robert Douglas *Seymour* Coates,' the man corrected him.

'Of course,' said Winter. 'I'll just make a note of that . . .'

Prick

'And your age?'

'Twenty-four.'

'Do you know why we're here?' Winter asked him, noticing the ticking of the carriage clock on the mantelpiece in the pause before he answered.

He nodded sadly: 'I heard on the news. You're here because of Alphonse.'

'That's right. So, you knew him?'

'I consider myself fortunate to say that I did.'

'And may I ask where you met?'

Chambers had to remove his jacket, having inadvisably chosen the chair closest to the radiator, which was pumping out heat at an uncomfortable rate.

'At the leisure centre.'

'Where you . . .?' Winter left the question dangling.

'Swim.'

'So, you were . . . friends?'

'I would call it more a teacher/student relationship in nature. I saw a lot of myself in him, the depths of his untapped potential.'

There was a slightly awkward beat in which both Winter and Chambers glanced around at the sum of Robert Douglas Prick Coates's depths of untapped potential.

'You live with your mother?' asked Chambers, earning himself a glare from Winter for muscling in on his suspect.

'Not any more,' answered Coates. 'She went into a home a month ago.'

'Do you mind me asking what happened to your foot?' asked Winter, taking back over. Coates showed no sign of even having heard the question until Winter went to ask it again: 'Mr Coates, do you mind me ask—'

'I cut it . . . on some glass.'

Both Winter and Chambers unconsciously leaned forward, mirroring Coates's unsettled pose.

'And where was this?' Winter pushed him.

'At the leisure centre. In the shower room of all places.'

The two detectives shared a look of anticipation, Winter trying to remember in which pocket he'd put his handcuffs.

'Of little interest to the police, I should imagine,' Coates continued, 'but it looked like a syringe that had been stamped into the floor. I sliced the bottom of my foot open on it. It was quite painful. I then brushed what I could find into the nearest drain to prevent anybody else injuring themselves. Needless to say, I haven't been back since.'

They both relaxed a little, disarmed by the man's very plausible story.

'You're a lecturer at Birkbeck College?' Winter asked him, changing tack.

'That's correct.'

'Art History?'

'Broadly speaking.'

'So, you must know quite a bit about . . . *sculpture?*'

Coates gave nothing away, both men watching him closely as Winter continued.

'Rodin's *The Thinker*? Michelangelo's *Pietà*?'

'Of course. They are two of the most famous and celebrated works ever created.'

'And as an expert—'

'Art History is *quite* a broad subject,' Coates interrupted him.

'In comparison to us then,' Winter corrected, Coates nodding along to his logic. 'Can you think of any link between those two pieces of art?'

'Link?'

'Anything at all?'

Coates looked puzzled: 'I thought this was about Alphonse's murder?'

'Humour me.'

The lecturer seemed to zone out for a few moments, chewing on his fingernail as he mulled it over.

'I believe that *The Thinker* was originally just one small part of a far more ambitious piece entitled *The Gates of Hell* . . .' A little disconcerted, Winter wrote it down. 'Many believe that it depicts Dante, but there are those who suspect it to be, in fact, Rodin himself. *Pietà*, meanwhile, captures Mary cradling her dead son in her arms,' he pondered out loud. 'One resides in Paris, the other in Rome. They were created centuries apart. One bronze, one marble . . . I honestly can't think of a single thing that connects them.'

'We're going to need a sample of your blood,' blurted Chambers, catching both Coates and Winter off guard.

'My . . . blood?'

'In order to exclude you from the investigation.'

'Of course. I'll co-operate in any way that I can.'

'Appreciated. May I use your bathroom?'

Again, Coates didn't answer right away, as if disappearing into his own head to calculate his response.

'Upstairs. First door on your left. You'll have to excuse the mess.'

Chambers nodded and got up, leaving Winter to finish off. He glanced into the dated kitchen on his way out, noticing nothing unusual, and made his way up the staircase to the landing, where the carpet was caked in dog hair of various colours. He suspected that the entire house normally looked the same, only the ground floor hastily prepared for their visit. Disappointingly, both bedroom doors were closed and he didn't dare risk trying them, the house creaking and groaning, reporting his every movement to its owner downstairs.

Walking into the bathroom, he closed the door and hurried straight over to the medicine cabinet. There was an impressive selection of pills, most belonging to a Mrs M Coates, but none of any significance. Frustrated, he looked around the sparse room for any further insight into the strange man's life. With no better ideas, he stepped into the bathtub to reach the frosted window, forcing the rusted catch to peer out over the back garden. In comparison to the well-tended gnome-fest to the front, the rear of the property was a state – overgrown and wild, bar an area of disturbed soil at the very far end.

Knowing he'd already taken too long, Chambers pulled the window closed, flushed the chain and washed his hands for good measure. He reached for the door handle but paused on seeing the home-made decoration hanging from it. He flipped it round to read the inscription etched into the wood:

'Though your sins are like scarlet,
they shall be as white as snow.'

ISAIAH 1:18

Frowning, he twisted the handle and headed back downstairs, where Winter was already on his feet, ready to leave.

'I haven't seen your dogs yet,' said Chambers, collecting his jacket.

Coates looked at him guardedly.

'Saw the hair on the carpet,' he explained.

'Dog. Just one,' Coates told him. 'Sadly, he passed away. Quite recently, in fact. I think that may have been the final straw for my mother.'

'I'm sorry,' said Chambers. 'What sort of dog was he?'

'A mutt. We have always taken in strays.'

'"Do unto others as you would have them do unto you,"' said Chambers, ignoring the enquiring look Winter shot him.

Coates appeared momentarily lost, but then smiled for the first time since their arrival.

'Now you sound like my mother,' he said, showing them to the door.

Climbing into the car, Winter looked to his colleague expectantly:

'So . . . what did you think?'

'OK. I was wrong,' admitted Chambers, starting the engine. 'I get why you're interested in him.'

CHAPTER 9

Wearing a derisive sneer, Mrs Chambers pushed her main course around her plate, the single spoonful she'd managed of the starter apparently filling her up.

'What is it again?' she asked, sticking an exploratory finger into the sauce.

'Chicken,' Eve replied curtly. 'A flightless bird we have back home. One of my mother's recipes.'

'And where *is* home again?'

'Content, Jamaica.'

'*Hmmm*,' the older woman replied, turning her disapproving glare to her clearly objectionable surroundings. 'So, they call this a "loft" do they?' she asked, pushing her plate away from her.

'They do.'

'Just a fancy word for "flat", isn't it?'

'I suppose it is.'

'One that costs as much as a house.'

'Depending on the house.'

Making another snort of general displeasure, Mrs Chambers took a moment to regard her hostess sitting across the table from her, Eve squeezing her husband's hand in anticipation:

'You're quite pretty . . .'

'Thank you. How *quite* kind of you to notice.'

'. . . for one of them.'

'*Oww! Jesus!*' blurted Chambers, Eve's fingernails finally breaking his skin. He glanced between the two woman, neither looking particularly happy, and suspected he'd missed something.

'Are you finished, Lucile?' asked Eve, getting up from the table.

'Oh, most definitely,' she replied, handing over the plate as if she couldn't get it away from her quickly enough.

'Want to help me with dessert?' Eve asked Chambers.

'I thought it was already made up in—'

'Help me with dessert!'

He obediently got to his feet: 'Mum, can I get you another . . . tap water?'

'No. Thank you,' she said, covering the top of the glass with her hand as though he might try to stealthily top it up without her consent.

'Did you hear that?' tutted Eve as they carried the plates through to the kitchen. 'She doesn't even like the water!'

'I think it's going well though, don't you?' smiled Chambers hopefully, receiving a 'you're sleeping in the spare room' glare in reply.

'Have you *not* been at the same dinner table as us?!'

'*Shhhhh.* What's wrong?'

'Don't *shhhh* me!'

'I'm sorry. Do you not like her?'

'Like her?!' spat Eve, again, a little too loudly. 'I hope she chokes on my mango tart!'

Chambers looked a little taken aback . . . and then a little nervous: 'She doesn't really like mango . . . or tarts.'

Dropping the beautifully presented plate into the sink, she punched him in the arm.

'*Oww!*'

'Why didn't you stick up for me?'

'I didn't even hear what she said!'

'Because you were daydreaming . . . like usual,' she huffed.

'Look,' started Chambers, 'Mum's just . . . a bit old-fashioned. She's very proud of her Ghanaian heritage *and* of being British.'

'And doesn't like you wasting yourself on any old "Jamo"?'

Chambers sighed: 'I didn't say that.'

'You didn't have to . . . And what about our children? Is she going to treat them the same way?'

Chambers looked shell-shocked: 'Are you . . .? Are you saying you're . . .?'

Eve folded her arms: 'What would you say if I was?'

'I'd say . . . that's wonderful.'

'Well, I'm not.'

'Oh, Jesus *Christ*! Thank God!' he gasped, holding his hand to his heart.

She cracked a smile: 'What's going on with you? Did something happen with the case today?'

Chambers glanced across the room to ensure his mother was still looking as bored, disgusted, and outraged by the single-flooredness of his living space, as before.

'The blood and hair I snatched from the rope didn't match our victim . . . *any* of our victims.'

'Still, blood and hair though. What is it doing there?'

'What *is* it doing there?' agreed Chambers.

'Let's talk about this later,' Eve told him, squeezing his bleeding hand. 'Just get me through this first. I need you.'

The next morning, Chambers hobbled into the office, the spare bed apparently taking Eve's side in the argument. Skipping the pleasantries, he gestured for Winter to follow him into the meeting room, closed the door and then lay down with a groan of relief.

Unfazed, Winter removed his notebook and took a seat on the floor beside him, gazing up at the stained ceiling tiles:

'How did anyone manage to spill coffee up there?' he asked.

'Boss threw it at someone he didn't like.'

'Who?'

'Me.'

'Oh. Kinda looks like the Millennium Falcon,' he said, squinting up at it.

'I was thinking the blade of an axe,' said Chambers. 'But as a prospective homicide detective, it's good to know where your head's at. So, Robert Coates's alibi for the night of the first murder?'

'Home alone.'

'Doesn't matter. I've got a new angle for us to look into,' announced Chambers, reaching into his jacket pocket and handing Winter a bright orange rubber chew toy. 'Dogs.'

'Great,' he said encouragingly. 'Wait . . . What?'

'Dogs,' repeated Chambers. 'I picked this up from his front garden on the way out.'

'Maybe you should take a day off,' suggested Winter.

'Just look at the teeth marks,' Chambers told him. 'There's one set of seven close together, another of four further apart, and then another couple of deep punctures completely different to the rest.'

'OK?'

'At least three different dogs have been chewing on this thing. And when I went upstairs, the carpet was matted with fur of every colour under the sun.'

'OK?'

'And there's a grave in the back garden.'

'A grave?'

'. . . Area of disturbed soil.'

Winter looked dubious: 'That doesn't make it a grave.'

'Remember what we said the night we found Henry John Dolan up on that podium?'

'*Errm?*'

'"Non-committal". A tentative first kill perhaps? Setting up the pieces but then letting the weather do the dirty work for him. Do you know where most serial killers begin before moving on to real people?'

'With animals,' said Winter, catching up.

'And one of our two prime suspects seems to be going through dogs at an alarming rate.'

'But what about Tobias Sleepe?' asked Winter. 'He's got a pulley system easily capable of lifting a person covered in hair and blood. He seems equally as guilty.'

'You like *my* guy now?' Chambers asked him.

'Of the two of them, yeah, I think he's the more likely.'

'Well, I like yours.'

'So, which do we go for? Make the wrong choice and we lose our case.'

Chambers considered it for a moment:

'Both. Simultaneously. One of us digs up the garden while the other seizes the pulley.'

'Without a warrant?' asked Winter sceptically.

'Without a warrant,' nodded Chambers. 'In and out. Confidence is key.'

'One of us will be wrong.'

'But one of us will be right,' Chambers pointed out. 'Even Hamm can't ignore that. There's no doubt in my mind that one of these two freaks is our killer . . . You?'

'No doubt.'

'Then we can't lose, can we? Are you in?'

'I'm in . . . When?'

'No time like the present,' said Chambers. 'The longer we wait, the longer they have to kill again.'

The meeting room door swung open as Lewis entered, stumbling over the two men on the floor and slopping his coffee over the wall:

'What are we doing?' he asked them while shaking off a painful scald.

'Fixing my back,' replied Chambers, making no attempt to move. 'Better half made me spend the night on the spare bed.'

'Well, join the club,' said Lewis, setting his coffee cup on the table before lying down next to him. He let out a sigh of relief. 'Can't remember the last time I was allowed in my own bed . . . Boss's looking for you.'

'What else is new?'

A peaceful silence descended over the three men, only interrupted when Winter pointed up at the fresh stain on the wall:

'Anyone else seeing a lightsabre?' he asked.

'Screwdriver,' replied Lewis.

'Yeah, definitely a screwdriver,' agreed Chambers. 'Don't worry,' he told Winter. 'You'll get it.'

Chambers was parked fifty feet down the road from Robert Coates's cottage and had fiddled with every button on the dashboard twice while waiting for 1:45 p.m. to come around, the time agreed upon with Winter to allow him to get into position. He looked up at the dark clouds: 'Come on. Don't rain. Please don't ra—'

As if on cue, the heavens opened, flooding the street in seconds.

'. . . Thanks, God,' he muttered, glancing once again at the dashboard clock:

13:42

Close enough, he decided, grabbing the shovel from the passenger-side footwell and climbing out. Utterly drenched by the time he'd passed the neighbours' houses, he marched through the front gate of the cottage under the watchful gaze of the grinning gnomes. The sound of the raindrops striking their ceramic bodies seemed to bring them to life – like tiny tools hard at work under the cover of the rain.

The side gate splintered apart with a single kick, allowing him to negotiate the overgrown rear garden, brambles snagging on his trousers, trying to drag him back. Noticing the curtains twitch in the adjacent properties, Chambers finally reached the eight-foot patch of soil at the far end. Conscious that the clock was already ticking, *he raised his hands high and then drove them down hard*, the metal sinking deep into the saturated earth.

'Police! Open up!' yelled Winter, banging against the metal shutter of Sleepe & Co. Restoration. 'Open up!'

The roller door released its grip on the wall, Tobias Sleepe appearing in the gap looking as grubby and dishevelled as ever. Dark goggles covered his eyes as he held a blowtorch in his hand.

'Put that down on the ground!' ordered Winter, eyeing it warily.

'Put it down!'

Following his instructions, Sleepe removed the goggles, a confused look on his face.

'I'm seizing your pulley system,' Winter told him, entering the building.

'I need it for my work.'

'I bet you do,' said Winter knowingly. 'It's evidence in a murder investigation.'

Reaching the suspended length of rope in the centre of the room, he tried to conceal his alarm, seeing no trace of either blood or hair anywhere, but noticing the conspicuously unsoiled frayed end protruding from an elaborate knot:

'When was this cut?' he asked Sleepe urgently.

'My memory's not what it was,' he replied insincerely. 'I can't recall.'

'Go up to your office and wait for me there!' Winter barked at him, a quiver of desperation in his voice, the victorious sneer on the other man's face confirmation that he had heard it too. 'I need access to your rubbish bins.'

'You'll find them in the alleyway round the back. Please do help yourself,' said Sleepe, making his way up the staircase.

Staring back down at the rope, Winter looked ill.

They'd staked everything on this.

'Shit,' he whispered, only hoping Chambers was having more luck.

'Excuse me, Detective! . . . Excuse me!' called Robert Coates from under his umbrella as he squelched through the garden to reach an exhausted Chambers still taking ineffectual blows at the floor of a five-foot pit. The mound of sludge above him was dissolving in the downpour, filling his excavation back in faster than he could get it out. 'What on earth do you think you're doing?'

'Investigating . . . the murder . . . of Alphonse . . . Cotillard,' panted Chambers, flinging another spadeful of dirt behind him.

'I presume you can show me a warrant?'

Ignoring him, Chambers continued to dig.

'Detective?'

'What have you got buried under here?' Chambers asked him, stumbling unsteadily into the soil wall.

'It was my mother's vegetable patch,' answered Coates, crouching down to meet his eye, the rain ceasing as his black umbrella eclipsed the sky. 'Detective. Do . . . you . . . have . . . a . . . warrant?'

Giving up, Chambers tossed the shovel to the ground and met the beady black eyes above him defiantly:

'No. I don't.'

'In which case,' started Coates calmly, 'remove yourself from my property immediately and expect a call from my lawyer before the end of the day.'

The relentless rain returned as he got back up and headed for the house.

Barely able to stand, Chambers watched the water rising around his feet, the irony of his career ending in a grave that he had dug himself not lost on him.

He'd fucked up.

CHAPTER 10

The busy platform was displaced by darkness.

James 'Jimmy' Metcalf felt as though he was watching the journey happen rather than undertaking it himself, as the woman he'd been staring at for the past five minutes got up and moved away. Resurfacing from his daze, he realised that he'd drooled all over himself but didn't particularly care, relishing every moment of this farewell high, the last he would enjoy for a good long while, perhaps ever. Truth be told, he wasn't at all sure he'd survive the withdrawal process this time round. Even if he didn't, it would still be preferable to the alternative.

Stumbling off the Tube at Westminster, he emerged out onto the busy street, a sensory overload: traffic, voices, drilling – all vying for attention beneath a dazzling grey sky, the world all the more vivid after his subterranean journey. He forced himself to focus:

'Excuse—'

The young man walked by as though he were a ghost.

'Excuse me,' he tried again.

'No. Sorry,' a woman replied, turning away until he left her alone.

After years living rough, the sum of his worldly possessions filling a pathetic two-thirds of the rucksack on his back, he was well-accustomed to such dismissive salutations.

'Excuse me, please,' he smiled, surprising a man counting his change as he emerged from a newsagent. He could see the cogs

turning: the man glancing from the handful of money to the insa-
lubrious character before him. Seeing no way out, the stranger
removed the pound coin and then unenthusiastically offered up the
rest. 'No. But thank you,' he smiled. *He wouldn't be needing it.*
'Could you tell me the way to New Scotland Yard, please?'

Less than ten minutes later, he passed through the restless shadow
of the iconic revolving sign, immediately attracting the attention of
the officers standing guard. Staggering a meandering path over to
them, he nodded in greeting and then swung wildly, the makeshift
knuckleduster unremorsefully dismantling bone, the man unconscious before he'd even hit the ground.

Bursting into the building, he leapt over the security barrier before
anyone had time to react, shoving several people off their feet as he
tore across the atrium, officers closing in from all directions, some
wielding firearms, most just approaching with batons raised.

'Stop where you are!' one of the armed officers shouted. 'Stop or
I'll shoot you!'

Accepting that he was completely surrounded, the homeless man
froze and dropped the bloodied weapon to the floor:

'OK!' he panted. 'You got me! You got me!' He raised his arms, a
small plastic bag visible in his left hand.

'What is it?' the officer asked him, approaching cautiously.

He was still catching his breath: '. . . Proof.'

'Of . . .?' Snatching the transparent bag away from their prisoner,
one of his colleagues restrained the man's arms.

'My guilt,' the homeless man replied, smiling as the handcuffs
tightened around his wrists. 'I did something very, very bad.'

'. . . And now two complaints in a single afternoon!' bellowed
Hamm, Chambers and Winter remaining advisably quiet on the
other side of the desk. 'We've already got Coates's lawyer suing us
for harassment. Think Sleepe's will be far behind? And hey, want to
know how I'm spending my Friday night now? With my boss and
the legal team working out how much keeping this from the papers

is worth to us. I told you to treat these as two . . . separate . . . incidents!' Winter raised his hand. 'If what's about to drop out of that stupid bloody hole in your face includes the word statues,' Hamm warned him, 'I'd suggest you close it.'

He did.

'There's something else,' started Chambers.

'*Else?*' scoffed Hamm. 'You mean *on top* of the man paid to restore damaged statues carrying out the very job he was employed to do, and the fact that two leisure centre members sometimes spoke to each other in passing?! There is no "else". You . . . have . . . nothing!'

'There's something else,' Chambers repeated, poking at the bear, 'something we haven't officially documented yet. We found a needle and broken glass where the teenager was murdered. We believe that—'

'You're wrong.'

'But—'

'I said: you're wrong!' Hamm shouted him down, startling everyone out in the main office pretending not to be listening in.

'Sir?'

Hamm tossed a wad of paper across the desk at him:

'A full confession from one James Metcalf in relation to the murder of Henry John Dolan in Hyde Park.'

Chambers and Winter shared a confused look: 'Who?'

'Twenty-five. Homeless. That park was his spot,' explained Hamm. 'He saw an opportunity and he took it.'

'You're saying this was just a robbery?' asked Chambers. 'There's no way that's right.'

'Really?' Hamm reached over, took the paperwork back and started flicking through. 'Here, he explains how he lured the victim into the park under the pretence of selling him some drugs. Here, it describes how he got Dolan to climb the podium himself, telling him it was where he'd hidden his stash. And *here*, he injects him in the back of the neck, paralysing him, taking his wallet, watch and clothing, then leaving him there to die.'

'But,' started Chambers, 'how—'

'He had the *fucking* needle!' screamed Hamm, silencing him. 'Covered in our victim's blood, the syringe still wet with the drug. Case *fucking* closed!'

Chambers looked crushed.

'These murders were never related, you stupid glory-hunting prick,' Hamm told him, clearly savouring this part. 'There never was any statue connection. You got yourself suspended for nothing.'

'Suspended?'

'You heard me.' Hamm turned to Winter: 'I'll let your chief decide what to do with you. You're not my problem any more.'

'What about Alphonse and Nicolette Cotillard?' asked Winter while Chambers processed the news.

'That investigation is still ongoing. Thought I might go in a new direction this time and try handing it over to someone *actually* competent.'

'And the blood we found on the rope?'

'Oh, I'm sorry,' said Hamm sarcastically. 'I didn't realise it was your first day. It's *completely* meaningless. You two *idiots* obtained it illegally. We can't prove where it's come from, and now you say the pulley's clean anyway. It's a dead end! Just get out of my sight, both of you!'

Still a little dazed, Chambers followed Winter out into the main office, ignoring the snide smirks and even snider remarks from their eavesdropping peers.

Lewis was waiting for them by the lifts and patted his friend on the back as they stepped inside.

Chambers stared at him vacantly: 'I was *so* sure.'

'I know you were,' he smiled pityingly as the doors juddered closed between them.

Chambers heard the front door slam, and quickly poured a glass of wine before Eve entered the room. Her eyes darted from the pans sizzling on the hob – to the candle flickering in the centre of the table – to the wine glass in his hand – to his excessively bandaged thumb – to the practised smile Chambers had fixed upon his face:

one part 'I'm so sorry', two parts 'what are we like?', a sprinkling of 'I'm just so happy to see you', with just a dash of 'I really badly burnt my thumb cooking for you and am smiling through the pain'.

Her frown softened and after a moment she even smiled back.

Nailed it.

'I thought you were working tonight,' she said, accepting the glass from him.

'Funny story about that,' he began, before taking several procrastinating sips of his own drink.

'. . . Yes?'

'We'll talk about it after dinner.'

'No. We'll talk about it now,' Eve told him, setting her drink down on the side.

'OK. But don't get mad. You know this case I've been working on? And you know how you've always told me to just follow my gut, to stay true to myself and what I believe in?'

'Those words have literally *never* left my mouth.'

'Well, I was paraphrasing.'

'The time I said *do not* follow your gut, just make sure whatever you do you keep your job? *Don't* stay true to yourself, 'cos we've got bills to pay? And *screw* what you believe in; we can't afford this place on my wage alone?!'

'*Ummm.*'

'Ben, did you get yourself fired?'

'No! Of course I didn't get fired!' he laughed, Eve relaxing ever so slightly. '. . . Just suspended.'

'I'm going out.'

'What?'

'I'm going out. You were *meant* to be working,' she told him, marching towards the bedroom. 'It's my night out with the girls from work.'

'What, those stuck-up partners and associates who always talk down to you?'

The door slammed in his face. Knowing better than to pursue her any further through the loft, he took a seat on the floor:

'I'll go in and grovel first thing Monday morning. I promise,' he called through the door. 'I screwed up. I mean, really, *really* screwed up. I just wanted to . . . I wanted to catch him before he could hurt anybody else. I know you think I was out to prove something, prove I'm smarter than them, but that's not it.' He sighed, a moment's reflection in his impromptu monologue. 'I just thought I could stop something bad happening to somebody who didn't deserve it. I had to try. And I'm sorry you're cross with me, but I'm not sorry for that.'

The bedroom door creaked open and Eve stepped out wearing her second-favourite dress. She smiled down at him and reached out to take his hand:

'And I wouldn't expect anything less from you.'

'Still want me to grovel to Hamm though?' he asked hopefully.

'Still grovelling,' she told him. 'The truth: I'm just glad it's over. This case was getting under your skin.' She frowned at him: 'It *is* over?'

'It's just, it doesn't make sense.'

'You've got to leave it be now. For your job . . . For me.'

Chambers hesitated.

'Ben! Tell me it's over!'

'It's over. It's over,' he said in surrender.

'You promise?'

'. . . I promise.'

At 8.15 p.m. Chambers was parked outside Birkbeck College as a raucous group of students passed either side of his car. He barely noticed, however, even their elaborate fancy dress failing to pull his attention away from the second-floor window where Robert Coates flickered in and out of view as he worked into the night.

Deciding there was little to be gained from sitting in the cold watching him mark papers, he started up the engine and pulled away, intending to use the time to drive by Sleepe & Co. Restoration on his way home. Had he not been playing with the temperamental heater, he might have taken one final look up, might have noticed

Robert Coates's waspish face framed in the illuminated window, beady eyes fixed on the car as it moved off . . . watching Chambers leave.

Monday

CHAPTER 11

'Hey. It's me,' said Chambers, feeding the slot another ten-pence piece as he clamped the receiver between his shoulder and ear.

'What?'

'It's me!'

'What?'

'Ben! . . . Benjamin Chambers . . . We live together.'

'Ben? The connection's terrible. Where are you?'

He peered out through the panes and was rewarded with the sight of a breakfast drunk urinating against the wall of a job centre.

'Westminster,' he lied. 'Got The Houses of Parliament to my right and to my left . . .' He turned his head and pulled a face: a feral-looking cat appeared to be eating a dead rat. 'Well, you get the picture. I wanted to call you straight away. Guess who's got himself a probationary period!'

'You're not suspended any more?'

'No. You should've seen me. I calmly stormed right into Hamm's office, gently slammed the door, helped myself to a chair when asked, and then told him to his face just how truly sorry I was.'

'Thank you.'

'First shift back tomorrow.'

'I need to go, but that's such good news. Life can start getting back to normal again now, can't it?'

'Yes, it can,' replied Chambers, almost managing to tell her he loved her before she hung up on him. 'Back to normal. Back to normal,' he muttered to himself as he crossed the street to enter the run-down butcher's shop.

The man behind the counter eyed him suspiciously when, like a coiled snake, a length of thick rope attempted to break free of the bag he was carrying.

'What can I get you?'

'Two pints of your finest pigs' blood, please.'

Winter really, really could've done without being late for work. Dressed in jeans and a jumper, he leapt off the bus at Uxbridge Road and jogged past the shops towards Shepherd's Bush Green Police Station in too much of a hurry to notice Chambers waiting outside for him.

'Winter!' he shouted.

'Oh. *No. No. No.* I'm not talking to you,' he said, continuing by. 'Haven't you got me in enough trouble?'

'Not suspended though, I take it?'

'No,' he conceded. 'Strike two.'

'I need your help.'

Laughing bitterly, he turned to Chambers with furious eyes: 'No.'

'Come on. We *both* know something doesn't add up here. You *know* these two cases are related.'

'I don't *know* anything!' Winter bit back as it started to drizzle. 'The guy confessed, Chambers!'

'But what if we could prove he's lying? Show them we were right all along?'

Winter glanced at his watch: 'How?'

'We provoke them. We force them to react emotionally, to make a mistake.'

'And why does *that* sound so familiar?' he replied drily, looking his dishevelled colleague up and down.

'I'm OK.'

'You've got blood on your shoes.'

Chambers' eyes flicked downwards, but he didn't explain himself.

'I can't do this on my own. I can't watch both of them at the same time.'

'I'm sorry,' said Winter, turning away.

'Look, you've met these people. They're unhinged. I know if we push them, one of them is going to snap. They'll finally show their true colours. And when they do, we'll be waiting.'

'*You* sound unhinged.'

'Is that a *yes*?' Chambers asked him, wearing a desperate smile.

Winter shook his head: 'I'm not helping you. Please don't come here again . . . Goodbye, Chambers.' And with that, he turned round and walked away.

Tobias Sleepe left the alarm blaring in the darkness as he hurried back inside, a trail of blood winding its way behind him as he dropped the saturated rope onto the floor. Tied into a neat noose, it had been dumped on the bonnet of his van – a clear message of intent from a homicide detective who didn't know when to quit, one that would cost him dearly.

Wiping his hands on his apron, he climbed the metal staircase up to his office, taking a seat in front of the flickering security monitor. He clicked through the feeds, rewound the relevant tape a couple of minutes and then hit the *play* button. The untouched van stood just about visible in the bottom corner of the screen. Thirty uneventful seconds passed, Sleepe edging closer and closer to the black and white image in anticipation . . .

A shadow spilled across the concrete in front of the vehicle, seemingly appearing from nowhere . . . And then the heavy rope landed in a heap on the bonnet, tossed from the bridge above in order to evade his cameras.

Sleepe screamed in anger and slammed his fist on the desk, the monochrome recording scrolling down the monitor like the credits at the end of a movie.

Chambers was still scrubbing his hands in the sink when Eve arrived home from her evening class. Setting her weighty law books down, she gave him a quizzical look:

'You're doing *washing*?' she asked, the machine whirring away in the cupboard.

'Yeah.'

'Of your own free will?'

'Yeah.'

'. . . Why?'

'Being helpful.'

'Why?'

'Just was,' he shrugged, struggling to remove the last of the blood from under his fingernails. 'Want to go out tonight?'

'I'm tired.'

'Pictures?'

'I'll just fall asleep.'

'Can go and see something *I* want for a change then.' Turning the tap off, he dried his hands on a tea towel. 'Come on. I feel like celebrating.'

'Only *almost* getting yourself fired?'

'Not *just* that.'

'What then?'

Chambers walked over and embraced her:

'I don't even know: us . . . you . . . everything. I'm in a good mood. I just feel like everything's going to be all right.'

Robert Coates passed beneath the street lights that fended off the bitter night. Noting the absence of the silver MG Maestro he'd seen parked outside his cottage twice over the weekend, he turned into his garden. Spotting the envelope placed neatly in the centre of the doormat outside rather than posted through, he crouched down and picked it up, pulling the paper apart to unfold the short note written in what appeared to be blood:

Though your sins are like scarlet,
they shall be as white as snow.

Looking back at the deserted road, his eyes scanned the line of dark
cars: empty, still and cold. The only sound came from the trees, the
wind rustling through the leaves as their branches danced shadows
in the patches of orange light. Unconcerned, he carefully folded the
note up, placed it back inside the envelope, and opened the door to
his little house.

Tuesday

CHAPTER 12

Almost nine hours into his shift, Chambers' enthusiasm was starting to wane. The forecast snowfall had manifested instead as a relentless deluge of sleet and rain, reducing the number of calls he was being asked to attend while quadrupling the travelling time between those he did receive.

His mind was all over the place. He'd spent an hour in the office that morning but had thought better of enquiring about the Alphonse and Nicolette Cotillard investigation, conscious that he was already on very thin ice. It had been the most sensible course, a rare flicker of self-preservation, but after an entire day driving himself crazy wondering whether there had been any progress, he was beginning to regret not taking his chances.

Giving up on the traffic jam otherwise known as Great Portland Street, he parked up, fate depositing him directly across the road from a pet shop. An idea coming to him, he decided to brave the weather, weaving between the stationary traffic to reach the unassuming little store.

'It's raining cats and dogs out there!' the owner greeted him.

Presuming this an attempt at that infamous pet shop humour, Chambers smiled politely and made his way over to the accessories, immediately drawn to a dog lead with the silhouettes of different breeds decorating the leather.

'Need any help over there?' the owner asked him.

'No,' replied Chambers with a smirk. 'I think I've found just what I was looking for.'

Two-and-a-half hours later, Chambers found himself in the vicinity of Birkbeck College. Hoping to avoid catching a call with just thirty minutes of his shift remaining, he figured he'd sit tight, instinctively heading back to the same spot he'd parked in the other evening to stare up at the same second-storey window.

A familiar bespectacled face turned to peer out over the street. Although confident there was no way Coates could see him inside the dark car, Chambers slumped down in his seat until the window was empty once more. Nervously checking the time, he fiddled with the radio, having to turn it right up just to hear it over the storm.

Three songs later, whatever heat had been trapped inside the car with him had found a method of escape, and although Coates's office remained illuminated, Chambers hadn't actually laid eyes on the man himself for a little while. He watched the window, finding some solace in knowing precisely where either Coates or Sleepe were at any given moment.

The inevitable hiss of static crackled through the speakers, interrupting Bon Jovi's latest offering. He glanced at the dashboard clock and sighed.

'All units. All units,' the dispatcher called over the airwaves. 'Possible attempted murder in progress at the British Museum.'

Typical, he thought, knowing he was just around the corner from it:

'Yeah, it's Chambers. Allocate to me.'

'Received. Caller states he was attacked by a man with a syringe and can no longer feel his legs.'

Chambers sat up straight and turned on the engine, the wiper blades springing into action as he switched his lights on.

'Any further details?' he asked, already accelerating down the road.

'Caller is hiding in a staffroom in the Greek sculpture section . . .

Now saying he can't feel anything below his navel. He says he can hear his attacker, but he's trapped.'

'All received.'

'Backup en route.'

'Much obliged.'

Four miles away, Winter and Reilly were listening to the short exchange over the radio, Winter still gazing down at the little black box long after the static had dissipated.

'Don't even think about it,' Reilly warned him, for the first time ever, her terse tone giving way to genuine concern for him.

Fifteen minutes from the end of their shift, they were already going to finish late, and there would be dozens of resources far closer to back Chambers up.

'Winter . . . Winter!' He stared at her blankly. 'They won't tolerate any more. They told me as much. Let it go.'

He rolled them to the end of the street and paused at the junction – left would take him home, right to Chambers and more than likely the end of his career . . .

Abandoning the car in the middle of the pedestrianised square, Chambers sprinted up the steps towards the columns that lined the museum's grand façade. Passing through doors so massive they looked ready to welcome a proud God dropping in to admire his handiwork, he looked up at the list of exhibition halls pointing in all directions.

'Greek sculpture?!' he yelled, ID card held out on show. The woman behind the desk just stared at him. 'Greek sculpture?!' he demanded again.

She pointed across the hall.

Entering the maze of hushed corridors, Chambers followed the arrows overhead, surreal images flashing past but lingering in his mind: an open sarcophagus, dragon-like creatures carved from stone, the colossal half-head of a bearded deity. Finally, he reached a sign pronouncing: *Greeks and Lycians 400–325 BC.*

Taking out his non-issue flick knife, similar to those carried by half the force as a last resort, he entered the first moodily lit hall, a gauntlet of gods waiting for him like sleeping giants. Feeling worryingly exposed, he stuck to the thin pathway of light running the length of the room, as though it were a bridge spanning a void, to reach the entrance to the Mausoleum of Halikarnassos.

Long shadows were thrown from spotlit sculptures, incomplete and ravaged by time. Noticing an inconspicuous door set into the wall, he made his way over, finding only cleaning supplies inside. Sensing something move behind him, Chambers raised his weapon and spun round, the gallery looking every bit as still as before . . . but then heard hurried footsteps coming from the next hall.

Chasing the sound, he found himself in yet another deserted room, the ambiance disrupted by a rectangle of warm light spilling from an open doorway. Conscious of his surroundings, Chambers approached slowly, more of the room coming into view with every step until he reached the threshold: the office empty, a phone off its cradle and left to sing its disconnected tone.

The sound of running footsteps returned.

Chambers reacted too late, feeling a sharp pain in the back of his neck, but lashing out with the knife as he fell forward and somehow managing to kick the door into his attacker as he hit the floor. The flimsy wood sprang back, but Chambers kicked again. This time, the catch reached the frame as he scrambled up to twist the lock. The door trembled and split as it was assaulted from the other side, the handle jerking back and forth of its own accord as it was tried repeatedly to no avail.

And then, as suddenly as it had begun, everything went quiet.

Chambers held his hand up to his neck, fingers returning wet with blood. Trying to remain calm, he reached round and squeezed the wound as per his training, bleeding it as he would any other needle-stick injury, feeling the warm droplets run down his back. Ignoring the pins and needles in his fingers and toes, he picked the knife up off the floor and pulled the door open: no trace of his attacker anywhere until an alarm went off nearby.

Feeling as though he were drunk, he ran towards the noise, bursting out through the emergency exit and into a service alleyway. As a vehicle started up, he was thrown into stark light, the sleet distorting the air around him as the Ford Transit reversed aggressively. Chasing it out to the front of the museum, Chambers' vision felt slightly delayed, giving his movements an almost dreamlike quality, the tingling in his fingers spreading to his palms. The burnt-orange van bounced down the kerb backwards and then sped off as he dashed back to his own car.

Groping blindly for the handset, he fired up the engine and took pursuit:

'Control? . . . Control?!'

'Receiving.'

'Chambers. In pursuit of orange Transit heading east on Bloomsbury Place,' he slurred.

'Repeat. Which street?'

'*Boom . . . sby Pace.*'

'Detective Chambers, I can't make out what you're saying. I *need* to know where you are.'

The van accelerated, speeding through a red light. Chambers stamped on the pedal in response, his left arm hanging limply at his side as bright lights blurred past the windows, the engine screaming at him to change gear, the car continuing to gain speed: 50mph . . . 55mph . . .

Slumping against the steering wheel as they passed the Kimpton Fitzroy Hotel, Chambers pulled up alongside the speeding van, unable to make out the figure in the driver's seat. Feeling the numbness climbing his neck, he pulled on the wheel in a final act of desperation.

The car smashed into the back end of the van and sent it into a wild spin while his own vehicle hit the crossing and flipped, rolling devastatingly again and again, spraying metal and glass into the air before finally coming to a rest on its side.

Chambers regained consciousness. He was lying face-down on the road, having been thrown from his crumpled mess of a car that was still rocking precariously beside him. He couldn't move a single part of his body, couldn't speak, couldn't do anything more than watch as the damaged van reversed back up the street towards him.

He tried calling out, a feeble groan all he could muster as a set of boots came into view, retrieving something from the back of the vehicle before strolling over. He tried to shout, to plead, tears of frustration running down his face as a rusty saw was placed on the ground beside him. Sensing the figure standing over him, he watched its shadow kneel down, overcome with panic and helplessness when a gloved hand reached over to pick up the saw.

Unable to feel any pain, Chambers could still feel the hair pulling against his scalp when the shadow repositioned his head, just as he could feel the pressure of the serrated blade against the back of his neck, the vibration of the teeth catching on bone . . .

The roar of an engine preceded the arrival of a patrol car skidding around the corner, blue flashing lights making the carpet of broken glass sparkle beneath him. The sirens blared in warning, the shadow releasing Chambers' head and running back towards the van.

'Orange van, damage to the rear end, currently on Bernard Street!' Winter shouted into the radio as Reilly flung her door open and took off after the suspect. 'And I need an ambulance to the Kimpton Fitzroy! Now!' he added as he climbed out, taking a few seconds to process the devastation before him. The wrecked car was littered all over the road, its one working headlight shining back over its chaotic path.

His mouth fell open when what appeared to be a large snake started slithering towards them, piercing green eyes catching in the light.

'Police! Stop!' he heard his partner yell.

Forcing his attention away from the surreal scene, he rushed over to Chambers, on first glance believing him to be dead – pale bone visible from within a horrific wound across his neck, the sight of his right leg stripped of flesh and still partially crushed beneath the unstable car stealing his breath away.

'Stop!' shouted Reilly as the orange van crunched into gear, its tyres squealing and rear door hanging uselessly as it skidded down the street.

Winter knelt beside Chambers and was relieved to find a weak pulse, the smell of petrol intensifying as the car bled out over the tarmac. Quickly removing his belt to form a makeshift tourniquet, he watched a sea of flashing lights appear in the distance, the retreating van slamming its brakes on and turning round before accelerating back up the road towards them.

'Hey. It's Winter,' he told his gravely injured colleague. 'You're gonna be all right,' he promised, one eye on the vehicle heading straight for them while an obliterated bollard threw sparks at the growing puddle of petrol and oil. He pulled the leather belt as tight as he possibly could, only slowing the bleeding.

The van's throaty engine growled as it gathered momentum.

'Get out the road!' yelled Reilly, sprinting back towards their patrol car.

Winter attempted to lift Chambers but couldn't, his foot firmly pinned beneath the upturned vehicle. He tried again just as a single spark landed in the dark puddle, setting the road alight, the van less than a couple of hundred metres away.

'Leave him, Winter!' his partner cried. 'Leave him!'

Wincing, Winter grabbed hold of what remained of Chambers' leg, twisting it as he pulled, the trapped foot finally coming free. Grasping the incapacitated detective's hand, he dragged him away from the car only moments before it caught light, the ruptured fuel tank combusting almost instantly.

The explosion momentarily blinded them all, Winter rubbing his eyes and watching in horror as the orange van swerved off course, now heading directly for the patrol car.

'Reilly!' he called out, his dazed partner folding under the wheels like a ragdoll as the van mowed her down and sped off into the night. 'Reilly?!' he yelled, staring at the motionless heap bathed in firelight. Taking a step towards her, he noticed the fresh pool of blood he was standing in, still flowing copiously from Chambers' leg.

In stunned shock, he dropped to his knees and readjusted the tourniquet, adding his entire weight above the artery just to stem the bleeding, only to be faced with an impossible choice when his crumpled partner reached out for him, Winter unable to move, unable to go to her.

'Help's almost here!' he shouted desperately, the flashing lights closing in fast. 'I'm here, Reilly! Just hold on! Thirty seconds, I promise! Just hold on!'

Her hand flopped to the concrete.

'Reilly?' he called. '. . . Reilly?!'

A chorus of sirens filled the night sky. Breaking down, he watched the sleet fall in the glow of the boutique shops that lined the road, such a mundane setting for so life-changing a moment, no sign of the jet-black serpent he'd seen only sixty seconds earlier. Wondering whether it had even been real, whether *any* of it was real, Winter closed his eyes, willing himself to wake up.

Seven years later . . .

Friday 15 November

1996

CHAPTER 13

She wasn't quite sure what had woken her up: the tainted sunlight jaundiced by the stained curtains, the November chill breathing over her exposed shoulders, or the slamming of car doors out on the street.

Freeing her arm from under her emaciated friend-cum-dealer-cum-casual companion, she sat up on the ripped mattress, the bed sheet slipping away bit by bit, as if unveiling a work of art. Intricate tattoos fought to stake their claim to goose-bumped skin, pouring the length of both arms and even spilling onto her hands once they'd completely filled her back and chest. Careful not to tread on the discarded needle she had to thank for her restful night's sleep, she got up to put some clothes on, hearing the front door burst open downstairs:

'Police!'

'On the floor! I said: on the floor!'

As heavy footfalls stormed up the stairs, she left her unconscious acquaintance where he lay to peer round the wall, pulling a string jumper over her head as along the corridor another door was separated from its frame:

'Police! Get on your knees!'

They were in her friend Greg's room – a treasure trove of narcotics, counterfeit goods, and dubiously acquired high-end bike parts.

Cursing when she spotted her rucksack and boots in the doorway, she cautiously stepped out to retrieve them, creeping into the hall just as more officers came thundering up the staircase.

Rushing into the next room along, she pushed the door to and waited for them to pass.

'What . . . What's going on?' asked a girl she didn't recognise from the threadbare sofa, hair hanging over mascara-smudged eyes, needles still hanging out of either arm.

'*Shhhh!*' she whispered back. 'It's nothing. Go back to sleep.'

More than happy to oblige, the girl lay back down and pulled the duvet over her head.

Rolling her eyes, she didn't feel the least bit guilty. There was no way she'd make it out with one of her old school friend's half-fried floozies in tow.

Seizing her opportunity, she tiptoed back out into the corridor and started heading down the stairs, freezing when four more officers entered the squat house, filling the hallway below and blocking her exit. With no other option, she hurried back up, returning to the room she'd just come from as a commotion broke out: Greg, as addicted to poor decisions as any drug, deciding to put up a fight.

She gently shut the door and rushed over to the frosted window, pushing the stirring girl's head back down onto the pillow on her way past. Opening only at the very top, she squeezed her rucksack through the narrow gap first and then dropped her boots out one at a time. Clambering up onto the windowsill, she scraped several neat white marks across her skin as she fell out onto the fire escape.

London was its usual grey self as she stepped into her boots, threw her rucksack over her shoulder and started climbing down towards the street, the devil on her shoulder convincing her to skip the last ten rungs by dropping onto the bonnet of a police car, which turned out to be less unoccupied than first thought.

The young officer in the driver's seat stared up at her with his radio handset hovering in front of his open mouth.

'Oh, shit,' she muttered before leaping down off the vehicle and sprinting into the alleyway opposite.

She emerged out on Parliament Street and joined the procession of office workers marching down the road. Conscious that she was still far too conspicuous among the suited and booted, she tied up her chin-length hair and swiped a pair of plastic sunglasses from a street vendor's display.

Seeing a police car pull up at the junction ahead, she forced herself not to react and continued walking straight towards it, watching out of the corner of her eye as it turned onto the main road and rolled by. She'd made it at least another five paces before hearing the sirens wail.

Breaking into a sprint, she shoved a businessman out of her way and tore across the street, car horns blaring in her ears as she entered The Red Lion pub, exiting through the back onto Derby Gate. As she hurried up to the rear entrance of a nearby building, she could hear the sirens getting louder . . . the patrol car speeding around the corner after her.

'Come on. Come on. Come on,' she whispered, stepping forward one place in the queue.

Handing the man at the entrance her ID card, she stepped through the doors of New Scotland Yard just in time, a smirk on her face as she watched the police car give up the hunt and turn round.

Performing her morning ritual, she got off the lift two floors higher than she needed to, the short walk to the stairwell providing an opportunity to peek through the glass doors of the Homicide department. A recent recruitment freeze coinciding with a one-off opportunity to progress in the Narcotics team had diverted her career path temporarily, but if there was one thing she had learned during her short time on the force, it was that it was always easier to move sideways than upwards.

Coming out of the stairwell, she headed into the toilets to make herself look a little more presentable, washing her face and removing her nose and lip rings ahead of facing her achingly conservative training officer, Dennis Trout, who'd no doubt already be sitting at his desk raring to go.

*

'Goodness. Goodness, Ms Marshall,' he exclaimed as she slumped into the chair opposite. He was well into his fifties and was an inherently kind-natured, gentle and dull human being. Dennis didn't smoke. He didn't drink. He liked model aeroplanes. How on earth he'd survived a career in Narcotics, when he looked like someone who'd water down cough mixture, was beyond her. 'You're almost an hour early!' he informed her before eyeing the rather see-through jumper and ripped jeans disapprovingly. 'Ummm, Marshall.'

'I know. I know,' she cut him off. 'Hey, was there a raid this morning I didn't know about? Thought I passed something on my way in.'

With a frown, Dennis clicked about on his computer before glancing around the room. 'Not us,' he shrugged.

'As long as I'm not missing out,' she smiled. 'Coffee?'

'That would be grand. But first . . . And I know it's not really my place to say, but . . .'

'Go ahead,' she huffed.

'It's just, I never realised you had so many . . .'

'Tattoos?'

'Yes.' She waited for the point that was presumably on its way. 'Perhaps I could give you a bit of friendly advice from someone who's been "inked" himself.'

'I would *really* like that,' said Marshall sarcastically.

'Don't get any more.'

'Great.'

'Don't get me wrong, you look great, and you've got your whole angry biker *thing* going on. But over time they're going to fade and turn blue, and by the time you're my age you're going to look like a . . .'

'A . . .?' she prompted him as he searched for the right word.

'. . . Smurf.'

Unable to help cracking a smile, she got up and squeezed Dennis's shoulder affectionately:

'Duly noted. So, how about that coffee?'

*

At 7.15 p.m. Chambers climbed the driveway up to his front door, the framework of scaffolding standing between him and the house an unwelcome reminder of prison cells and work-related stresses every time he returned home. Suffering with a streaming cold, eyes watering and nose rubbed raw, he was back almost forty-five minutes late, time enough for the atmosphere inside to frost beyond saving.

Kicking off his shoes, he assessed the battlefield: Eve was slaving away in the kitchen, a half-empty bottle of wine on the worktop, while his mother made unhelpful remarks from the dining-room table:

'You'll kill us all if you reheat that.'

'I should be so lucky,' muttered Eve under her breath before calling back: 'I'm not *re*heating it. I'm just *still* heating it. There's a difference.'

Mrs Chambers scoffed at that: 'Maybe where you come from.'

'Evening both,' he greeted them, taking his cue to intervene. 'I'm sorry I'm late,' he said, hurrying over to assist Eve, who gave him a distracted kiss to the eyeball.

'Something going on at work?' she asked.

'There's *always* something going on at work,' they chimed in unison, much to the un-amusement of the elderly woman.

When they finally sat down to eat, Chambers sighed in relief, rubbing his right knee as Eve watched him in concern.

'You've been overdoing it,' she told him, slurring ever so slightly, deciding that having tried sticking up for herself, killing her with kindness, and one eventful time even threatening to deprive the old bat of grandkids just to spite her – she'd try drinking her way through her mother-in-law's biannual visit. 'You need to tell people you can't be on your feet all day.'

'I'm fine. And I don't want everyone knowing my business.'

'It's your leg, not your hopes and dreams!'

'I don't want them to know!' His expression turning sad, Chambers took her hand, his mother looking as though she might lash out with the knife to separate them. 'Because it's a constant reminder of the only time I *ever* broke a promise to you. And I *hate* that.'

Eve squeezed his hand tightly.

'So, "bungalow" is just a fancy term for a flat with a roof then, is it?' blurted Mrs Chambers, crapping all over the touching moment.

'Why do you love stairs so *fucking* much?!' Eve snapped back at her, patience apparently exhausted.

Even the extractor fan cut out to partake in the stunned silence that followed.

Deciding it best to pretend as though it never happened, Chambers let go of Eve's hand, picked up his cutlery, and smiled:

'This looks delicious. Shall we?'

Thirteen hours and an uneventful shift later, Marshall made it back to her tiny studio apartment, the concrete sliver of balcony looking out over the river its only redeeming feature. Tossing her bag onto the sofa, she commenced her nightly ritual: putting a meal-for-one in the microwave as she lit up a cigarette and stepped outside to watch the city lights on the water.

Shovelling the tasteless lasagne into her mouth, she opened a bottle of beer and took a seat on the floor beside the archive boxes, the contents of which were already strewn across the rug. She picked up a copy of the signed confession of James 'Jimmy' Metcalf, the homeless man who had admitted to murdering Henry John Dolan in the park and who had now served over seven years of his life sentence as a result.

Pulling the telephone as close to her as the cable would allow, she dialled the number for Belmarsh Prison scrawled at the bottom of the page, absent-mindedly shading in part of a sketch she'd been working on as she waited for someone to answer.

'Hi. It's Trainee Detective Mar— . . . Yeah, me again. So, did you ask him? . . . Yeah . . . You're shitting me?! Sorry. I mean: that's great! How about tomorrow? . . . I'll see you then.'

Placing the receiver back on its cradle, she looked down over her paper floor: the unsolved case file of Alphonse and Nicolette Cotillard; a pharmacological encyclopaedia's dog-eared page describing the effects of pancuronium bromide; the report on the assault of one Detective Sergeant Benjamin Chambers; and three overdue art history books, one lying open on a double-page spread of *The Gates of Hell*. She raised her bottle in toast to Rodin's beautifully crafted representation of torment and suffering, the darkest parts of her yearning for a fleeting peek inside.

Taking a celebratory swig, Marshall smiled.

Finally, she was getting somewhere.

Saturday

CHAPTER 14

'Morning all. We've got a white male, bulky, dark-blond hair . . . quite handsome apparently.'

'Sounds like me,' quipped Winter, responding into his walkie-talkie as he surveyed those in his vicinity.

A static click:

'Yeah, if by "dark-blond" you mean "losing his", and by "bulky" you mean . . . "just fat". Plus, this guy's not old.'

Winter looked confused: 'Old? You think I'm old?'

Radio silence.

'. . . Guys?' Only a shrill alarm responded, however, as someone fitting the description sprinted out through the doors. 'We've got a runner!'

Bursting out onto Fulham High Street, Winter's strip-light-strained eyes took a moment to adjust. Spotting the tracksuit-wearing man tearing past the cracked windows of Argos, he took off in pursuit, weaving between the traffic as he followed his suspect into the park.

'Hey!' Winter coughed unhealthily, already severely out of breath and losing ground. He went to vault a bench, but then thought better of it, making a beeline instead for an elderly gentleman wheeling an even elderly-ier bicycle: 'Sir, I need to commandeer your vehicle.'

'My wife gave me this bike.'

'I'm sure you can get another one.'

'Wife?' The old man seemed quite taken with the idea.

'Bike.'

'Oh . . . Then no.'

'Fine. I'll bring it back. I promise.'

With reluctance, the pensioner allowed Winter to straddle his ride home and, after a shaky start, pedal away after the untiring criminal.

Building up some speed, he was only a few metres behind when the man flung the gate open and headed towards the playing fields.

'Stop!' panted Winter, now feeling quite sick. 'Stop, you bastard!'

But when he failed to comply, Winter stood up on the pedals to accelerate harder – a final burst of speed as he aimed the handlebars at his quarry's back.

Wincing, he closed his eyes . . . colliding painfully with the criminal and landing in a confusing heap of wheels and limbs in the middle of the road.

Winter slapped a limp arm across his suspect's chest: 'By the power vested in me by the multinational conglomerate of Sainsbury's plc. I now pronounce you: not really allowed to go.'

'OK. OK. You win.' As the queue of traffic grew by the second, the man unzipped his jacket to surrender the can of Irn-Bru and copy of *Jurassic Park* on VHS.

'I've still got to take you in,' Winter told him, struggling to free his leg from between the spokes.

'Fair enough.'

'. . . Although, you might have to carry me.'

With his detainee's assistance, Winter hobbled proudly back through the doors of the supermarket, the alarms announcing his triumphant return like a chorus of trumpets. His boss, Dan, an acne-ridden grease slick of a teenager, looked decidedly unimpressed as he handed over the recovered merchandise.

'One can of carbonated unpleasantness and "an adventure sixty-five million years in the making",' he announced, reading the quote off the front cover. 'You're welcome.'

'You've been gone for like an hour!' Winter was a little thrown by the reaction. 'The alarms went off at least *five times* while you were off playing cop.'

'He smashed up some old geezer's bike and all,' added the inarticulate shoplifter, sensing the tables turning in his favour.

'Thanks,' Winter told him sarcastically.

The man smiled.

'Let him go,' said Dan.

'What?!'

'Let him go. I'll have saved up a house deposit, and you'll be six-feet under by the time the police get round to turning up.'

'I'm not old!'

'We got the stock back. And anyway, I know him. His nan lives down my road. Marcus, right?'

'*Uh-huh*,' grunted Winter's walking aid.

'But—'

'That's a *direct* order from your superior,' Dan told him.

One finger at a time, Winter released his grip on the young man, who adjusted his shell suit as though it were a fine three-piece. Looking bemused, he slowly backed away.

'Know what makes me manager material? I can read people. He won't do it again,' said Dan knowingly, watching Winter's capture roam the aisles like a rehabilitated animal he'd just set free.

'He's heading straight for the videos,' Winter pointed out.

'You're on your final warning. Understood?'

'Yes, sir.'

The alarms tripped once again, Marcus the shoplifter now nowhere to be seen.

Turning back to Dan, Winter had to physically bite his tongue in self-preservation.

'Well,' said the teenager, as though he were in no way to blame. 'Get after him then.'

Winter could actually taste blood now:

'Shoplifter – I'm in pursuit!' Hobbling towards the open doors, he muttered to himself: 'Maybe I *am* too old for this.'

*

Marshall wasn't sure how long she'd been staring into space when the metal door clunked loudly and a prison officer escorted a vaguely familiar man into the visitation hall. He looked well, far healthier than in the mugshot attached to his arrest file. He was of average height and build, clean-shaven, his long straggly hair now cut just above the ear. Even the dark-blue jumpsuit looked almost tailor-made on him.

'James Metcalf?' she smiled, getting to her feet and extending a hand. 'Trainee Constable Jordan Marshall.' She figured it best to drop the 'detective' bit.

'Jimmy,' the man replied. 'And . . .' He held his cuffed hands up apologetically.

'Can we take those off please?' she asked the guard, who looked uncomfortable with the request. 'It's all right. I've already cleared it with the governor and signed a waiver. Take them off please.'

The man did as he was instructed.

'Cheers, Frank,' said Jimmy pleasantly.

'Want me to stay with you?' the guard asked Marshall.

'No. Thank you. We'll be fine.'

'You behave yourself, Jimmy,' the man smiled. 'And don't think I've forgotten about the Spurs game.'

'Yeah, yeah,' laughed the younger man, the door closing on them as he turned back to Marshall. 'He might be a screw, but he's all right, Frank.'

She gestured for him to take a seat opposite the stacks of paperwork, where a chilled bottle of water was already waiting on the table for him:

'First off – let me say thank you for agreeing to speak to me.'

'Couldn't really keep saying no, could I? After you'd asked so nicely almost twenty times.'

'Twenty-two,' Marshall corrected him, 'but who's counting?' she said breezily but knowing full well why he had agreed to meet with her on this particular occasion. He was surprisingly well spoken for someone who had lived on the streets much of their adulthood. But then she felt like a judgemental bitch for even thinking it. She knew

better than most how a single decision could change the course of a
person's life. 'Can I get you anything before we begin?'

'I'm good.'

'OK. As I'm sure you've already gathered, I'm the minion they've
tasked with dotting the i's and crossing the t's on a warehouse-worth
of old case files. It's just a formality, but as I explained to your governor the other day, during my consolidation work, I came across a
discrepancy that could have a major bearing upon the evidence that
led to your conviction. So, obviously I felt it important to come in
and clarify some of the details surrounding the murder of Henry
John Dolan that you allegedly committed and confessed to.'

'I did it,' blurted Jimmy.

'I'm sorry?'

'I'm just saying I did it. There's no "allegedly" about it. I did it,
and I confessed. End of story.'

'Of course,' smiled Marshall. She glanced over one of the piles of
paperwork in front of her. 'I see from your file that you've been in
and out of prison since the age of eighteen, juvenile detention centres
before that. All for non-violent offences: theft, burglary, trespassing.'

'That's right.'

'And you made an attempt on your life back in eighty-six?'

'Just a cry for help,' Jimmy replied dismissively.

'You jumped off a bridge.'

'But not a very high one.'

'According to this, you were in hospital for the best part of five
months.'

He simply shrugged, so Marshall moved on:

'Your longest stint back out in the real world was from January
eighty-seven until the October of that year. What was different?'

'For the first time ever, I had someone looking out for me.'

'And what happened?'

'He didn't look out for himself.' Jimmy looked crushed, the memory still too raw. 'But that's the streets for you,' he continued, his guard
back up. 'One way or another, you lose everybody.' He picked up the
bottle of water and broke the seal, clearing the frog in his throat.

'I'm sorry,' said Marshall genuinely, before appearing a little distracted. 'I hope you don't mind me saying, but you're not at all what
I was expecting.'

'And what were you expecting?'

'Oh, I don't know. That wild-eyed, half-starved, dirt-encrusted
drug addict in the arrest file. But you don't look anything like that
man, quite the opposite actually. It would seem prison suits you,'
she complimented him with just a hint of flirtation, but enough to
make an incarcerated man crack a smile.

'They say it's supposed to be like purgatory in here, but they look
after us.'

'I'm glad to hear it,' said Marshall. 'Why did you give yourself
up?' she asked bluntly, changing pace to throw him off guard.

'I *ummm*. Guilt . . . I suppose.'

'The same guilt that failed to materialise the entire *twelve* hours
you knew Dolan was up on that podium slowly freezing to death?'

'I guess,' he replied, folding his arms defensively.

'Oh, I almost forgot,' said Marshall, placing her papers down
and moving a little closer to him. She lowered her voice: 'Could you
maybe do something for me? You know, on the quiet.' He looked
wary. 'An old friend of mine got himself locked up in here a while
back. I can't really be seen coming to visit him, for obvious reasons.
So, I just thought you might be able to pass on a message. Just that
his mum and Sammy are doing fine.'

'Mum and Sammy?'

'Yeah. Would you mind?'

'Sure. What's his name?' asked Jimmy, uncrossing his arms.

'You'll probably know him as "Roady" . . . Auguste Rodin?'

She watched him very closely as a blank expression formed on his
face on mention of the celebrated French artist.

'I don't,' said Jimmy. 'But I'll ask about.'

Marshall smiled sweetly: 'Where'd you get the paralytic from?'

'I told the police when they arrested me – a guy I knew who used
to work the park.'

'Oh, right. Was that Big Tony or Micky D again?'

'Big Tony.'

'Otherwise known as Anthony Stuart Baker,' she said, picking up another file, 'who just so happened to get busted a week after your arrest for pushing pills to schoolkids.' She flicked through to a book-marked page. 'Now, I'm looking at a list of his entire seized inventory, and while I'm seeing an impressive array of different drugs, there's no mention of pancuronium bromide. That's weird, right?'

'. . . I guess.' Jimmy held a hand to his stomach. 'You know what? I'm not feeling so good. I think I might need to go lie down.'

'Last question.'

'I'm sorry. I've really got to go.' He went to get up.

'One final question,' said Marshall, 'and you'll never have to hear from me again. I swear.'

'. . . One question,' nodded Jimmy, sitting back down and recrossing his arms.

'OK. So, Jimmy, do you *actually* think I'd have had the guard remove your handcuffs and then gone on to send him out of the room if I believed for even *one moment* you'd really murdered someone?' Now Jimmy looked legitimately unwell. 'Don't worry. Your secret's safe with me. I get it. It's tough out there. And I bet if you spend enough time in hell, purgatory's going to start looking mighty tempting.'

'I have no idea what you're talking about,' he said unconvincingly, taking another sip of water to cover his poor poker face.

'You're right-handed,' noted Marshall, and Jimmy looked confused. 'The bottle of water,' she explained.

'Yeah? . . . So?'

'Forensic science has come a long way in the seven years since you've been locked up in here. Our killer was left-handed,' she told him simply, risking everything on a weak bluff. 'Left-footed too, according to the footprints on top of the podium. It's all to do with weight distribution and all sorts of other clever stuff I don't really care about.' She picked up a file at random to read from a blank page:

'"Considering the angle of injection and clear finger marks in the bruises around the neck, there is almost no physical way that the murder could have been carried out by a right-handed assailant."'

She closed the file conclusively and tossed it back onto the table. 'Aside from the fact that I can *prove* your innocence and ruin this whole cushy little life you've set up for yourself in here, there's a person who *did* do this to Henry Dolan, who then went on to murder a woman named Nicolette Cotillard and her son, Alphonse, who was someone very special to me. This person is *still* out there. Christ knows how many others he's hurt over the years. We can stop him, but I need your help.'

'With what?'

'The truth, off the record, of course. I need to know *everything* that happened that night: how you ended up with the needle and syringe covered in Dolan's blood, how you knew it contained a paralytic.'

Putting his face in his hands, Jimmy sighed heavily.

'Jimmy, you've won. You got what you wanted; you escaped the streets for little more than a convincing lie and punching one police officer in the face. But you're not blameless in this any more . . . not now. Not when you know he's done this to other people.'

He looked back up at her unsurely: 'Off the record?'

'Off the record . . . and this,' she said, gesturing to the table of paperwork, 'all goes away.'

'You swear?'

'I swear.'

Taking a deep breath, he nodded: '. . . OK.'

'Goth, aisle two. Repeat: goth, aisle two. Wants to speak with security.'

Only partway through washing the mud off his face in the toilets, Winter picked up the walkie-talkie:

'On my way.'

Uniform ripped and caked in dirt, he headed back out onto the shop floor where the black-haired, leather-clad young woman was waiting for him at the end of the aisle, looking like something out of a horror movie.

'Hi!' Winter greeted her pleasantly, noticing her judgemental eyes take in his untidy appearance. 'Yeah, sorry. It's been a busy day.

I had to chase down a shoplifter . . . twice.' She didn't look particularly interested. 'People were *pretty* excited,' he assured her, starting to babble. 'Said I was very brave. One person even clapped!'

'That person you, by any chance?'

'What can I say? I was impressed . . . You wanted to talk to me?'

Manager Dan poked his unpleasant head around the baked beans:

'*Dos minutos* then back on the door!'

Winter waved in acknowledgement.

'I think there's been crossed wires,' Marshall told him. 'I'm looking for Police Constable Adam Winter.'

'*To* . . . put a spell on him?' he asked, immediately regretting provoking the scary young woman when she fixed her dark eyes on him.

'Detective Constable Jordan Marshall,' she announced, holding up her ID, her thumb tactically positioned over the word *Trainee*.

'Well, in that case, I am he . . . me . . . I mean, I'm Adam Winter.'

She looked at him dubiously: 'Oh . . . *Oh!* We need to talk.'

'We *are* talking.'

'Thirty seconds,' muttered Dan as he walked past, one of his larger zits actually popping when he scowled too vigorously.

'I mean talk, talk,' Marshall clarified.

'You *do* know I'm not currently on active duty, right? Hence the . . . this.'

'Yes. I gathered that.'

'OK. I've got a break at two.'

She checked her watch and went to leave: 'I'll see you then.'

'Hey, wait! What's this about?'

With a huff, she turned back to him:

'You don't remember me, but we've met before – Bridge Street Leisure Centre, more than seven years ago. You were "investigating" the murder of someone, but I doubt you'd—'

'Alphonse Cotillard,' mumbled Winter, lost in thought, 'and his mother Nicolette. And you . . . You were the girl with the cigarettes.'

'Yeah,' said Marshall, trying to hide her surprise. 'While you're on a roll, does the name Jimmy Metcalf mean anything to you?'

'It does. He admitted to the murder of Henry John Dolan, blowing our entire case out the water.'

'That's right. Well, I spoke with him this morning.'

'Why?'

'Because I needed to hear it from the horse's mouth. I needed to hear him confess.'

'*Errrm*. He already confessed.'

Marshall shook her head:

'Confess that he *didn't* do it . . . because it means you and Detective Chambers were right all along: that they had the wrong man behind bars, about the murders being linked, the killer replicating famous works of art . . . You were right about all of it.'

CHAPTER 15

'You ready?' asked Marshall as she stepped through the doors of the supermarket.

Winter nodded, zipping a fleece top over his uniform:

'There's a café down the road, if you wanted to—'

'Actually,' she interrupted him, 'I had somewhere a little further afield in mind. Got a ride?'

'Nope.'

'Guess we're taking mine then.'

They stepped outside, Winter watching in confusion as Marshall made her way over to the motorcycle parked illegally in front of the store. She unhooked a helmet from the back of the bike and handed it to him.

'*Errrm.* I don't know how to . . .'

'Hold on?' she asked impatiently. 'Get on.'

Still limping from his disagreeable experience on two wheels earlier in the day, he unenthusiastically obeyed:

'So, I like . . . *hug you* from behind?' he asked her.

Marshall looked at him as though he were a pervert:

'You hold here and here,' she showed him, eyeing him warily for several seconds afterwards.

Winter had his arms wrapped so tightly around Marshall she could barely breathe as she turned them into Old Mortlake Burial

Ground, the trees that marked the outer boundaries a thousand different shades of red and brown.

The moment she stopped the bike, he leapt off, removing the helmet and gasping for air, collapsing to the ground with the elation of an astronaut returning to earth.

'A graveyard?' he asked angrily. 'You put me through *that* to bring me to a graveyard?!'

'It's peaceful,' reasoned Marshall. 'And it's private. Let's go for a walk.'

Getting back to his feet, they started ambling between the rows of gravestones.

'How long have you been away from the force?' Marshall asked conversationally.

'*Ummm*. Five months . . . this time. It's a medical thing,' he explained.

'Oh. Sorry. None of my business.'

'It's fine. I'm actually in the process of coming back. But until then, Sainsbury's is a pretty good gig. I like my sleep, and now I never have to finish beyond nine o'clock. Life's good! So . . . Jimmy Metcalf?' Winter prompted her, changing the subject. He was also conscious that he'd already had a third of his lunch break and seen a big red cross next to his name in Dan's office earlier on.

Marshall hesitated.

'I've literally got seventeen minutes,' he reminded her.

A gust of wind blew across the cemetery and the sound of death rustled through the trees, the corpses of countless leaves discoloured and petrified as if in rigor mortis above them.

Marshall took a deep breath, feeling apprehensive now that it actually came to sharing her solitary venture with another person . . .

Jimmy Metcalf couldn't stop shaking. The cold no longer merely engulfed him – it had infected him.

'Stanley?'

He gave his friend a gentle shake, the elderly man slumping lifelessly against the doorway where he had unknowingly chosen to spend his final hours. The two of them had only spoken that afternoon, when the veteran rough sleeper had promised to check himself into a hostel, but the half-spent bottle on the step beside him suggested he had decided on another way of trying to make it through the night.

'Oh, Stanley,' Jimmy sighed sadly before kneeling down to rummage through the old man's pockets, relieving him of £3.72 in small change, the bobble hat he would no longer be requiring and the remainder of the bottle of whisky.

Taking a swig in honour of his friend, Jimmy squeezed his hand affectionately, got back up, and walked away without looking back.

Two hours later and barely able to keep his eyes open, Jimmy forced himself to keep moving, intending to walk the city the entire night, knowing that to stop was to freeze. He turned the corner into Bayswater Road, familiar turf, and was surprised to hear voices, unsure why anybody would choose to be out so late in such bitter conditions.

A little way up the street, two men were walking adjacent to the park – one large, muscular, the other slimmer and shorter. Clearly intoxicated, the larger man lost his footing on the ice, the other unsuccessfully attempting to catch him before they both landed in a heap on the pavement. Bursting into fits of laugher, the two figures made no effort to get back up, the slimmer man rolling on top of the other as they shared a kiss . . .

'Woah. Woah. Woah,' said Winter, who'd stopped walking. 'I take it the larger man is Henry John Dolan? So, you're saying there's some gay lover out there that we knew nothing about?!'

'Are you going to let me finish the story or not?' Marshall asked him.

'Sorry. Please continue.'

*

Feeling uncomfortable interrupting the intimate moment, Jimmy slowly started making his way over, deciding that the desperate circumstances justified the intrusion and conscious that drunk people tended to be more generous than sober ones.

As large snowflakes took it in turns to eclipse the street lights, Jimmy was still twenty feet away when the pair climbed back to their feet, the slimmer man leading Dolan through the entrance of the park.

Oblivious to his presence, the two silhouettes staggered along the meandering path as Jimmy watched them from the gates. Reaching into his pocket, he wrapped his fingers around the handle of his knife, deliberating. He'd never use it, of course. He just needed to scare them a little. The one time he'd done it before had all been over in less than thirty seconds, the red-faced businessman handing over the wallet as if he'd been expecting him, no harm done and an exciting story to tell his colleagues the next morning. The guilt, however, still weighed in the pit of Jimmy's stomach. He was a lot of things, and his life certainly hadn't turned out as he planned, but he'd never thought of himself as a bad person.

Still undecided, he followed them down the path, keeping his distance, Dolan's voice carrying in the silence:

'I'm so glad you made me come out with you.'

'And you thought you were going to have an early night!' laughed the other man.

Seeing his chance, Jimmy took the knife out and quickened his pace. But then the thin man took hold of Dolan's hand, leading him off the path and into the trees.

Curse words misting in front of his face, Jimmy glanced back the way he had come – the park still completely deserted. It was far too rare an opportunity to pass up, and if he'd ever needed a room for the night, it was tonight.

He crunched over the fresh snow into the treeline. The two men entered a small clearing, where a large stone pedestal stood ominously vacant, as if its occupant might be off roaming the park somewhere under the cover of darkness. Squatting down to avoid being seen, Jimmy watched as the slim man scaled the empty podium.

'Where are you going?' Dolan called after him. 'Are you crazy?'

'Come on,' the other man told him. 'I've got a surprise.'

'No! There's no way on earth you're getting me up there!'

'No way?' he asked playfully, disappearing from view before returning with a picnic basket and blanket he must have stashed up there earlier in the day. He took out a bottle of champagne and popped the cork. 'Suit yourself.'

Dolan huffed, feigning irritation as he started to ascend the frozen ladder towards the safety of the stone summit.

Chuckling at his own bad luck, Jimmy tucked the knife back into his pocket, feeling relieved more than anything else. He turned to leave, when an abrupt change in the slim man's body language caught his attention; as Dolan continued to climb, he retrieved something from the basket, all trace of the debilitating alcohol gone as his steady hands assembled the apparatus.

Jimmy was almost tempted to call out a warning, unsure what he'd even say – just that something didn't feel right? So, he remained quiet, watching in morbid anticipation as Dolan finally reached the top rung.

'A little help here!' he laughed, struggling to scramble over the ledge.

The other man slowly made his way over, extending his left hand to heave his bulky companion onto the stone as he brought his right hand down, sinking something into the back of his neck.

'What the fuck?!' bellowed Dolan, jumping unsteadily to his feet as the other man backed away. 'What did you do?!' he yelled, wincing as he rubbed the puncture wound.

The man in shadow remained silent as Dolan dropped to his knees.

Jimmy had unconsciously edged forward, out of the cover of the treeline and into the open, mesmerised by the events unfolding ten feet above.

'I can't feel my legs,' gasped Dolan in fear and confusion.

'*What did you do to me?*' *he asked. 'I can't feel . . . anything. I can't . . . I . . .*'

Coming to his senses, Jimmy hurried over to the base of the podium, out of sight of the man somewhere above him. As he tried to organise his thoughts enough to remember where the nearest working phone box was located, a pair of smart brown shoes dropped onto the ground beside him. Moments later, a black sock fell from the sky . . . and then another.

Deciding he needed to get out of there, Jimmy hesitated when a shredded shirt flapped ineffectually in the wind like a bird with a broken wing, something small and solid dropping into the very centre of it as it landed.

Edging as far as he dared from the safety of the stone pedestal, Jimmy peered down at a wet syringe attached to a crimson-tipped needle. On hearing something being dragged across the surface above, he darted out into the open, heart racing as he grabbed the expensive-looking shoes and the bloody syringe before tearing back into the trees, leaving the sobbed mutters of 'I'm so sorry' in his wake.

'He was . . . *crying?*' asked Winter incredulously.

'Apparently.'

He looked lost: 'So . . .?'

'Jimmy Metcalf takes the shoes for himself, the syringe and needle to give to the police, but by the time he'd reached the phone box, another idea had come to him. He believed Dolan to be dead already and was standing there with the murder weapon in his hand, seeing it as a one-way ticket off the streets for good. Did you ever listen to the tape of his interview?'

Winter shook his head.

'The detective clearly thought Christmas had come early: he asked leading questions, prompted him on details he was struggling with, and signed it off without another thought.'

'No doubt following Hamm's instructions. He'd have admitted to the murder himself before he would acknowledge that Chambers was right.' Winter sighed just as the sun managed to break free of the clouds. 'Please tell me Metcalf gave you a description of the killer.'

'Not much of one,' replied Marshall. 'Caucasian. Six-foot-ish. Possibly between twenty and thirty-five years old but perhaps even older. Dark hair. Sounded posh. And he was slim.'

'That's it?'

'That's it.'

'You said the killer handled the syringe,' he tried.

'And then Metcalf wiped it clean before covering it in his own prints. He didn't want to risk there being any doubt over his story.'

'*F-ing* Jimmy Metcalf,' he tutted.

'F-ing Jimmy Metcalf,' concurred Marshall.

'And he won't let you use this to get the case reopened? He'd do a good few years just for destroying evidence and lying about—'

'It's not gonna happen.'

'*F-ing* Jimmy Metcalf,' Winter reiterated. 'OK. Moving on to the elephant in the . . . graveyard: why are you telling *me* all this? Why not go to Chambers?'

'Ideally, I'd rather not come to either of you,' said Marshall bluntly. 'But needs must.' Winter frowned at the bitterness in her voice. '. . . I'm going to be a homicide detective one day. But the fastest way to ensure that *never* happens is to march in there and ambush my future superior with a half-baked theory. The reason I need *you* is because we both know how this job works – there are things that happened which didn't make it into the reports. I need you to fill in the blanks.'

'Such as?'

'What was Chambers looking for the day he decided to dig up Robert Coates's back garden? He can't realistically have expected to find a body?'

'Dogs.'

'. . . Dogs?'

'Chambers had his reasons for believing Robert Coates was going through rescue dogs at a worrying rate and that Henry John

Dolan was a first tentative kill, someone's graduation from animals to real people.'

'Interesting,' said Marshall, the cogs turning. 'Next one: I've read two differing accounts of what happened the night Chambers was attacked . . . both from you.'

'OK?' said Winter, a little defensively.

'One was the transcript of your interview on the night, the other: your official written statement the next day . . . What happened to the snakes?'

He looked tempted not to answer:

'The truth is: I don't know if they were real. Chambers was lying there bleeding out all over the road. The car was an inferno, and Reilly was . . .' Winter returned there for a moment. 'It was the worst night of my life. It still feels like a dream now. And I honestly wouldn't be surprised if I'd been seeing things. When no reports came in overnight about snakes roaming the streets of Bloomsbury, I thought I'd save myself the psych review and leave that detail out.'

'You know what you saw,' Marshall pushed him. She stopped walking. 'Did you see snakes?'

'I just told you—'

'Did . . . you . . . see . . . snakes?'

Winter shuffled self-consciously: '. . . Yes.'

'I believe you . . . They still refused to link the three incidents even after Chambers was attacked?'

'From my *very* limited involvement after that night, I know by the time Chambers was in any fit state to tell them he'd been injected with something, it was three days later, he'd been in surgery twice, and had a blood transfusion.'

'The evidence was gone.'

'The evidence was gone,' nodded Winter. 'And I don't think he pushed the matter.'

'Why not? Why would Chambers never make any effort to find the person who tried to kill him?'

'You'd have to ask him that.'

'I will. So, you didn't keep up with the investigation into Alfie and Nicolette's murders at all?' she asked with a judgemental barb.

Winter shook his head: 'Not really. They didn't want me anywhere near it. I know they liked a local dealer for it for a little while, even arrested him I think, but that all fizzled out to nothing.'

Marshall nodded: 'I've got the file.'

'And then there was that stalkery type who lived in the flats across from the leisure centre,' he recalled, 'but they were really scraping the bottom of the barrel by that stage. There's no shortage of bad people out there, doesn't make them the ones we're looking for.'

'I'm going to interview Henry Dolan's girlfriend,' said Marshall, thinking out loud, 'see what she knows about him holding hands with strange men in dark parks. Then I want to find out where Robert Coates is these days. He was the prime suspect then; he still is now.'

'What about Tobias Sleepe?' asked Winter. 'Are we discounting him just on Jimmy Metcalf's vague description of a seven-year-old memory?'

'Not *just* that.' Marshall nodded towards the gravestone they had stopped beside as another gust of wind rattled through the trees:

TOBIAS PERCIVAL SLEEPE

1932 – 1996

Devoted to his work.

'It still could've been him,' Winter pointed out while reading the inscription with disdain.

'Could've been,' agreed Marshall, looking a little pale. '*God*, I hope it was. But I need to know for sure.'

Sunday

CHAPTER 16

Winter awoke in the darkness.

Skin wet with sweat, he realised he was sitting bolt upright, the duvet a bloated heap halfway across the room. Still panting, he reached in panic for his legs, feeling the need to check they were still intact before switching on the lamp, but finding the insipid four walls of little comfort.

'*Shit*,' he whispered, wiping his eyes as he climbed out of bed and went over to the window, peering out to find the high street still dark, the sound of the bakers downstairs already hard at work the only sign of life.

When he let go of the curtain, the framed award perched on the windowsill landed face-down on the carpet. Tempted to leave it where it was, he crouched to pick it up, unsure why he had ever kept it so long – a celebration of his 'bravery', a constant reminder of a night he only wanted to forget.

How brave he had been while watching his partner die in the road like an animal.

How bravely he had cried as he held Chambers' leg together.

And what bravery he had shown during his five separate periods off work because he wasn't man enough to cope with his own memories.

Carrying it through to the kitchen, he dropped it into the bin, instantly feeling a little better.

A draught entered freely through the ill-fitting window in his bathroom, where he found a box of paroxetine at the back of the shelf – the fact that he had kept the medication proof of how little faith he had in himself.

He took two tablets with a mouthful of water and then regarded his reflection in the mirror: overweight, hair thinning, unable to perform his job and now, like so many times before, afraid to even go to sleep.

Pathetic.

Determined to be better, he returned to the bedroom and put on a pair of jogging bottoms and a sweatshirt, heading out for a run before the world woke up. Tiptoeing, so as not to disturb his neighbours, he quietly pulled the door to behind him.

Marshall stomped down the hallway, setting her neighbour's dog off, and kicked the front door open, too tired to even remove her boots as she collapsed onto the bed face-first.

Over the years, her non-conformist appearance had often drawn comparison to that of a vampire, that likeness never more accurate than when working the winter night shifts, where she could go days without seeing the sun, negating the need to even touch the blinds, her coffin-sized studio reduced to a dark box in which to sleep away the days.

She was so tired – teetering on the precipice of sleep and yet resisting, stuck in that no-man's-land in-between where one loses all control of where their mind takes them . . .

It was snowing, it had been for days, great drifts laying siege to the old railway arches, the road borderline impassable as she continued under the bridge where a torn banner curled towards the ground like a hanging snake:

ppy New Year 1996!

The adjacent units stood frozen and forgotten, either vacated long ago or still closed up after the extended Christmas break. So she was relieved when the lone pair of footprints she had followed down from the main road veered off to the right, ending abruptly at the rusted roller door of Sleepe & Co. Restoration. The snow-dampened silence was clearly playing with her mind as she could easily imagine a ghost still standing there, waiting to be invited in. She walked up to the shutter and banged against the metal, the thunderous echo sounding deceptively more confident than she was feeling . . .

The temperature plummeted as she crossed the threshold into Sleepe's world, her misting breath betraying her unease as she gazed up at the roof above them – razor sharp and surreal – punctured by a million icicles.

Her ID card felt firm in her hand – still brand new, as the hunched man gestured to the sparkling staircase – ice-covered metal climbing into the dark . . .

The office was warm, an ancient heater glowing like fire as they spoke over the case files laying open on the desk.

He was taunting her, every word laced with malevolence, mistakenly believing himself beyond reproach, protected by his advancing years.

Repulsed by his rotting smile, she looked down at the black-and-white image of Alfie – just a collection of printed shapes on a photocopied document, rage building inside her as the man who may have been responsible relished this last opportunity to toy with the police . . .

They were both on their feet, the frail man retreating from the little room as she screamed at him, Metropolitan Police Service-headed paper falling over the main workshop like giant snowflakes as she followed him out . . .

The small body lay at the bottom of the stairs, an island in the crimson puddle still spreading across the floor.

She stared at it for what felt like a long time, waiting to feel something, but it failed to come.

Stepping back into the office, she collected up the case files and removed the security tape from the VCR. Using the sleeve of her jumper, she wiped down the table, remembering the doorknob and the handrail on her way out. After fishing the last of the sodden documents from Sleepe's blood, she wrapped her scarf around her neck and headed back out into the snow.

Monday

CHAPTER 17

Marshall was feeling a little jealous of Winter's nine o'clock finishes after two particularly demanding shifts; three raids and a co-ordinated operation with London City Airport taking precedence over her after-hours enquiries. In desperate need of sleep, she'd been quite relieved when Henry Dolan's former girlfriend, Rita, wasn't available to meet until after work.

Braving the torrential rain, Marshall knocked on the door of the beauty salon, feeling a little self-conscious when the immaculately presented woman invited her to take a seat on the reception-area sofa, all the while regarding her with thinly veiled pity. As she unpacked her bag, she tried to ignore the similarly judgemental stares from the other women pottering around as they cleared up for the evening.

'Oh, I hope you don't mind; I asked Dave to join us,' said Rita with an Essex twang to match her Essex tan.

'Dave?' enquired Marshall.

'Dave Thornton. My boyfriend. He knew Henry almost as well as I did.'

Marshall scribbled a note as the largest man she'd ever seen in the flesh came over to sit with them. He looked simultaneously impressive and absurd, shuffling around with the limberness of a robot, while looking likely to burst should Rita be too careless with one of her talon-like nails.

'I like bodybuilders, don't I, love?' she said, giving Dave a risky squeeze as the first street lights came on beyond the windows.

'Thank you for meeting with me,' started Marshall.

'Don't have much choice when the police ask, do you?'

Marshall swiftly moved on:

'I'm not here to open old wounds, and I know your original statement inside out so don't intend to go over things discussed before.'

'What's this all about then?' asked Dave, leaning forward, alpha male to his core.

'Some new information has recently come to light,' explained Marshall. 'And it's *that* I'd like to focus on.'

'They caught the guy, didn't they?' Dave asked her, seizing any excuse to get riled up. 'That homeless bloke. He admitted it!'

'And my job is to ensure he never sees the light of day again,' she lied, reading the room. 'I need to make sure *every last box* is ticked or you know the lawyers will find a way in . . . They always do.'

'So, this is just a box-ticking exercise?' enquired Dave.

Marshall couldn't help the face she pulled.

'She *literally* just said that, didn't she?' Rita scolded him.

'I was just saying,' he shrugged, leaning back as far as his body would permit.

'What's this new information then?' asked Rita, turning back to her.

Conscious of the ears listening in at the back of the room, Marshall lowered her voice:

'It regards Henry's . . . sexual orientation.'

Rita looked blank-*er*: 'What? Like which way up he did it?'

'*Ummm*. No. Sexual orientation, as in . . . straight or gay.'

She noticed Dave take his girlfriend's hand.

'What you on about?' Rita asked her, but in a way that suggested she already knew.

'That he was seen with a man on the night of his murder.'

'Well,' Rita laughed, 'that doesn't mean—'

'A witness saw them holding hands,' Marshall cut her off. 'He saw them kiss.'

'I knew it. Didn't I say?' she asked Dave. 'I *bloody* knew it!'

'You *knew*?' Marshall asked her.

'Well, not "knew" knew, but I had a feeling.'

'There were . . . rumours,' added Dave mysteriously, putting his arm around Rita.

'I need to identify who that man was,' Marshall told them.

'How should I know?!' replied Rita, getting upset, tears threatening to spoil her perfect make-up.

'Anyone he'd been spending a lot of time with?'

'No.' She shook her head. '. . . Only . . .'

Marshall sat up in her seat: 'Only?'

Rita turned to Dave: 'There was that new guy . . . at his birthday party, remember?'

'Yeah,' he nodded. 'I remember.'

'Know his name?' asked Marshall.

They both shook their heads.

'He took off pretty sharpish once I turned up,' said Rita bitterly. 'Guess it makes sense now.'

'Do you remember what he looked like?'

'White guy. Sounded southern. You know, posh like. He wasn't big – just normal size. Dark hair. Pretty good-looking, I suppose. It was a long time ago.'

'Do you recognise either of these people?' Marshall asked them, handing over photographs of both Tobias Sleepe and Robert Coates. She held her breath expectantly . . .

'. . . No,' replied Rita.

'Nah,' said Dave, giving the pictures back.

Unable to hide the disappointment in her voice, Marshall picked her notebook back up:

'Anything else you can recall about this man? Anything at all?'

Dave clearly had a thought, the street light behind his head coming on as if on cue:

'He drove a van of some sort.'

'A . . . van?' asked Marshall excitedly.

'How do you know that?' Rita asked him.

'At the birthday party,' explained Dave. 'He got me to move my car to let him out. You know what parking's like at The George.'

'Colour?' Marshall almost shouted at him.

Dave screwed his face up as he wracked his brains: '. . . Orange. I think.'

'Thank you,' said Marshall, already packing up her bag. 'You've been very helpful.'

By 8.40 p.m. Sainsbury's was almost deserted, meaning that Winter had been roped in to stacking shelves, and had in turn enlisted the help of Marshall.

'This is big, right?' she said, holding an armful of PG Tips. 'You and Chambers both called in an orange van on the night of his attack, and now we learn someone fitting the description of Henry Dolan's killer drives the same vehicle!'

'It's something,' nodded Winter.

'It's more than just "something",' she argued as they moved on to the Nescafé, seeing as no one had bought any of the weird herbal stuff.

'We still can't link this to Alphonse or his mother.'

'You don't think both Rita and Jimmy Metcalf's descriptions could apply to Robert Coates?'

'No. Not at all. Dolan's girlfriend said he was "good-looking".'

'Well, that's subjective.'

'Not *that* subjective. The guy looks like a praying mantis.'

'OK then, how about this? Both Henry John Dolan and Alfie had someone new come into their life in the weeks leading up to their murders, a person who managed to remain completely detached from their social groups while still forming rapid and unusually close relationships with them: romantic in the case of Dolan, a strong male role model in Alfie's. That *can't* just be coincidence.'

Winter looked impressed: 'You're good at this whole "police" thing, aren't you?'

Marshall smiled: 'That's what you told me seven years ago.'

'You *are* forgetting one vital detail though,' he told her. 'You showed both the girlfriend and the friend a photograph of Robert Coates and *neither* recognised him.'

Marshall didn't really have a response for that small technicality: '. . . We're missing something.'

'Then perhaps it's time to bring Chambers in?'

She gave him a reluctant nod: 'You want to call him?'

'It's your revenge mission. Why don't you?'

'I don't know him!'

'Fine,' Winter huffed. '. . . *I'll* call him.'

The following evening, Marshall and Winter were sharing a taxi to The Black Dog in Camden, Chambers agreeing to a meeting with a man he hadn't seen in years and a woman he didn't even know on the most limited of information. Foot tapping nervously, Winter chewed his nails, watching the rain as the city scrolled past the windows.

'You seem a little on edge,' said Marshall as the cabbie argued with the radio in the front.

'I'm fine. Just haven't seen him since . . .'

'Since . . .?'

'Since I helped lift him into the back of an ambulance.'

'But weren't you partners?' she asked in confusion.

'No.'

'You didn't . . . visit him in hospital?'

'No.'

'Think he's forgiven you for that?'

'No.'

'And you didn't think *perhaps* you should've mentioned this before?'

'. . . No.'

The Wet Dog would have been a more apt name for the dank little establishment on the banks of the canal, the musk originating from damp shoes, complemented by stale beer and the resident Doberman by the fireplace, a nauseating cocktail as Winter and

Marshall squeezed into a nook beside the window. They sipped their beers in silence, watching the rowdy regulars exchange good-natured insults across the bar.

'Here he comes. Here he comes,' whispered Winter, getting to his feet, his nervousness catching, Marshall too getting up to greet him. Between them and the man waiting for the toilet, it must have looked as though they were receiving royalty in the far corner. 'Chambers!' he smiled as they shook hands.

'Been a long time,' he replied, catching Marshall glance down at his leg.

'Thanks for coming. I'd like you to meet Detective Constable Jordan Marshall.'

'Chambers,' he introduced himself, shaking her hand for a moment longer than felt natural as he regarded the intricate tattoos climbing her arm, her dark clothing and numerous piercings. 'Homicide?'

'Narcotics . . . at present,' she answered.

He smiled pleasantly and sat down.

'We took a guess,' said Winter, pushing a pint in front of him.

'Not even close,' smiled Chambers. 'But thanks.'

Silence fell over the group as he took a long sip of his drink. Wiping his Guinness moustache away, he looked up at them patiently.

'So . . .' Winter hesitated . . . and then chickened out: 'Your local?'

Marshall rolled her eyes.

'Used to be,' nodded Chambers, taking a fond look around the room. 'Not been back in years though. Seemed appropriate somehow . . . Are you still out at Shepherd's Bush?' he asked.

'Sainsbury's,' Winter replied cheerily. 'But hopefully coming back soon. Had a meeting with occupational health today, in fact.'

'Good,' nodded Chambers. 'That's good.'

The tense atmosphere returned as they all took a greedy chug of their drinks this time.

'So,' started Winter, trying again, 'as I mentioned, we wanted to talk to you about—'

'Henry Dolan, Alphonse and Nicolette Cotillard,' Chambers finished on his behalf.

'Right.'

'And as *I* mentioned,' said Chambers firmly, 'I'm not interested, and the only assistance you're getting from me is what you can extract over the next two-and-a-half pints.'

'Why bother coming at all then?' Marshall challenged him.

'I can go now, if you'd like?' he offered, getting to his feet.

'Of course not,' said Winter, glaring at Marshall. 'We need your help.'

Chambers looked at the young detective expectantly, whose begrudging apology was just about sincere enough to convince him to sit back down.

'It's a good question though. The *only* reason I'm here at all is because seven years ago, *this* man saved my life. But please, go ahead and say whatever it is you came to say.'

Over the course of the next twenty-five minutes, and another round of drinks, Marshall explained her connection to the case. She told him about Jimmy Metcalf's off-the-record confession and Henry Dolan's secret lover, about the orange van, and the official line on Tobias Sleepe's death, and then went on to share her theory about mysterious strangers suddenly entering each of the victim's lives.

'I think the next step is to speak to Robert Coates again,' she told him. 'Tomorrow. I'll engineer a "chance" meeting under the guise of a student, begin establishing a rapport.'

'"Establishing a rapport"?' Chambers nodded enthusiastically before picking up his pint, gulping down the rest and slamming the glass on the table. 'Well, be careful,' he said, standing up and walking out without another word.

Marshall turned to Winter: 'What the *hell*?'

'It always was a long shot,' he told her.

'He *really* doesn't give a flying fuck, does he?' she snapped, grabbing her coat.

'*Errr*. Where are you going?'

'To tell him *exactly* what I think of him.'

'Wait. I don't think that's . . . Wait!' he called too late, struggling to free his legs from under the table as he watched her storm out after Chambers.

'Hey!' barked Marshall as she marched along the dark canal path. 'Chambers!'

With a sigh of exasperation, he stopped walking and turned round, Winter rushing over to intervene.

'You should be ashamed of yourself,' she told him.

'Is that right?'

'How many years, precisely, does it take to become so bitter and detached that victims stop feeling like real people any more?' she asked him. 'You were able to just walk away so easily, weren't you? You didn't give a shit about Alfie or finding his killer. Neither of you did!' she shouted, glaring at Winter as well. 'You just went through the motions, collected your payslips, waiting to get reassigned to something easier . . . or skive off on the sick again,' she added, eyes on Winter once more.

'You don't know what you're talking about,' Chambers told her calmly but with a fire in his eyes.

After the hour's reprieve, the first raindrops began to fall, ripples forming across the surface of the water as if the canal had started to simmer.

Chambers turned to Winter:

'You think I'm getting dragged into this angry girl's crusade?' he asked before focusing back on Marshall. 'You're no detective. Not really. Think I didn't notice Mary and Jesus painted up your inner arm . . . over the track marks? Where did the Rodin end up?'

Marshall's eyes involuntarily flicked to her other arm.

'. . . You've been telling yourself you're doing all this for your teenage crush?' Chambers asked her. '*Bullshit*. I bet you don't even remember what he looked like. You're just a lost little girl who latched on to the first thing that came along to give her life some meaning, using it to justify how "messed up" you *act* like you are. If anyone doesn't give a shit about the victims here, it's you.'

'Chambers!' said Winter, his tone implying that he'd crossed a line.

On the verge of tears, Marshall turned away.

Looking a little guilty for the outburst, Chambers sighed:

'I just want to put it behind me. Every *fucking* time I take a step, it's a reminder. I don't need any more.'

'And you think I *do*?' Winter asked him. 'Why do you think I never came to visit you in the hospital? Why do you think I only managed to struggle on for another month before going off on the sick? It's because *every time* I closed my eyes, I was back there – wrapping my belt around your mangled stump of a leg, black snakes slithering around us as if Hades had finally spilled over, watching Reilly die alone in the street twenty feet away from me because I was holding your artery together! . . . I couldn't face seeing you.' With tears rolling down his cheeks, the heavens opened above them. He looked up and laughed bitterly: 'And guess what?! The nightmares are back again. But I'm still here, aren't I?'

Marshall couldn't meet his eye, as the one responsible for dragging him into her obsession.

'I had no idea,' said Chambers, giving his former colleague a reassuring pat on the back. He cleared his throat: 'While we're all sharing, there's something I didn't tell you . . . didn't tell anybody. When I said seven years ago you saved my life, I wasn't just talking about the leg. Maybe I'd have bled out, maybe not, it's irrelevant because as I was lying there . . . helpless . . . he came back for me.'

'The killer?' asked Marshall.

Chambers nodded:

'He reversed back down the street. He climbed out of his van, and he walked over to me.' Now even Chambers had bloodshot eyes as he revealed a secret he'd kept for so many years. 'He had a hacksaw in his hand . . .'

Marshall raised her hand to her mouth.

'He grabbed a handful of my hair and put my head in position . . . I felt the teeth of the blade pressing into my skin . . . That wound to the back of my neck – it didn't come from the car crash.'

Winter looked ill. 'But then you came skidding round the corner when you weren't even meant to be there . . . Saved me.'

'*Jesus*,' said Winter, rubbing his face as Marshall remained quiet, realising that she had unfairly judged these two men, who had already pursued this killer through Hell and back.

'This case almost cost me my life once,' Chambers told them, drenched to the bone, 'all because I broke a promise to my wife. I'm sorry. I can't make the same mistake again. Now, if you'll excuse me – I feel like shit.' He turned round to walk away but not before adding: 'Be careful. I mean that . . . Both of you.'

Wednesday

CHAPTER 18

The blade sliced through the skin with such ease, the first droplet of blood running down his cheek like a crimson tear.

'Shit,' muttered Chambers, unsure how long he'd been staring at himself in the mirror. He placed the razor down and washed his face off in the sink.

'I liked your beard,' Eve told him from the bedroom as she pulled her tights on.

'It went white,' he reminded her, speaking into a towel.

'I thought it made you look very . . .'

'Old?'

'. . . wise.'

'Same difference.'

As he dabbed at his newest injury, Eve called: 'I'll make us healthy omelettes.'

'With cheese?' he asked hopefully.

'You're not having cheese.'

Still holding a tissue to his cheek, Chambers absent-mindedly poked at his breakfast.

'Something going on at work?' Eve asked over the top of her coffee cup, opening her mouth to chime the inevitable answer with him.

'. . . *Huh?*'

She put her drink down: 'What is it?'

He gave her a weak smile: 'Nothing. Just didn't sleep that well.'

'Your leg keeping you up again?'

'Yeah,' he lied.

Downing the dregs of her coffee, Eve checked the clock:

'I've got to get to work. I'm in court today. Are you done?' she asked him, reaching out to take his plate.

'Sorry. What?' he replied dazedly.

'Are you done?' she asked again. 'Or are you going to finish this?'

Looking up at Eve with a pained expression, Chambers squeezed her hand: '. . . I haven't decided yet.'

Rucksack over her shoulder and dressed in shredded jeans and a flannel shirt, Marshall walked the halls of Birkbeck College, having made worryingly little effort to fit in amongst the sea of Nirvana and Rage Against the Machine T-shirts. She followed signs through glass-roofed corridors that sprouted ancillary buildings like off-shoots that had come into bloom.

Her plan: only to make contact for now. Her cover: a teary humanities student convinced she'd chosen the wrong discipline and thus completely ruined her life, seeking guidance on trans-ferring to a course that would allow her to specialise in her true passion: sculpture. Having only spent the previous evening revis-ing to complement what little she remembered from A-level art, she didn't feel confident for anything more than the most superfi-cial of conversations and planned on bursting into tears every time the gargantuan gaps in her knowledge were threatened to be exposed.

There was a part of her that feared somehow Robert Coates would recognise her. It was absurd, of course; she had been no more than an inconsequential leisure centre employee back then, and yet, the truer barbs in Chambers' derisive summation of her had made her feel closer to that directionless teenager than she had in a very long time.

The musty smell returned as she left the modern extension and entered a quiet corridor, the name plaques on the doors a hopeful sign that she was in the right place.

Approximately halfway down the long hallway, she stopped:

Prof. Robert D. S. Coates Ph.D.

Taking a deep breath while trying to summon some tears, Marshall knocked on the door.

. . . No reply.

She knocked again, waited, and then tried the handle to find it locked. A glance to the left . . . and then to the right, she slid her Swiss army knife out of her pocket, confident that it was more than capable of overcoming the antiquated mechanism. Jamming the nail file attachment between the door and the frame, she jimmied it until she heard a click.

'Can I help you?' someone asked from the next doorway along.

Dropping the tool into her back pocket, Marshall turned round, red-faced and committedly snotty:

'I'm looking for Professor Coates,' she sniffed.

'He's not here,' the tank-topped little man informed her, voice full of suspicion.

'But I *need* to speak to him. It's urgent!'

'Wednesday's his day with his mother. He'll be in again in the morning.'

'OK,' she sobbed, already starting to back away.

'Can I let him know who stopped by?' the man called after her.

'OK!' Marshall shouted back unhelpfully, marching straight for the nearest exit.

Parked just across the street from the main entrance, Winter was part-way through stuffing a breakfast bap into his face when he spotted Marshall come rushing out through the doors. Binning the remainder, he sucked his fingers clean and went to cross the road, hesitating when he saw Chambers making a beeline across the courtyard for her. Electing to stay well out of it, he sat back down on the wall, watching their body language in interest, lip reading, convinced he was picking up the gist despite the distance between them:

'You, sir, were really rather rude to me the previous eve!' Marshall probably said, gesticulating wildly.

Chambers held his hands up, either in peace or for an optimistic, and frankly inappropriate, high-five. He moved his right hand over his chest:

'My heart aches, for I am so sorry.'

'I'm good at this,' Winter complimented himself, peering down into the bin at his half-eaten breakfast. None of it looked to have escaped the packaging, at least not enough to come into contact with anything else in there. Checking no one was looking, he reached in and retrieved it, missing several lines of dialogue in the process:

'. . . you made it *quite* clear *blah blah blah . . . blah*,' Marshall almost certainly said.

Chambers shook his head regretfully:

'I *something* didn't *something* to *something* you.'

Winter was pretty distracted with his breakfast at this point, which, on closer inspection, had most definitely come into contact with something else in there.

'Did you find Coates?' Chambers asked her.

That was an easy one.

'No,' replied Marshall. 'He spends Wednesday's at McDonald's.'

'McDonald's?'

'McDonald's,' nodded Marshall.

'Then let's go. Wait, where's Winter?' Chambers asked her.

'Over there,' said Marshall, pointing in his direction.

He raised his bin breakfast in greeting.

'I really respect that guy,' Chambers might have said. 'He's the best.'

Marshall nodded in agreement: 'Yeah, Winter's the coolest.'

'I *am* the coolest,' smiled Winter, binning the sullied bap for good this time and getting to his feet as they crossed the road. 'Morning,' he said conversationally.

'Sorry about last night,' Chambers told him, sounding better, but without the aching heart bit, which didn't feel quite as sincere somehow. Winter waved it off. 'This yours?' he asked, frowning at the U-Drive van he seemed to be clambering into.

Winter patted the dashboard proudly and then wiped his sticky hand on the seat:

'Rented this morning . . . In case we needed to transport a prisoner in the back.'

Seeing as they'd only just made up, Chambers diplomatically bit his tongue. Following Marshall up into the cabin, he strapped himself in, the three of them sitting in a row like an audience watching the dullest movie ever.

'We'd better catch you up on what we were discussing,' said Marshall.

'No need,' said Winter knowingly. 'McDonald's anyone?'

Both Marshall and Chambers looked blank. Suspecting his lip reading skills still needed more work, he started up the engine.

'Perhaps you'd better catch me up.'

The parking bays at Tall Oaks Nursing Home hadn't been designed with poorly driven, long-wheelbase rental vans in mind.

'You're going to hit it,' warned Chambers, peering down at the shrinking gap between them and a new Fiesta.

'No, I'm not,' insisted Winter.

'Why would I lie?!' Chambers asked him.

'Just reverse and try again,' Marshall told him.

'Fine!' huffed Winter, searching for the gear. 'Give me a break; I haven't driven in a while.'

'*Caution: vehicle reversing. Caution: vehicle reversing . . .*'

'*Jesus Christ,*' muttered Chambers, shielding his face. 'If Coates spots *either* of us, we're blown. Just park out on the road.'

Finding a space directly across the street from the nursing home, the three of them climbed out and then bundled into the back to finalise their plans.

'Notice the maroon Vauxhall Cavalier Winter almost backed into?'

Chambers asked them. 'It's Coates's. He's in there.' He removed something from his coat pocket.

'Is that . . . a wire?' Winter asked excitedly.

'Didn't want you going in there *alone* alone,' he told Marshall, passing it to her.

Feeling a little foolish for not thinking of it herself, she set about feeding it under her shirt.

'We'll be listening,' Chambers assured her. 'First sign of trouble, me and Winter will come running.'

'I'll be fine,' she said, lifting her collar towards her mouth, Chambers holding a set of headphones up to his ear: 'Testing: One. Two. One. Two.'

He nodded: 'So, what's your "in"?'

'I'm looking around the home with a view of moving my mother there. Taking care of her the past year has finally got too much and prevented me going to uni to study my one passion in life . . .'

'*Sculpture*,' the three of them chimed together.

'I like it,' said Chambers.

'Do we know what condition his mother is suffering with?' asked Marshall.

'Afraid not.'

'Shame,' she sighed. 'Could've used it as common ground. Oh well, wish me luck,' she said, getting up and jumping out without a moment's hesitation, sliding the door closed behind her.

'Bye then,' mumbled Chambers.

He handed Winter a pair of headphones, who eagerly put them straight on.

'Good thing you came back!' he yelled across the van while playing with the volume controls.

'I'm not back,' muttered Chambers, more to himself than the man who quite clearly couldn't hear him, as he pulled his own headphones over his ears.

It was mid-morning coffee; perfect timing. No one even gave Marshall a second look as she ambled among the residents and assorted relatives in the crowded recreation room. Quickly discovering that Coates wasn't there, she edged towards a set of doors labelled Residential Wing.

Waiting for an opportune moment, a conveniently timed Scrabble dispute broke out, distracting several of the staff as she hurried through unnoticed, a scruffy whiteboard on the wall proving useful:

Room 20 *Judith Hart*

Room 21 *Meredith Coates*

Room 22 *Carol McNiell*

Distressed shouts filled the corridor, growing louder as the room numbers ascended. By the time she passed room seventeen, Marshall was able to decipher occasional words:

'It's poison! It's all poison!'

There was a loud crash and then a healthcare worker emerged a few doorways along, wearing both a cup of coffee down their uniform and a pissed-off expression. Marshall froze guiltily, but the man stormed by without paying her the remotest bit of attention.

Passing rooms nineteen and twenty, she stopped outside the open door to room twenty-one, the commotion inside jarring with the soothing sound of someone singing:

'If all . . . we have . . . is the time. . . we share . . . then I . . . have all . . . I need.'

The shouting subsided as a frail voice joined the first:

'And if I . . . could spend . . . all my time . . . with you . . . then time . . . is a friend . . . to me.'

'Is that better, Mum?' the man asked, Marshall able to see him take the woman's wrinkled hand in his. 'Come on. Shall we sit you up and get some of this coffee into you?'

Deciding there was no way to engineer a 'chance' encounter under the circumstances, Marshall turned back and hurried out before she was seen, something about the exchange she'd witnessed niggling away at her as she climbed back into the van.

'Forget what you went in there for?' Winter asked jokingly. 'Serial killer. You went in there . . . for a serial killer.'

'It wasn't the time,' she bit back. 'He was feeding his mum in her room. She seemed confused.'

'Think we'll get anything out of her?' asked Chambers.

'Based on what I just saw: not likely. But she could be different later.'

He nodded: 'Let's see where he goes next.'

Another forty minutes passed before they watched Robert Coates come out of the nursing home, whistling as he spun his keys on his finger. His hair was shorter now, his insect-like features softened considerably by modern glasses that suited him far better.

'Looks like someone found some swagger since we last saw him,' said Winter.

Marshall frowned, the same nagging doubts returning as she watched the university professor get into his car and drive away.

'OK,' said Chambers. 'Follow him.'

Winter crunched the van into gear.

'*Caution: vehicle reversing . . .*'

'He's going home,' Chambers told them, recognising the area.

'Can you get ahead of him?' Marshall asked Winter, who turned the corner and put his foot down, the sound of his security deposit rattling into the road as he hit the speed bumps at forty-five miles an hour.

'What are you thinking?' Chambers asked her in interest.

'Chance encounter . . . of sorts.'

'We're here!' announced Winter, stamping on the brake and pointing towards the house. 'The one with the gnomes.'

Grabbing her rucksack, Marshall flung the door open.

'Hey,' Chambers called after her. 'We'll be listening.' She slammed the door and hurried through the front gate. 'Again: goodbye,' he muttered, Winter parking them a little way down the street, both ducking under the dashboard when the familiar maroon car rolled by.

Winter was first to put his headphones back on.

'. . . One. Two. Testing: One. Two,' Marshall whispered through the speakers, sounding uncharacteristically anxious. 'I *really* hope you can hear me . . .' They watched in the wing mirror as Coates climbed out of his car, pausing as he approached the open gate. '. . . Because he's coming.'

CHAPTER 19

'What are you doing?'

Startled, Marshall dropped her sketchbook, which landed open on the apparently ironically intended *Welcome* mat. She spun round, looking both guilty and embarrassed.

'I asked what you were doing?'

'I *ummm* . . . Mr Coates?' she asked timidly. 'Sorry. I should say *Professor* Coates.'

The moment the words left her lips, she watched the man before her transform into a different person entirely: posture stiffening as he grew another two inches taller, mouth pursing to accommodate the buck teeth, eyes appearing to shrink back behind the glasses. Although playing the part of the flustered student, for a moment Marshall was genuinely rendered speechless.

'That's correct,' he replied, studying her every bit as intensely as she was him.

'Oh! I was just putting a note through your door,' said Marshall. 'I wasn't expecting you to . . .' She extended a hand and took a step towards him. 'Let me start again. Hi! I'm Laura.'

Giving her a feeble handshake, he immediately took a step back, re-establishing the space between them as he awaited an explanation.

'. . . I'm going to be moving into the street. Number sixty-five,' she lied, having spotted the *Let* sign in the garden as they'd sped past. 'I was talking to the lady next door . . . You don't happen to know her name, do you?'

Coates shook his head, in no way appearing to warm to his unexpected visitor.

'Anyway,' she continued, 'we got talking about art and the such, and I showed her some of my drawings,' she gestured to the sketchbook in her hands. 'And then *I* said I was hoping to study it at university, at which point, she told me a Birkbeck College art professor lived just a few doors down!'

'I see,' said Coates, relaxing ever so slightly.

'So, being neighbourly . . . or just brazenly cheeky, depending how you want to look at it, I was hoping we might be able to have a chat over a cup of tea or something? Just to get some advice about the best courses for me to apply for, what I might be able to do to give myself the best chance of being accepted.' She smiled hopefully.

Coates glanced down at his watch: 'Regrettably, today isn't—'

'Just one cup of tea,' Marshall pressed him, interrupting his excuse. 'Everybody needs tea!'

He looked torn: 'I don't have long.'

'Oh my God. Thank you *so* much!' He turned back towards the front gate. 'Actually!' she blurted. 'I *probably* should've mentioned that I don't have any furniture in there yet . . . or crockery . . . or a kettle – ulterior motives for accosting you like this!' she laughed, knowing that she was pushing her luck.

Coates fixed his insect eyes on her, Marshall unable to help but shift uncomfortably, it feeling as though he were staring straight through her laughable charade.

'Your medium?' he asked, testing her.

'Sculpture,' she fired back.

'Modern? Abstract?'

'Classical.'

He nodded in approval: 'A woman after my own heart . . . Artist?'

'Not a fair question. Could you pick just one?'

'Bernini.'

'Then I'll say . . .' She took a deep breath, deliberating how far she dared push him so soon: '. . . Cellini.'

A hundred yards down the street, Winter noticed Chambers tense up and close his hands together as if in prayer, for some reason behaving as though she'd given the wrong answer.

Marshall didn't dare breathe as she watched Coates consider her response, his emotionless features giving nothing away . . . But then a toothy smile broke across his face:

'One of the few true masters of the discipline,' he agreed, the approval as much a compliment of Marshall's taste as it was of the artist.

He gestured towards the front door.

'Oh, shit!' exclaimed Winter, far louder than he needed to. 'She's going inside!'

'She's fine,' said Chambers despite the concern painted over his face.

'Thought about something to say?' Winter asked vaguely, lifting his headphones.

'What?'

'You know, if we have to burst in there,' he explained. 'It's been seven years. Seems like one of us should say something cool, don't you think?'

Chambers looked at his colleague as though he were an idiot:

'All yours,' he told him, trying to focus on the feed from Marshall's wire as she stepped into the house.

As Coates crouched down to collect up the post and crumpled note, Marshall's eyes scanned the precarious piles of paperwork, years-worth of bills and correspondence covering every inch of surface along the hallway, one letter in particular catching her attention. But just as she took a step towards it, footfalls came charging down the stairs at her.

The black Labrador almost knocked her off her feet as it jumped up excitedly.

'Hello,' she laughed, rubbing its ears. 'He's gorgeous,' she told Coates, who showed no affection whatsoever when the puppy pawed at his legs. 'What's his name?'

'I haven't got round to choosing one yet,' he replied, leading the way into the kitchen, the Labrador bounding after him.

'Should I take my shoes off?' Marshall called, loitering in the hallway.

'No need.'

The house was uncomfortably hot and smelled old and fusty, time-weathered wallpaper climbing to elaborate Artex ceilings, passé ornaments laying claim to every spare space; an unconventional way for a thirty-one-year-old professional to choose to live. She carried on through to the 1960s kitchen, where Coates was scooping dog food into a bowl.

'Do you live here alone?' Marshall asked conversationally.

'I do,' he replied, washing his hands and filling the kettle. 'My mother had to go into a home,' he explained. 'I kept it just as she left it in case she ever came back, but that seems unlikely now.' He lit the hob and placed the kettle on top. 'May I?' he asked of the sketchbook in her hands.

'Oh,' said Marshall uncomfortably, feeling foolish for not anticipating this eventuality, knowing that the three pictures contained within could obliterate her cover in an instant. 'They're not very good,' she said shyly.

'Still. I'd very much like to see them.'

'I'm sorry, but no,' she laughed, putting it down on the surface behind her.

As the water began to simmer, Coates removed his glasses and rubbed his eyes, the Labrador whimpering and taking shelter beneath the kitchen table.

Also sensing the abrupt change in atmosphere, Marshall was tempted to make her excuses and leave, but instead managed to force a bashful smile onto her face:

'OK. OK. But be nice,' she said, picking the sketchbook back up and handing it over.

Replacing his glasses, Coates took the book to the table and sat down, the hiss of steam escaping the spout hitting occasional notes, as if still learning to whistle. Marshall watched anxiously from across the room as he opened up the first page to Rodin's *The Thinker* brought to life in pencil and negative space.

'It's good,' he told her as the kettle started to sing.

Marshall smiled back nervously: 'OK. That's enough. Could I have it back now?'

Ignoring her, he turned the page, showing no discernible emotion when he was presented with the tragic scene of Michelangelo's *Pietà*; mankind's saviour sprawled pathetically across his mother's lap.

The kettle began to shake, as if trying to escape the flame. Coates remained where he was, however, as he flicked to the unfinished final drawing: Benvenuto Cellini's dark imagining of *Perseus with the Head of Medusa*, the serpent-haired Gorgon depicted in gruesome detail, the decapitation now the trophy of a half-god.

Finding the subsequent pages blank, Coates closed the book and got to his feet, the steam now screaming out of the kettle behind him. Finally taking it off the heat, he stood there looking at her.

Conscious that he had just armed himself, Marshall didn't take her eyes off the container of boiling liquid in his hand.

'You're a very clever young woman, Jordan,' he told her.

'Thank you,' replied Marshall before realising her mistake. With a frog in her throat, she corrected him: '. . . It's Laura.'

'I didn't recognise you at first,' he said, his repellent little mouth curling into a sneer.

Marshall felt as though she'd been kicked in the stomach. She glanced down the hall to the front door longingly.

'It's not like me at all,' he continued, still just standing there with the bubbling kettle. 'I remember everyone . . . What does that say about you, I wonder?'

You're just a lost little girl who latched on to the first thing that came along to give her life some meaning – Chambers' words from the previous evening returning to side with their enemy.

When he took a step towards her, she backed into a unit, sending one of the ceramic figurines tumbling to the floor:

'God! I'm so sorry,' she said, crouching down to collect up the pieces but slicing her shaking hand open in the process. 'I think you're mistaking me for somebody else,' she told him unconvincingly as a steady trickle of blood ran down her arm.

'I think not. Alphonse's friend,' he nodded, closing his eyes to revisit the memory. 'You worked together at the leisure centre. He used to talk about you a lot – not all good things, I'm afraid to say.' Feeling tears prickling her eyes, Marshall shook her head. 'Why are you *really* here?' he asked, positioning himself between her and the doorway.

'I'm sorry. I really don't know what you're talking about. I have to go now. Excuse me.'

Coates showed no sign of moving as he watched the emotions play across her face in fascination.

'You're free to do as you please,' he told her, the kettle twitching in his hand.

Marshall remained where she stood, unwilling to pass within such close proximity of him:

'I can't get by.'

'Of course you can,' he assured her, smile collapsing as he watched her lift her collar up to her mouth.

'I can't get out,' she said loudly. 'I need help.'

The front and back doors burst open simultaneously as Chambers and Winter rushed inside, surrounding their prime suspect in his own kitchen.

'You OK?' Chambers asked her on noticing the wet blood on the floor.

She nodded and moved over to stand beside him.

'I'll be taking those Custard Creams now,' Winter told Coates, but knew in his heart of hearts that it hadn't been the Schwarzenegger-ism he'd been aiming for.

Placing the kettle down on the surface, Coates regarded his guests in turn:

'*Ah*. Chambers.' He nodded in greeting. 'And Detective Constable . . . Adam Winter,' he recalled, as if it all made sense now. 'I thought we had moved past this.'

'We were in the area,' Chambers shrugged. 'Thought we might come and collect our friend.'

'And the dog,' Marshall added, gesturing to the terrified animal in the corner.

'And the dog,' Chambers agreed.

'The animal stays with me,' Coates told him simply. 'I suppose I'd be wasting my breath to ask whether you have a warrant to be in my house?'

Their lack of response was answer enough.

'Then I demand that you leave. Goodbye,' he said curtly before turning to Marshall. 'It was a pleasure seeing you again, Jordan,' he smiled before herding them out, watching from his broken front door as they crossed the garden.

But as they reached the gate, Chambers stuck his fingers into his mouth and whistled loudly:

'Come on, boy!' he called, the puppy tearing down the hallway, barging past Coates, and following them outside without needing to be asked twice.

'I'm sorry,' said Marshall as they piled into the van.

Winter started the engine: 'Where to?'

'Just get us out of here,' replied Chambers, watching Coates watching him as they pulled away.

'Cellini?!' bellowed Chambers as Winter parked up opposite a recreation ground, now pretty confident he was missing something.

'I knew he'd approve,' argued Marshall.

'It was too much too soon, and it blew your cover!'

'It wasn't that,' sighed Marshall, knowing the truth wasn't any better.

'Either way,' said Chambers, 'we're done.'

He climbed out, slammed the door, and walked away.

'. . . Cellini?' asked Winter as the dog jumped up to claim the vacant seat.

'I didn't realise he knew,' she said, pressing her sleeve over the painful cut to her hand.

'Coates?'

'Chambers,' she answered sadly, watching him pace the treeline. '*Perseus with the Head of Medusa*. The night he was attacked, I think that's what the killer was trying to recreate – his third "work of art".'

'Medusa?' asked Winter. 'As in . . . snakes?'

'And the fresh head of an enemy,' she nodded, reaching for her sketchbook, only to realise that in her haste to leave she'd forgotten it in Coates's kitchen.

'*Jesus*,' huffed Winter.

'It's him – Coates,' Marshall said decisively, an image of Tobias Sleepe's broken body falling uninvited into her mind. 'It's always been him. And now I'm even more sure of it. That wasn't the same Robert Coates I met seven years ago.' She paused, trying to organise her thoughts. 'I mean, it *was* the same man, but it *wasn't* the same person, if that makes any sense?'

'None at all.'

'That wasn't even the same Robert Coates I saw at the nursing home earlier.'

'What are you saying?'

'That I think I know why Henry John Dolan's girlfriend didn't recognise the picture I showed her . . . Coates is a chameleon.'

'A chameleon?'

'He assumes personalities, alters his appearance, he becomes whatever somebody needs him to be.' She turned to Winter, who looked a little out of his depth: 'What do *you* think?'

'I think . . . we should tell Chambers.'

They climbed out beneath a tree so red it tainted the light around it, and made their way over, while their new pet burned off some energy.

'You all right?' asked Marshall.

'Just needed a couple of minutes,' said Chambers. 'This was a mistake. It's my fault. I shouldn't have let myself get sucked back in. And it was all for nothing anyway.'

'I wouldn't say *all* for nothing,' argued Winter. 'We *did* get a dog out of it,' he pointed out, watching it chase a squirrel up a tree . . . then do an enormous poo.

Chambers looked unimpressed.

'And *I* got this,' announced Marshall, taking a crumpled letter from her pocket and handing it to him. 'His mother's been renting an allotment in West Putney since before he was born,' she explained. 'Maybe you weren't wrong to be looking for something that day you dug up his garden . . . I wonder if you were just digging in the wrong place.'

CHAPTER 20

Having waited over seven-and-a-half years for so significant a break in the case, Chambers felt it a little anticlimactic when the address at the top of the stolen letter led him to a drab hallway in the bowels of the Wandsworth Borough Council offices. From behind a, surely unnecessary, security window, the woman on the desk had instructed him to take a seat, the council leaders apparently expecting their constituents to storm in and rob the Parks and Open Spaces department of their dubious treasures at any moment.

With time being of the essence, Robert Coates no doubt already phoning in his complaints and instructing his bulldog of a lawyer, they had a matter of hours to come up with some tangible evidence before red tape and disciplinary proceedings rendered their prime suspect untouchable. So, the team had split up. While Chambers followed the allotment lead, Marshall and Winter had gone back to Tall Oaks Nursing Home to pursue her theory, Coates's mother seeming a logical place to start.

The stale stench of a thousand cigarettes announced the arrival of the begrudging 'volunteer' who came out to deal with him. Unashamedly scratching the exposed underside of his beer belly, the man reread the crumpled letter:

'Plot eight-six-one,' he said in greeting, shunning social niceties. 'That's *errrrrr* . . . Doverhouse Road.'

He handed the letter back to Chambers and went to walk away – another job well done.

'Great,' said Chambers, getting up. 'Let's go.'

The man looked as though he'd just been slapped.

'I'm going to need you to take me there,' Chambers clarified. '. . . Right now.'

'Did you crack a window?' asked Marshall after flashing her badge at a member of the nursing home staff and requesting to be taken to Mrs Coates.

'I told you,' Winter replied defensively, 'I barely hit it!'

'I meant for the dog.'

'Oh. Then yes.'

Someone came to escort them down the corridor: 'Hi! I'm Maisey!' the woman greeted them as if they'd just arrived at a house party. 'I'm Meredith's primary carer. Come with me. I'll show you to her room.'

The yin to Marshall's yang, the woman seemed off her face on the joys of life – the sort of person who took photographs of flowers and nursed birds with broken wings back to health – well-meaning but oblivious to the world that would one day eat them up and spit them back out.

'Oh, who dropped that?' asked the bubbly carer, stopping ahead of them in the corridor. A little too large for her uniform, she struggled to pick the hairbrush up off the floor, exposing her lower back to Winter and Marshall in the process.

'Is that . . . Marvin the Martian?' asked Winter on being confronted with the unusual tattoo.

'Yes, it is!' Maisey smiled. 'Are you a fan?'

He looked a little awkward: 'I mean, as much as . . . anyone is.'

'I hear Mrs Coates can be a bit of a handful at times,' said Marshall, breaking up the inane conversation but being careful not to mention how she knew that to be the case.

'Oh, she's a *lovely* lady,' Maisey told her. 'But yes, she has her *moments*. That's why I took on the role as her primary carer.

You know, her son once told me that there were only two people he's ever met who are better with his mother than he is, and I was one of them.' She smiled proudly. 'It's the little things like that, that make it all worthwhile. Right. Here we are,' she said, knocking twice before entering Meredith Coates's private room, where the elderly woman was lying on her back staring vacantly at the ceiling.

'I'm afraid this conversation is confidential,' Marshall told their escort.

'Of course. Then I won't come in or she'll want me to stay,' whispered Maisey.

'Thanks for your help,' said Marshall, closing the door on her before taking a seat beside the bed. 'Mrs Coates?' she asked. '. . . Mrs Coates?'

The frail woman turned her head but then looked through her as though she wasn't even there, lost somewhere within her own mind.

'May I call you Meredith?' she smiled, recognition flickering across the blank face. 'Meredith it is. I'm here to ask you some questions about your son.'

While Marshall persevered with her futile endeavour, Winter moved over to the dressing table. Catching a glimpse of himself in the mirror, he self-consciously brushed his hair forwards, pausing to check his receding hairline didn't look any worse than the last time he'd checked. Forcing himself to focus on the more imminent problem, he turned his back to it, subtly sliding the top drawer open a crack to find a collection of nighties and underwear inside. Pushing it closed, he moved on to the next one down: more clothes. Unable to reach the bottom drawer discreetly, he quickly knelt down and pulled on the handle . . .

As he stood back up with an old photograph album in his hands, something dropped out onto the floor. He stooped down to pick it up.

'*Ummm*, Marshall,' he interrupted, handing her the envelope of more recent pictures that hadn't yet made it into the album's yellowed pages, the first of which captured a handsome-looking

Robert Coates with his arms around an attractive woman. They appeared genuinely happy. 'Looks like she might've been one of his students,' he told her when the second photograph showed the same woman wearing a graduation gown, *Class of '94* written across a banner in the background.

After sharing a significant look at this latest development, Marshall turned back to the elderly woman:

'Meredith, can you tell me who this is?'

Raising a shaky hand to the picture, she replied: 'That's my Robert.'

'But the woman?' she asked patiently. 'Who is Robert with?'

Catching the vulnerable woman in a fleeting moment of lucidity, Marshall watched her smile sadly before meeting her eye for the very first time:

'. . . Eloise. Such a wonderful girl.'

'Eloise? Do you happen to know her last name?' Marshall asked softly.

She shook her head: 'She used to visit me.'

'Here? When was the last time she came to see you?'

And with that, she was gone again, a blank expression spreading across her face as if she'd just been reset.

With a hefty sigh, Marshall got back up and joined Winter as he flicked through the delicate photo album, the assorted pictures of Robert Coates from over the years looking more like those of a set of brothers, his appearance going through drastic chan-ges, weight fluctuating, his taste in clothes varying from home-made hippie hemp to smart business attire and hitting every trend in-between.

'We're going to be needing that,' Marshall told him quietly, checking the coast was clear as Winter stuffed it inside his jacket.

Huffing with every step, the groundsman led Chambers through a gate to an unremarkable patch of land:

'Eight-six-one,' he announced, already reaching for his next cigarette.

A rickety shed presided over some browned vegetables, spent for the year, and a tangle of brambles laying siege to the neglected far end.

'Do you mind?' Chambers asked him, gesturing to a spade in the adjacent plot.

The man shrugged, evidently not giving a damn.

Collecting the tool, Chambers returned to the same spot, driving it into the damp earth as he began to dig.

The nursing home's old visitor books were stored off-site. And without even knowing which year to start looking through, it felt a dead end under the time-sensitive circumstances.

'You take the van to the university,' Marshall told Winter as they hurried out into the car park. 'Find out anything you can about this Eloise.'

'OK. Just one thing . . . I'm a security guard, not a police officer right now.'

'So improvise! Use your imagination. We're running out of time! And I need the photo album.'

Unzipping his jacket, Winter handed it over: 'Why? Where are you going?'

'If we want to get the case reopened, we *need* to link Coates to the Henry Dolan murder,' she explained. 'And *this* is going to get us our positive ID.'

The rusted metal struck something solid just three feet below the surface.

Tossing the spade aside, Chambers dropped to his knees and leaned into the hole. Excavating the rest by hand, the patch of chalk-white almost looked to glow against the dirt as he brushed it clean. Digging his fingertips below the smooth surface, he carefully pulled it from the earth: no more than a few inches long, sharper at one end, it was undoubtedly bone.

Leaping to his feet, he looked out across the deserted allotments for his resentful borough council representative:

'Hey!' Chambers called to get the man's attention. 'Can you drive that?' he shouted, pointing to the mini-digger by the entrance.

Armed with three photographs of Eloise, Winter entered Birkbeck College still trying to come up with a way of walking out of there with personal information on a student without a badge, let alone a warrant. His most promising ideas so far: the estranged relative routine, pulling the fire alarm, or (and this one was admittedly dependent on a vast and wide-ranging number of factors) . . . seducing the filing clerk.

Approaching the main staircase, he slowed to a stop and then retraced his steps back to a huge trophy cabinet. Holding one of his photos up to the team picture of the women's lacrosse champions 1992, he looked between the young woman lifting a gold cup above her head – to the graduation picture – and back again, a caption below reading: Eloise Brown (Team Captain).

'*Huh,*' he smiled, feeling pretty pleased with himself. 'That was a freebie.'

It seemed to have gone dark in the space of the ten-minute taxi ride. Climbing out in front of the beauty salon, Marshall tried the door to find it locked, a lopsided Closed sign reminding her to check the time. Cursing under her breath, she rapped against the window until she was finally bathed in light as three immaculate faces peered out at her.

'I'm sorry to turn up like this unannounced,' said Marshall, sitting down opposite Dolan's former girlfriend for the second time in as many days. 'But I need to ask if you recognise any of these people' – these people seeming simpler than trying to explain it was all the same man.

Rita began flicking through the photograph album, Marshall losing hope as she watched photo after photo being dismissed . . . But then she turned back a page and squinted down at one of the pictures:

'This one,' she said, tapping her blood-red nail against it.

'You're absolutely sure?' Marshall asked her.

'One-hundred-and-ten per cent,' she nodded. 'That's him. That's Henry's "special" friend.'

The cold had set in, making his leg ache, the tablets just about holding the pain at bay. Barely able to grip his coffee, Chambers watched the team of council workers excavate the site by torchlight. Two diggers had been shifting earth for the past couple of hours while others dug by hand, the commotion attracting an audience of bored teenagers and gossiping residents from the houses behind. The patrol cars he'd requested had cordoned off the area and, thus far, done an admirable job of keeping people away.

'Excuse me, Detective,' said a man covered head-to-toe in dirt. 'You wanted to know when the first quadrant was cleared?' he asked, looking a little traumatised.

Chambers nodded and followed him down into the five-by-five-metre patch carved out of the ground, stepping carefully through the carpet of bones, the skeletons of dozens of animals, many still perfectly assembled – a mass grave accrued over years.

'How many more diggers can you get here?' he asked the man.

'Quadrant three's almost done,' he replied. 'Two's not far off. I think we can do it with what we've got.'

Chambers stared out over the sea of allotments with a pang of guilt. Sheds bordered by evenly spaced fences. It looked like a miniature village in the darkness:

'That's just tonight's job,' he said. 'Tomorrow we start on the rest.'

'*Errrr* . . . I'm sorry?'

'You heard me. Rip it *all* up.'

The dog had curled up in the footwell, the U-Drive van a surprisingly cosy way to spend the evening, with the heater billowing hot air into the cabin and the engine rumbling gently beneath them. Winter had parked them up beneath the same tree as earlier, the quiet park just around the corner from Coates's house a logical place to rendezvous with their Metropolitan Police contingent.

The dog lifted its head when there was a knock on the glass.

'Marshall?' a uniformed officer asked when she wound down the window.

'Yeah?'

'Got a Detective Sergeant Chambers on the radio for you.'

'Thanks.' She turned to Winter: 'You coming?'

'Nah,' he yawned. 'I'll look after the dog.'

Following the officer back to his car, she climbed in and took the handset, the man and his colleague going off for a smoke to give her some privacy.

'Chambers?'

A click: 'Just checking in . . . Over.'

'Still waiting on the armed response unit, but we've got people watching the house. Over.'

'They've granted the arrest warrant . . . Over.'

'Just in time. You should be here for this. Over.'

'I've got my hands full here. Over.'

'I take it no human remains yet? Over.'

'Negative. I still suspect Dolan was his first. Over.'

Marshall had to shield her eyes as a set of headlight beams swung around the corner:

'Looks like they're here. I'd better get going. Over.'

'Be careful. Over.'

'Copy that . . . Out.'

'Go! Go! Go!'

Winter felt a little redundant as he watched the team of armed police storm Robert Coates's property, the first officer in claiming credit for the broken lock *he'd* kicked open earlier in the day, dark shapes moving across net curtains as they diffused through the little house; a shadow puppet police raid.

Marshall was the last through the door and had argued solidly just for that honour. Shouts of 'Clear!' started coming from all directions as she walked the bare hallway in confusion; the furniture remained, but the stacks of paperwork had disappeared. Glancing into the lounge on her way past, it looked similarly sparse.

'Someone's had a bonfire,' an officer commented as she entered the kitchen, a cluster of four metal rubbish bins still smouldering out on the patio.

She frowned on seeing her sketchbook waiting ominously on the table and made her way over as frustrated officers began filing back out of the house. Coates appeared to have burned everything he owned, and yet, he'd left this – an act of kindness she considered him incapable of, which could only mean he'd left it for another purpose.

Tentatively, she opened it up, flicking past her sketch of *The Thinker* . . . and then *Pietà* . . . her unfinished drawing of *Perseus with the Head of Medusa*. Holding her breath, she turned the page, feeling her heart sink as Winter came bundling into the room behind her.

'They said he's gone?' he asked, out of breath. 'Marshall? What is it?' He joined her beside the table, peering over her shoulder as she flicked to the next new picture . . . then the next . . . and the next. 'What *are* those?' he asked, but she didn't seem to hear. '. . . Marshall?'

Slowly, she turned to look at him:

'Jesus, Winter,' she said vacantly. 'What have we done?'

Thursday

CHAPTER 21

Eve got up five minutes before her alarm was due to go off. She tended to on these early starts when she had an entire day in court ahead of her. Fumbling around in the dark so as not to disturb Chambers, she successfully switched off the alarm clock, retrieved her clothes from the back of the chair, and made it out of the bedroom, only stubbing her toe twice in the process – a new personal record.

She pulled the door to and relaxed a little, switching on the countertop television in the kitchen, its volume set to a constant murmur. Filling up the coffee maker, she was surprised to find it still warm from the previous morning – *yet another thing that needed replacing*. As she took the milk out of the fridge, the morning news came on in the background:

'. . . residents of this sleepy riverside development have awoken to the aftermath of a horrific crime this morning . . .'

Yawning, she added two heaped teaspoons of sugar to her favourite mug . . . and then a third.

'. . . the body of a young woman. Reports coming out of the cordoned area suggest that *at least* one of her limbs appears to be missing. As yet, we don't know if this was a prior injury or whether it was sustained during an attack . . .'

Ears pricking as details of the horrible story continued to buzz from the speakers, Eve picked up the remote control:

Vol IIII

'. . . Again, these reports are, as yet, unconfirmed. But we have been told by several sources now that the positioning of the body bears an uncanny resemblance to that particular work of art . . .'

With a foreboding sense of déjà vu, Eve muted the television, as if not hearing any more would somehow make it go away. Desperately not wanting to tell her husband, she stood there deliberating for a few moments, resigning herself to the fact that he needed to know. Ignoring the click of the coffee maker getting up to temperature, she headed back to the bedroom door, a sliver of light dissecting the darkness as she crept over to the bed.

'Ben,' she whispered. '. . . Ben.' Sitting beside him, she reached out . . . her hand sinking down to the mattress before pulling back the duvet to discover the bed empty. Leaping to her feet, she switched the bedside lamp on, calling into the quiet house: '. . . Ben?!'

Thermos of coffee in hand, Chambers ducked underneath the police tape and showed his ID card to the first officer to come running over:

'Chambers. Homicide,' he announced.

'Christ!' the young man sighed in relief.

'. . . *Chambers*,' he reiterated, concerned that in his sleep-starved delirium he might have somewhat oversold himself.

The officer smiled:

'I mean, *Christ*, am I glad to see you! Come on. It's this way.' He led Chambers down the hill towards the river, where a grubby blanket had been draped over a human-sized shape, making it look like a half-arsed Halloween costume against the cold dawn sky. 'It's the only thing I had in the car,' he explained, picking up on the detective's expression.

'Take it off.'

'But . . . the press—'

'Are for people paid a *lot* more than us to worry about,' Chambers told him, 'and are a distant concern compared to preserving the evidence.'

'Yeah, but—'

'Look!' Chambers barked at him. It was *way* too early. 'If you're *that* bothered, you have my blessing to stand there holding your manky blanket up until we get a screen down here. But, take . . . it . . . off.'

As the scolded young man went to uncover their victim, Chambers walked to the water's edge, bracing himself as always before laying eyes on any dead body: a soul ripped from existence against its will, a ripple effect of sorrow, loss and anger touching an untold number of other lives – those who knew them . . . those who now never would . . .

Snapping out of his musings, he shook his head, Eve's philosophies really starting to hinder him in his chosen career.

He watched the reflection in the water lapping at the bank as the blanket fell away to reveal the disfigured masterpiece he had been fearing. Feeling his heart sink, he finally forced himself to look at it.

Hair plaited around her crown, leaves woven into the intricate design, the beautiful woman stood topless, only a sheer cloth, brought to life by the breeze, hanging loosely around her waist. Somehow, she looked peaceful, happy even, the hint of a smile curling at the corner of her mouth all the more haunting for the fresh dismemberments just below either shoulder. With both arms missing, the figure cast an uneven shadow, the skin ending abruptly, unnaturally, like broken marble – the *Venus de Milo* reborn in mutilated flesh.

Having seen enough, Chambers started trudging back up the grassy bank, the inexperienced officer still gallantly holding up his holey blanket:

'Hey!' he called after Chambers. 'Where are you going?'

'To get someone out of bed who can help you.'

'So . . . not you?!'

Without looking back, Chambers shook his head: 'Not me.'

*

'OK,' started Detective Chief Inspector Wainwright, 'who wants
to tell me what a trainee Narcotics officer . . .' Marshall self-
consciously avoided the others' eyes, having almost forgotten herself that she was still only a trainee, '. . . an experienced Homicide
detective, and a . . .' the stern woman double-checked the sheet of
paper in front of her, '. . . Sainsbury's security guard, are doing con-
ducting an unsanctioned investigation into a seven-year-old case?'

Wainwright was the Homicide department's third DCI since
Hamm, who had punched out of the force, in a move no one had
seen coming, for 'Personal reasons' – a reason Chambers personally
didn't feel captured the force with which he'd punched out one of
his constables . . . who, likewise, had not seen it coming. That had
all been swept under the carpet, of course, an old acquaintance
ensuring that the underqualified, unsuitable and unhinged Hamm
left with his head held high, a full pension and a send-off worthy
of a hero.

Wainwright was a welcome breath of fresh air in comparison, a
little by-the-book at times but generally fair and approachable. A
position she'd earned through hard graft, the years of night shifts,
junk food and employer-issued alcohol dependence had taken its
toll on her, as it had them all, the deep creases running through her
skin like dried-up riverbeds making her look ten years older than
she actually was.

'. . . Well?' she prompted them when nobody answered.

Winter cleared his throat:

'It all started right after I got back from a high-speed pursuit
. . . Well, medium-speed would be more accurate; we were both
still pretty tired following his first attempt to nick *Jurassic Park* on
video, which I . . .' Sensing he was losing his audience, and actually
hearing Chambers' hand slap against his forehead, he trailed off.
'Yeah, you probably want to hear it from one of them,' he concluded, sitting back in his chair awkwardly.

Wainwright turned to Chambers:

'Explain to me why you were even looking into a man who had
already been cleared of suspicion?'

Chambers frowned: 'But who actually *did* do it.'

'But who you shouldn't have been investigating in the first place,' argued the DCI, the other two watching the debate bounce back and forth across the desk.

'But who, if we hadn't, would've gone undetected because no other bastard was going to look into him,' Chambers pointed out, getting irate.

'You should've asked permission first.'

'Would you have given it?'

'No.'

Looking about to blow, he raised his arms in exasperation.

'Look,' said Wainwright calmly. 'I'm not saying I'm not glad you did what you did, only that I'm going to have to punish you for doing it. Does that make sense?'

'Literally, none at all.'

Winter tentatively raised a hand.

'Yes?' asked Wainwright, turning to him.

'Could my punishment be dished out by the overlords of Sainsbury's plc.? 'Cos I'm late for work again and my manager, Dan, is going to shit a brick.'

'Fine.'

'Great. So, I can go?'

'No.' Wainwright looked exhausted already. '*You*,' she said, addressing Marshall. 'You haven't annoyed me yet. Why don't *you* bring me up to date?'

'. . . and he added five new pictures?' asked Wainwright, looking ill, speaking for the first time in over fifteen minutes. 'So, still four more murders?'

'I think we have to assume that's his intention,' nodded Marshall, the same ball of nausea twisting inside her that she'd been experiencing all day.

'Jesus,' she groaned, slumping in her chair. 'Why would he tell us this? Why leave the sketches at all?'

'I don't know,' shrugged Marshall. 'To taunt us? To test us?

Either way, after our reunion party in his kitchen he knew we were coming for him and that he had nothing left to lose,' she finished guiltily.

'OK,' said Wainwright decisively, turning back to Chambers. 'I'm making you lead on the case.'

'I'm sorry?' he asked in surprise.

'It's your case.'

'*No. No. No,*' he said. 'Give it to someone else.'

'You worked the original investigation,' she reasoned. 'And you were right about everything all the way through, which makes you the most qualified to catch this man. Can you give me one good reason why you're not up to this?'

Shifting uncomfortably, Winter glanced over at his colleague, while on the other side of him, Marshall's eyes flicked down to his leg . . .

'. . . No,' he replied, shaking his head in frustration.

'Then it's settled,' said Wainwright. 'Do you want me to request that Marshall be transferred over to assist? . . . If that's all right with you, of course?' she asked the Narcotics officer, who nodded eagerly.

'Sure,' grunted Chambers. 'The more, the merrier.'

'And Winter . . .' the detective chief inspector started. He sat up excitedly. '. . . you should probably get back to work before "Dan" passes that brick you mentioned.'

'Oh,' he said, looking a little disappointed.

'So, what's next?' Wainwright asked.

'Eloise Brown,' replied Marshall. 'We believe she was in a relationship with Coates at some point. We need to speak to her.'

'And, now that we're official,' started Chambers bitterly, 'I want to search his office at the university.'

'They're jobs number two and three,' Wainwright told them. 'First: we need every set of eyes in the country looking for this man. I'll need you to supply me with a selection of photos to circulate to the media.'

'Sure you want to go to the press with this?' Chambers asked her.

'"Want" has nothing to do with it. But I don't really see what choice we have. As Marshall so eloquently put it: the man's a chameleon. We're not going to find him alone.'

'And how much are you going to tell them?' he asked, wondering what his chances were of keeping any of it from Eve.

'Enough,' said Wainwright thoughtfully. '. . . The truth. That today, after seven years undetected, Robert Coates *officially* became a serial killer.'

CHAPTER 22

Chambers had offered to drop Winter off at work en route to their meeting with Eloise Brown, the relentless London traffic predictably turning the gesture into a massive inconvenience.

'Hey, guys?' Winter piped up from the back seat.

Marshall turned round but instantly regretted it:

'Jesus, Winter! Put some trousers on!'

'I wasn't expecting you to look!'

'You said "hey, guys" – of course I'm going to look!' she snapped, eyes fixed firmly on the car in front while he planted his feet against the window to wriggle into his uniform.

They sat quietly for a few moments.

'. . . Hey, guys?'

'What?!'

'I was wondering . . . well, more *thinking* that maybe you could . . . you know, wait until I finish work to go see Eloise Brown.'

'You're joking, right?' asked Chambers.

'I just thought—'

'This is a *murder* investigation. Coates has already told us he's going to kill again. *Every* second counts. And you want us to *wait* for you?'

'Now that I hear it out loud . . .' said Winter awkwardly. 'Yeah, you're right. Ignore me.'

'Go easy on him,' Marshall told Chambers. 'We wouldn't even

know Eloise Brown existed if it wasn't for Winter.' She turned to give him an encouraging smile: 'For Christ's sake! Where's your top?!'

'It's trapped in your door,' he replied, belly hanging over his waistband.

Marshall quickly opened and closed the passenger door before tossing the polo shirt into the back:

'How about, with Chambers' permission, of course,' she looked over at him, 'I stop by later and catch you up on everything? . . . OK?'

'You would?' Winter smiled hopefully.

Chambers gave a reluctant nod as he pulled up outside the doors to the supermarket.

'See you later then,' said Winter, jumping out onto the pavement.

'Bag!' she reminded him.

'Thanks. Bye!' he called after clambering back in to retrieve it, Chambers and Marshall waving him off like proud parents as he practically skipped into work.

'Sure this is the place?' asked Chambers, unenthusiastically regarding the entrance to the set of underground toilets.

'Pretty sure,' replied Marshall, gesturing to the brand-new signage:

Gallery.sw7

Pushing the metal gate open, they made their way down the stone staircase towards the sound of building work, the smell of stale urine intensifying, literally stinging their eyes by the time they reached the crowded subterranean space.

'Oh! Hey!' smiled an attractive woman, her light-brown hair tied up in playful bunches, oversized shirt covered in dried paint. 'Are you the toilet guy?'

Glaring at Marshall when she sniggered, Chambers took out his ID, feeling a little self-conscious – those were his smartest trousers:

'No. I'm the homicide detective.'

'Was that today?' she laughed dizzily before frowning: 'So, when's the toilet guy coming?'

The three of them stood in silence for a moment, as though she actually expected Chambers to know.

'. . . I really can't help you. Are you Eloise Brown?' he double-checked, feeling it necessary with the scatter-brained woman.

'Yeah. That's me. I'd shake your hand but . . .' she looked down at her own, 'I'm not *entirely* sure what this is.' Wiping whatever it had been on her shirt, both detectives looked a little repulsed. 'Sorry. Am I being gross again? I can't even tell any more. I know it doesn't look much now, but a few coats of paint and this'll be the edgiest gallery in the city.'

The expression *you can't polish a turd* sprung a little too easily to mind, but Chambers decided to keep it to himself.

'Above ground, I wouldn't be able to afford this much space in a million years,' she told them cheerfully, surveying her well-plumbed empire. 'But this place . . . It's like striking oil in central London.'

'I'm not so sure that's oil,' muttered Chambers as he stepped over an unpleasant-looking puddle. 'Do you think we might be able to talk somewhere a little . . . else?'

Eloise shrugged: 'Sure.'

Both Marshall and Eloise had looked longingly at The Rembrandt Hotel, but seeing as Chambers was paying, they'd politely agreed to his suggestion, the three of them sitting down at a sticky table in the McDonald's down the road. Stuffing his face, Chambers listened in as Marshall conducted the interview:

'I'll start with a few easy ones,' she told Eloise. 'Were you in a relationship with Robert Coates?'

'Yes . . . That *was* easy!'

'From when until when?'

She thought about it and then started counting on her fingers:

'March until November, ninety-four. Eight months. We'd talk in the corridors when no one was around, steal a few minutes here and there whenever we were able. He didn't want anybody knowing about us. He was paranoid about it – a real stickler for the rules. Our first "official" date was the evening of my graduation.' She scowled at Chambers: 'Is that your *second* burger?'

'I've been up since five!'

'And how would you describe Robert?' Marshall continued, both women edging away from the lump of chewed meat Chambers had spat across the table.

Again, Eloise took her time to consider the answer:

'Handsome, charming,' she blushed as though he'd just walked by and paid her a compliment, 'fiercely intelligent and . . . intense.'

'Intense? In what way?'

'In every way. Like how he asked me to marry him after just three months . . .' Marshall raised her eyebrows – she was intending to wait until her chosen suitor had proven their worth and was buried six feet under before lamenting the fact that perhaps they should've got hitched after all. '. . . And then *every single day* after that,' Eloise added sadly. 'I thought it was romantic at the time. Now, I'm not so sure.'

'Were you two often . . . intimate?'

'*Woah!* As much as I'd *love* to share details of my sex life with you and the Hamburglar here, I think you need to tell me what this is about.'

'Your ex is a serial killer,' Chambers replied bluntly. 'He murdered three people back in eighty-nine and another this morning: a young woman . . . cut off her arms.' Marshall pulled a 'Are you crazy?' face at him. '*What?*' he said, picking up a handful of chips. 'It's going to be all over the news anyway.'

Taking a few moments to process the revelation, Eloise merely nodded in response.

'Forgive me for saying,' started Marshall, 'but for someone who spent eight months of their life with this person, you don't seem overly shocked.'

'And *as* someone who ended that relationship and then went out of their way to try to ensure they never saw that person again . . . I'm not.'

'*Try* to?' asked Marshall.

'Robert still contacts me from time to time: letters . . . flowers. I just tend to ignore them.'

'When was the last time?'

'I don't know. Months ago,' she shrugged.

'You had your suspicions about him then?'

'It was only a small thing,' said Eloise, gazing out of the window, as if watching the story unfold somewhere out on the street. 'He'd been staying round at mine more often. Things were good. We were happy. Every night, though, there'd be this scratching in the walls, the sound of something scrabbling about right by our heads.'

'A mouse?' asked Marshall.

'Right. So, what do you do when you have a mouse? You go and buy traps. Which is precisely what I did – not even the humane, trap it and let it go outside, sort. I went for the proper metal bar on a spring, crush-it-to-death type. I wanted that creature dead . . . until the morning I noticed the trap had gone that is.

'I went downstairs, headed into the kitchen, and had never felt so disgusted with myself – seeing that harmless little animal pinned but still thrashing around in pain. I just wanted to turn back time, nurse it back to health, build it a cosy little home in the wall – put a little light in there for it. Because now that I thought about it, hearing him scratching away at night was reassuring. It meant that I was never really alone.

'Anyway, Robert had clearly just found it and decided to put the poor thing out of its misery before I could get upset. I was just about to sneak back out of the room when I saw him remove the cheese knife from the drawer. One of the really sharp curved ones with the two prongs at the end? And that's when I spotted two other knives out on the work surface, both stained with blood. I gasped, and he turned to look at me. He didn't say anything . . . just stood there with this emotionless expression and these dead eyes. It was like I was seeing him for the very first time . . . The *real* him.

'You know when a child picks the wings off a crane fly? It's a cruel act of dominance dismissed as "normal naïve interest", justifiable by a developing mind's lack of understanding of consequence, of coming to terms with one's place in the natural order,' she said, the ditzy persona giving way to an articulate university graduate's mind, the change in her as dramatic as anything Robert Coates could conjure. 'It was like that – not so much that he was *enjoying* torturing a tiny animal, more that he *needed* to do it.'

Hamburger ruined, Chambers placed it back in the wrapping.

'Did you report it?' Marshall asked her.

'To whom?' Eloise asked impatiently. 'The police? And tell them what exactly – about an already dying mouse and a creepy look? I don't think they'd send the helicopters in, do you?'

Marshall looked a little embarrassed.

'Did the two of you have a dog?' asked Chambers, when a more pressing concern came to mind. He quickly turned to Marshall: 'What happened to our dog?'

'Winter's mum has got him for now.'

'Oh,' he said in relief.

'She named him Bertie.'

'*Bertie*? He's not a Bertie,' he scoffed disapprovingly before returning to the original question: 'So, did the two of you have a dog?'

'No. Why?'

'No reason.'

Eloise watched him for a moment, but then took the opportunity to ask one of her own questions:

'You said he . . . cut a girl's arms off?' she whispered, appropriately appalled.

'While she was incapacitated . . . a bit like your mouse,' replied Chambers, an accusatory barb to his voice, as though she should have seen the signs.

'My God.'

'. . . Before posing her like *The Venus de Milo*,' he added.

Eloise didn't even flinch, her colour fading as, outside, threatening clouds moved in, casting gloom over the entire restaurant.

'What is it?' asked Marshall on seeing the look on her face.

'It's just . . . It's just so like Robert,' she replied. 'He has this . . .

need to create something beautiful out of ugliness. It's probably the thing I loved about him the most,' she laughed bitterly. 'How sick is that? It's weird, I suppose, but it's like his way of coping with the things he can't accept.'

'Such as?' Marshall pushed her.

'Such as when there was a fire at the university. They lost half the art block – all those years of work, irreplaceable . . . unrepeatable. And do you know what Robert did? He spent an *entire* week knee-deep in the debris recreating what he could from memory – these incredible ashen sculptures.'

'Sculptures?' asked Marshall, sharing a look with her colleague.

Eloise nodded, smiling wistfully at the memory despite what she had just learned about the hero of her story:

'It was truly amazing . . . truly. *Oh!* Or the time I broke my arm and was told I couldn't paint for months. I was utterly inconsolable. But Robert, he sat by my side for almost two days straight creating one of the most incredible paintings I've ever seen on my cast to cheer me up.'

'What did he paint?' Marshall asked her, sounding more like an envious friend than a police officer.

'Us,' smiled Eloise, eyes glistening. 'Us as Apollo and Daphne . . . What?' she asked, noticing the concerned looks on the faces of the two detectives opposite. '. . . *What?!*'

'We're going to need you to come with us.'

'Think you could've thrown some fake blood around? Made it look a little more nightmarish in here?' Chambers asked Constable Dogsbody (no one knew his actual name) in irritation, on being confronted with the gallery of enlarged crime-scene photographs alongside commanding works of art. Struggling for room, the overzealous young man had even covered the windows, lending the pictures against the glass an eerie glow as the light seeped in around the edges.

They had brought Eloise back to New Scotland Yard for further questioning, the terrifying room in Homicide their base from which to investigate the murders alongside their rapidly expanding team. Transfixed by the haunting images surrounding her, Eloise walked a lap of the evidence wall while Chambers evicted his subordinates and switched on some lights.

'Is this *all* Robert?' she asked, her voice distant and dazed.

Adopting a respectful whisper, Marshall nodded: 'Yes.'

'They're sort of beautiful in a way, aren't they?' said Eloise. '. . . I mean, it's terrible, of course. These poor people,' she added quickly but unable to hide the spark of wonderment in her hazel eyes.

'Take your time,' Marshall told her. 'Any insight you can give us, no matter how small, could be significant.'

'I really don't know what I'm going to be able to tell you beyond these clearly being Robert recreating the defining moments of his life . . . But I guess you already knew that.' She was met with two very blank expressions. '. . . You *didn't* already know that?'

'Perhaps you could elaborate a little?' suggested Marshall, figuring it sounded better than outright admitting they'd had no idea.

'They were found in this order?' Eloise asked her.

'They were.'

She took a pair of glasses out of her pocket and pushed them onto her nose, analysing Henry John Dolan's autopsy pictures as though critiquing a painting:

'Robert always had an affinity for *The Thinker*; this lone figure sitting deep in contemplation in the midst of the chaos depicted in *The Gates of Hell*: immersed and yet separate somehow,' she told them. 'There are different interpretations: some believe the figure to be Dante reflecting on his nine circles of hell, whereas others believe it to be—'

'Rodin himself,' Chambers finished on her behalf, wishing more people had been around to hear the most cultured thing he was ever likely to say.

'Robert conformed to that second school of thought because that was how he saw himself . . . intellectually . . . creatively – as one who didn't belong in the scene in which they were trapped, his potential squandered by a world that didn't appreciate him.'

'And that didn't set off any alarm bells?' Chambers asked her.

'Arrogance and the arts tend to go hand in hand,' shrugged Eloise. 'He used to draw it all the time. Like obsessively. Where other people sit there daydreaming, doodling rubbish, he'd scribble these incredible sketches without even realising.' She moved onto the area of wall dedicated to Nicolette Cotillard holding her dead son in homage to Michelangelo's masterpiece. '*Pietà*. This is clearly a reference to his mother,' she announced.

'Meredith?' blurted Marshall in surprise, feeling a six-foot garden gnome might have been more apt.

'No. I mean his *biological* mother.' Chambers and Marshall glanced at one another; it was probably a good time to say the 'could you elaborate' thing again. 'She was a drug addict,' continued Eloise, Marshall unconsciously scratching the pockmarks on her inner arm. '. . . Heroin, a vice she passed on to her son when he was born. Meredith didn't tell you any of this?' she asked them, surprised.

Marshall simply shook her head in response, not wanting the conversation to veer off onto the topic of an elderly woman's worsening dementia.

'Long story short: Robert was an incredibly tiny and unhealthy baby, who stopped breathing *twice* in his first few days of life. He always struggled to get his head around it, how close he came to barely existing – everything he would go on to achieve and create just erased like *that*,' she snapped her fingers, 'lying in the arms of a woman too far gone to even notice.'

'The Virgin Mary wasn't an addict though,' Marshall pointed out.

'But Nicolette Cotillard *was*,' Chambers reminded her. 'And *I* don't need to tell *you* how much Alphonse had going for him.' Picking up on the bizarre comment, Eloise glanced between the two detectives inquisitively but neither elaborated. 'Perhaps even worthy of playing Robert Coates in one of his "masterpieces",' he suggested.

'As was Henry John Dolan by that logic,' said Marshall sceptically. 'I'm not seeing much of a resemblance there.'

'Maybe we're being too literal,' said Chambers. 'Maybe it's more symbolic than that. Henry Dolan was undoubtedly an impressive specimen of a man. In another time, he'd have been a gladiator or a warlord rather than "wasted" as a backing dancer and television extra.'

'*Now* you're thinking more like Robert,' Eloise told him. 'The truth is we're deep in his head here, and I doubt we're going to make head nor tail of it. What we *do* know is that in his own twisted way, he's trying to find meaning and beauty in the ugliness of what he's doing. And, for whatever reason, he's chosen *this* image,' she pointed to a photograph of the actual sculpture, 'to associate with that trauma.'

'What about this one?' asked Chambers, moving her on.

'*Perseus with the Head of Medusa*,' said Eloise. 'Why is there no photograph of the bodies?'

'Because he didn't get to finish.'

'Oh. Best guess: this is him finally freeing himself of her once and for all.'

'His mother?' asked Marshall.

Eloise nodded: 'Even though Meredith had adopted him, he had scheduled weekly visits with his mother up to the age of eleven. She still had a huge amount of influence over his life until . . .' She trailed off. 'I suppose it makes no difference now: he stole some of Meredith's opioid medication from the medicine cabinet and slipped it into his recovering mother's cup of tea. By the end of the week, she'd been found passed out in a squat house and denied access to him until she could prove she was clean . . . which never happened. That small act represented him emerging victorious over the greatest monster in his life . . . Who did he select as his Perseus?'

'We never found a body,' said Chambers.

'Then who did he choose to be the severed head of Medusa?'

'. . . Me.'

She looked troubled: 'Wow. He must *really* hate you.'

'I think so, yeah.'

She walked over to the next set of crime-scene photographs – the half-naked and disfigured body of the *Venus de Milo* perched on the banks of the river:

'Who was she?'

Marshall didn't even need to consult her sheet of paper: 'Tamsin Fuller, a technician from the art department at the uni.'

'Must have joined after I left. And these?' she asked, gesturing to the collection of waxy green leaves that had been scooped into an evidence bag.

'They were scattered all around the victim,' explained Chambers, 'but didn't appear to match any of the trees in the area. I've got someone trying to identify—'

'Laurel,' she interrupted him. 'They're laurel leaves . . . It's a message,' she said, staring up at the mutilated corpse, for the first time with an appropriate degree of revulsion and sorrow.

'A message?' Marshall asked her.

With a nod, Eloise took a deep breath: '. . . That this one is me.'

CHAPTER 23

Barry 'shit job' King was living up to his name. Where his fellow Rangers would spend their days talking to girls, planting trees and making friends with squirrels, it somehow always fell to him to put out the fires, evict the groups of underage drinkers and deal with the wildlife on its last legs. And it was this disagreeable task that had him bouncing his 4x4 down the gravel track to the lake at two minutes past finishing time, following a report of blood and feathers on the footpath. Typically, the caller hadn't been able to wait, which meant he had a half-hour traipse through the dark for whatever the foxes had left for him to find.

He stopped the engine when the headlight beams skipped across the water like skimmed stones, the handbrake creaking dubiously as he climbed out and set off on his lap of the lake. Sweeping his torch over the uneven terrain, Barry prayed it was only one of the bastarding Canada Geese:

'Not Big Bob the duck,' he whispered. 'Please not Big Bob.'

Approximately a quarter of the way around the lake, in a predictably muddy area of the bank, the first fluffy white feathers caught the torchlight, trembling in the breeze as if still reeling from whatever ordeal they had just witnessed. Like snowflakes in the dirt, he followed the greatest concentration into the treeline, whiteness gradually replaced with crimson – those feathers perfectly still . . . saturated . . . dead.

Noticing a trail of blood glistening up a felled tree, he clambered over the trunk, twisting his ankle on what awaited him on the other side: the remains of two adult swans, their long necks slack and twisted, gaping dark holes where their wings had once attached to their bodies.

'What the *hell*?' he muttered, shining the torch around in search of the missing parts, despite knowing that no fox in existence could take down two large cobs in one go.

Beginning to feel a little vulnerable alone with the silence, he scrambled back over the tree trunk and hurried towards the lake, deciding it was a job that could wait until the morning.

Marshall glanced down at the multicoloured display tent . . . and then back up at Winter:

'I'm not getting in that.'

'Come on,' he told her. 'I don't finish for another forty minutes.'

'I am a police officer. I'm not going to hide from your—'

'Shit! Dan's coming!' whispered Winter, apparently through his ample back end as it disappeared through the opening.

'Winter! I'm not going to . . .' However, she trailed off as voices rounded the corner:

'If he's with that scary goth girl again, I swear I'm gonna fire him here and now.'

'Oh, for Christ's sake, move over,' she huffed, diving inside just in the nick of time, watching as two pairs of legs marched by. Unimpressed, she glared across at Winter: 'This is *ridiculous*.'

'Welcome to my life,' he shrugged. 'So, you were saying?'

Marshall caught him up on their unexpectedly productive conversation with Eloise Brown and, with Chambers' prior agreement, invited him along to their meeting the next morning, where she was going to take them through the remaining sketches one by one.

'I still don't get the laurel leaves,' he whispered, shooing off a trespassing toddler when it attempted to climb in with them.

'It's just a thing the two of them had,' she explained, without explaining anything at all. 'He scattered leaves all around our *Venus de Milo* . . . Something to do with art and marriage and *nymphs* maybe?'

'Well, that clears it up.'

'It went over my head, OK? But she's adamant it relates to her.'

'So . . . we've put her under protection, right?'

'Chambers sorted it. She's convinced Coates would never hurt her though.'

Winter looked sceptical . . . and then a bit hungry:

'Want something to eat . . . a drink maybe?'

'What have you got?'

'Literally anything,' he told her, gesturing to the supermarket beyond the zipped opening.

'A bottle of red to share?'

'Coming up.'

'. . . Malbec or a Bordeaux Blend.'

'*Ummm*. I'll see what I can do,' smiled Winter, pretty sure he'd already forgotten it.

'. . . But French not Argentinian if you go for the Malbec.'

Already hanging halfway out of his hiding place, Winter looked back at her with an exasperated expression.

'My dad was big into his wines,' said Marshall apologetically.

'Sommelier?'

'Drunk. *Oh*, and some cheese and biscuits wouldn't go amiss . . . And, Winter!'

'Yes?' he asked from somewhere outside the tent.

'Could you grab some plasters and painkillers? . . . My hand's *really* starting to hurt.'

Winter returned a few minutes later with their 'borrowed' supper. Fortunately, he didn't notice Marshall's look of horror when he handed her a bottle of Merlot from . . . she didn't even bother finishing the label to discover who had admitted responsibility.

'I had a thought,' said Winter, 'over at the cheese counter,' he revealed, not entirely sure why that detail was pertinent himself.

'At the risk of sounding like a snob . . .'

They were dining on Merlot and Dairylea Triangles.

'. . . it seems likely that Robert Coates and his biological mother, being an addict, might've lived in council housing . . . until he was taken away from her.'

'I can certainly check. Why? What are you thinking?'

'That Alphonse and his addict mother *also* lived on a council estate.'

'You think the same one?' asked Marshall, intrigued.

'It just seems from what you've said, that if the statues represent *events* in his life, and the victims share qualities with the *people* in his life, then it follows that the locations might be important in some way as well.'

'*Hmmm*,' said Marshall, part pondering but mainly because her mouth was full. 'You know, if you said some of this clever shit around Chambers once in a while, he *would* wait for you and we probably wouldn't be having this conversation in a tent right now.'

'But where would be the fun in that?' he smiled, toasting cardboard cups with her.

'Honey, I'm—' Chambers froze in the doorway. Eve was waiting for him, arms folded and already changed for bed. '. . . Sorry for something?' he asked with a weak smile, having spent their evening together alone searching Coates's office instead. 'What did I do?'

'What did you do?! What did you do?!'

'I . . . I don't know,' he stuttered.

She marched over to the television and pressed *play* on the VCR:

'. . . serial killer. Lead investigator on the case Detective Sergeant Benjamin Chambers is pictured here attending the scene of the latest brutal murder in which . . .'

She switched it off.

'Oh,' said Chambers. '*That*.'

'This is him again – the statue man! The one who did *this* to you!' She pointed down at his leg. 'You *promised* me.'

'Honey, I—'

'Don't *honey* me!'

'All right,' he said, holding his hands up. '*Eve* . . . I tried to say *no* but—'

'You tried?' she laughed bitterly. 'You didn't try hard enough! Did you tell them this case nearly killed you already?'

'They have the files.'

'And did you tell them you still can't walk across the reception at work in the mornings without stopping for a rest?'

'I—'

'Did you tell them you'd quit if they tried to make you do this?'

Chambers sighed: '. . . No.'

'Then you didn't really try at all, did you?'

He opened his mouth, but then hesitated, knowing that he wouldn't be able to get to sleep should he break a promise *and* lie to her on the same day.

Irritated by his silence, Eve stormed away, slamming the bedroom door behind her.

Back in the recently named Sainsbury's Homicide HQ, Marshall and Winter had put an impressive dent in their bottle of wine and assortment of cheeses aimed primarily at children. Unpeeling a Babybel, the combination of alcohol and the sombre greenish light inside the tent had put Marshall in a melancholy mood:

'She'd still be alive if it wasn't for me.'

Winter looked confused: 'Who?'

'Tamsin Fuller.' He still looked lost. 'The *Venus de Milo*!' she snapped, angry with him for already forgetting the name that was all she could think about. 'If I'd just left it alone . . . He'd stopped. He was done until I turned up at his house.' She stared into her blood-red drink. 'They're on me. From this point on . . . whoever he hurts. They're all on me.'

Winter huffed and topped up her party cup:

'With all due respect, that's the biggest load of rubbish I've ever heard. We're police officers,' he told her proudly, apparently forgetting that he currently wasn't. 'And police officers catch bad guys, even when they might react badly to that. Robert Coates is to blame for that woman's death – no one else. And it's tragic, but no more tragic than the three lives he's already taken and got away with. So stop thinking like that.'

Marshall tucked her dark hair behind her ear, as if she'd been hiding behind it.

'Can I ask you something?' Winter said, lowering his voice to a whisper.

'Sure.'

'That night we met Chambers in the pub, he made a comment.' Marshall knew full well what was coming next. 'He said you had track marks up your arms.'

'I remember,' she nodded. 'He doesn't miss a thing, does he?'

'So . . . it's true?'

'*Uh-huh.*'

'Is it like a *work* thing?' he asked awkwardly. 'Like from being undercover?'

'You've watched too many movies.'

He looked confused: 'But . . . you're a narcotics officer.'

'Which makes me *very* good at hiding it.'

'Don't they check you for things like that?'

'Frequent random urine testing,' she revealed, the look on his face not improving any, 'nothing one to three days and a repeat prescription for codeine can't cover,' she smiled. '. . . Back pain.'

Winter knew he was out of his depth: 'Are you . . . OK?'

'You mean: am I a drug addict?'

'Yeah.'

'No. I'm not an addict and, yes, I'm OK.'

'Then . . .?'

She sighed heavily: 'There's this social stigma around heroin that anyone who takes it instantly becomes a gaunt, sunken-eyed zombie, when the truth is, it's far more like alcohol than they'd like to admit. There are those with the self-restraint to dip in and out and know their limits. Just as there are those who become a slave to it and let it consume them. I'm fortunate enough to fall into the former category. Anyway, they're old. Most of them. Souvenirs of a misspent youth, bar *very* occasional relapses.'

'How occasional?'

'Do you ever have those days? Those days where it feels like your mind is screaming at you? When you have so much of everything going on at once that you feel like you can't cope, can't concentrate, like you're going to explode? . . . Days when you're just so fucking tired of pretending and all you want to do is go home, pack a bag and go . . . and then keep going? Just leave it all behind and never look back?'

'I . . . Maybe you should talk to someone,' suggested Winter.

'I'm talking to you, aren't I?' said Marshall. 'So yes, there are track marks on my arms, tactically covered by tattoos, and each and every one of them represents one of those days. And do you know what? I'm thankful for them because they saved me from doing something far worse.'

'Saved you?' he asked in genuine interest.

'Some people have friends, others a myriad of other addictions. I . . . have this.' Marshall closed her eyes and took a deep breath, experiencing a phantom surge of euphoria just at the memory of sinking a needle into her skin. 'It's like . . . like puncturing a balloon. Not putting something *into* you but taking something away: a sharp prick here and then from the very top of your head it starts to work its way down, all those problems and worries and stresses and regrets washing out of you, resetting you just for one night . . . It is peace, and that is a *very* precious thing.'

She opened her eyes to a concerned-looking Winter, realising that her right thumb was still poised over an imaginary plunger:

'Hey,' she shrugged. 'You asked.'

Fifteen minutes later, they reconvened out on the street, Winter having finally finished his shift.

'It's not that late,' he said, zipping up his jacket. 'Still hungry? Fancy a drink somewhere?'

'No. But thank you. I'm exhausted. I'd better get home.'

'OK,' he smiled, now a little worried it had sounded like he was asking her 'out' out.

'Don't worry,' she assured him, reading his expression with unsettling accuracy, 'I know you didn't mean it like that.'

'*Huh?* No! Of course. I didn't think . . .' He trailed off. 'Anyway, I'll see you tomorrow.'

'Yeah. See you tomorrow.'

'Hey, Marshall!' he blurted when she went to walk away. '. . . Jordan,' he corrected himself. 'I'm your friend,' he told her genuinely.

She smiled: '. . . I know.'

Winter nodded and headed off in the other direction as Marshall's expression collapsed. Mind screaming, she desperately tried to work out whether she was nearer to the squat house in Maida Vale or the strip club in Farringdon but was unable to concentrate on anything.

There was no way she was going home tonight.

Friday

CHAPTER 24

'You are a genius,' Marshall greeted Winter when she came to collect him from the well-worn sofas of the New Scotland Yard reception area wearing the same clothes she had been the previous night.

'I know,' he nodded as they started walking towards the lifts, relieved to get away from the assorted newspapers left lying around – all featuring the same snap of their *Venus de Milo* on the front pages. '. . . Why though?'

'Alfie and Nicolette's council estate – you were right. It *was* the same one Coates's mother lived on. I don't think that's a coincidence.'

Having worn a suit for the occasion in an attempt to impress Chambers with his professionalism, Winter was feeling rather uncomfortable. Apparently, he had put on a few pounds since its last outing, and made a mental note to loosen his belt another notch the next time he got a chance.

'What about the other locations?' he asked as they started to ascend the building.

'Coates only ever lived at two addresses, but we're compiling a list of past employers and asked his bank to flag any recurring or notable transactions . . . But our best bet is Eloise Brown.'

'And what did she say?' he asked, wanting to catch up on everything he'd missed before he could get in there and embarrass himself like the third wheel he was.

When the lift doors juddered open, Marshall stepped out and looked back at him in surprise:

'We figured you'd want to ask her that yourself.'

The expression of pride on Winter's face immediately gave way to suspicion:

'And Wainwright's OK with that?'

Marshall took a moment too long to answer: '. . . Of course.'

'She doesn't know I'm here, does she?'

'Not so much.'

Winter couldn't stop staring at Eloise.

It was getting a bit creepy.

Everyone had noticed.

But how Robert Coates had ever managed to woo such an intelligent and beautiful woman was beyond him. Even in the confines of the drab investigation room, she seemed to radiate fun and positivity, effortlessly brightening the day of anyone fortunate enough to come into contact with—

'You're doing it again,' Marshall nudged him.

'Sorry.' He forced his eyes back down to the list in front of him.

The office was buzzing. People rushed in and out with armfuls of paperwork, while the ringing phones, overspill from the tip line, didn't pause for breath – the nationwide press coverage rapidly gathering momentum.

It felt as though they were getting somewhere. After showing Eloise on a map where their *Venus de Milo* was discovered, a memory had been jogged free: she and Coates getting off the Tube at Pimlico station to walk along the river. Assembling a selection of crime-scene photographs absent of the newly built block of flats in the background, she had recognised it as the spot where the two of them had shared their first kiss. And then, when the list of past employers revealed that Coates had spent three consecutive summers working at the British Museum, there could be no doubt that the locations were every bit as significant as the works of art he was mimicking.

'I think I've got something!' called Marshall, grabbing the map off the adjacent desk. 'Tyburnia Grammar,' she announced, pointing just to the right of a vast expanse of green space. 'His secondary school. And it's only a few roads over from Hyde Park.'

Chambers leaned in for a closer look, but then frowned, the four roads standing between it and the park troubling him. Struck with an idea, he headed back over to his own workspace to retrieve one map of the London Underground network and one showing a confusing tangle of bus routes knotted around the city:

'He'd have been coming in from the gnome house in Wandsworth, right?'

'Right,' replied Marshall.

He tapped his finger in satisfaction: 'No nearby Tube stations. The number twenty-eight bus would've got him there but dropped him on the wrong side of the park . . . The murder site would have been on his daily walk to school.'

'We're getting closer,' smiled Marshall in relief, Chambers nodding in agreement:

'We're getting closer.'

People are shallow, simple creatures, and beauty no more than a tool to exploit that fundamental flaw – to fit in with a specific group, to project a deceptive impression of oneself, to attract a viable mate – animalistic behaviour in its most primitive form, and Robert Coates understood that concept better than most.

Where a gangling and awkward university professor could repel the majority of close encounters in situations where attention is inevitable, a handsome and charming stranger will form new friendships with ease – with those who want to be *with* him – with those who want to be *like* him, while leaving behind a lasting impression.

Neither were appropriate for today, however. Today, he would slouch and shuffle around as though the weight of the world was bearing down on him. He would smile hopefully at anyone who caught his eye, as if to say '*please to God* let me unload some of my troubles onto you', and watch them retreat from his vicinity. He had shaved the stubble that cast such a flattering shadow across his jawline and picked out his earthiest clothing, a rainbow of beiges and browns, making him resemble a lump of rock whenever he stopped moving.

Because today, he needed to be invisible.

*

Statue	Location	Victim	Event
The Thinker	Hyde Park	Henry John Dolan	His birth? An artist and intellectual who would never belong
Pietà	Cranbrook Council Estate	Alphonse and Nicolette Cotillard	A drug dependent baby almost dying in his mother's arms
Perseus with the Head of Medusa	The British Museum	(Benjamin Chambers) and ???	Finally ridding himself of his drug addict mother
Venus de Milo	Riverside Walk	Tamsin Fuller	

Chambers clicked the lid back onto his pen and turned to Eloise:

'Tell us about the *Venus de Milo*.'

Dressed in another paint-spattered shirt, she got up, holding the presentation she'd been working on all morning:

'The *Venus de Milo* is a marble sculpture attributed to Alexandros of Antioch somewhere around 100 BC. It is a little larger than life-sized and is displayed in The Louvre in Paris.'

Giving her an encouraging smile, Winter scribbled down a detailed set of notes on her introduction, which even the most thorough detective couldn't deny was all utterly useless to their investigation.

'She also goes by the name *The Aphrodite of Milos.*'

'Aphrodite?' asked Chambers in recognition.

Eloise nodded: 'The goddess of love and beauty.'

'Which is how we know it's meant to be you,' said Winter, both Chambers and Marshall turning round to look at him. 'I mean, why *we* think *he* thinks it's you,' he added quickly but going bright red even quicker.

An embarrassed smile broke across Eloise's face.

Marshall rolled her eyes.

Chambers shook his head.

They both turned back to face the front.

'So, is it Aphrodite or Venus?' asked Chambers.

'Both,' replied Eloise. 'Aphrodite is Greek. Venus is Roman. Same goddess, different names. But, of course, this is art and there are different interpretations. Some – Robert included – don't believe it's Aphrodite at all, but *Amphitrite*, who, when Poseidon asked for her hand in marriage, fled to Atlas on the far side of the world.'

'Like you rebuffing Coates's proposals,' said Marshall, now understanding why Eloise had been so adamant that the statue represented her arrival in his life.

'Precisely.'

'Makes sense,' concluded Chambers, removing the lid from his pen again to scribble the name of the next statue on the list. 'Moving on then: *Psyche Revived by Cupid's Kiss.*'

Eyes lowered to the floor, hair left to its own devices in a non-descript style, even the modest bunch of flowers in his hand an insipid collection of muted hues, Robert Coates roamed the halls of Queen Elizabeth Hospital unnoticed. The rucksack he carried was far heavier than he'd been expecting. Pulling it back up onto his shoulder, he watched with interest as two sleep-starved order-lies approached, their conversation building to a crescendo as they passed him:

'... already late. Seriously, if I miss this train, she's going to kill me. Would you mind dropping these off with ...'

Coates turned back the way he came to follow them, the talkative man already slipping his white tunic off in anticipation of leaving. He paused to read a noticeboard when they reached a door labelled *Staff Only*, watching them key in a four-digit code before disappearing inside . . .

Catching the heavy door before it could click shut, he waited for the voices to fade and then entered the changing rooms, their conversation audible once again as he stalked them through the maze of lockers:

'Worst . . . striptease . . . ever!' laughed a new voice as a pair of trousers landed in a heap on the floor. 'Go! Go! Hurry!'

The slap of bare feet against the tiles gave way to the hiss of the shower bursting to life.

Placing the rucksack down, Coates continued to the end of the next row, hovering just out of sight, the man mere inches away, flashes of skin teasing from round the corner as he hung his clothes up in a locker.

'Shit!'

The clatter of something dropping to the tiles echoed around the room.

Sensing that this was his opportunity, Coates stepped out into the open, the man on his knees oblivious as he groped beneath a bench covered in clothing.

Silently, he started to approach . . .

'The story goes that once upon a time, in a great city that's name has long been lost to time, there were three princesses, the youngest of which was named Psyche, whose beauty was said to rival that of Venus herself, a compliment that the goddess did not take well. In jealous retribution, Venus sent her son, Cupid, to shoot the princess with one of his arrows in a devious plan to make her fall in love with some hideous beast; however, Cupid accidently scratches himself in the process, causing him to fall madly in love with the very first thing he lays eyes on, which, of course, was Psyche.

'*Yada. Yada. Yada.* Something about a helpful ant, golden sheep and invisible lover hostage-type situation. It all gets a bit weird in the middle until we reach the scene depicted in the sculpture, where Venus demands that Psyche venture into the Underworld with a flask to retrieve a scrap of beauty from Proserpina.

'Successfully carrying out her task, Psyche returns to the earth but is overcome with burning curiosity. Ignoring all of the warnings bestowed upon her, she lifts the lid and peeks inside – the flask filled *not* with beauty but with The Night of Styx, which sends her into a deep and lasting sleep, where she remains until discovered by Cupid, who takes her in his arms and revives her with a single prick of his arrow.

'With Venus's hold on her finally broken, Psyche is granted immortality so that she and Cupid may be wed and spend the rest of eternity together.'

Pulling his towel around him, the late-running orderly emerged from the showers just in time to see his colleague reclaim a can of deodorant from under the benches.

''Scuse me,' he said, squeezing past to reach his crumpled pile of clothes, but immediately noticing that he was one item short. With a puzzled expression, he turned back to his friend: 'Hey, have you seen my uniform?'

The ceramic cups rattled on their saucers as though the decrepit refreshments trolley were enduring an earthquake rather than rolling across a smooth floor. Dressed in a white tunic and dark trousers, Robert Coates pushed the cart through the doors of the recovery ward without a single person batting an eyelash, helped by the whir of a powerful floor fan which had made him invisible once more. Surveying the ward like a sentinel, it billowed cold air out in all directions as he parked up beside the nurses' station and plugged the kettle into one of the available sockets. Distracted and harassed, several people hurried past, but none paid him the slightest bit of attention as he calmly flicked the switch and headed back out.

'So . . .' started Chambers, looking perplexed. 'We're thinking you're Psyche in this?'

'Yes,' replied Eloise.

'And this relates to that time you popped out to the Underworld to pick something up?'

'It's my accident,' she responded sadly. 'It was autumn and had gone dark a good hour before I'd even left work. I was riding my bike home as usual on my favourite route through Greenwich Park when . . .' she took a breath, 'I was hit by a car.' She paused, as if she still couldn't quite believe what happened next. 'I heard them stop . . . only for a moment . . . and then drive away. They just left me there.

'Both the bike and I had gone over a ridge. No one knew I was down there, lying helpless, barely conscious and badly hurt.' But then she raised her head and smiled: 'He found me. When I didn't come home, Robert spent the entire night searching for me. I can still remember the feeling of him picking me up and putting me in the back of his car.'

'Which part of the park?' asked Marshall, pen poised to add it to the list of significant places.

'Right by the Royal Observatory,' Eloise told her. 'That was how I broke my arm. And he painted a masterpiece across my cast with just a children's novelty art set he'd found in the hospital shop . . . He never left my side.'

Chambers and Marshall shared a significant look:

'Which hospital?' they chimed in unison.

*

**DO NOT ENTER
DEEP CLEAN IN
PROGRESS**

'What's going on?' asked a porter, on being confronted with the sealed set of doors and scattering of yellow cones that fortified the entrance to the ward.

'Highly infectious patient,' replied Coates, sounding bored as he loitered out in the corridor.

The man pulled a face: 'Did they say how long?' He looked down at the elderly man in the wheelchair he was pushing, as if considering fly-tipping him somewhere.

'Half an hour . . . Forty-five minutes,' he shrugged. 'But I'd probably give it longer,' Coates advised with a knowing nod, exploiting the loyalty among the lower ranks. 'Let the others know too, yeah?'

'Will do. Thanks,' said the man, needing no further information to start spreading conspiracy theories that the 'higher-ups' wouldn't want them knowing about. 'Let's get you back to the waiting room then, Des!' he bellowed down at his patient, who appeared to be able to hear perfectly well.

Coates watched them wheel away just as the five-minute timer on his digital watch reached zero.

Crossing his own barricade, he ensured that no one was watching and then slid inside, stopping to pull an oxygen mask over his face and open up the cylinder to a sharp hiss of air. Picking it up by the handle, he strolled down the short connecting corridor and through the set of double doors at the end.

The bustling ward was now completely still, bar the pivoting floor fan still breathing tainted air over the collection of people sprawled across the floors and desks. Stepping over a stocky staff nurse attempting to crawl on all fours, he walked over to the refreshments trolley, switched off the kettle and then opened up the storage compartment beneath to retrieve his rucksack.

Following the felt-marker guest list scribbled behind the nurses' station, he made his way into one of the six-bay rooms. After a disdainful glance at the frail woman asleep in the bed to his left, he continued past three empty bays to reach the two people at the far end of the room – both unconscious, both pathetically helpless, both entrusting their lives to banks of outdated machinery – one of the beige boxes literally held together with tape.

He approached the woman in the bed beside the window and, without hesitation, switched off her screens one by one, silencing the various warnings and alarms. In fascination, he watched as the bag squeezing air into her lungs simply ceased to do so, the warm blood being pumped back into her body growing viscous and slow.

Moving to the bed opposite, he stared down at the man – peaceful in his medicated sleep despite the fresh bandages to the contrary. Closing his eyes, he realised that he had matched his breathing to the wheeze of the ventilator, finding it strangely soothing in the otherwise hushed ward. He was almost loath to turn it off.

Raising his thumb to the machine, he paused to take a final look down at one of the few people on this living Hell of a planet he could actually relate to . . .

He deserved more – a more beautiful end.

Taking his hand away from the switch, he set the oxygen cylinder down to unzip the rucksack, revealing the metal shapes and bulging plastic bag inside before pulling the curtain across the end of the room.

For he still had much to do.

CHAPTER 25

'Wait in the car!' barked Chambers, skidding to a stop outside the entrance of the hospital, joining three other police vehicles abandoned in the road. He, Marshall and Winter all went to climb out: 'I said: wait in the car!'

'Sorry. I thought you were talking to . . .' started Winter, but they were already out of earshot, running through the crowd of journalists being held at bay outside the wide glass doors. 'Yeah, you don't care.' Feeling a little embarrassed, he got back in beside Eloise, giving her a 'what can you do?' shrug.

She pulled on the handle and climbed out.

'Hey!' he called after her as she hurried inside after them. '. . . Hey!'

Identifying themselves to a man on the door, they made their way through the chaotic ward. With maintenance staff ruling out a gas leak before removing the suspect kettle, the unflappable nurses had opened all of the windows and were now carrying out their duties as normal around their recovering colleagues and the crime scene in the adjacent room. Rounding the corner, Chambers hadn't had time to compose himself, the scene awaiting them stealing his breath like a physical blow.

Surreal . . . Elegant . . . Brutal.

'Oh my God,' gasped Marshall at his side, not having made it any further into the room than he had.

Standing equidistant between the two bays at the far end of the room, a set of fanned white wings looked to have burst from the spine of a kneeling man. Reaching for the ceiling, they eclipsed the light pouring in through the windows, casting long shadows that both detectives instinctively stepped out of.

'Chambers?' whispered Marshall. '. . . Chambers?'

'I need a minute,' he admitted.

She nodded understandingly and then went to intercept their colleagues before they could notice him standing there.

'Marshall,' she introduced herself to a uniformed officer, who looked at an utter loss at where to begin. 'I work with Detective Chambers.'

'Oh! *Literally* never been happier to see anyone!' he told her before turning back to the winged abomination beside them: 'I mean, seriously, what the *fuck*?!'

She looked down at the two bodies – one male, one female, realising that what had resembled a careless heap from across the room was, in fact, an all too familiar and carefully staged pose. Completely nude, the male victim's weight was supported by his outstretched right leg as he held the woman's lifeless body in his arms.

Marshall stepped around the bodies towards the windows, the tiny strings that held the wings in place catching in the sunlight, and was revolted to discover that the angelic appendages were actually protruding from the male victim's body, a ring of dark blood still oozing from the wounds.

'Swans . . . *I think*,' commented the officer.

She nodded, crouching down to inspect the intricate metal framework that looked to have grown up out of the floor, curving and clasping at various points to hold the two 'subjects' in position.

'He didn't make this here,' said Chambers, startling Marshall, who clearly hadn't heard him approaching. He pulled on a pair of gloves and reached out to touch the end of one of the metal shapes, remoulding it with only moderate force. 'Malleable though. Some sort of aluminium? Any obvious brand names or symbols on the quiver?' he asked.

'Quiver?' replied Marshall. She hadn't even got to that yet.

'There were these as well,' mentioned the officer, pointing to the floor.

'The arrow he used to wake her and the flask containing The Night of Styx,' he mumbled.

'*Errrr* . . . I beg your pardon?'

'Don't worry about it,' Marshall told the officer. 'When were they found?'

'About thirty minutes ago, when one of the cleaning staff walked in to discover everyone passed out on the floor.'

'Passed out or awake but unable to move?' she asked him. 'There's a difference.'

'*Errm*. I'll check. Nobody seems to remember seeing anyone coming in *or* out. It's like they were invisible or something.'

'Perhaps they were,' muttered Chambers despondently.

The officer glanced at him, clearly unsure whether it had been a dig at his police work or if he genuinely believed in ghosts:

'This is Robert Coates again, isn't it?' he asked them. '. . . The statues?'

Chambers calmly turned to address him:

'The press are already here. I trust I can rely on your discretion?'

'Of course, sir.'

'Great . . . Now, get out.'

'Yes, sir.'

Through Cupid's wings, he and Marshall looked at one another.

'I'd seen the pictures,' she said, dazed, as the officer's footsteps retreated from the room. 'I knew what to expect. . . . And yet, I wasn't expecting *this*.'

'Have you checked the flask yet?' somebody asked from the doorway.

Eloise was standing at the far end of the room, not a trace of fear or repulsion to be found on her face – only awe.

Winter came bounding into the room after her, closely followed by the officer they'd managed to evade on their way in.

'They're with me,' said Chambers, calling the constable off, before turning his attention back to the others: 'I told you to stay in the car.'

'I tried to stop her,' wheezed Winter, not a trace of awe to be found on his face – only fear and repulsion.

'You can't be here,' Chambers told them.

'Have you checked the flask yet?' Eloise asked again, as if she hadn't heard him.

'This is a crime scene!'

'This is *Robert!*' she bit back, edging towards the winged god and his princess, bright eyes drinking in every detail of the scene before her.

With a look of intense displeasure, Chambers walked round to where the ceramic flask lay atop the bed sheet that spilled across the floor. He crouched down and grasped the lid, hesitating for a fleeting moment as stories of vindictive goddesses and curses from the Underworld raced through his mind.

He gently removed the top . . . and peered inside.

'What is it?' Winter called from the safety of the corridor.

'Leaves,' replied Chambers, looking to Eloise in concern. '. . . Laurel leaves.'

'I don't like it,' said Chambers. He and Marshall had stepped outside for a coffee and breath of fresh air in a courtyard that the smokers among the staff had staked a claim to long ago.

'She's been invaluable to us so far.'

'You saw her face in there. Not exactly subtle, is she? She's getting off on this every bit as much as Coates is.'

'Doesn't mean she's involved,' Marshall pointed out.

'And helping us doesn't necessarily mean she *isn't*.'

She nodded, squinting as the November sunshine made a reappearance: 'I agree it's *one* possibility.'

'And then,' continued Chambers, 'there's the leaves he keeps dropping around the place for us to find for her like little love notes.'

'Say you're right – why would she be helping us?'

'For the same reason *he* is. Why would Coates leave us your sketchbook?'

'Like we said before: as a taunt,' suggested Marshall. 'A threat? . . . A cry for help?'

Chambers shook his head: 'I don't think Robert Coates gives a damn about playing games. He could've gone to the press at any point, but he hasn't. He's not looking for notoriety and wouldn't expect the world to understand anyway. He's doing this for *him*.'

'Then why do *you* think he left it?'

'I'd feel a *hell* of a lot better if I knew. But whatever the reason, he left it for *his* benefit, not ours. And we'd do well to remember that.' He checked his watch: 'Wainwright will be here in a few minutes. I've got to explain why we've got *another* two corpses and an entire hospital ward drugged up on what sounds like his paralytic.'

'I'll come with you.'

'I can handle it. You should have a talk with Eloise, make up your mind whether we keep her around or not.'

'You're trusting *me* with that decision?' she asked in surprise.

'I've got enough to do,' he told her simply, heading back inside.

'Who were they?' asked DCI Wainwright, still watching the faux-god's wings intently, as if expecting them to start flapping again at any moment.

'Javier Ruiz and Audrey Fairchild.'

'The ones from the news?!' she asked urgently.

Chambers looked down at his notes for help, realising that he hadn't had time to pick up a paper or sit down in front of the television since this had all begun.

'The transplant couple?' she prompted him.

'Then yes. Lung transplant. She had—'

'Cystic fibrosis,' Wainwright interrupted him, regarding the two victims with a very different expression now. 'They gave her six months to live.'

'OK,' said Chambers, folding up his useless sheet of paper.

'Her boyfriend offered to be a donor. The doctors said it wasn't as easy as that: that he'd have to be a perfect match and without a second donor, they'd have to take a life-altering amount of tissue from him. But he pressed ahead regardless, and somehow the stars aligned . . . It made the news because they booked their wedding before going in for the surgery – six months to the day from Audrey's diagnosis,' Wainwright said sadly, looking almost tempted to embrace the tragic lovers. '. . . Why them?'

'Wrong hospital, wrong time,' shrugged Chambers. 'Marriage seems a recurring theme. It might even be as simple as "man saves the woman he loves". Truthfully, who knows?'

His boss looked a little surprised by his candour.

'The guy's away with the fairies,' continued Chambers, a slight edge to his voice. 'We have no real idea how his twisted mind is forming these vague connections to the victims, no way of predicting who he might fixate on next, no pattern of behaviour to work to because he's not an actual person; he's a mirror that can only mimic others . . . The locations,' he said decisively. 'It's *all* about the locations. They're our *only* constant, our only advantage over him.'

Wainwright nodded along to his logical summary: 'What do you need?'

'We have a list of significant places from his ex. I'd like surveillance at each of them twenty-four hours a day until this is over.'

'How many locations?'

'Four perhaps.'

'You've got a week,' Wainwright told him. 'If you've still got nothing by then, we'll all probably be reassigned anyway.'

Marshall and Eloise had found a table in the back corner of the hospital canteen, the two women a conspicuously mismatched pairing – Eloise effortlessly beautiful in no make-up at all, clothing colourful and comfortable, her wavy hair scrunched into a messy ponytail;

Marshall, as always, sporting her monochrome warpaint, her every movement restricted by layers of dark clothing and leather.

Winter had held on for as long as he could, giving himself a whole fifty minutes to make the hour-long journey into work, but at least meaning he should make it in before acne-face Dan. He'd be all right just so long as Sophie, the stuck-up new girl from the other store, didn't snitch on him.

Marshall shook her head, wondering why on earth she even knew any of that.

Consciously avoiding more obvious and unpleasant topics, the two women had been making small talk, mainly about the gallery – Eloise enthusing over her plans for it, Marshall somewhat pissing on her fireworks when she put it down as another location Coates might choose to leave them a body.

During a natural lull in the conversation, Marshall broached the real issue on her mind:

'It's strange . . . seeing a dead body for the first time,' she started. 'It's not like it is on TV, not just a person lying still. They've *changed* somehow.'

'I'm fine,' Eloise assured her.

'You do seem to be handling it remarkably well: those crime-scene photographs back at the office . . . and now *this*.' She paused expectantly . . .

'I'm not sure what you want me to say.'

'Why aren't you freaking out right now?' blurted Marshall. 'You just saw one of the most disturbing crime scenes either I *or* Chambers have ever been to.'

Leaning back in her chair, Eloise fiddled with the plastic stirrer from her cup of tea:

'Because it was beautiful.'

'Beautiful? They were dead bodies.'

'Some things can be both tragic *and* beautiful at the same time.'

Marshall watched Eloise carefully, deliberating over her next move, deciding that bluntness was the best course:

'Chambers is worried about you. And, frankly, so am I.'

'Worried how?'

'That you want Coates to succeed.'

'. . . I do.'

Taken aback, Marshall folded her arms and locked eyes with the other woman:

'Then *we* have a serious problem.'

'I don't really see why. Morally, I want to help you stop him before he hurts another person. But from an *artistic* standpoint, I feel we're all honoured to witness his genius in any form, and there's certainly a part of me that wants to see him finish his . . . collection.'

'Collection?' asked Marshall, appalled. Her head was starting to hurt. 'OK. Tell me this: when push comes to shove and you have to choose, which side is going to win out?'

'Honestly, I don't know.'

She shook her head in exasperation:

'Are you still in love with him? . . . Even after *all* of this?'

'. . . Yes.'

'Are you not scared of him?'

'He absolutely terrifies me.'

'Because he's a monster!' snapped Marshall, feeling as though they were going in circles.

'Oh, no doubt,' agreed Eloise. '. . . But he's *my* monster.'

CHAPTER 26

Wearing an off-beige shirt and a jacket so moth-eaten it was a wonder how it was still hanging together, DS Phillip Easton was the very picture of a burnt-out police officer desperately holding on for retirement.

He had seen it all, done it all, and come to the inevitable conclusion that ignorance was indeed bliss.

After what had already been a non-stop morning, he returned to Harrow on the Hill Police Station, bakery meal-deal in hand as he made his way back to his desk.

'You've got a customer,' one of his colleagues greeted him.

He sighed: 'I need food. Can't you handle it?'

'Missing person,' the man shrugged. '. . . Your remit.'

Raising his head to the heavens, Easton gazed up through the skylight, conveniently placed to more effectively shoot God the stink-eye.

'Can I *not* get one *arseing* moment to myself?!' he spat, continuing with his rant as he stormed through the office: '*All* I wanted was to eat one *bloody*— Good afternoon!' he smiled pleasantly, placing his lunch to the side as he sat down. 'I'm Detective Sergeant Easton. Or you can call me Phil, if you like?'

The frumpy woman sitting across from him gazed back as though she hadn't understood a word.

'Right then,' he said, glancing at the few details his colleague had bothered to scribble down. 'You're Greek?' he commented in forced interest. 'So, what can I do for you Mrs . . .' he squinted at the form, '. . . Pap . . . a . . . dop . . . ou . . . lou.'

'Papadopoulou,' she told him with a very strong accent.

'Papadopoulou,' he corrected himself. 'I understand you're here to report a missing person?'

'My son,' she answered in broken English, but the worry in her voice crystal clear. 'He no come home from . . .' She appeared to get stuck.

'. . . Work?' Easton guessed.

'Yes! Work. He no come home from work today.'

'Today?' he asked, a slight strain to his voice. 'The thing is, we wouldn't normally—'

'He has . . . mind . . . of child,' she interrupted him.

'I see,' said Easton, circling the *Vulnerable Adult* section of the form. 'And has he ever done this before?'

'No!' she replied, bursting into tears.

He gave her a tissue and his best attempt at a reassuring smile:

'Let's get some details from you then. Could I have his full name please?'

'Evan Ioannou Papadopoulos.'

'Not Papadopoulou?'

'Papadopou*los*.'

He got her to spell it out for him.

'Date of birth?'

'October seven, nineteen seventy-three.'

'Making him . . . Twenty-two,' said Easton a little more loudly than strictly necessary to show off his Rainman-like abilities. '. . . Wait. No. Twenty-three?' In the end, he resorted to counting it out on his fingers. 'Moving on: height?'

'Oh! Eight and four.'

Easton looked lost: 'In feet and inches, if possible?'

'Yes. Eight and four.'

He placed the lid back on his biro and tapped it impatiently against the desk:

'Tell you what – we'll come back to that one. Do you have any recent pictures of Evan with you?'

'Yes,' she replied, rooting through her handbag and passing him a photograph of her son standing with the rest of the Papadopouli.

Easton stared down at it, looked back up at the distraught woman, and then checked around him for sniggering colleagues. Guardedly, he removed the lid from his biro again:

'Height: eight feet, four inches.'

*

The Royal Observatory (the accident)
Fire-Damaged Art Block (Birkbeck College)
His Mother's Grave
The Laurel Tree Wood

Having seen to the safe removal of the bodies from the Recovery Ward, the sight of white feathers dragging along the floor from beneath a blanket fuel for at least the next year's worth of nightmares, Chambers had requisitioned the hospital's lecture hall. Before the others arrived, he scribbled the list of locations significant to Robert Coates on the whiteboard in a pen he now suspected to be permanent marker.

DCI Wainwright, looking a little jaded after addressing the press, was the first to join him, taking a seat at the very front. She was closely followed by Marshall, who was quite clearly deliberating how far she could sit from the formidable woman without appearing rude – the answer, apparently, two empty chairs away.

'Is that all of us?' Chambers asked her significantly, as they hadn't had a chance to catch up since their talk in the courtyard.

As if on cue, Eloise hurried through the doors:

'Sorry!' she said, out of breath, a takeaway coffee cup in her hand as she took a seat two empty chairs away from Marshall.

'OK,' said Chambers. 'Eloise Brown, my boss – DCI Wainwright.

Boss, Robert Coates's ex – Eloise Brown,' he introduced them before getting straight to business. He gestured to the whiteboard behind him: 'These are our *four* potential sites for the *three* remaining murders.'

'Maybe five sites,' Marshall piped up. 'Eloise's gallery?'

Chambers glanced over at Wainwright, who gave him a begrudging nod.

He added it to the list.

'The boss has signed off on surveillance at each for the next week, on the proviso we pick up some of the slack,' he said, looking in Marshall's direction.

Keen to make a good impression in front of her future superior, Marshall looked practically ecstatic at the prospect of losing the next seven days of her life to sitting around in freezing cold cars.

'. . . Winter too, hopefully,' he added as an afterthought, having persuaded Wainwright to expedite the occasional constable's return to work, subject to an HR interview and his doctor's blessing. 'The question is,' he continued, 'where to focus our efforts?' He turned to Eloise: 'Think you could place these locations in order of *most* to *least* likely in your opinion?'

'I . . . don't . . . really . . .' she stuttered, clearly feeling that he had put her on the spot.

'Your best guess,' he encouraged her.

Setting her drink down, she got up, taking the marker pen from him on her way past. She stared at the whiteboard for a few moments and then decisively went to rub out the top line:

'. . . It's not coming off.'

Chambers winced:

'Make a new list,' he advised, pointing her towards the flipchart instead.

1. The Fire
2. The Grave
3. The Woods

4. The Observatory
5. The Gallery

She handed him back the marker.

'Talk us through it,' said Chambers.

'Well, the gallery is significant to me, but not really to him. So, I think, while a possibility, it's the least likely. And it feels like my accident has already been covered here at the hospital.' She glanced back at her reordered list. 'The most important thing to Robert, the thing that *defines* him, is his art . . . followed by his hatred of his mother . . . and *then* me and our relationship,' she finished bitterly.

'The laurel leaves would suggest otherwise,' argued Chambers. 'That perhaps he's doing all of this for you . . . or to get to you.'

'Robert would never harm me.'

'That's not a chance I'm prepared to take. We're agreed,' he said, looking again to Wainwright. 'From this point onwards, you're on twenty-four-hour protection detail. If you're not with us, you're with a competent uniformed officer . . . Or Winter, of course.' He turned back to the whiteboard. 'I think we need to prioritise—'

Wainwright cleared her throat:

'Forgive me, Detective, but it sounds an awful lot like you're already moving on to the next dead body without doing *a thing* to investigate the two we just put in the back of a van.'

Chambers glared at her challengingly: 'There's nothing we're going to learn from them.'

'You're being callous.'

'I'm being *realistic*.'

'I'm not sure the families of our two victims will be reassured by that.'

'Or the millions passing judgement sitting on their fat arses in front of the telly,' he bit back. 'But it doesn't really matter what they think, does it?'

'And *I* thought you were being "realistic",' said Wainwright calmly. 'We have the entire country watching our every move. Are they expecting too much wanting to see the lead detective on the case making *some* effort to find out what happened?'

At that moment, the doors swung open into the wall and a flustered man wearing a pinstripe suit burst into the room:

'Is this the talk on . . .' he glanced down at his visitors pass, '"Pre-emptive versus Unwarranted Colonoscopies"?'

'No. But it's certainly starting to feel like one,' muttered Chambers, gesturing for the man to get out. He turned back to address Wainwright: 'We have limited resources and can't save the dead. These people were murdered by Robert Coates, we know that, who will have altered his appearance as required to gain access to them. None of that helps me in the least.

'We've requested the CCTV footage, prioritised the external cameras in case he was stupid enough to climb into a car or get onto a bus. We've got people contacting all the local parks with lakes to find out if they've had any swans hacked up, and we found traces of soil on a few of the leaves inside the flask. I've asked the lab to analyse it for a detailed breakdown of its components in the hopes we might be able to at least narrow down which part of the city it came from. Javier Ruiz and Audrey Fairchild's deaths *are* being looked into, but I wouldn't be doing my job if I wasn't already looking ahead.'

. . . Silence.

The tense stand-off eventually ended when Wainwright gave him a curt nod.

'Tell us about the next statue,' Chambers prompted Eloise, putting her on the spot for the second time in five minutes. He looked down at his notes: '*The . . . Winged Victory of Samothrace?*'

'I don't have my presentation with me, but I can certainly give you an overview,' she smiled, but with a sharp edge to her voice.

'I'm not loving the word *winged* right now,' commented Marshall. 'Another god?'

'Goddess,' Eloise corrected her. 'Nike, to be precise.'

'Never heard of her,' said Chambers, taking a seat.

'Sure you have: who do you think the sportswear brand is named after? And you must have seen the Silver Lady she inspired on the

front of every Rolls-Royce? She even features on the Olympic medal. Nike is the goddess of victory, the daughter of Pallas and Styx.'

'Not Styx again!' huffed Chambers, rubbing his face wearily.

Wainwright gave him an enquiring look.

'It's the name of the river that separates the earth from the gates
of Hell . . . *Eugh! The Gates of Hell!*' he complained, wishing he'd
just kept his mouth shut.

'The Greeks believed that Nike could make them invincible and
give them the strength and speed to succeed in any endeavour,'
explained Eloise. 'She would then reward the victors with a wreath
of laurel leaves.'

There was a beat in which no one bothered to voice the significance of the leaves in this third female statue.

'Which event does this relate to?' asked Chambers.

'I don't know,' she replied.

'She's you, isn't she?'

'Yes.'

'Then you *do* know,' he challenged her.

'Give her a break, Chambers,' snapped Marshall.

He got to his feet, realising that he had already made up his own
mind about Coates's ex, regardless of what Marshall thought:

'People's lives are on the line!' he shouted. 'Think!'

'Detective!' said Wainwright firmly, but still he pushed her:

'What did you give to Coates? How did you reward him? What
did he need your support with that he couldn't have done without
you?!'

Close to tears, a look of comprehension suddenly dawned over
Eloise's face:

'The fire!' she gasped. 'Building the ash sculptures . . . It's the
fire!'

'And the reward?' he asked.

Eloise revisited a memory that she hadn't in a long while:

'He asked me to marry him again on the night we finished them,
surrounded by these monochromatic shapes and figures grown out
of the dirt. It was as if Robert and I were the only two flashes of

colour in an otherwise black and white picture . . . it was the only time I ever said *yes*.'

Satisfied, he looked to Marshall expectantly: 'Then what are we waiting for?'

Her three escorts talked amongst themselves, Eloise trailing several steps behind as they traipsed the hospital's endless corridors in search of a less public exit. Being forced to confront that particular memory had stirred up some surprising feelings in her, reminding her of the lies that she had been telling herself – branding one of the most magical nights of her life as a mistake best forgotten – blaming her younger self's impulsiveness for accepting his proposal, when the truth was she had never been more sure of anything.

They were talking about her. She could tell because Marshall kept looking back and smiling. Presumably intended nicely, it was a rather sinister look on her pale, Bride of Dracula, Halloween costume of a face.

Smiling back sweetly, Eloise noticed a man who seemed overly interested in her distracted entourage as he approached from the opposite direction. Dressed in earthy colours and carrying a rucksack, something about him felt vaguely familiar: *not his walk . . . nor his hair . . . not even what she could make out of his face – but something.*

As the gap between them continued to close, Eloise made eye contact with the stranger and then audibly gasped, recognising him instantly, Coates looking equally stunned to see her there behind the wall of detectives, his stride faltering as Marshall glanced back to check on her.

She couldn't breathe. She opened her mouth but no words came, Coates now only a few metres away. But he didn't stop, instead, he continued walking right at them – a show of his utter trust in her as he subtly extended his left hand away from his side.

Marshall frowned: 'Eloise? Everything OK?'

She felt as though she were being ripped in two, still unable to take a breath as their group unknowingly drew level with Coates, Marshall's earlier words repeating in her head:

When push comes to shove and you have to choose, which side is going to win out?

Honestly, I don't know.

Remaining silent, she nodded, Marshall turning back just as Eloise mirrored Coates's gesture, opening her hand, their fingers brushing for the most fleeting of moments . . . and then he was gone.

Heart racing, she forced herself not to look back, wanting to so badly she thought she might burst, an invigorated smile on her face the entire way out.

Because now she knew.

'I want that gate locked, someone in that window there, another in the building opposite,' barked Chambers, a tideline of dust climbing his shoes the longer he paced over the ash-covered earth.

He and Marshall had left Eloise with Wainwright back at the hospital before speeding across the city to Birkbeck College in order to assess the location while they still had the light.

Like a fresh stem growing from a damaged plant, the new extension had found its own path, wrapping itself around the existing structure, only its shadow tumbling into the building site that the fire had left behind.

The School of Arts premises in Gordon Square had been able to accommodate the vast majority of displaced classes, negating the urgency for redevelopment. The area now consisted of little more than metal fences, brightly coloured health and safety signage, and skips overflowing with debris. The ash had turned the ground underfoot black, a long-departed digger pushing the excess filth into three large mounds in the centre. Chambers had to count his blessings that it hadn't rained in the previous couple of days, the site no doubt an inaccessible quagmire the vast majority of the time. A large fence separated the university premises from an identical scene on the other side, to which the fire had spread like a contagion.

'Find out how we gain access to this floodlight,' he ordered one of the officers, pointing to the sealed control box that several thick wires retreated into.

'Yes, sir.'

'I want *all* personnel and vehicles in position and out of sight in half an hour!' he shouted to the rest of the team. 'And you . . . Yes, you!' he called someone over. 'It looks like an army's been through here. When everybody's out, grab a broom and cover our tracks as best you can. We can't risk spooking him.' Spotting Marshall by the gates, he made his way over: 'You all right?'

'One way in. One way out,' she informed him, the other two entrances now secured.

'Good,' he said, regarding the scene in satisfaction, which now less resembled a worksite in his eyes – more a giant cage. 'But you didn't answer my question. Are you all right?'

'It's just . . .'

'Just what?'

'This is all well and good but—'

'But someone else is still going to die,' he finished on her behalf. She nodded:

'And there's nothing we can or are doing to prevent it. Doesn't feel right somehow . . . I know. I know,' she added before he could say anything. 'There's no way of knowing who he'll target next. It just doesn't feel very good. But it's like you said back at the hospital "we can't save the dead".'

Chambers leaned against the wall beside her: 'We've got the whole country looking for him, officers interviewing everyone he's ever known.'

'They won't find him.'

'No . . . No, they won't,' he said thoughtfully. 'But, this is it. This is where it ends after all these years . . . Thank you.' Marshall looked confused. 'I'd walked away from this,' he explained, '. . . from him. But now here we are, and for the first time ever, *we* have the upper hand. Coates is coming; he can't help himself. And when he does, we'll be waiting. So . . . thank you.'

Appreciating the sentiment, Marshall patted his arm affectionately:

'Thank me when it's over.'

'Detective!' called the officer crouched beside the floodlight control box. 'Think they're trying to reach you!' he said, gesturing to
his radio.

Frowning down at his own, Chambers turned the volume up to
catch the end of a distorted transmission:

'. . . is now requesting your attendance. Over.'

He took it off his belt: 'This is Chambers. Was that for me? Over.'

'Affirmative. We've had a call from a council worker at some
allotments in Putney,' started the dispatcher, Chambers holding the
radio up for Marshall to listen in as well. 'He says they've uncov-
ered some bones that he believes to be human. Over.'

He and Marshall shared a look.

'Received. Advise caller to cease activity at the site immediately,
and please request a forensics team meet me there. Over.'

'Wilco. Out.'

'No rest for the wicked,' yawned Chambers. 'We've got a long
night ahead of us,' he told Marshall. 'Don't feel you have to—'

'I'm coming with you,' she cut him off.

'Suit yourself.'

'It wasn't buried anywhere near as deep as the others,' the bearded
council worker co-ordinating the excavation told them.

The oasis of green was unrecognisable: uprooted sheds stood in
crooked clusters beyond the work lines, the vast majority of the
plots now either tossed soil or exploratory pits. The man led the
way. Just past where one of the mini diggers was parked, the three
of them spread out around the edge of a shallow grave, a partially
exposed corpse at its centre – almost skeletal, being in the advanced
stages of decomposition. A stone sword lay atop the body, reminiscent of the knights of old, and tattered pieces of clothing still hung
over the pale bones, the grave itself perhaps three feet deep at most
– clearly dug in a hurry.

'Think I can guess where that sword's from,' said Chambers. 'This has been here for years. It's not going to be easy to get an ID.'

'Christopher Ryan,' their bearded guide informed them.

Chambers shot the man a strange look:

'Do you . . . *recognise* him?' he asked dryly, glancing again at the Iron Maiden album cover at their feet.

The council worker handed him a laminated badge covered in dirt:

'We found it before they told us to stop work,' he explained. 'It was sticking out from beneath him. I guess it must've been in his back pocket or something.'

The fact that Coates had missed it further supported the theory that he had disposed of the body in haste.

Chambers nodded in thanks, the man going to re-join his colleagues, leaving them in the company of the hollow-eyed corpse.

'It's not like Coates to waste a dead body,' said Marshall, deciding there and then that she wanted to be cremated. 'What do you think?'

'That without his Medusa, he no longer had any use for a Perseus,' replied Chambers, feeling the scar tissue on the back of his neck pull taut. He looked up at the November sun hanging low in the sky. Feeling the warmth on his face, he took a deep breath and smiled: 'It's going to be a lovely sunset,' he commented, Marshall frowning at the non sequitur as he turned his back on the grave and ambled off in the direction of the car.

CHAPTER 27

The last patch of sky burned orange and pink against the encroaching night, the dark clouds bringing with them a predator on the hunt, an undignified and violent end for his prey.

Chambers watched the fire above go out, replaced by his own exhausted reflection in the window. He'd still been a young man when this had all begun, not the greying, pill-popping mess he now saw staring back at him. Where he had once been a formidable presence, he now stood tall but unimposing. Where he used to be able to stay awake for two days straight and still function, he now looked perpetually drained. And where his mind had always been razor-sharp, he could feel himself slowing down . . .

He knew he was missing something.

'Oh, good! You're here,' someone exclaimed, making their way down the corridor towards him.

He turned to see Doctor Drew Sykes approaching. Having always got on with his mother, he'd had high hopes when the young man assumed her position. Unfortunately, the cocky and abrasive medical examiner had inherited scarce few of the retired doctor's personable qualities. He seemed to like Chambers well enough though, who tended to encounter less problems with him than most.

They started walking towards the doors at the far end.

'Do you want the good news or the bad news?' Sykes asked him.

'Good.'

'That girl I told you about, Fiona? Third date tonight. And you know what that means!'

Pretending not to see his invitation for a high-five, Chambers asked patiently:

'Regarding the bodies?'

'Oh, God, no. No. That's *all* bad news.'

'Fantastic.'

They entered the forensic lab, where the victims from the hospital were already lying out on metal gurneys. Beside them, a table had been dragged from the wall to display the two heaps of blood-spattered feathers. In revulsion, Chambers recalled something Eloise had said in her summation of Robert Coates – him being like a child picking the wings off a crane fly.

'He's getting sicker,' said Sykes, puffing out his cheeks. 'Both were heavily sedated anyway, so no puncture marks. The chick—'

'Audrey Fairchild,' Chambers enlightened him, irritated by his unprofessionalism.

'OK; Audrey Fairchild then. She's a clear-cut case of asphyxiation. He just switched off her ventilator and . . . game over. The *male* however . . .' They moved over to the other gurney. 'His wings were *attached* while he was still alive . . . Unconscious, but alive.'

Chambers glanced over at the pile of white feathers, a long broken bone protruding off the edge of the table like a blade: '*Jesus.*'

'I know, right? The wings punctured his lungs either side from behind, hence the blood-spotting over the feathers, causing a catastrophic hemopneumothorax.' Chambers looked blank. 'He basically drowned in his own blood,' explained Sykes, the thought even appearing to shake his arrogant façade.

'Asphyxiation and drowning the day after a lung transplant,' Chambers pondered out loud. 'I suppose there's some twisted poetry in there somewhere.'

He checked his watch.

'You look terrible. How are you holding up?' asked Sykes, in what actually sounded like genuine concern.

Things must be bad.

'I'm fine. Just got somewhere to be. What about the kettle?' he asked, noticing the evidence they had confiscated from the hospital next to the piles of feathers.

'Absolute genius,' replied Sykes, glancing over at the innocent-looking appliance.

'So, that *is* how he drugged all those people at once?'

'Oh, definitely,' nodded the medical examiner. 'No doubt about it . . . It's not a kettle though.'

Chambers looked blank: 'You've lost me.'

'It was once, but it's been tampered with: rewired, the heating element replaced with an ultrasonic membrane and the spout narrowed, segregated and shaped to achieve greater dispersal.'

'So . . .?' started Chambers, none the wiser.

'It's a diffuser masquerading as a kettle. Boiling pancuronium bromide wouldn't work. You'd end up with the water evaporating at a hundred degrees and the drug just sitting at the bottom of the container. But set the ultrasonic membrane to the correct frequency, the water *and* the drug vaporise into a dry mist. Apparently, there was a fan close by?'

'I mean, maybe,' shrugged Chambers. He'd been a little distracted by the winged corpse in the other room at the time.

'Distributing it several metres in all directions, thus giving everyone in the vicinity a debilitating but non-lethal dose . . . As I said: genius.'

A little less enthused by the development, Chambers rubbed his eyes wearily:

'So, now he doesn't even have to inject someone to paralyse them. That's just great. As if he wasn't already holding all the cards.' But then he frowned as a thought came to him: 'There's a treatment, right? . . . To reverse the effects of the paralytic?'

'There is – a mixture of atropine and neostigmine.'

'And do ambulances carry those drugs?'

'The atropine perhaps, but they'd never know to give it . . . Why?'

'Then, as the likely first people on scene, don't you think we should have it?'

Sykes shuffled uncomfortably, finally catching up: 'You're not a doctor.'

'That doesn't mean I can't save someone's life,' countered Chambers, 'especially if he's now gassing rooms full of people in one go.'

Sykes still looked unsure.

'Come on, Drew. This could save someone's life, maybe even one of ours.'

He huffed: 'No promises. But I'll look into it.'

'Thanks.' Knowing he had pushed the matter as far as he could, Chambers moved on: 'Any progress with the soil yet?'

'We've broken it down into its parts but are still waiting on samples.' Chambers checked his watch for the second time in two minutes. 'I had a thought though,' continued Sykes. 'We could apply the same principle to locating where this swan came from.' He walked over to the table where the wings were piled. 'There are still trace amounts of water all over these feathers. I could take a sample, break *that* down into a percentile chart of its composition, and then compare it to other samples collected from around the city.'

Without pausing for breath, he hurried over to a computer: 'It's labour-intensive, sure. And obviously going to take a while. But as they say, "good things come to those who . . ."' He looked up from his screen to discover that he was alone. Checking beneath the gurneys in confusion, he wondered how long he'd been talking to himself: '". . . wait."'

'I'm fine.'

'And returning to the investigation after all these years hasn't triggered dreams about the incident again?'

'No,' lied Winter.

The Human Resources form filler filled in her form.

'And working alongside Detective Chambers – how has that been so far?'

'Fine.'

'No tensions?'

Winter remembered him walking out on them in the pub in Camden.

'. . . No arguments?'

He pictured the three of them yelling at each other in the rain on the banks of the canal.

'. . . No heightened emotions?'

He, Marshall, and Chambers all in tears.

Winter stuck out his bottom lip and shook his head: 'Not that I can think of.'

'Your doctor tells me you haven't renewed your prescription for . . .' she glanced at the fax, '. . . paroxetine in some time. You don't believe you need them any more?'

He could feel the container in his pocket pressing against his leg: '. . . No. Like I said: I'm fine.'

Easton had been waiting in the entrance of Thornbee's Garden Centre for over ten minutes, watching the Christmas lights flash hypnotically from a darkened corner of the store.

'Detective Easton?' asked a moustached man, snapping him out of his daydream. 'Justin Hume. I'm the manager here.' They shook hands. 'We're all worried sick about Evan. I'm not just saying this because he's missing: he is genuinely one of the nicest, most gentle human beings I have ever come across.'

He showed Easton through a doorway that led to a tatty striplit service corridor.

'What does Evan do here?'

'Back of house mainly,' the man told him with just a hint of guilt. 'That probably sounds awful, but I assure you it's nothing to do with his size. I mean, the kids adore him, and he adores them. A real-life giant to play with! But Evan's English isn't up to much and he's a little . . .' He took a moment to find the appropriate word, '. . . slow,' he explained, failing to do so.

'And is that a common feature of gigantism?' asked Easton, it dawning on him that as Evan's employer, they probably held his medical history on record, which might fill in some of the blanks that his mother's limited English could not.

'Evan doesn't have gigantism.'

On that bombshell, Easton stopped walking and turned to the other man:

'He's eight-foot-*bloody*-four!'

'In the medical sense of the word, I mean,' the manager clarified. 'He *actually* has something called Sotos syndrome, which, as I understand it, involves abnormal growth in children that usually slows down by adulthood . . . Usually. *That's* the reason for his—'

'Learning difficulties?' offered Easton before he could say anything else inflammatory.

'Right.' He opened the door to a cramped room, where a pile of videotapes had been stacked on the desk. 'These are for you. That's all the camera footage from this morning.'

'I'll collect them on my way out,' Easton told him. 'Does Evan have a locker or any personal possessions here?'

'Of course. This way.'

They went through into a depressing staffroom, the entirety of the far wall covered in flimsy blue doors. When the manager unlocked one, seemingly at random, a leg of the missing giant's jeans spilled out onto the floor like a tentacle. A photograph of Evan bent double to embrace his mother was taped to the inside.

Easton regarded the manager and then his identically dressed employees sitting at the table:

'He wears a uniform like this?' he asked.

'Yes.'

He nodded, noting that with his clothes still there, the missing man was more than likely still dressed for work:

'And what shift was he on today?'

'Five 'till ten a.m. It's an unpopular one, but we need someone here to take in the deliveries.'

He closed the locker door: 'Show me.'

Easton shivered as they entered the loading bay, where three large roller doors banged noisily every time the wind blew, utterly failing to keep out the cold.

'Cameras?' he asked, not seeing any.

'Outside, but not in here,' the manager informed him, ill-advisedly wearing only a polo shirt.

Easton ambled in and out of the neatly stacked boxes, noting the cigarette butts on the ground, a bicycle propped against the wall, and two red buttons beside each of the metal shutters:

'Are today's deliveries here?'

'Yes.'

'All of them?'

'Yes.'

'Can these doors be shut from the outside?'

'No.'

Easton nodded in interest and then continued wandering the maze of stock.

'May I ask what you're looking for?'

'Nothing in particular,' he replied, pausing when he came across a sprinkling of fresh soil on the floor. Crouching down, he ran his thumb over a dark crack in one of the ceramic pots . . . realising that the one next to it was completely broken in half . . . a sizeable chip taken out of the one beside that. Frowning, he began dragging the heavy pots out one by one to expose the crimson stain smeared into the dirt.

'I'm no expert,' said the moustached man, peering over his shoulder, 'but that's not good, is it?'

Easton sighed. *Why did he always cop the shitty jobs?*

'No, Justin. That's definitely not good.'

Still sporting his work uniform, Winter took a moment to catch his breath, peering down over the seven floors of stairwell as if he'd just conquered Everest. His self-congratulatory mood was short-lived, however, when one of the frailest old women he had ever seen followed him up without even breaking a sweat.

'Excuse me, dear,' she addressed his rear end, Winter moving aside as a younger man with long black hair and overladen with shopping bags struggled up behind her. He looked Marshall's type – black boots, sandpaper stubble and a leather jacket – and nodded in greeting to Winter before accompanying the elderly woman to her door. Still recovering, Winter was unable to help eavesdropping on their short exchange:

'You are a sweetheart. I don't know what I'd do without you.'

'Do you need me to bring them in?'

'No. No. You've done enough.'

'OK. Just give me a knock if you need anything.'

'I will.'

The door closed.

'Those stairs are a killer,' the man told Winter understandingly, who wasn't overly thrilled by the proximity of a handsome rock and roll neighbour to Eloise as he swaggered into one of the two remaining doors on the landing.

'*Prick*,' he muttered jealously.

As recovered as he was ever going to be, Winter double-checked the address scrawled across the back of his hand and knocked on the door to flat twenty-three, hearing the voices inside fall silent.

'Who is it?' someone called.

'Adam Winter – Sainsbury's finest.'

The lock clicked and the door opened a crack, a female officer looking him up and down from behind the taut chain.

'Hey,' he smiled pleasantly.

'You're late.'

'*You're* seven floors up.'

The ill-tempered woman removed the chain to allow him inside, already pulling on her coat to leave:

'All quiet today. I'll be back tomorrow at . . .' she looked up at the clock, '*twelve minutes* past eight,' she said pointedly, slamming the door behind her.

'She seems nice,' he said, turning to Eloise, who was curled up on the sofa.

He thought she looked stunning, wearing cosy jogging bottoms and a slouchy jumper at least two sizes too big for her, and where she had tied her hair up, stray strands of chestnut curled down her neck.

He was definitely staring again.

'So, guess who aced their HR-imposed back-to-work interview!'

'You?'

'. . . No. But I scraped through, and that's good enough for me,' he said before raising the bag in his hand. 'Thought you might be hungry. I got us pizza, ice cream and Doritos.'

'Sounds like movie food,' said Eloise, getting up to take it from him.

'Funny you should say that because . . .' He produced a black box from behind his back. '*Jurassic Park* on video!'

'Amazing!' she smiled, walking through to the kitchenette to switch the oven on and put the ice cream in the freezer.

Removing his jacket, Winter relocked the front door and kicked his shoes off on the mat.

'I met the neighbours,' he said conversationally. 'They seem nice.'

'Yeah, Doris is a character all right, and I don't think I've ever said more than five words to Chris in the two years he's lived here. He's never around.' Winter relaxed a little. 'You always know when he is though. I hope you don't mind falling asleep to the sound of Metallica,' she joked.

'You've been painting,' he commented, noticing the canvas set up on an easel in the bedroom.

'Had to do something to take my mind off things.'

While Eloise sorted dinner, he moseyed around the sparse room regarding the whitewashed walls and the industrial-looking piping proudly on show, her few items of furniture simple, practical, free of unnecessary clutter.

'I like what you've done with the place,' he told her.

'What?' she asked through a mouthful of crisps.

'I said I like what you've done with the place. The whole "arty" minimalist vibe you've got going on.'

'*Ah*. Yeah. No. It's not really a "vibe" as such. I'm just completely broke. I can't actually afford any stuff.'

'Oh,' he said, a little embarrassed.

'Turns out being a controversial artist out to challenge people's preconceptions of what art is while living in the most expensive city in the world isn't quite the money-spinner one might think,' she joked, pouring them each a glass of wine.

'I'm working,' said Winter.

'So, you're getting paid?'

'I hope so.'

'Then you're only *hopefully* working, aren't you?' she teased him. 'To say thank you for dinner. You're not going to make me drink alone, are you? Come on! Just one.'

He made his way over.

'Fine,' said Winter, crumbling like the Dorito he'd just stepped on. He took a glass as Eloise raised her own in toast:

'Cheers!'

'We can turn this off if you want?' Winter offered, tactically pausing the movie at one of the talky bits.

'*Huh?*' asked Eloise, who'd been gazing out at the street lights since the brachiosaurus. 'No. I'm enjoying it.'

'You're worried . . . about Robert.'

'No . . . Maybe . . . I don't know.'

Winter nodded understandingly, before blurting: 'I once had a guinea pig.'

Eloise looked bemused.

'Del Boy Trotter,' he continued, making her laugh.

'You named your guinea pig Del Boy Trotter?'

'*Uh-huh.*'

'Why not just Del Boy?'

'That's a little overfamiliar, don't you think?' he asked her, straight-faced. 'I believe only his close friends and family called him Del Boy. To the rest of us, he was always Del Boy Trotter. Are we going to have a problem here?'

'No,' she smirked. 'Please, continue.'

'Anyway, Del Boy Trotter started to go a bit strange, walking in circles . . . into things . . . off things. We took him to the vet, who told me he was going to put Del Boy Trotter down. I burst into tears, of course. I *pleaded* with him. I offered to pay for his treatment with my pocket money, but Death-Vet wasn't having any of it. And worse, my mum agreed with him. So, guess what I did.'

'What?'

'I waited for Death-Vet to leave the room to fetch his injection, snatched Del Boy Trotter off the table and sprinted home. I ran upstairs, packed a bag of essentials . . . pretty much just pants and chocolate bars, and filled the basket of my bike with food and bedding for him.'

'Your bike had a basket?'

'Yes,' said Winter defensively. 'For life-and-death emergencies such as this. And then we were off – two devil-may-care fugitives on the run, out to make a new life for ourselves in a strange foreign land. I made it two towns over and spent the night in someone's greenhouse before I called my mum for a lift home.'

'Impressive. And what happened to Del Boy?' Winter frowned at her. '. . . Trotter.'

'Oh, he died. I suspect the stupid thing was dead before I'd even passed my school. He was a very poorly guinea pig and undoubtedly needed putting down.'

Eloise hurt herself holding in a laugh: 'That's a very sad story.'

'My point is . . . sometimes you have to let the things you love go. Learn from my mistakes. Don't Del Boy Trotter it.'

She smiled at him affectionately.

'What?'

'Nothing. I liked your story. That's all.'

Winter watched her suspiciously for a moment and then picked up the remote control:

'Now, do you want to watch this lawyer bloke get eaten off a toilet?'

Snatching the Doritos back, Eloise shuffled in her seat to get comfortable:

'You're damn right I do!'

*

While Eloise brushed her teeth, Winter made up his bed on the sofa. He'd checked in with someone at New Scotland Yard and made sure, yet again, that the front door and windows were all secure.

Emerging from the bathroom wearing long pyjama bottoms and a vest top, Eloise had removed her make-up and somehow looked even more beautiful for it.

'. . . What?' she asked.

'Nothing,' he replied, plumping his pillow.

'Well, I'm going to . . .'

'OK. I'll be here . . . *obviously*.'

'Goodnight.'

'Night.'

She smiled bashfully and headed into the bedroom, closing the door behind her.

A few minutes passed, in which Winter got himself a glass of water, switched off the lights and climbed fully dressed into bed. But then, there was a creak as the bedroom door inched open.

'Adam?' whispered Eloise.

'Yeah?' he replied, sitting up in the dark.

'I . . .' And then, despite her unwavering insistence from the outset that Coates would never harm her, she asked: 'Would you mind if I left the door open?'

'No. Of course not.'

'Thanks,' she said, returning to her bed and rolling onto her side to face away from him.

Winter just sat there for a moment listening to the hushed cacophony of humanity: doors slamming somewhere in the building, a moped buzzing along a nearby street, and then lay back down, missing her already.

10.34 p.m. – Chambers and Marshall had been sitting in the dark for over two-and-a-half hours, plenty of time to replay his latest fight with Eve a hundred times over in his head, their second in as many days.

She was afraid for him . . . after what happened, his car accident forever emasculating him in her eyes. He could see it every time she looked at him. Before that, he'd been invincible as far as she was concerned, superhuman, now she regarded him as weak, fragile – as one of the victims. The thought made him feel physically sick, which was perhaps the reason why he'd lashed out so venomously over the phone.

Parked beneath the scaffolding that scaled the new art block, the car was cloaked in shadow, its windscreen framing the one open gate like an oil painting. He picked up the radio:

'Alpha to all units, check in,' he said quietly, conscious that the three black mounds of ash were partially obstructing his view.

'. . . Beta: all clear.'

'Charlie: clear.'

There was an electronic hiss.

'Delta: Yeah, we're clear up here.'

Replacing the handset, Chambers huffed impatiently: 'Where the *hell* is he?'

11.14 p.m. – Stifling his first yawn of the night, Chambers finished the dregs of his lukewarm coffee.

12.22 a.m. – Unable to risk switching the engine on, both Chambers and Marshall had wrapped themselves up in musty-smelling blankets.

'Shouldn't have had that coffee,' she told him as ice crystals started to form on the windshield.

'Why not?'

''Cos if you go for a piss, your thingy's gonna drop off.'

Chambers looked annoyed: 'Thanks a lot . . . And *now* I need a wee.'

1.37 a.m. – Marshall was snoring softly in the passenger seat while a resentful and bleary-eyed Chambers scowled at her, counting down the minutes until his turn.

2.44 a.m. – Chambers was snoring loudly in the driver's seat while a contemplative and wide-eyed Marshall gazed up at the sky.

3.33 a.m. – 'You awake?' asked Marshall, giving him a prod. 'Chambers! Are you awake?'

'Yes, I'm awake!' he snapped, giving himself a firm slap to the face just to make sure.

'Time for a comms check,' she reminded him.

'All right,' he said, dropping the handset twice before finding the *transmit* button: 'All units,' he yawned, 'comms check.'

'Beta: receiving you loud and clear.'

'Charlie: receiving.'

'Delta: still awake . . . *just*.'

4.18 a.m. – 'I told you you shouldn't have had that coffee,' Marshall said smugly as Chambers got back into the car, his frozen fingers still struggling with his fly. 'Feeling better?'

Teeth chattering, he turned to her: '. . . Much.'

5.05 a.m. – 'Movement at the gate!' a voice buzzed through the radio. 'Movement at the gate!'

Instantly wide awake, Chambers and Marshall peered into the darkness, the gate still trembling, whoever or whatever had disturbed it nowhere to be seen.

'See anything?' whispered Marshall, without taking her eyes off the abandoned site.

'Nothing,' replied Chambers, tentatively picking up the radio: 'Delta: was that you? Do you have a visual? Is it Coates?'

There were several static clicks before he answered:

'Negative. Apologies. It's a cat. Just a cat, everyone. Go back to sleep.'

'Easy for him to say,' muttered Chambers, shifting uncomfortably in his seat. 'I need another wee.'

6.46 a.m. – The first patch of sky burned orange and indigo against the retreating night.

Chambers looked as though a zombie had bitten him during one of his four 'rest breaks', Marshall not faring much better.

'Maybe we were in the wrong place,' she said, the dawn giving her the confidence to raise her voice a little.

'This is the place,' Chambers replied confidently.

'Then maybe he knew we were here.'

'Or someone *we know* warned him we were,' he countered, punching the dashboard in frustration. 'What a *waste* of a night!' he spat, climbing out of the car.

'Chambers!' Marshall stage-whispered. 'Where are you going?!'

'. . . To bed.'

CHAPTER 28

Remembering it was Eve's Saturday in the office, Chambers had tried so hard to make it home in time, but a city bursting at the seams had had other ideas, slowing his progress at every step. Rounding the corner to discover her car already gone, he traipsed up the driveway and let himself into the silent house.

No longer needing to keep up the act, he limped over to the fridge to find it absent of messages, not even a terse instruction or reminder for him to add to his secret stash of keepsakes. He considered heading over to her work, picking up a drink from her favourite coffee place on the way – a gesture to show her he was sorry, that he hadn't meant any of the hurtful things he had said, that he'd missed her terribly over the past week. Dismissing the thought, he smiled at just how much she would hate that – 'airing their dirty laundry in public' as she would say, giving her gossiping colleagues a subject to dine out on – an unannounced visit as incriminating as guilt-given flowers or chocolates laced with regret.

When he noticed a perforated envelope waiting out on the counter for him, he didn't bother to open it, knowing precisely what his payslip would say: he'd sacrificed his body, his mental health, and was well on the way to derailing his marriage – all to earn less than his neighbour who taught at the primary school down the road.

Tossing it onto the pile of junk mail, he took three painkillers, hobbled through to the bedroom, and collapsed onto the bed.

*

True to her word, Officer Resting-Bitch-Face knocked on the door to Eloise's flat at precisely twelve minutes past eight.

'Right on time!' Winter greeted her pleasantly despite knowing he was going to be late for work.

'Not really. I've been sat out here reading my book for a quarter of an hour.'

His smile crumbled: 'I really hate you.'

Unfazed, she just watched as he pulled his coat on.

'*Blade Runner* tonight?' he called back to Eloise.

'And don't forget you promised me a curry!' she reminded him.

Chuckling, he was about to say something witty when O-R-B-F got bored and slammed the door in his face.

Managing an entire three hours of sleep, Chambers' first stop on arriving back at work was the Forensic Lab, where Sykes was living up to his reputation, scoffing a bag of crisps while the decomposed remains from the allotment lay out on the table.

One of their colleagues had run a check on the name from the ID badge, Christopher Ryan, and found a very likely match: a celebrated London-based artist whose modern-day subject matter created using traditional materials and techniques had gained him international recognition. His most famous piece – *Strangers at a Bus Stop* – was said to be lit with the beauty and skill of Caravaggio himself, while his painting of rioters torching a police car had invoked the atmosphere and theatrical staging of a Jean-Antoine Watteau.

He had also been officially declared dead in absentia in 1995, having been missing for over six years by that point.

'What do you want me to say?' Sykes asked him, screwing up his crisp packet. 'That it's definitely him? I can't.'

Chambers sighed:

'Someone's going to speak to the family. We'll get you some fingerprints.'

'Fingerprints?!' he laughed. 'For what fingers? I'll never pull anything useful off these!'

'Blood then . . . or hair . . . or clothes,' Chambers corrected himself.

He was so tired.

'*Thank you!*' replied Sykes in exasperation. 'Because if you were to ask me to ID him right this second, my best guess would be . . .' he glanced down at the collection of bones, '. . . Skeletor.'

Having had enough, Chambers headed for the door.

'And for the Cluedo aficionados amongst us,' Sykes called after him, 'I think He-Man did it . . . in Castle Greyskull . . . with the Power Sword!' Chambers slammed the door behind him, but Sykes's voice carried out into the corridor: 'Get me some DNA!'

'Detective Chambers!'

He barely made it two steps into the office before a small crowd had gathered around him:

'The sword recovered from the grave was almost certainly taken from the damaged statue at the first murder scene,' someone half-shouted.

'Thought so.'

'The contact details were out of date,' another piped up, 'but I've tracked down Christopher Ryan's sister and I'm heading there now.'

'Good,' he replied. 'Forensics need DNA samples. Ask her specifically about anyone new who came into his life and take some photos of Coates with you . . . And when you get back, I want everything you can find on him: financials, previous addresses, employment history . . . the lot.'

'Yes, sir,' replied the woman as a gawky man took her place.

'We might have a lead on the orange van,' he said, thrusting a printout into Chambers' hand. 'Came through the tip line – a garage owner who remembers fixing the damage described on the press release.'

Glancing over it, Chambers handed it back:

'Seven-year-old memories aren't much use to us. Tell him to dig out his records. If he can't give us a registration number, payment details, or an alternative name or address Coates was using, don't waste any more time on it.'

'I'll call him now,' said the man, making way for the next expectant face.

'Three more possible sightings: Islington, Camberwell and Highbury.'

'Prioritise Islington and Highbury as they're relatively close to each other.'

The officer nodded and hurried away, leaving just one left.

'Yes?' asked Chambers.

'I was wondering if I could get you a coffee, sir?'

'Oh, *Jesus*, yes! Thank you!' he said, finally reaching his desk, a handful of colourful, and no-doubt important, sticky notes taking to the air like butterflies as he collapsed into his chair. 'Shitty *bloody* things,' he complained, leaning down to pick them up.

Sitting in the shadow of the tower stacked precariously in his post tray, he was tempted to phone Marshall but didn't want to disturb her if she was sleeping. Recalling that Winter had gone straight to his other job, he conceded that it fell to him to call Eloise, wanting to ask her about the man in the grave and whether she knew why Coates might have targeted him.

He dialled the number and waited, letting it ring at least twenty times before giving up.

'Hey!' he called, waving someone over.

'Yes, sir?'

'I need you to get on the radio. Find out who's with Eloise Brown today. First, check all's OK and then find out why the hell they didn't pick up the phone when I called.'

'Yes, sir.'

The gallery's metal gates rattled shut, Eloise's police escort watching, arms folded, as she threaded the chain through several times before ensuring it was locked.

'Thank you for this,' said Eloise, picking up the canvas and carrying it over to the car. 'It's always exciting to sell one.'

'What is it?' the other woman enquired as they climbed in, Eloise holding it up proudly.

'It's an abstract painting of a famous abstract painting,' she explained. 'So, the museum, the people, the walls and frame have all been reduced to simple forms, while the painting within the painting has been returned to a naturalistic state.'

The officer squinted at it: 'And someone bought that?'

'Yes.'

'For money?'

'Yes.'

'How much?'

'Three hundred pounds . . . including postage.'

Shaking her head, the woman started up the engine:

'Be worth a fortune when you're dead,' she said, at least twenty seconds passing before realising the comment could *perhaps* be perceived as a tad tactless: '. . . of old age.'

'They were at the gallery,' blurted an officer Chambers didn't even recognise the moment he stepped out of his meeting with Wainwright.

'Huh?'

'You asked me to find out why Eloise Brown wasn't at home earlier.'

'Oh, right,' he nodded, stopping just short of saying: *was that you?*

'They went to her gallery.' Chambers frowned. 'Something about collecting a painting,' she shrugged.

Now even more confused, recalling the state of the unsanitary underground worksite, he thanked the officer and walked all of four paces before spotting his next intrusion:

'Why is there a scarecrow at my desk?'

'That's no normal scarecrow,' Lewis informed him. 'That's Detective Scarecrow from Harrow on the Hill. He was asking for Marshall, but I think you ought to speak to him,' he told his friend with a significant look.

'Like I don't have enough to do,' muttered Chambers, heading over to his dishevelled visitor.

'Detective Chambers?'

'The one and only . . . *regrettably*,' he said, shaking hands and taking a seat.

'Phillip Easton . . . Phil. I know how busy you must be right now so will get straight to the point. Does the name Popilopadopaluss mean anything to you?'

'. . . Dinosaur?'

'Human. Evan Ioannou Popilopidi . . .' He gave up.

'No. Why? Should it?'

'I got the impression from your colleague that it might.' Chambers looked lost. 'See, I'm working this missing persons case and . . . it's a bit of a strange one if I'm honest: an eight-foot-four Greek giant with learning difficulties.'

'Giant?' asked Chambers, sitting up, but at a loss as to why Easton had come to them with it. Details regarding the remaining sculptures were a closely guarded secret and, as far as he was aware, nothing had been leaked to the press.

'So, it *is* one of yours?' enquired Easton in interest.

'Perhaps,' replied Chambers. With another statue promised before then, the team had had little time to think about Robert Coates's penultimate creation. 'I'm going to need everything you've got. When he went missing. Where from. Any information you have on his—'

'My apologies,' the other detective interrupted him. 'I think we've got crossed wires. I'm not here to help you with your investigation. I'm here for *you* to help *me* with mine.'

Folding his arms defensively, Chambers leaned back in his chair: 'Go on.'

'There was blood found where my missing giant was last seen. I called in a favour and got someone to work on it overnight.'

'You got a blood match overnight?' he asked sceptically.

'OK. It was a *big* favour. And, of course, it helps that Narcotics officers get screened regularly.'

'Why?' he asked, not liking where this was going. 'Whose was it?'

'Trainee Detective Constable Jordan Marshall's.'

In panic, Chambers reached for the phone, but then paused:

'When did you say you found the blood again?'

'I didn't,' replied Easton. 'But it was yesterday afternoon.'

Pretty sure he'd spent an entire night with Marshall since then, Chambers summed up his melange of emotions, confusion and exhaustion quite succinctly:

'Wait! What?!'

Winter had jogged all the way up to the seventh floor and, if the stabbing pains in his chest were anything to go by, the spot where it all ended for him. Hoping that Eloise's chicken korma hadn't exploded when he'd stumbled (the first time), he composed himself and knocked on the door, the rumble of heavy rock music coming from the noisy neighbour's opposite.

'Who is it?'

'Who do you think?'

Swinging the door open, O-R-B-F regarded him with contempt:

'Have you done something *different* with your hair?'

'No. Leave me alone.'

'She's in the shower,' said the miserable woman before taking another sneering look at him. 'Just a word of advice: *this* is never going to happen. She's like an eight-and-a-half, a nine maybe, and you're like a two . . . in the right light . . . which is very low light.'

'Yeah, but I'm funny . . . on occasion.'

'Good point. I was just thinking what to book for my sister's hen do – The Chippendales or Jasper Carrot. *Hmmm.*' She rubbed her chin: 'Which one? . . . Which one?'

'Oh my God, just go!' snapped Winter. 'Be sure to give Adolf and Vlad the Impaler my regards when you get home!'

'Just trying to stop you embarrassing yourself,' she said as she headed out.

'And for your information – Eloise is clearly a stone-cold ten!' he shouted after her, slamming the door.

'I'm a what?' she asked from the bathroom doorway, her wet hair wrapped up in a towel.

'Nothing,' he smiled bashfully. 'So . . . food then?'

8.00 p.m. – 'Here we go again,' sighed Chambers, pulling the car door closed while the day shift snuck through a fire exit. 'Get any sleep?'

'Some,' replied Marshall. 'I was going over old files in case there was anything we missed. You?'

'A little.' He hesitated. 'I had a visit from a Detective Easton today, who was actually looking for you. He's investigating the dis-appearance of an eight-foot-something giant.'

'A giant?!' Disturbing images of Robert Coates's promised sculp-ture filled her mind.

'Ever been to Thornbee's in Harrow?'

'No. What is it?'

'The last known location of the missing man . . . Your blood was discovered at the scene.'

'*My* blood?' She looked dumbfounded. 'That's . . . That's impossible.'

'Is it?' asked Chambers knowingly, having had hours to think on it. His eyes flicked down to her hand.

'The figurine I broke!' gasped Marshall, catching up. 'And he . . . kept my blood from it?' she asked, disgusted. 'Why would he do that?'

'I'm not sure. But you've got to look at this from where I'm sitting.'

'Come on, Chambers. You can't!' she told him, pre-empting what he was about to say.

'I've got a missing giant, when we know he needs one. And I've got your blood where it shouldn't be . . .'

'You *need* me on this!'

'. . . when we know he has *two* female figures yet to cast.'

'Chambers!'

'I'm sorry,' he said firmly. 'I'm putting you on desk duty after tonight and assigning an officer to your home.'

Shaking her head, Marshall stared out at the three mounds of ash, feeling as though she knew every bump and curve of their silhouettes by now, the only focal point in an otherwise featureless vista.

'I'll help you with Easton,' said Chambers, 'come with you to the interview. We'll sort that mess out in no time.'

'Thanks, but I can take care of myself.'

Giving up, he pulled a blanket over his shoulders and settled into his seat for the night.

8.33 p.m. – Bored of the silence, Chambers risked switching the radio on, turning the volume down until it was barely audible over the wind.

'. . . Ioannou Papadopoulos – last seen yesterday morning at his place of work: the Thornbee's Garden Centre in Harrow. Anyone with any information should contact the . . .'

'Sounds like Wainwright's done her bit,' he commented, receiving nothing back from Marshall. 'Probably the right move. If the public are ever going to find anyone for us, it's going to be an eight-foot giant with a cartoon bumblebee on his back.' He twisted the dial, finding them a UB40 song to listen to. But reminding him of Eve and their fight on the phone the previous evening, he switched it off again, preferring the silence after all.

9.10 p.m. – 'I do get it, by the way,' blurted Marshall, making Chambers jump, having not uttered a word in over an hour. 'If I was in your shoes, I'd take me off the case as well.'

'I'm not taking you off the case.'

She looked at him impatiently.

'OK. I'm *sort of* taking you off the case.'

'It's just . . . you know what this means to me.'

'I do. But I'd rather have you angry with me than dead. It's not worth your life, no case is.'

Marshall raised her eyebrows: 'That's rich, coming from you.'

Looking affronted, he then thought about it and nodded: 'Yeah. Fair enough.'

10.04 p.m. – The first patters of rain struck the windscreen.

'*Perfect*,' yawned Chambers, conscious that aside from their car sinking in the mud and getting drenched every time he had to relieve himself, the entire team's visibility would be impaired. He wound down the window and stuck his hand out. 'It's only spitting,' he assured Marshall moments before the heavens opened, a deluge of biblical proportions threatening to wash them all away. Swiftly winding the window back up, he reached for the radio: 'Alpha to all units: receiving? Over.'

A static hiss.

'. . . Alpha to all units: receiving? Over.'

This time, a single broken transmission answered him: 'Ch--ie re--ing --ver.'

'Alpha to last speaker: you are broken and unreadable. All units: we are blind down here. Repeat. We are blind . . . Out.'

He placed the handset back in its cradle and leaned forward in his seat, attempting to peer through the torrents of water washing over the glass.

'See anything?' asked Marshall.

'I think . . . it's raining,' he deadpanned, when the radio crackled loudly:

'L--ts -- Tu-- t-- Li----.'

'Guess they didn't hear me say "out",' huffed Chambers. He grabbed the handset: 'This is Alpha: you are broken and unreadable. Over.'

'--i-- on --rn the Li-- --n.'

He turned to Marshall for help, who gave him a 'don't look at me' shrug in response.

'*For Christ's sake*,' he muttered, hitting the *transmit* button once more: 'This is Alpha: we *do not* read you. Repeat message. Over.'

Straining to hear anything over the downpour, he turned the

volume knob all the way up as they both leaned in close to the speakers . . .

'Tu--n th-- li--s on! . . . Turn the lights on!'

'*Shit*,' he spat, firing up the ignition and flooding the building site with the car's full-beam.

Marshall was already gone. Leaping out after her, he dashed through the sparkling rain as the floodlight overhead burst to life like a white sun in the darkness.

'Got anything?!' he yelled over the roar of the rain.

'Nothing!' Marshall shouted back before looking down at the river of black dirt washing over her feet, her gaze following it uphill to the three large mounds of ash. Struggling to see as freezing water streamed down her face, her eyes began to climb the dissolving peaks . . . all the way up to the headless bust erupting from the central mountain of earth, blackened wings billowing in a two-thousand-year-old wind, the absence of arms creating an inhuman silhouette.

Before she could even say anything, Chambers had raced over to the nearest mound, desperately digging the dirt away by hand.

'There could be others!' he yelled while Nike's sullied robes continued to emerge from the filth. 'Check the last one!' he ordered the first of his team to reach them. 'Check the last one!'

Giving the bemused officer a subtle shake of the head, Marshall made her way over to her superior, now on his hands and knees as he clawed away at the earth. She crouched down beside him.

'Why aren't you digging?!' he asked her. 'Help me!'

She placed a calming hand on his shoulder:

'She's been here for at least two days, Chambers, right in front of our faces. And if there *is* anyone else buried here, then they're already dead too.'

He looked at her blankly at first, but then comprehension dawned as he sat back on his knees, partially submerged by the flood. Gazing up at the decapitated goddess like a grovelling worshipper seeking favour, he admitted: 'I'm *so* tired.'

'Me too,' Marshall told him. 'Me too.'

He looked down at himself in surprise, sodden to the bone, his clothing and shoes most likely unsalvageable.

'We can finish up here,' she said, the body not yet even fully revealed. 'We'll check for other victims and get forensics on scene. Why don't you go and dry off?' She held a hand out to him.

Nodding, he reached out and took it, Marshall heaving him onto his feet:

'I've got this,' she assured him.

'I know you do.'

'. . . What's up with him?' asked one of the officers as Chambers walked away.

'Nothing. He's fine,' Marshall replied curtly, turning back to the goddess towering over them. She moved round the heap of wet ash: black water coursing off the outstretched wings, the robe fashioned from the same ethereal cloth as used in the previous two murders – see-through where it clung to the skin. 'Hey!' she called, waving the man over. 'Help me up,' she said urgently, eyes fixed on a dark shape beneath the sheer material.

Accommodatingly, the officer held out his hands to give her a leg-up, Marshall careful to only balance herself against the solid plinth on which the figure was standing. She strained to bring her eye level up to the goddess's lower back, focusing intently on the eerily familiar image: an oversized pair of feet, a skirt protruding from a slight frame . . . and two bright eyes emerging from a darkened helmet.

'*Shit*. Let me down! Let me down!' she called.

'What is it?' the officer asked her, wiping his filthy hands on his uniform.

'Marvin the Martian,' she replied, looking a little dazed, the man staring back at her blankly. '. . . I know who she is.'

Wiping his face with a grubby hand, Chambers left the outermost reaches of the floodlight and wandered back towards the car, seeing a flash of movement out of the corner of his eye. As the rain abated, he glanced back at his colleagues, counting them up. Slowly, he approached the chain-link fence that separated them from the adjacent plot, the high-pitched chimes of raindrops striking the metal almost musical as he watched the darkness on the other side for any sign of life . . .

Stillness.

He turned to head back to the car, when a soft voice mused behind him:

'I thought it was never going to rain.'

Chambers spun round, seeing nothing beyond the repeating criss-cross pattern. He looked over to the white glow of the floodlight, debating whether to call out to his team but knowing there was no way of gaining access from their side. Thinking better of it, he walked up to the fence, feeding his fingers through the gaps, pressing his forehead against the cold metal. Letting his eyes adjust, a dark shape separated from the blackness and started to approach.

'I had to be sure you'd found her,' said Coates proudly, stopping just a few feet from the wire mesh between them, his face cloaked in shadow like the blank canvas that it was.

He went to walk away.

'You won't get to her, you know?' Chambers called into the void. 'Eloise. We've got her. She's safe . . . We know about the laurel leaves!' he blurted in desperation, several moments passing before Coates returned.

His curiosity getting the better of him, he stepped right up to the fence this time to meet Chambers' eye, their faces mere inches apart.

'So, we *were* right?' Chambers smiled tauntingly. 'The statues *are* about her.'

A look of loss and regret, belonging to no other, filled the mimic's face:

'It was *always* all about her – the killing . . . the *not* killing.' Coates seemed to retreat into a memory. 'Do you have *any* idea what it takes to deny what you are? To change yourself from your very core outwards for someone? Have you ever loved anyone enough to do that?'

Chambers remained ashamedly silent because he knew, breaking promises to limp after serial killers in the dark, that he hadn't
changed at all.

'Seven years I went without,' Coates continued, confiding in
Chambers as though they were old friends. '. . . When I was pursuing her, while we were together, even afterwards when all I wanted
was to win her back. I tried *so* hard to be normal . . . And then you
returned to me. You showed me how deluded I had become, that
I was never going to get my happy ever after no matter how hard
I tried.' He laughed wistfully. 'You know, for a little while there, I
think even *I* believed I'd changed.'

Chambers could feel the fabric of the other man's coat brushing
against his fingertips:

'I won't let you hurt her.'

'Hurt her?' asked Coates, puzzled. 'Why would I ever want to
hurt her?'

'Because you're a sick fuck who blames everyone but himself for
his inherent mediocrity.' Even in the shadow, Chambers saw the
surge of anger cross his face. 'So, you *are* capable of emotion?' he
goaded him. 'I wasn't sure.'

Coates took a moment to consider his response. He glanced
down:

'How's the leg?' he asked with a sneer, and then outright smiling
when Chambers shifted uncomfortably. 'Rest assured, Detective, I
wouldn't want to spend a single day on this earth if she wasn't on
it.'

Chambers frowned – something in the impassioned way he'd
said it ringing true.

Suddenly, Coates grabbed the wire fence between them, a ripple
effect rattling off into the distance as he clawed onto Chambers'
hand, pressing his face up to the metal:

'I would no sooner hurt her than I would you,' he spat as
Chambers struggled. '*For only the living can suffer as you will,*'
he smiled before releasing him.

There were shouts from the team over by the floodlight and the sound of their footfalls running towards them. Instinctively glancing in their direction, Chambers looked back to discover that he was alone once more.

'Coates?' he called desperately. '. . . Robert?!'

'Not long now, Detective,' a voice hissed from the shadows, moments before the team reached them. 'It's so very nearly over.'

CHAPTER 29

Chambers hesitated on the doorstep.

He'd spent years politely entertaining Eve's whimsical miscellany of beliefs and customs but had never really put much stock in them, or in anything for that matter. And yet, he hesitated, knowing that if there was even a glimmer of truth to any of it – if all the evil in the world was in fact the work of malevolent demons at play, guiding the impious towards damnation – then they would be circling now, waiting upon that dark doorstep with him – all the things he'd vowed to never bring home.

Taking an irrational glance over his shoulder, he crouched down to retrieve the bag of rice from behind the plant pot: another peculiarity of Caribbean folklore. Pouring a generous pile out onto the ground for the obsessive Jumbee, who would count every grain until sunrise, he fumbled with the lock and slammed the door behind him – the dirty footprints stalking him down the hallway suggesting perhaps not quickly enough. Attempting to kick his shoes off, he turned his ankle and landed in a heap on the floor, the minor inconvenience enough to bring him to tears.

Half-asleep and wielding her husband's cricket bat, Eve poked her head round the corner:

'Ben?' she asked, wincing in the offensive light. 'What on earth are you . . .' She trailed off, however, on seeing the state of her sodden husband. 'Ben!' she gasped, rushing over to him. 'What's wrong?'

'Nothing,' he replied, wiping his tears away in embarrassment. 'I slipped. That's all. Go back to bed. I'm fine.'

'Bullshit,' she said while rubbing at a patch of the dark mud that caked his skin. 'Are you hurt? Is it your leg?'

Chambers' eyes filled with anger. He pulled himself back to his feet, leaving an applause of black handprints on the walls en route to the bathroom. He turned the shower on and stepped into the cubicle fully clothed as Eve hurried into the room after him.

'Ben, you're scaring me!' she said, watching him struggle to remove his ruined shirt before tossing it into the bathtub. 'Tell me what happened.'

Closing his eyes as the water began to steam, he lowered his head in disbelief, in failure, in lament of his own dulling brilliance:

'Why would anyone pile the ash in the middle of the site?' he asked himself in frustration. 'It's in the way. It's nowhere near any of the entrances for removal.' He laughed bitterly: 'It was *uphill* of the cleared area!' Smacking himself repeatedly in the side of the head, he whispered: '*Stupid*! *Stupid*! *Stupid*!'

'Hey!' yelled Eve, grabbing his hand before he could hurt himself further. 'Stop that! What are you talking about?'

With a vacant look in his eyes, he turned to her:

'The winged girl . . . He got to her.'

Eve didn't say anything but moved her hand to his chest, resting it over his heart.

'Cut off her head,' he continued, looking sick. 'Took her arms as well.'

'Oh, Ben,' she whispered in pity.

'I had him,' he revealed as the water gradually turned from black to grey around his feet. 'I *touched* him. I could feel his breath on my face . . . And I was powerless to do anything about it.'

Looking understandably concerned, Eve made a valiant effort to keep her voice even:

'What do you mean you touched him? Him who?' she asked; although, fearing she already knew the answer.

'Coates!' he spat in revulsion. 'He spoke to me.'

'A serial killer spoke to you?' Struggling with the button on his waistband, Chambers nodded. 'Let me,' she offered, but he slapped her hand away.

'I can do it!' he bellowed. 'And don't look at me like that! I can take it!'

'Take what?'

'All of it!' he shouted, ripping the button clean off and stepping out of his soaked trousers. 'More of it! . . . Anything anyone can throw at me! Because, despite what *you* may think, I am *not* weak!'

Eve looked simultaneously worried, hurt, and confused:

'Why would I, of all people, think you're weak?'

'Like you haven't treated me differently ever since *this*,' he scoffed, gesturing to the scars snaking from the bottom of his boxer shorts all the way down his right leg.

'Is *that* what this is about?' she asked him, throwing his dripping trousers into the bath with his shirt. 'You trying to prove something? Is that why you agreed to take this case on? Is that why you're having private conversations with serial killers now?'

'It's not like I went looking for him.'

'And still, you somehow ended up in a situation where he could get you alone.' Watching him as though he were transparent, she sighed: 'You *are* right though. I have looked at you differently since the accident. And it's true, perhaps with less respect than I had for you before.'

Even though he'd always suspected it, Chambers felt wounded on hearing her say it out loud.

'But not because I think you're weak, Benjamin,' she continued. 'But because I think you're reckless. Because I think you're too proud for your own good. Because I don't think you know when to stop . . . and wouldn't even if you did.'

'That's the job,' he told her.

'Then quit,' she replied simply. 'Can you remember the last time you came home with anything positive to say about it anyway?'

'I can't just leave!'

'Why not?'

'Because . . .'

'Because what?'

'Because!'

'Because our little life isn't enough for you without the thrill of nearly getting yourself killed every time we're not together?'

Realising that he had no response for her, he couldn't meet her eye.

'Do you know what I wish?' she asked him. 'I wish you'd walk away from this awful case. I wish you'd tell them to just get somebody else. I wish you'd take some days off while this whole thing blows over. I wish you'd stay here . . . with me.'

Chambers looked guilty: 'I can't do that.'

'You could. But you won't.'

He reached out a wet hand to stroke her cheek: 'I don't deserve you.'

'No. You don't,' she said matter-of-factly: 'But I'll still be here waiting for you all the same.'

Marshall gradually came to, lying on an unfamiliar floor.

With a groan, she forced herself upright, not recognising any of the other people passed out around the room.

She didn't feel right – her head muzzy, co-ordination gone as she tried and failed to get up, wondering what toxic shit she had put into her body this time. In her desperation, she had gambled and lost on an unknown and evidently inferior product, the guilt returning anyway, just as it always did.

She reached for her bag, but then panicked on realising how light it felt, pulling it open to discover that it had been cleaned out: her purse, her keys; they had even taken her travel card.

'*Shit*,' she whispered, laying back down to reach into her jeans pocket for loose change but coming up empty. 'Shit!'

Desperate times calling for desperate measures, she glanced around at the sleeping people, but then noticed their tossed possessions strewn across the floor – the self-comatose dregs of society an easy target for those one precarious rung up the social ladder.

'You *stupid* . . .' she chastised herself, pulling a face when she sniffed her T-shirt, the room a sweatbox of discontent.

Unsteadily getting to her feet, she stumbled along the corridor and out through a metal door at the end, emerging in a dark alleyway. The drizzle soaked through her clothes in seconds as she vomited against the wall and then staggered towards the main road, still having no idea where she was as her ghostly reflection searched the shop windows for a clue:

HOLLOWAY ROAD STORES

She had to support herself against a lamp post, unable to remember how she had ended up so far out.

Shivering uncontrollably, she calmly tried to assess the situation: it was the middle of the night. She was stuck miles from home in the freezing cold with no money, no bank cards, no travel tickets, and barely able to function.

She was screwed.

Looking down the deserted street, she spotted the red roof of a phone box.

'*Please. Please. Please*,' she whispered, opening up her bag to root through the rubbish, receipts and worthless tat they hadn't deemed worth taking, overcome with relief to find the official Metropolitan Police business card and, more importantly, the two phone numbers scrawled on the back.

She hurried across the road to the phone box and shut the cold outside, the standard montage of sex line numbers and call girl adverts decorating the back wall as she picked up the receiver and dialled the operator:

'Hello? Yes, I'd like to place a call please but reverse the charges.' She gave them the number and waited. 'Come on, Winter. Come on.'

Thirty seconds passed before the operator returned:

'I'm afraid they're not picking up.'

'*Shit*!' yelled Marshall, slamming the receiver down and remembering, of course, he would be with Eloise.

Feeling as though she were about to cry, she looked down at the other number scribbled below it, knowing she had no other options left.

She spotted the headlights approaching and apprehensively made her way over to the kerb as the car pulled up beside her. As she climbed in, Chambers looked utterly exhausted in the driver's seat, the weak smile he attempted for her benefit only making her feel worse.

'Hey,' she greeted him, pulling on her seat belt to the squeak of the windscreen wipers against the glass.

'Hey,' he replied, turning the heat up for her, the dashboard clock reading 5:55 a.m. as he pulled back out onto the road.

Neither of them spoke as he drove them through the empty city, Marshall unsure whether she appreciated him keeping to himself or if a part of her wanted him to be angry with her:

'Aren't you going to ask what happened?'

'Figured you'd tell me if you wanted to.'

She nodded self-consciously: 'How are you feeling?'

'Like I can't take much more,' he answered with surprising honesty.

'Same,' she admitted, Chambers again missing his prompt to enquire about her night. 'Thank you for coming to get me.'

'I need you,' he said simply, coming to a stop at a roundabout as the only other car on the road rolled by.

Marshall felt like she was going to burst, now under no illusion that the weight of the secret she had been carrying was going to cost her her life if she didn't get it out:

'This isn't me, you know?' she told him, Chambers concentrating on the road. 'Maybe when I was younger, but not now. I've only been using again since January . . . and then with everything going on . . .'

'You can make all the excuses you like,' Chambers said thoughtfully, 'but if tonight has taught me anything, it's that people *don't* change . . . None of us do. There will always be another excuse, and after that – another. And when they come along, we'll all pick up right where we left off: Coates starts killing again; I'll deliberately put myself in harm's way just to prove something; Winter will return to the job that ruined his life; and you'll keep on doing whatever it is that you're doing. We're all just waiting for an excuse.'

Letting his depressing epiphany settle for a moment, Marshall turned down the heater and gazed out at the twinkling lights:

'There's something I need to tell you . . . tell somebody.' She took a deep breath. 'The night Tobias Sleepe died . . . I was there.' Chambers raised his eyebrows but didn't interrupt. 'I had your old case files. It was freezing inside his workshop – ice everywhere, so we went up to speak in his office, but I got angry and he asked me to leave. I was screaming at him. He turned to me and . . . It was the tiniest of slips, but I can still remember the sound of him falling down that staircase. And I just stood where I was, looking at him . . . I left him there,' she finished shamefully.

Chambers didn't take his eyes off the road as he considered his response:

'Don't *ever* tell anyone else that story. Understand?' Marshall nodded. 'Tobias Sleepe isn't worth . . . *this*,' he continued, looking his dishevelled colleague up and down. 'I've been in this job a long time. I know a bad person when I see one – he was, and you're not. Maybe we'll never know who that blood on the rope belonged to, but I'm reasonably confident the world is an ever so slightly better place without him in it.' She still looked broken. Chambers sighed: 'As the *only* person you will *ever* tell about this, I absolve you of your sins. *Fuck him.* Now, let's never talk of it again,' he said, taking a right-hand turn.

'Oh, I'm that way,' she said, looking off to the left.

'I know. I just want to make a quick stop on the way.'

'What are we doing here?' she asked him, the rainclouds dispersing across the dawn sky as they parked outside Eloise's gallery.

Climbing out, Chambers walked over to a car on the other side of the road and tapped on the glass, Marshall following him out as a bleary-eyed officer wound down the window.

'Morning, Detective Sergeant.'

'I need the logs from yesterday,' said Chambers, the man handing over the uneventful surveillance reports.

'Anything I can help you with, sir?' he asked as Chambers flipped back one sheet and ran his finger down the page.

'"Eloise Brown and her police escort seen entering the gallery with a painting and leaving nine minutes later with a different one",' he read aloud. 'What painting?' he asked Marshall rhetorically. 'There aren't any paintings in there!'

'That's not entirely true, sir,' the man in the car interjected. 'There's always been one over the entrance.'

Chambers glanced back at the gallery and then tossed the clipboard through the window: 'Keys!' he demanded, the sleepy officer taking a moment to find them.

'What's going on?' Marshall asked him, jogging to keep up as he marched over to the metal gates, Chambers peering through the bars at the illuminated painting sealed in a Perspex box above the door:

'Son of a *bitch*!' he spat, unlocking the gate before pulling the box down off the wall.

'Chambers?' Prising the plastic apart, he removed the canvas. 'What are you doing?' He switched his torch on and shone it over the painting in explanation. '. . . What?' Marshall asked, bewildered.

'She's warning him.'

'She's what?'

He moved the beam over the grey blocks amid a sea of green: 'Graves?'

'I . . . Perhaps.'

'. . . Fire,' he said, highlighting the orange form in the corner.

'*Ummm.*'

'And trees.'

'. . . So?'

'His mother's grave, the fire at the university, and the laurel tree wood. She's warning him we know!'

'I mean this with the utmost respect,' said Marshall diplomatically, 'but I think you're reaching. These are just shapes. You're seeing what you want to see.'

'I don't trust her!'

'You don't have to! But we *need* her. This isn't enough to jeopardise that. Where would we be right now without her?' He had no comeback for that. 'I'm just saying, let's not make any rash decisions.'

'We need to watch her closely.'

'We will,' she assured him, Chambers staring at the painting in disdain:

'And I'm still taking this down.'

'Good morning,' chimed Eve, making a beeline for the coffee machine, Chambers hunched over a book at the kitchen table. 'What time did you get back?'

He glanced up for a moment: 'About an hour ago.' . . . And then back down.

'How is she?'

'She'll be fine.'

'Why don't you try to get back to sleep?' she said, though he showed no sign of hearing her. Pouring herself a drink, she took a seat beside him, moving two other books aside to make way for her mug. 'What are you reading?'

'The Bible,' replied Chambers without taking his eyes off the page. 'David and Goliath, to be precise.' It was too early for a Sunday; Eve looked utterly lost. 'The penultimate statue,' he explained, a pained look on his face.

'What is it?'

'It's just . . . I don't get it . . . the meaning behind it.'

'I'm not an expert,' said Eve between sips of coffee, 'but isn't it a tale of good triumphing over evil against all odds?'

'"Good" and "evil" are a matter of perspective,' yawned Chambers.

'Then a clearly biased underdog story,' she corrected herself.

'That's just it,' he said, turning another book towards her, which lay open on a dramatic picture of a young boy facing down a ferocious foe while an entire army watched on. 'The story goes that every day for forty days the giant, Goliath, emerged from the Philistine ranks to challenge the Israelites' best warrior to one-on-one combat to decide the outcome of the battle, and every day the king, Saul, declined, being both cowardly and unfit to rule.

'That is until David, a young shepherd boy, takes up the challenge, walking out onto the battlefield to face the giant with nothing but his sling and five round stones from the creek. Striking him squarely in the forehead, he brings Goliath down before relieving him of his head with his own enormous sword . . . all in the name of God.'

'What's the problem?' asked Eve.

'The problem is, according to the book beneath your elbow, a slingshot can produce almost as much energy as a twenty-two-millimetre long rifle round, meaning that David basically brought a gun to a sword fight . . . "Fight" is the wrong word: *execution*. That poor giant never stood a chance.'

'You're saying Goliath was the underdog in the story?'

Chambers nodded: 'And was dispatched with accordingly.'

'OK. What do *you* think it means then?'

He pushed the hefty book away from him and reached for his own tepid drink:

'That when faced with the prospect of a fight he can't win, even God isn't above cheating like anybody else.'

Someone's leftover Indian food had stunk up the investigation room.

'What's going on there?' asked Chambers, fourth coffee of the day in hand.

'I'm not sure,' replied Marshall, wearing the exact same expression, as Eloise slapped Winter's arm playfully.

'I mean, I like the guy,' he continued, transfixed, 'and he said that one funny thing that time, but he's like a—'

'Right?' nodded Marshall.

'And she's like a—'

'I know!'

'If you didn't think she was up to something before . . .' Chambers gave her a significant look. 'Anyway . . . murder then?' he suggested flippantly.

'Murder,' she concurred, sitting two empty chairs away from Wainwright, who too was staring over at the mismatched pairing as though she had to be missing something.

Unsurprisingly, things had felt a little awkward between them – Marshall knowing she was forever indebted to him, Chambers still embarrassed over his meltdown at the university. Of course, he had also made it worse by not recognising her from three feet away – absent of her usual heavy make-up and leather – and asking her to fetch him a sandwich from the canteen.

Still cringing about it, he assumed his place beside the scribbled table at the front of the room.

Statue	Location	Victim	Event
The Thinker	Hyde Park	Henry John Dolan	His birth? An artist and intellectual who would never belong
Pietà	Cranbrook Council Estate	Alphonse and Nicolette Cotillard	A drug dependent baby almost dying in his mother's arms
Perseus with the Head of Medusa	The British Museum	(Benjamin Chambers) and ???	Finally ridding him-self of his drug addict mother

Venus de Milo	Riverside Walk	Tamsin Fuller	Eloise coming into his life/ their first kiss/ refuses to marry him
Psyche Revived by Cupid's Kiss	Queen Elizabeth Hospital	Javier Ruiz and Audrey Fairchild	Eloise's accident/ He saves her
The Winged Victory of Samothrace	Birkbeck College	Care worker from Tall Oaks ?	Rebuilding his professional home out of ash/ Eloise agrees to marry him
The Bronze David			
Apollo and Daphne			

'Here's where we're at,' he started with a sigh. 'I've got someone going through the hospital security footage and another working the Christopher Ryan angle. The orange van is a dead end, and we're still trying to work out where and when he might have got to the Tall Oaks care worker. We've got two statues to go, a giant who's been missing for over forty-eight hours now, and Marshall's blood on the floor where said giant went missing. I've decided to take her off active duty for her own protection. She's very unhappy with me about that.'

'It's true,' Marshall confirmed to the others. 'He's being a patronisingly overprotective jerk.'

'Told you. *Oh*, and as you all know, Coates and I got to have a little catch-up last night as well,' he added in faux-bravado, consciously avoiding Marshall's eye, who knew just how thin that façade really was.

'And how is the old bugger?' asked Winter, playing along.

'He's good. He's good. For what it's worth, he said he hadn't killed anyone else over the last seven years. We talked about the weather, my leg, and then he went on to tell me how he couldn't live a day on this earth if Eloise wasn't on it.'

'Well, that's sweet,' muttered Winter sarcastically; although, judging from the look on Eloise's face, he'd just been well and truly upstaged by a narcissistically delusional serial killer.

'We took a hit last night,' continued Chambers, adopting a more serious tone. 'A bad one. We're confident the body is that of Maisey Jeffers, who worked at the nursing home, but without a head or any fingerprints, we're waiting on blood tests for confirmation. But the plan is solid. We're on the right track. Last night proved that; the locations are the key. And it was only blind luck on Coates's part that he'd already hidden the body before we got there.'

'He must suspect we're surveilling these places now,' Wainwright pointed out, Chambers and Marshall sharing a look.

'True,' nodded Chambers. 'But he can't rewrite his past, and I don't believe he'd leave one of his "works" anywhere that wasn't of great significance to him.'

Everyone turned to Eloise expectantly.

She looked a little awkward: '. . . I agree.'

They turned back to the front.

'Then we still have four locations left,' Chambers announced, pointing to their other list.

1. ~~The Fire~~
2. The Grave
3. The Woods
4. The Observatory
5. The Gallery

'. . . Eloise was right about the fire, so we'll be focusing our attention on Coates's mother's grave and the laurel tree woods—'

'Which is where precisely?' asked Wainwright.

'Wimbledon Common,' answered Eloise. 'A little west of the windmill.'

'. . . While maintaining passive surveillance at both the other sites,' Chambers finished as though he hadn't been interrupted. He looked to Winter: 'I'm going to need you to take Marshall's place with me tonight. I'll find a constable from a local station to sit with Eloise.' With the exception of Wainwright, no one looked particularly pleased with the new arrangements. 'Good. It's decided then.' He hesitated, again sharing a look with Marshall. '. . . Ms Brown?'

He stepped aside to give her the room.

'*The Bronze David*. Donatello. Mid-fifteenth century,' began Eloise, delivering her now trademark but always superfluous introduction. Marshall opened the sketchbook to the relevant page and held it up for the others to see. 'The original is housed in the Museo Nazionale del Bargello in Florence, but there are copies in both the Victoria and Albert Museum and in Kew Gardens right here in London, if anyone's interested.'

They were not.

'. . . It depicts a young and undeniably effeminate David in the moments after defeating Goliath in battle. Wearing only boots and a laurel-topped hat, he stands with one foot resting upon the giant's severed head.'

'Is it just me,' blurted Winter, 'or does using a giant to portray a giant seem just a little too "on the nose" for Coates?'

'*That* and thematically it's strikingly similar to one of the earlier statues – *Perseus with the Head of Medusa*,' added Marshall.

'Which he never got to finish,' Chambers reminded them, feeling the familiar prickles across his neck return, as they did every time he recalled the memory. He looked over to Eloise: 'Any theories?'

'That's what I was up all night thinking about,' she told them. 'Up until this point, all the statues have symbolised the most significant events in Robert's life in chronological order,' she said, gesturing to the list. 'So, it stands to reason that whatever event this relates to either happened *after* I left him or . . .'

'. . . Or?' Wainwright prompted her.

'. . . *Or* . . . we've finally caught up.'

'Caught up?' asked the chief inspector. 'I'm sorry. I'm not following.'

'As in, it's still happening . . . right now,' explained Eloise. 'Robert has already cast Chambers as the greatest monster in his life before. Perhaps this next sculpture represents Robert finally besting him, or the police as a whole, once and for all.'

Marshall raised her hand.

'*Ummm,* yes?' said Eloise unsurely.

'I think, for safety's sake, we should remove Chambers from active duty.'

He shot her a look that suggested he wasn't amused.

'Hang on,' said Winter with a puzzled frown. 'If that's true and the next statue is based on what's happening *now* – on him beating us . . . then what the *hell* is the final one about?!'

The room turned back to Eloise, who just stood there for a moment looking uncomfortable:

'I suppose, by that logic, we should prepare ourselves for the fact that Robert's big finale, the point to which his whole life has been building, the defining moment of his existence . . . is yet to come.'

A heavy silence fell over the meeting as each of them tried to contemplate what kind of atrocity Robert Coates might conjure to surpass all of the horrors that had preceded it . . . each of them bar Winter anyway, whose rumbling stomach betrayed that he'd been thinking about something else entirely:

'Anyone got dibs on the last onion bhaji?'

CHAPTER 30

'I don't really see how that's relevant.'

'With all due respect, I don't really see what you do or do not deem to be relevant . . . as being relevant. So, why don't you humour me? Is it, or is it *not*, true that you have a personal interest in the case you are currently investigating?'

'As does everyone on the team.'

'And you think that's appropriate?'

'I think it's motivating.'

'*Motivation* is such a broad term though, incorporating everything from long hours – to enacting vengeance – to uncharacteristic and desperate behaviours. How about we focus in on *that* for a moment?'

Following the team briefing, and feeling she already owed Chambers enough, Marshall had packed up her belongings and headed straight down to the fourth floor – home to the ever-unpopular Department of Professional Standards. They had been more than accommodating in providing a private room for Easton to conduct his interview of a fellow officer while a characterless man in a cheap suit, her union representative, sat mutely at her side. Marshall had pictured an assertive and eloquent lawyer-type, poised to jump in and throw the detective's more awkward questions back at him, not the useless, mouth-breathing mass of flesh they had provided her.

The interview had begun as the casual box-ticking exercise she had hoped it would be, but then quickly taken a different turn: statements laced with accusation being fired across the table at such pace, she wasn't even sure which one she was addressing any more. It was curious that the very tactics Marshall herself had been trained to employ could still work so effectively on her.

'You say other members of your team have their own "motivations",' started Easton, as if bringing up a provocative topic of conversation at a dinner party. 'Is that something you've discussed amongst yourselves?'

'Of course,' answered Marshall. 'We wouldn't be doing much of a job if we didn't know the history of the case, would we?' It had come out with far more venom than she'd intended, and she knew he would be watching her reaction with interest. 'Why are you even asking me about this?'

She gave the man to her left an elbow to the gut to make sure he was still awake.

'It *would* be helpful if you'd clarify why this detail is of importance,' he told Easton. 'Detective Marsham—'

'Marshall,' she whispered.

'. . . Marshall is involved in an active and very high-profile investigation, and as a result, there will inevitably be details that she is unable to share at this time.'

Not exactly Johnnie Cochran, but it was a start.

'Look,' said Easton, reverting to his friendlier demeanour, 'I'm trying to help here. I'm on your side. But I've got a missing person and *your* blood at the scene. It's been over forty-eight hours now, escalated to a kidnapping if not a potential murder, and you're not giving me anything.'

'I already told you—'

'You cut your hand during an undocumented visit to Robert Coates's home before you were even assigned to the case,' he finished on her behalf.

The union official took a sharp intake of breath, as if finally having enough, as if about to explode, as if gearing up to shut down

Easton's desperate attempts to implicate her in the absence of their actual suspect . . .

He sneezed.

Rolling her eyes, Marshall peeled back the plaster to show Easton the healing wound encircling her thumb.

'I presume you have witnesses to corroborate when you sustained that injury?'

She went to answer, when there was a knock at the door, smiling in relief when a familiar face stepped into the room.

'Detective Chambers,' said Easton coolly. 'I wasn't aware you'd be joining us.'

'No. Neither was I.'

'Had I been, I'd have told you not to bother. This is a private—'

'I want him here!' blurted Marshall.

'That may be the case, but as you can see, we're all full up.'

'That's all right,' said Chambers. 'I'll just take Marty's seat. He's next to useless anyway.'

'I resent that,' the union representative told him.

'But don't deny it,' Chambers pointed out. He held the door open for the man he'd had the misfortune of having dealings with in the past, while he packed his bag and got up to leave.

'. . . Benjamin.'

'. . . Marty.'

Letting the door shut on him, Chambers took a seat beside Marshall.

'Thought I told you I could take care of myself,' she whispered.

'You did. But you *also* told me I was a "patronisingly overprotective jerk",' he reminded her, turning his attention to the scruffy man rapidly losing confidence across from them.

Having successfully placated Easton for the time being, Chambers and Marshall had got to enjoy a leisurely lift journey back up to Homicide before sitting down to their next engagement.

'. . . My hands are tied,' said Wainwright unapologetically. 'The assistant commissioner blocked it herself.'

'On what grounds?' asked Chambers, not making any effort to hide his frustration, having requested additional resources be posted at Eloise's building.

'On the grounds that the press are tearing us apart out there! That we *still* have more officers than we can spare sitting about at *four* different locations around the city, one constantly with Ms Brown, one with Detective Marshall now, and are yet to make *any* tangible progress towards actually capturing Coates!' she bit back, her own desk-centric pressures getting the better of her.

'Robert wouldn't hurt me,' insisted Eloise for the umpteenth time, the words starting to feel like a catchphrase at this point. 'He even told you as much.'

'This *whole* thing is about you!' argued Chambers, sounding more accusatory than concerned.

'Detective,' said Wainwright firmly while nursing the beginnings of a headache, 'if you're *that* concerned about Ms Brown's safety, you are welcome to reassign some of the surveillance team.'

'I need them where they are!'

She raised her hands, giving up.

'I'll stay with her,' offered Winter. 'The whole time.'

'No. I want you with me,' said Chambers.

'You could let *me* help,' suggested Marshall as pleasantly as she could, not wanting to alienate the man who had come to her rescue twice already that day.

'Don't start,' he warned her before turning to Eloise: 'Why not come in? You're safe here. Just until this is over.'

'What, *live* here?' she scoffed. 'No, thank you.'

'Can I suggest a compromise?' Marshall interjected. 'Are we agreed, based on all that's come before, that all signs are pointing towards Coates's mother's grave as the location of this next statue? It is, without doubt, the most fitting setting to display his vanquished monster. Coates has made a credible threat against *me* by going to such lengths to leave my blood where it was bound to be discovered, and we know he already has his giant. Therefore, it seems highly unlikely that this penultimate statue involves Eloise in any way.'

She met Chambers' eye, a whole separate discussion occurring in the subtext:

'So . . . how about if Eloise remains at home with her one officer protection detail *for now*, but if we can't stop him, if he somehow manages to complete *The Bronze David* and escape, she comes in immediately and doesn't leave until he's in custody?'

There was a pause in which they each took a moment to consider her logical plan of action.

'I'd be prepared to go along with that,' said Eloise.

Winter smiled at her.

'Chambers?' asked Wainwright. He gave her a reluctant nod. 'Fantastic. The assistant commissioner *will* be happy,' she said dryly, looking up at the clock. '. . . Bit past your bedtime, isn't it?'

'*Way* past,' agreed Chambers despite the early-afternoon sun warming the room. 'I'm going to drive over to Margravine Cemetery and check in with the day shift, make any changes we might need for tonight, then head home for a few hours' kip. Marshall, mind finishing off the paperwork from last night?'

'Love to,' she said bitterly.

'Eloise, you should probably get an emergency bag packed as soon as you get home. Winter, drive her back. Update whoever's looking after her on what to do if we call to say she needs to come in.'

'Will do,' he said cheerily.

Chambers let out an exhausted sigh: 'Suppose I'll see you in the graveyard then.'

By no more than mere coincidence, Chambers' route out to Hammersmith and Margravine Cemetery had taken him through South Kensington and the museum district, where immense faux-palaces clustered together while the rest of the world transformed around them.

Switching off the engine when he hadn't moved in over five minutes, he glanced across the street to the Victoria and Albert Museum, recalling with almost no interest whatsoever Eloise's presentation and her excitement that a life-size replica of *The Bronze David* resided somewhere within its labyrinthine halls.

Turning back to the stationary traffic and the unpromising wail of sirens up ahead, he swore under his breath, turned the ignition on, and made a dubiously legal right-hand turn towards the car park on Prince Consort Road in search of coffee and toilets.

Staring up at the onyx-black cast of Donatello's masterpiece, Chambers felt the same sense of awe combined with his own inconsequentiality that he had back in Tobias Sleepe's warehouse seven years earlier. Rendered in painted plaster, the sculpture was exactly as Eloise had described it on first inspection, but the longer he looked at it, the more intricate details began to reveal themselves: the broken sword – its blade no doubt snagging on some bone or cartilage on its path through its owner's throat, or the care that had gone into carving each and every one of the laurel leaves atop the young victor's hat.

It was undeniably beautiful and violent and delicate and gruesome all at the same time: the way that Goliath's long beard curled up around his slayer's foot, suggesting that the boy had been standing there for some time, perhaps even running his toes through his felled foe's hair – the darker side of God's victory that the stories neglected to mention . . . the telltale signs of a psychopath in the making.

Marshall shielded her tiny flame from the wind as she stood in the collective candlelight of Tamsin Fuller's friends and relatives. The vigil, taking place on the banks of the river where her body had been discovered, was a private affair that she'd only learned of through the investigation. Armed with a time and place, she had wanted to pay her respects to their late Venus de Milo, feeling it the very least she could do for the woman she had failed.

The grieving parents had accepted her vague explanation of being 'a friend from work', handed her a candle and a hot drink, and welcomed her in like family. After stuffing the collection bucket with her grocery money for the month, Marshall listened to those closest to Tamsin tell their stories, sharing in their frozen tears and sentimental laughter, not one of them aware of the blood on her hands – that it was she who had provoked *Death*.

Once the final person had spoken and Mr Fuller had thanked them all for coming, the small crowd dispersed like fireflies disturbed from the grass.

'Jordan?' Pretending not to hear her name, Marshall continued up the hill. 'Jordan!' repeated Tamsin's mother, who had remained a stoic presence at her tearful husband's side throughout. 'It *is* Jordan, isn't it?' she asked, finally catching up.

'Yes. Sorry. I was miles away,' said Marshall, the candle flickering in her hand only emphasising the mascara all over her face.

'You said you work . . . *worked* with Tammy at the university?'

'*Uh-huh.*'

'So, will you be seeing Ted on Monday?'

Marshall hesitated: 'I'm not sure.'

The older woman's look of suspicion was confirmation that it had been a trap:

'Who are you? Really? . . . Press? . . . Some weirdo who heard about our tragedy and thought you'd come along for a nosy?'

'No. Nothing like that.' Marshall looked up at the gate, tempted to run away.

'Well then?'

'Just someone who needed to look you in the eye and tell you how truly sorry I am,' she said, feeling more tears building. 'Because I think what happened to Tamsin was my fault.'

'Why on earth would you think that?'

She took a deep breath:

'I'm a police officer. And the person who did this to Tamsin did the same thing to someone I cared about very much seven years ago.'

'I'm sorry,' said Mrs Fuller, taking her hand, the gesture too much for Marshall, who started to babble, now on the verge of tears:

'I just wanted to catch him so badly. I never stopped to think about . . . about what it might cost. And now she's gone and we haven't caught him and . . . I'm so sorry!'

'*Shhhh. Shhhh*,' whispered Tamsin's mother, embracing her tightly. 'Do you know what Tammy was doing the night she went missing? . . . Returning a dress she'd bought me for my birthday,' she revealed, releasing Marshall but taking her hands once more. 'Would we be having this conversation now if I hadn't stubbornly said I preferred the blue one?

'And do you see that man over there talking with my husband? That's her ex-boyfriend, Stephen. He broke up with her a month ago. Every Wednesday night, without fail, they went to the pub quiz with their friends. She'd have been safe with them . . .

'And did you see her sister talking up there?'

Marshall nodded, in awe of this woman who could remain so rational and composed while everybody else fell apart around her.

'. . . They hadn't spoken in over four months. The last thing she said to Tammy was that she hated her. She didn't mean it, of course, but can't ever take it back either. Worse, she ignored a call from her that night.

'My point is: there is more than enough guilt to go around. Each and every one of these things led to Tammy's death, and at the same time, none of them at all. Do you think it's *my* fault that my daughter is dead?'

'No. Of course not!'

The older woman smiled sadly: 'Then it isn't yours either.'

The graveyard was completely still – silent bar the rustle of wind-strewn leaves, the occasional hoot of an owl somewhere in the trees opposite, and the slurp of Winter sucking up the dregs of his Burger King fizzy brown water.

'Could you *not* do that?' whispered Chambers, missing Marshall's company at only forty minutes in.

Removing the straw from his mouth, Winter placed the paper cup on the floor with the rest of his rubbish:

'Sorry.'

They both turned to look back out over the sea of gravestones flickering in and out of the moonlight, bodies bedded down in the earth like fresh bulbs awaiting spring.

Earlier in the day, Chambers had walked the entirety of the churchyard in search of any disturbed soil or fresh lawn, there being no better place to conceal a body ahead of its grand unveiling, his hour in the company of the dead still playing on his mind:

'I found her grave,' he mumbled, uncharacteristically sparking conversation. '. . . Coates's mother's,' he clarified.

'Wonder if we'd still be sitting here if she hadn't been such a train wreck.'

'I was wondering the same thing,' said Chambers, leaning forward as if he'd spotted something, but then relaxing as a jogger passed the gates. 'Know what the inscription said?' he asked rhetorically. 'Elizabeth Marie Hallows. Nineteen forty-nine to nineteen seventy-seven.'

'That's it?'

'That's it. Nothing about being a degenerate junkie . . . even throughout her pregnancy, about almost killing her own baby by passing on her tainted blood along with her addictions, that because of her weaknesses *nine* innocent people are now dead.'

'Yeah, they tend to leave those sorts of things off,' said Winter.

'Maybe they shouldn't,' mused Chambers. 'Maybe if they started etching a list of *each* and *every* one of a person's sins into the stone they were going to spend eternity under, people would stop and think twice before committing them in the first place, take some fucking responsibility for the horrible shit they do to each other.'

Winter looked over at his morose colleague: 'Are you OK?'

'Just tired, I guess.'

'On a cheerier note, at least one positive has come out of this whole thing.'

Chambers groaned, in no mood to have a discussion about Winter's flourishing love life.

'. . . I've been feeling for a while now like something's been miss-ing,' he continued all the same.

'*Uh-huh.*'

'. . . Unsatisfied.'

Chambers pulled a face.

'Think that should go in the letter?'

'Letter? Be a man. They like that,' Chambers told him wisely, unsure himself why he was getting involved. 'You should do it in person.'

Winter picked at his fingernails nervously:

'I'm just not sure I can handle the rejection face to face . . . and then, even if it's a *yes*, what if I'm not as good as I used to be?' Chambers looked outright appalled now. '. . . It's been a while. And it's not like I was even that good at it to begin with.'

'*Jesus!*' complained Chambers, who had shuffled as far away from him as he could in such close quarters.

'. . . Either way. I think I'm ready,' Winter nodded confidently. 'And I'm not dreaming about your leg as much as I used to either.'

'. . . *What?!*' Chambers asked him, feeling partly confused, partly violated. 'What the *hell* are you talking about?'

'Transferring to Homicide,' answered Winter.

'Oh . . . *Oh!*'

'Why? What were you talking about?'

'Yeah, that. The job thing.'

An awkward silence followed, in which both men replayed the previous couple of minutes' conversation over in their heads.

'You know,' blurted Winter, swiftly moving on as a bank of mist rolled across the grass like the tide coming back in. 'I still think about that time when we found Alphonse Cotillard and his moth-er, which was horrible, obviously, but that's not what I remember about it. I remember *you*. You were so ridiculously good. You'd seen things in seconds that we hadn't noticed in ten minutes. I think that's why when what happened . . . happened, it affected me so badly. Not just because of your leg, which was gross by the way . . .'

'Good to know.'

'. . . but because if that could happen to you, when you were *that* good, what chance did I have?'

Chambers didn't acknowledge the compliment, keeping his eyes on the clichéd scene beyond the windshield:

'You're a good officer, Winter. I mean that. And you give me too much credit. I was reckless, and I was stupid. And that's what put me in that state, lying in the middle of the road. You can notice all the little details you want all day long, but none of it means anything if you can't take a step back and see the bigger picture.'

'And are we?' Winter asked him. 'Here? Now? With Coates?'

This time, Chambers glanced over at him, sad eyes now filled with worry.

He hesitated: 'No. I don't think we are. But let's just hope we're seeing enough.'

Monday

CHAPTER 31

'Chambers? . . . Chambers?'

He awoke with a start, aching all over, unsure where he was as the dirty light of an overcast sky stung his eyes.

'Day shift will be here in ten minutes.'

He gazed vacantly at Winter and then rubbed his face: 'Shit. Sorry.'

'Not to worry,' he smiled back, which only emphasised the dark circles under his eyes. 'Looks like you needed it.'

Sitting up, Chambers looked out over the churchyard, the building wind causing the carpet of amber leaves to undulate like water around stone buoys.

'No news?' he asked.

'Nothing.'

'Heard from the others?'

'They would've radioed it in if there was anything to tell.'

Still half-asleep, Chambers nodded while trying not to inhale too deeply, the smell of Winter's fast-food packaging turning his stomach:

'Is it just me or does it feel like he's playing with us?'

Winter shrugged: 'It always did.'

Stepping into her boots on her way out the door, Marshall jumped:

'*Christ!*' she gasped, holding a hand over her heart. 'I forgot you were out here,' she told the baby-faced officer.

'Glad to hear I made such an impression,' he joked.

With the exception of a glass of water and two toilet breaks, she hadn't heard a peep from the young man who had dutifully, and no doubt on pain of death from Chambers, remained outside her front door all night.

'Are we off somewhere?'

'*I'm* going to work.'

He looked at her patiently.

'. . . *We're* going to work,' she sighed.

Nodding, as if to say 'that's better', he asked: 'You're not wearing *that*, are you?'

Marshall peered down at her ensemble self-consciously: one of her more colourful numbers – the dark brown jeans really 'popping' against the black everything else:

'Yeah. Why?'

'You need a coat,' he told her, sounding like a fussing grandparent. 'It looks like the end of the world out there.'

As soon as he said it, Marshall noticed the low drone of the wind rushing through the ventilation system. With a huff, she stomped back inside, pulling on her woolliest winter jacket before picking up the sketchbook she'd left out on the table.

'Happy now?' she asked him, closing the door behind her.

'Outfit approved,' he smiled. 'Seriously, you haven't caught a weather forecast this week?'

'Been a *bit* busy,' she replied snippily as they walked along the corridor.

'Severe storms tonight,' he recited, morphing from eighty-year-old to weatherman before her eyes. 'Gusts of up to a hundred miles an hour.' He appeared frustrated by her blatant disinterest. 'They said by this evening there will be a significant risk of damage to property and danger to life.'

Marshall pulled her hood up over her head:

'Sounds like any other night in London then.'

*

'That's weird,' said the officer drafted in to collate information on the long-expired victim from the allotments.

'What?' her overly preened colleague asked, jumping at any excuse to scoot his chair over to her desk. A cloud of aftershave accompanied him as he shuffled uncomfortably close to look at her screen.

'He's still got regular payments coming in and out,' she explained.

'So?'

'He's been dead seven years.'

'*Oh*. Then it's one of two things: either the family never got round to cancelling his bank accounts . . . It happens.'

'. . . Or?'

'Or it's identity fraud. Happens a lot with inactive accounts when people snuff it. Flag it up,' he told her commandingly, despite them being the exact same rank.

As he rolled away, she printed off and highlighted a selection of the offending transactions, placing them in a dull blue folder. Crossing the office to the incident room, she knocked on the door:

'Is Detective Chambers about?' she asked the people working inside.

'He's not in yet,' one of them replied distractedly.

'Which one is his desk?'

Following their dismissive points, she walked over to a post tray overflowing with similarly dull folders, so tore off a sticky note to label it:

Christopher Ryan – Important!

Sticking it to the front, she carefully balanced the folder on top of the pile and headed out . . . one corner of the colourful note already beginning to curl back on itself as the ineffectual glue surrendered its hold.

Winter was lying on his breakfast. Sprawled across Eloise's kitchen table, he remembered heading to hers after finishing at the graveyard with a box of freshly baked delicacies that he'd subsequently crushed before either of them had taken a bite.

'Eloise?' he called, getting to his feet as the curtains billowed like sails across the room. 'Eloise!' he shouted when there was no answer. 'Eloise!'

The front door opened and she hurried in carrying an empty mug:

'You're up,' she greeted him.

'Where were you?!'

'Talking to Patrick.'

'Patrick?'

'The unlucky recipient of the Metropolitan Police's Short-Straw Award this afternoon.'

'Afternoon?' he asked, bleary-eyed.

'Ten past three,' she informed him, walking over to close the window on the escalating apocalypse outside. 'Wouldn't want to be out in this tonight,' she said, watching the rain slash horizontal scars across the glass while the few trees to miraculously survive the metropolis bent double, fighting for their lives against nature's mutinous mood. 'Apparently it's only going to get worse.'

She crouched down to collect up the handful of leaves and twigs that had blown across the floor, it reminding Winter of something:

'Hey . . . So, I never totally understood the whole laurel-leaf connection,' he told her, picking up the few strays that had made it as far as the kitchen table, 'like why they're so significant to him . . . to both of you.'

Hesitating, Eloise headed over to the bin before responding:

'Well, to understand that, you'd have to understand the final sculpture: *Apollo and Daphne*.'

Winter took a seat: 'I've got all day.'

'No, you don't.'

'No. You're right, I don't. I've got perhaps forty minutes if I skip a shower. All the same . . . I'd really like to hear it.'

'All right then,' she said, sitting down opposite him. 'Bernini's sculpture of *Apollo and Daphne* is widely regarded as one of the most beautiful works of art ever created. It captures the climactic moments of the myth as told in Ovid's *Metamorphoses*, which goes: arrogant and elated following his defeat of the great serpent, Python, Apollo stumbles upon Cupid—'

'Cupid again?'

'Yes, Cupid playing with his bow and arrow. He taunts the young god, belittling him by asking what use he has of weapons of war. In anger, Cupid draws two different arrows from his quiver – one to ignite love, the other to extinguish it – striking the mighty Apollo through the heart, who instantly falls madly in love with the nymph Daphne, daughter of a powerful river god. Cupid then takes up the lead-tipped arrow, sinking it into the beautiful girl, who, repulsed by Apollo's advances, escapes into the woods.

'Apollo longs for Daphne, finding no other her equal. So, one day, he follows her into the trees, pursuing her even when she flees from him. He pleads with her to stay, but still she runs, him only wanting her more with every step. "So flew the god and the virgin – he on the wings of love, and she on those of fear." But he was faster than her, and as her strength began to fail, she called upon her father for help: "Open the earth to enclose me, or change my form, which has brought me into this danger!"

'No sooner had she uttered the words than a stiffness seized all of her limbs. Her bosom enclosed in tender bark and her hair became leaves. And as her arms turned into branches and her foot struck the ground as a root, a faint heartbeat thumped from somewhere deep within.

'Heartbroken, Apollo embraces all that is left of Daphne, lavishing kisses upon the wood. And, no less in love, he bestows eternal life upon her, promising that her leaves will remain evergreen . . . that never shall she know decay.'

Winter puffed out his cheeks: 'Intense.'

'And do you know what the Greek word for *laurel* is?' she asked him: '. . . Daphne.'

'It's the same themes again, isn't it? Unrequited love, marriage, and escaping from a lover.'

'Robert used to call me his laurel tree,' she recalled sadly.

'Makes sense now,' said Winter, looking troubled. 'Does Chambers know any of this?'

'Some. But—'

'*Yeah. Yeah.* Robert wouldn't hurt you.'

'If he's doing all this for me. He wants me to see it.'

Winter didn't look as convinced: 'Have you packed a bag?'

'Yesterday.'

'The *moment* we call to say you need to come in . . . you come in. Understand?' he told her, sounding unusually authoritative. 'I mean it. You promise me.'

'I promise.'

He embraced her tightly. And then, with an unenthusiastic glance out at the storm, he headed for the door.

'Wait. Where are you going?'

'To end this thing, so I can stop worrying about you.'

Winter briefed Patrick on the door, before negotiating the slippery stairwell, giving Eloise's soaked long-haired neighbour a passive-aggressive nod when he passed him on the way down.

Stepping outside, the relentless wind was augmented with a strange drone as it tore through the city – both eerie and powerful – like the breath of God.

Chambers walked through the door of the Homicide department
. . .

'Medical examiner wants to see you downstairs.'

. . . huffed, and then headed back out.

'Detective Chambers, Christopher Ryan. Christopher Ryan . . . Yeah, you don't care. You're dead.'

'I take it the DNA was a match then?' he asked Sykes impatiently.

'It was indeed.'

'You could've just called.'

'Maybe that's not what I needed to see you about,' he replied, taking a step towards him. 'You did *not* get this from me,' he whispered, as if concerned the people in the freezer drawers might be listening as he handed over a small metal tin.

Opening it up, Chambers peered down at the contents.

'You've got one dose there,' Sykes informed him. 'And don't even ask how I got hold of this for you.'

'OK,' shrugged Chambers. He wasn't going to. 'Thank you,' he said, tucking it into his inside pocket before making his way over to the exit.

'And you owe me, Chambers! . . . *Big time!*' Sykes called after him as the door swung shut on their conversation.

'We'll reconvene here tomorrow at,' Chambers checked his watch, having lost all sense of time, 'Jesus, five o'clock again,' he said, adjourning the team briefing.

Wainwright promptly got up and headed to her next appointment while the rest of them remained where they were.

'Anyone else got a bad feeling about tonight?' asked Winter, watching the rain hammer against the windows.

Neither Chambers nor Marshall answered, apparently having similar thoughts.

'It's always the days like this when the bad jobs come in,' he continued, 'the days when you can physically *feel* the pressure building . . . the tension in the air.'

Shooting him a funny look, Chambers turned to Marshall:

'Fancy some overtime this evening?' he asked casually.

'To do what?'

'Catch up on paperwork. Do some filing. Sit in the break room all night watching *EastEnders* for all I care. I'd just rather you were here tonight.'

'You're letting Winter get to you,' she told him.

Not thinking anything of the crinkling sound as the wheel of his chair crushed an unstuck sticky note into the carpet, he shrugged: 'I know. But still . . .'

The howling wind sounded more like a scream as it rushed past the windows, the glass panes trembling more and more violently until it subsided.

'Yeah, sure,' she said, having an abrupt change of heart. 'I've got nowhere to be.'

Chambers reached for the blue folder and assorted loose documents at the top of his post tray, when there was an urgent knock at the door:

'Detective Chambers?' said a flustered constable without waiting to be invited in. 'There's something I think you need to see . . . Just . . . Chambers, please,' she added when all three of them went to get up.

With a frown, he followed the officer out, joining her beside her computer in the main office.

'I've spent the last two days going through the footage from Saint Mary's. Like you asked, I've logged every lone man entering the hospital within two hours of the murders and exiting up to two hours afterwards, using the security video, where possible, to track their movements in-between.'

'OK,' he said, not bothering to sit down.

'Which,' the woman continued, 'is exactly what I did with this person.' She played a three-second clip of a man with a rucksack and bouquet entering through the main doors, it was impossible to make out a face from the grainy image. 'Now watch this,' she said, swapping to another feed: two orderlies disappearing into a room, the same man running to catch the door.

Now intrigued, Chambers pulled up a chair and sat down.

'And this is three minutes later,' she said, skipping forward, the man re-emerging but now sporting a white tunic.

'That's him. That's Coates,' said Chambers excitedly.

'I was just about to come and get you, when I suddenly remembered seeing this man somewhere else.'

She clicked on a final video, Chambers tensing up on seeing himself appear on screen, Wainwright and Marshall at his side as Eloise followed behind.

She hit the *play* button.

Chambers leaned in, watching in dismay as Coates walked right by them. He put his head in his hands and exhaled.

'Did you see it?' she asked him.

'See what?'

'Watch Eloise Brown,' she told him, looking a little nervous as she played the clip in slow motion – the subtle but undeniable raising of Eloise's pixilated hand to meet his as they passed each other in the corridor.

The video continued to repeat on a loop as the officer turned to him:

'I'm sorry if I was rude back there. I just didn't know—'

'You did the right thing,' Chambers assured her, looking across the office to where Marshall and Winter were chatting in the incident room.

They didn't have the time to waste on another argument over Eloise – the laurel leaves, the painting in the gallery, and now this: he had already made his decision.

'I want you to keep this between us for now,' he told the officer.

'Yes, sir.'

He nodded: 'Could you give me a moment? I need to use your phone.'

There was a knock at the front door.

'Come in, Patrick!' shouted Eloise from the bedroom, hearing the careful officer slide the bolt across as she folded her washing into piles. 'Tea?' she guessed when he appeared in the doorway. She noticed him shuffle uncomfortably. '. . . Patrick?'

'I just got a message through from Detective Chambers,' he told her.

'Everything all right?'

'Not exactly.'

He removed a pair of handcuffs from his belt.

'*Oh.*'

'Orders,' he said apologetically as he entered the room. 'Eloise Brown. I am arresting you on suspicion of being an accessory to murder . . .'

Dazed, Eloise sat down on the edge of the bed, the officer's voice becoming distant, the sensation of the cold metal wrapping around her wrists barely registering as she looked out at the building storm – so anticlimactic an ending for such elaborate staging, yet knowing it was the fate of a muse to quietly fade from the light of the geniuses they inspire.

'I'm not really hungry yet.'

'Eat.'

'But—'

'Eat now or starve,' said Chambers simply. 'I'm not spending another night in the stench of your burger wrappers.'

Like a child forcing down a Brussels sprout, Winter shoved the rest of his Whopper into his face as Chambers picked at some chips. From their booth in Burger King, they watched a procession of headlights crawl past on roads flooded already and rising quickly.

'We'd better get there before we can't any more.'

'But you said—'

'I know what I said.' For the second time in thirty seconds, Chambers felt like a strict parent. 'But that was before a new river sprung up in the middle of Chelsea.' Foolishly, he had told Winter that they'd be passing the Victoria and Albert on their drive. And then, more foolishly still, had revealed he'd stopped in the previous day to visit the statue that Eloise had talked so passionately about. Winter looked dejected. 'OK. Fine,' he said irritably. '*If* . . . the traffic isn't too bad. And *if* . . . we can park, we can go and see it. But we've got to be in and out. Deal?'

'Deal,' Winter smiled back.

Marshall had made herself at home at Chambers's desk, the warm light of the desk lamp reflecting in the dark windows, the radiator by her leg billowing out hot air as the storm raged only inches away. It felt like being back in school again – the evenings she'd spent in Alfie's room while he tried, and failed miserably, to help her keep up in Physics.

Allowing herself to get lost in the memory, she was dragged back to the present by the muted ring of the phone. Tempted to let it ring off, she then noticed it was coming from an internal number, perhaps even someone in the office able to see her sitting there:

'Detective Chambers' phone,' she answered, confused by the sound that greeted her.

'Is Chambers there?!' a voice yelled, his words barely decipherable over the wind.

'No. He's not,' replied Marshall, trying to work out how an internal line could have made it outside.

'He's not here!' the voice relayed to somebody else. 'Who's that?' he asked her.

'Detective Marshall. I work with him,' she replied, still at a loss as to what was going on.

'Marshall!' the man shouted, the weather all but drowning him out. 'She said her name's Marshall!' A few moments passed before his voice returned, the storm abruptly abating as he presumably stepped back inside: 'Hi, Detective Marshall?'

'Still here,' she said.

'We've got a . . . situation. We're going to need you downstairs right away.'

'OK. You've seen it now. Can we go?' asked Chambers a little too loudly for the hushed gallery, earning himself a glare from the tour guide enthralling a group of pensioners about one of the other statues.

'One more minute?' said Winter pleadingly as he walked around the priceless replica again, hand on chin in consideration as if debating whether to put in a cheeky offer.

Shaking his head, Chambers unenthusiastically regarded the masterpiece himself, this time unable to see past the two subjects' opposing expressions – the smug smile on the shepherd boy's face, the look of surprise, horror and regret reflected in the giant's, having so willingly walked into the young man's trap.

*

'Detective Marshall?' asked an armed officer hurrying over to meet her as she crossed the atrium. 'Nighton,' he introduced himself, shaking her hand.

'What's going on?' she asked him, stepping over the phone wire snaking out from the reception desk all the way over to the doors.

'Is the name Evan Papadopoulos familiar to you?' He gestured for her to follow him.

'The giant?' she asked urgently. 'You found him?'

'Not exactly,' replied Nighton as one of his colleagues presented Marshall with a bulletproof vest and an in-ear radio transmitter. 'More like *he* found *us*.'

'He's here?' she asked, her mind still playing catch-up.

'He asked for Detective Chambers,' he explained, pausing at the door, 'but seemed to know your name well enough. Says he won't talk to anyone else.' Nighton hesitated: 'He's got a bag with him.'

'A bag? What's in it?'

'We don't know . . . Hence the vest.'

'Right,' she nodded anxiously.

'Look, I can't make you go out there. But I've been informed he's down as a missing person with learning difficulties, so I wanted to give him a chance.'

'A chance?'

'If he refuses to drop the bag and give himself up, he's leaving us no choice but to neutralise the threat,' he explained unapologetically. '. . . Protocol.'

An image of Goliath's head lying separated from his body flashed through Marshall's mind.

'No. Don't do that. I'll talk to him.'

'You're sure?'

She nodded: 'But do me a favour. Get Detective Chambers on the radio for me.'

'I'll keep trying,' promised Nighton, forcing the door open against the wind as Marshall stepped out into the storm.

CHAPTER 32

The ground shimmered underfoot, Marshall's every step sending ripples across the flooded walkway towards the man framed
in light: standing at over eight feet tall, his arms were wrapped
around a sack easily large enough to fit a grown adult inside. She
approached slowly, arms raised, passing within inches of an armed
officer. She didn't acknowledge him though, wanting to remain a
separate entity to those with their weapons trained on their unexpected visitor.

'No closer than ten feet,' Nighton advised in her earpiece.

While their own army of spectators watched from the windows
of the surrounding buildings, Marshall walked into the light, taking four more steps before stopping – David to his Goliath, facing
down the giant alone.

Winter moved aside as the tour group descended upon The Bronze
David and headed over to speak with Chambers, who looked to be
struggling with his radio.

'This is Chambers. Go ahead.' He received only an assortment
of clicks and crackles in response. 'Repeat: this is Chambers. Go
ahead!' he half-shouted, this time receiving an assortment of tuts
and headshakes from the geriatric crowd who were straining to
hear their guide as it was.

'Who was it?' Winter asked him.

'No idea. This *bloody* weather . . .' He huffed. 'I'm going to find a phone. You stay here.'

'OK.'

'Don't move.'

'Got it.'

'We're leaving the *second* I get back.'

'Right.'

Apparently satisfied, Chambers hurried away to flash a member of staff his ID card, Winter using the time to walk around some of the other pieces while the tour guide continued his spiel:

'. . . and of course depicts the biblical account of David and Goliath, which I presume we're all familiar with?'

A sea of grey hair bobbed up and down in reply.

'. . . Now, while not the original, this replica, cast in the late eighteen hundreds, is a work of art unto itself.'

Winter strolled over to the next statue, keeping one eye on the door for Chambers.

'. . . a perfect copy of Donatello's masterpiece in *every* way but one . . .'

Ears pricking, he joined the back of the audience.

'. . . Can anyone tell me what?'

Everybody looked blank, but then a frail hand rose in the air.

'Yes?'

'The sword . . . or lack thereof.'

'Very good! Front seat for you on the way home,' joked the guide. 'Now, does—'

'Hey! Excuse me!' called Winter, pushing his way to the front. 'Excuse me!'

'Can I help you?'

'What was that?'

'I'm sorry, sir, but as you can see, I've got my own group to—'

'About the sword!' Winter raised his voice over him. 'What about the sword?'

'That it doesn't have one,' replied the man irritably.

'Yeah, I can see that.'

'But the original does. In Florence, David is still holding the weapon he used to take the giant's head.'

A look of mounting concern on his face, Winter shoved his way free of the crowd and tore out of the hall after Chambers.

'Evan?' asked Marshall, the rain hammering painfully against her scalp. It was clear that he was afraid, his bloodshot eyes suggesting that he'd been crying as he grasped the bag tightly like a security blanket.

'Detective . . . Marshall?' he asked, his voice deep yet having a childlike quality to it.

'That's right,' she smiled. 'There are a lot of people looking for you.'

He frowned, unable to hear her over the rain.

She took a stride towards him.

'Do *not* take another step!' barked the voice in her ear.

Shooting an angry glare at the reception area, Marshall turned back to the giant:

'I said: there are a lot of people very worried about you!' she shouted. 'Where have you been?'

'With Robert.'

'Is he here?' she asked, looking up at their illuminated audience.

'No.'

'Do you know where he is?'

'No.'

'But he knows that you're here?' she asked him, edging a little closer.

'Yes,' Evan nodded, looking nervously at the armed officer to his left. 'He told me to give this to you or Detective Chambers only,' he said, patting the bloated bag in his arms.

Watching the bomb squad arrive on scene in the background, Marshall's face betrayed no reaction as she turned her attention back to the ominous gift from Coates. Fearing the answer, she knew the question she had to ask next:

'What's in the bag, Evan?'

*

The phone on Chambers' desk started to ring for a third time, prompting Lewis to actually get up and answer it on this occasion:

'DS Chambers' phone,' he said, taking a sip of his tea.

'Lewis?'

'Chambers?'

'Where's Marshall?'

'Apparently she went to deal with some sort of incident down in the lobby.'

'What sort of incident?'

'Some sort,' he reiterated.

'I need you to do something for me. Is there a sketchbook any-where on my desk?'

Taking another leisurely sip of his drink, Lewis glanced over the piles of paperwork besieging the computer:

'That would be a negative.'

'*Shit* . . . Is any of Marshall's stuff there?'

'Yes. Her coat and her bag.'

'Look in there,' Chambers told him.

'*Ummm*. I don't feel very comfortable with—'

'Just do it!'

'OK! OK!' said Lewis, stealing a quick look to see who was about before he started rummaging through a colleague's personal pos-sessions: '. . . Got it.'

'Good. Take it downstairs to Marshall.'

'But she's—'

'Put me through to reception and then take it straight down to Marshall. Tell her whatever she's dealing with, it can't be more important than this.'

'What's in the bag, Evan?'

He offered it out to her.

'Do *not* take it from him,' Nighton buzzed in her earpiece.

'Evan, you've done what Robert asked,' said Marshall softly. 'So, I need you to just put the bag down and step away.'

He shook his head: 'He told me to *give* it to you.'

'I can't take that from you. I need you to put it down for those people over there,' she said, gesturing to the bomb disposal officers waiting close by.

'No!' he yelled, beginning to get worked up.

As he retreated from them towards the building, a chorus of clicks emanated from the officers' weapons.

'Wait!' shouted Marshall, holding her arms out desperately on seeing the fear and confusion on his face.

Nighton was in her ear again:

'Don't you do it. I mean it, Marshall. Don't take that bag from him.'

'He'll run if I don't,' she told him decisively, forcing a smile onto her face before slowly approaching the terrified man.

Tentatively, he handed over the almost weightless bag.

'OK, Evan. You've done it. Now I need you to do *exactly* as I say, all right?'

He nodded.

'I need you to get down on your knees.'

'But . . . it's wet.'

'I know. But you have to.'

With great effort, the enormous man got down onto the ground yet still stood fractionally taller than her.

'And I need you to put your hands behind your head.' Watching her demonstrate, he interlocked his fingers. 'That's right . . . just like that.'

'Move in! Move in!' bellowed one of the officers, Evan shooting her a look of betrayal as he was shoved onto his front and his arms restrained.

'Detective Marshall,' buzzed Nighton. 'I want you to gently place the bag down and walk back towards me.'

Slowly, she followed his instructions, the bomb squad swarming in as Nighton came rushing out to meet her:

'I've got Detective Chambers on the phone for you.'

Re-entering the building, Marshall frowned on seeing her sketchbook out on the reception desk and picked up the receiver:

'Chambers?' she asked with a sniff, water streaming from her wet hair.

'What's going on?'

'Easton's giant just turned up outside.'

'. . . Alive?'

A puddle began to form around her feet, her saturated clothing freezing where it clung to her skin:

'He wanted to give us something: a bag . . . from Coates.'

'What was in it?'

She glanced out at the group waddling about almost comically in their cumbersome protective gear:

'Bomb squad's looking now.'

'. . . Have you got your sketchbook?' he asked her.

'Yes.' Picking up on the urgency in his voice, she decided not to enquire how it got there.

'*The Bronze David*,' he told her.

She flicked through the pages, each one another life lost, until she reached the penultimate picture:

'OK?'

'Is he holding a sword?'

'*Huh?*'

'A sword. Is David holding a sword?'

She stared down at Coates's sketch: '. . . No. Why?'

Turning to Winter, Chambers shook his head, both men sharing the same troubled look:

'He drew the replica,' said Chambers, desperately trying to put the pieces together. 'Why would he draw the copy?'

Across town, Marshall's expression mirrored her colleagues' as she watched a member of the bomb squad pick up the large sack and start walking towards the building.

'They're bringing in the bag now,' she told Chambers, the pages of the sketchbook flipping of their own accord as the officer came in from the storm.

Looking decidedly unimpressed, he dropped it at her feet:

'Safe,' he told Nighton, in a way that implied he'd wasted their time.

'What's in the bag?!' Chambers demanded.

With the phone clamped between her ear and shoulder, Marshall crouched down. Cautiously, she started to pull the drawstring opening apart to peer inside. And then she reached in, plunging her hand deep into the brittle contents.

'Marshall, what is it?!' he asked again.

'. . . Leaves,' she replied, removing a black and brown handful that cracked between her fingers. 'It's just leaves.'

'Laurel leaves?' asked Chambers as Winter paced anxiously.

'Hard to tell,' said Marshall. 'They're all dead. But . . . yes. I think so.'

'Why send us a bag of dead laurel leaves?' he pondered out loud.

'Eloise!' Winter gasped, grabbing Chambers' arm, his eyes wide with fear.

It took a moment for the pieces to fall into place – the bigger picture they had been missing all along: Coates leaving them the sketchbook, drawing a replica of a statue that never fit the pattern, the missing person guaranteed to catch their attention, and an empty threat against one of their own – all conspiring to push their already limited resources to breaking point, leaving him free to complete his work.

It was always all about her.

'Marshall,' said Chambers with an audible tremble in his voice. 'I need you to find out where Eloise was taken.'

Winter stared at him in confusion as Marshall asked: '. . . Taken?'

He hadn't wanted them to find out like this.

'. . . I had her arrested earlier this evening,' he admitted, now suspecting he had made a mistake.

'You did *what?!*' yelled Winter, shoving him backwards into the wall, his fists clenched.

'When were you going to tell us this?' asked Marshall, her concern outweighing her anger.

'Just find out where she is,' said Chambers. From the look Winter gave him, he knew that he would never forgive him for what he had done. 'Tell them he's coming for Eloise . . . Tell them to send everyone.'

CHAPTER 33

The city lights blurred into a neon dreamscape as Winter sped them through the traffic, Chambers relinquishing the keys, knowing that his own unresolved issues would only slow their progress. Feeling acutely aware of the pins that held his leg together, he gripped tightly to the seat with both hands, afraid that the car might flip every time they took a corner at speed.

'Can you get that? . . . Chambers? . . . Chambers, pick it up!' Winter yelled at him, swerving round the car in front, only narrowly missing an oncoming lorry.

The radio was chattering away, inaudible over the engine noise, its feeble orange backlight lost in the kaleidoscope of colour beyond the windows. Releasing his grip, he reached out for the handset:

'Chambers. Go ahead.'

'They never made it back to the station. No reply on Eloise's phone or the officer's radio,' advised Marshall, the panic in her voice evident, the wail of sirens coming through the speakers jarring with their own. Winter glanced over at him, too many emotions to read painted across his face. 'We're en route to the flat,' she continued. 'Local unit is three minutes out.'

'And the team at the woods?' asked Chambers, now holding a hand against the dashboard just to stay balanced.

'They've been alerted.'

Winter put his foot down when the traffic lights ahead turned red. Dropping the handset, Chambers grabbed hold of the door handle as they reached the junction, headlights coming at them from all directions, the sound of squealing brakes and car horns everywhere and then fading into the distance as they continued on.

Shaken, he groped around for the transmitter: 'Received. Out.'

'There they are!' said Winter, gesturing to the line of flashing blue lights tearing across the bridge.

Swinging the wheel round, they were both thrown fleetingly from their seats as the car mounted the kerb and careened over a pedestrianised area – and then again as they returned to the road on the other side, Winter accelerating aggressively up the ramp that led onto the bridge. As the traffic pulled aside to allow them past, he stamped his foot to the floor, quickly catching the rear of the convoy.

'*Come on. Come on. Come on,*' he muttered under his breath.

A road sign flashed by.

'Her flat or the woods?' Chambers asked him. It wasn't his decision to make with so much at stake.

The slip road started to form, the tarmac offshoot widening with every metre they travelled. Still undecided, Winter edged over the road markings, hovering half-in, half-out of both lanes as the fork in the road materialised.

'Her flat or the woods, Winter?!' cried Chambers, straightening his legs to push himself back into the seat.

Manoeuvring fully into the exit lane just as the metal barrier rushed past the windows like a train travelling in the opposite direction, Winter changed down a gear, the strobe of their colleagues' vehicles flickering in and out of view as he undertook them one by one.

Against the backdrop of a city sparkling in the rain, the summits of iconic skyscrapers claimed by the clouds, the cluster of blue lights continued along one of its countless concrete veins like the insufficient antidote to a systemic illness.

All but one: a single dancing light breaking away from the others.

A single dancing light, alone in the darkness.

Units were already on scene by the time Marshall jumped out of the car and sprinted inside, passing several of her colleagues on the stairs. She burst into the apartment to find two uniformed officers administering first aid to another, who was lying perfectly still, barely breathing, on the living-room floor. There were clear signs of a struggle.

'Eloise?' shouted Marshall. 'Eloise!'

'There's no one else here,' one of the officers told her. 'But the door was locked from the inside.'

She frowned at him.

'Neighbour heard screaming earlier,' announced one of the herd of people squeezing through the doorway. 'She presumed it was just music or on the TV.' He must have seen the look of utter desperation on her face because he then added: 'I'm sorry.'

She glanced down at the incapacitated man at her feet:

'Ambulance on its way?' she asked.

'Yes.'

'Tell them pancuronium bromide. Got that? Pan . . . cu . . . ronium,' she said, already heading through to the bedroom. 'We've got blood in here!' she called, following the crimson trail to a pair of stained scissors lying on the carpet.

'It's not his!' confirmed the officer tending to his colleague.

'Radio!' demanded Marshall, someone rushing over to hand her theirs.

'Chambers. Winter. Come in.'

Flinching when the passenger door glanced a wooden fence post, Chambers reached for the handset as Winter waterplaned them through the flooded entrance of Wimbledon Common and raced down the gravel track road.

'Go ahead,' he replied over the scream of the engine.

'She's not here. Repeat: she's not here!'

*

'Detective Marshall!' called the officer whose radio she'd borrowed, her heart sinking on seeing the look on his face as he gazed into the wardrobe in the corner.

'. . . Wait one,' she told Chambers, bracing herself for the worst as she rounded the bed, only now noticing the blood smeared on the wooden door. She took a deep breath as the officer moved aside. Expecting to see a body, her mouth fell open on peering straight through the wall into the apartment next door.

She turned to her dumbfounded colleague:

'Grab two others and go round the front . . . Go!' she told him when he failed to move, stepping inside the dark wardrobe and pushing the hanging clothes along the rail as she passed through an arch of carefully removed bricks into a nightmarish version of the room she had just left.

Discarded frameworks stood empty, lethal and open like giant mantraps waiting for her to stray too close. The dark walls, grey on first inspection, were in fact graffitied sketches layered atop one another . . . hundreds upon hundreds of them, each a work of art. And a head of human hair lay in the very centre of the room, as if the floor had swallowed a person whole. With hesitation, she knelt down and picked up the damp wig of tangled black hair as the front door burst open.

'*Jesus Christ*,' she muttered, holding the radio back up to her mouth: 'Chambers? . . . Chambers, come in.' The speaker just wailed with feedback. 'Chambers, come in!'

'Mr Christopher Ryan,' she heard one of the officers read aloud as he flicked through a handful of post addressed to the seven-year-old corpse currently residing in the medical examiner's freezer.

'Chambers!' she tried again, resting her face in her hands in defeat.

'Marshall?!' he yelled into the handset, gravel stones striking the car like bullets as they sped through a gauntlet of moving trees.

'It's the neighbour,' she told them. 'He must have been wearing a disguise of some sort. But Coates was her neighbour all along!'

Winter turned to Chambers with the expression of one who had slit her throat himself – recalling the hours-old memory of passing the long-haired man on the stairs.

'He's got her,' continued Marshall, 'and he's been right under our noses the entire time.'

Chambers held down the *transmit* button – broadcasting only background noise, at a loss as to what to say:

'. . . Copy that.'

Skidding into the parking area adjacent to the windmill, Winter leapt out before the car had even fully stopped moving, the headlights illuminating his path as he sprinted into the trees.

'Winter! Winter, wait!' shouted Chambers as he climbed out after him, his words hushed by the wind, dirt and debris pelting him from all angles, the sky literally raining leaves. 'Winter?!' he called again, following him into the woods but jarring his leg painfully only a few steps in on the uneven ground.

The sound was like nothing he had ever heard before: the rustle of a billion leaves like a rattlesnake coiling to strike, the creaking of branches overhead interspersed with sharp cracks as mighty centenarians lost another limb, and the roar of the wind ripping through the trees like great waves crashing on the rocks.

'Eloise?!' he heard Winter shout just a little way ahead. 'Eloise, where are you?!' In agony, Chambers staggered towards the sound. 'Eloise?! . . .Eloise?!'

But then, though sure he was catching up, the calls fell silent.

'Winter?!' he yelled, receiving no reply.

Ignoring the pain, he ran blindly through the drowned woodland with a building sense of foreboding on recognising the trees that now surrounded him: alive amid a forest of death.

Emerging from the treeline, he stumbled into a small clearing, complete with swollen stream fit for a river god, where Winter had collapsed to his knees in the dirt.

'Winter?' asked Chambers.

He didn't react.

'. . . Winter?'

Approaching slowly, Chambers looked to the area of disturbed leaves beyond his friend, now understanding the reason for his silence.

'Oh, God,' he whispered, limping over to the two bodies locked in position against the storm by an intricate metal frame: Robert Coates still in pursuit of his beloved, even in death, his left hand wrapped forever around Eloise's naked body as she turned away from him one final time.

Chambers gently pressed his fingers to her throat . . . the temperature of her skin telling him all he needed to know. He glanced back at Winter, wishing he had some words of reassurance for him, but nothing came.

Turning to regard Coates's lifeless form, he performed the same check, placing the tips of two fingers against his neck . . .

Startled, Chambers pulled his hand away and was overcome with a pronounced sense of déjà vu, of scaling an icy ladder up to the frozen *Thinker* all those years earlier, the static man's gaze now on him, unnervingly watching his every move, the shallow rise and fall of his chest gradually building pace.

'Winter!' Chambers called without breaking eye contact with the living statue. 'I need you here. Now!'

With trepidation, Winter got to his feet. Consciously avoiding looking in Eloise's direction, he made his way over as Chambers produced a small metal tin from his inside pocket, opening it up to reveal the thin vial, syringe and selection of needles contained inside.

'What is that?' Winter asked him, his voice breaking.

'The antidote. I had Sykes make it up.' Eyes instantly wide, he looked over at Eloise. 'Not for her,' Chambers told him sadly. '. . . For him.' As Winter slowly turned to face Coates, Chambers didn't even recognise his friend any more – all the rage, all the pain, all the power he suddenly held over the other man's life somehow transforming his features. 'He's still alive,' he explained, handing over the tin and stepping away. 'It's your call.'

'My call?' Winter asked in confusion, staring down at the metal box in his hands as the two statues rocked gently in the relentless wind.

Chambers nodded: 'Your call. But remember – *this* is what he wants. If he dies, he wins.'

Winter considered their predicament but only for a moment:

'Honestly, I don't even care any more. I just want him gone,' he said, a broken man, reaching in and removing the glass vial before dropping it to the ground.

When Chambers made no effort to intervene, he raised his foot to stamp Coates out of their lives once and for all . . . but then hesitated, the conflict clear on his face as he looked from the faux-god, powerless to stop him – to Eloise, so elegant and still – and then back to his partner. Foot trembling with indecision, he took a steadying breath and gritted his teeth, fixing his eyes on the fragile vial beneath him . . .

With tears streaking down his face, he screamed into the wind and stepped away.

'. . . Do it,' he said, closing his eyes as though he couldn't bear to watch.

'You're sure?'

'Just do it.'

Aware that it might already be too late, Chambers hurried over, the incapacitated man's fearful eyes following him as he knelt down to retrieve the vial, the rigid fingers twitching ever so slightly on being prised free from Eloise and laid down onto the ground. Assembling the injection, Chambers looked back at Winter, giving him one last chance to protest, but he remained silent. Sinking the needle deep into Coates's neck, he hovered his thumb over the plunger:

'Robert . . . Robert, can you hear me?' he whispered into the dying man's ear. Slowly, the dark eyes found him. '*Only the living can suffer as you will*,' Chambers recited in satisfaction, depressing his thumb and emptying the entire contents of the syringe into his bloodstream.

Handcuffing Coates to his own metal frame, he got back up to re-join his colleague as the trees bowed impossibly overhead, eclipsing the sky.

They stood in silence for a few moments.

'I'm going to go call an ambulance,' Winter told him, turning his back on the scene, the sight of Coates reluctantly coming back to life beside Eloise's dramatic corpse too much for him.

Unsure what to say, Chambers gave him a pat on the back and watched him walk away. Within just five steps, he had disappeared entirely into the moving trees.

Now alone, Chambers tentatively approached the woman that he felt he had so utterly failed – Eloise: delicate, beautiful, and frozen in flight, as he took a moment to regard Coates's final tragic masterpiece.

'I'm so sorry,' he whispered, now on the verge of tears himself.

Dazed, he wanted to cover her up, although he knew that he couldn't. The thin robe, placed with precision to look as though it had slipped naturally off her body, turned inch by inch into the mound of soil and twigs that now consumed her legs. And her hands, lovingly removed, replaced with two thriving branches of deep-green laurel leaves – the culmination of Robert Coates's life's work closing with the beginning of her metamorphosis.

Seven months later . . .

Thursday 3 July

1997

CHAPTER 34

Winter gazed up at the supermarket's bright-orange signage, supposing it had always just been a matter of time before he would have to step back through its doors. Cursing when he realised he was already late, he ceased his inane musings and hurried inside.

'. . . We have since discovered that Partridge was in the bar at the same time as this man,' said Marshall, holding the surveillance camera image up for the entire Homicide department to see, the nerve-wracking experience her first time presenting at their weekly progress meeting. 'No name as of yet, but a known associate of none other than Charlie Slattery,' she announced, catching Chambers' eye as the room erupted into excitable murmurs at her revelation.

She had asked him to sit at the front for moral support, not that it seemed she needed it – as the department's second-newest hire, she had just blown the case wide open.

'So, Detective,' started Wainwright from her spot perched against the windowsill. 'How do you intend to proceed?'

At that moment, the door swung open into Lewis as a flustered and dishevelled Winter came bundling into the room with two large boxes. There were jeers from his colleagues, who pelted him with screwed-up paper balls as he made his way to the front of the room.

'Hey! . . . Hey!' he complained, setting the boxes down.

'You're late, new guy!' someone heckled him.

'Because I was picking up you lots' *bloody* doughnuts!' he complained.

'Please just sit down,' Wainwright told him before addressing the rest of the boisterous room: 'OK. Settle down. Settle down!'

A few straggling projectiles bounced off Winter's head as he took a seat beside Chambers, who appeared mildly amused by the whole thing.

'Hey.'

'Hey,' replied Chambers.

'. . . Why is there a page ripped out of your notebook?'

Shaking her head, Wainwright turned back to Marshall:

'My apologies, Detective. How would you like to proceed?'

'I need to find the man in the photo. He's our only link between them, but that's going to take a lot of time and legwork. I don't think I can do it on my own.'

'Nor would I expect you to,' said Wainwright simply. 'So . . . who do you need?'

The question caught Marshall off guard. But then, from her position at the front of the homicide meeting room, having just apparently been handed her very own investigation to lead, she glanced over at Chambers and Winter bickering in the corner and smiled . . .

CHAPTER 35

Assuming her usual position between the fire alarm and that black scuff on the wall she couldn't get out no matter what she tried, Denise Smith waited as the prison officers escorted their inmate along the corridor for his thirty minutes of recreation time.

With bulbous white bandages wrapped around his forearms, another mess she had been asked to clean up, the prisoner shuffled by, Denise keeping her eyes glued to the floor as he passed, always feeling a little guilty about her daily visits.

'All yours!' one of the officers called back to her.

Pushing herself off the wall, Denise dutifully grabbed the handle of the mop and wheeled her bucket into the vacated cell.

She closed her eyes, took a deep breath in anticipation, and then opened them again.

As one of the only people to ever see inside, she felt it her responsibility to take a few moments to fully appreciate her surroundings, where every last inch of the insipid walls, ceiling and floor was now adorned in breathtaking artwork: delicate pencil sketches, moody smudges carving perfect shadows, pastel portraits alive with colour – every one unique, every one a work of unrivalled brilliance and, as always, every one depicting the exact same subject, the face of the same beautiful woman, time and time again.

But then she noticed something, something that didn't belong surrounded by so much love and lament: a lone figure formed out of charcoal and scratches, the anger in the careless scribbles and blurred lines radiating off it, as if it had been clawed out of the wall. Moving a little closer, she peered at the cheerless image, recognising the prisoner's own likeness captured in the face of the triumphant warrior, the severed head of his snake-haired adversary held high – dark-skinned and vacant-eyed – a trophy for all the gods to see.

Not liking it one bit, she pulled a face and stepped back to appraise the rest of her own personal art gallery.

'Incredible,' she muttered, shaking her head in awe. As she had come to expect, the detail in the beautiful woman's varying expressions was so lifelike that Denise almost felt as though she knew her. 'Just incredible,' she said again, wringing the mop out over the soapy water before raising it to her favourite of today's offerings and starting to scrub.

THE END

ACKNOWLEDGEMENTS

Firstly, I'd like to thank my new project editor Georgia Goodall for reminding me to actually include these this time, seeing as for *Endgame* someone somehow forgot to remind me not to forget to remind them that I most likely would (and subsequently did) completely forget – an unintentional F-you to all the wonderful people who made that book possible.

So, in no particular order:

A massive thank you to my editor Sam Eades. As someone who could be said to be editorial-adverse, I can honestly say it's been a blast working on this book together and I look forward to many, many more. Also on the publishing side of things: Ellen Turner, Yadira Da Trindade, Rachel Neely, Jade Craddock, Anna Valentine, Katie Espiner and the rest of the Hachette team.

As always, thanks to my amazing agent Susan Armstrong for her advice and guidance and to all the team at C&W: Dorcas Rogers, Tracy England, Jake Smith-Bosanquet, Alexander Cochran, Kate Burton and Matilda Ayris to name a few.

. . . To my ¾ feral cat, Chonky, for permitting me to live long enough to finish the thing, and to all the rest of my family: L2theB, Sarah, Ma & Ossie, Melo & Indiana B, Bob & KP.

Not forgetting my very good friends Rob Parsons and Matt Muschol for their endless support and for probably being even more excited about this whole 'being a writer' thing than I am.

A sincere thank you to my readers for their loyalty and tireless enthusiasm, and to all the book bloggers out there who are getting behind this book and helping make sure it gets noticed amid a world of noise.

... And finally, a very, very special thank you to Alexandra Limon for lending her talents to the beautiful illustrations that made this novel come alive.

'Til next time . . .

Loved Mimic?

Why not try the trilogy that began it all?

||||||||||||||||||||||||||||||||||||||||||||||||||||||||||||||||||||||||||||||||||||||||||||||||

Start with *Ragdoll* . . .

A body is discovered with the dismembered parts of six victims stitched together, nicknamed by the press as the 'Ragdoll'. Assigned to the shocking case are Detective William 'Wolf' Fawkes, recently reinstated to the London Met, and his former partner Detective Emily Baxter.

THE GLOBAL BESTSELLER

'SURPRISING AND ORIGINAL'
Sophie Hannah

'SUPERB THRILLER WRITING'
Peter Robinson

RAGDOLL

**ONE BODY.
SIX VICTIMS.
NO SUSPECTS.**

'A BRILLIANT, BREATHLESS THRILLER'
M J Arlidge

'A STAR IS BORN'
Simon Toyne

DANIEL COLE

The 'Ragdoll Killer' taunts the police by releasing a list of names to the media, and the dates on which he intends to murder them. With six people to save, can Fawkes and Baxter catch a killer when the world is watching their every move?

Devour *Hangman* . . .

A body is found hanging from Brooklyn Bridge, the word 'BAIT' carved into the chest.

In London a copycat killer strikes, branded with the word 'PUPPET', forcing DCI Emily Baxter into an uneasy partnership with the detectives on the case, Special Agents Rouche and Curtis.

Each time they trace a suspect, the killer is one step ahead. With the body count rising on both sides of the Atlantic, can they learn to trust each other and identify who is holding the strings before it is too late?

Finish with *Endgame.*

A locked room.

A dead body.

A secret that went to the grave.

W hen retired
police officer
Finlay Shaw is found
dead in a locked room,
everyone thinks it's
suicide. But disgraced
detective William 'Wolf'
Fawkes isn't so sure.

Together with his
former partner detective
Emily Baxter and private
detective Alex Edmunds,
Wolf's team begin to dig
into Shaw's early days on
the beat. Was Shaw as
innocent as he seemed?
Or is there more to his past
than he'd ever let on?

But not everyone wants Wolf back. As his investigation draws him ever deeper into police corruption, it
will not only be his career on the line, but the lives of
those he holds closest as well.

Go back to where it all began . . .

Read on for an extract from
Ragdoll

CHAPTER 1

Saturday 28 June 2014

3.50 a.m.

Wolf groped blindly for his mobile phone, which was edging further across the laminate floor with every vibration. Slowly the darkness began to disassemble itself into the unfamiliar shapes of his new apartment. The sweat-sodden sheet clung to his skin as he crawled off the mattress and over to the buzzing annoyance.

'Wolf,' he answered, relieved that he had at least got that right as he searched the wall for a light switch.

'It's Simmons.'

Wolf flicked a switch and sighed heavily when the weak yellow light reminded him where he was; he was tempted to turn it off again. The tiny bedroom consisted of four walls, a worn double mattress on the floor and a solitary light bulb. The claustrophobic box was sweltering thanks to his landlord, who still had not chased the previous tenant up for a window key. Normally this would not have been such an issue in London; however, Wolf had managed to coincide his move with one of England's uncharacteristic heatwaves, which had been dragging on for almost two weeks.

'Don't sound so pleased,' said Simmons.

'What time is it?' yawned Wolf.

'Ten to four.'

'Aren't I off this weekend?'

'Not any more. I need you to join me at a crime scene.'

'Next to your desk?' asked Wolf, only half-joking as he hadn't seen his boss leave the office in years.

'Funny. They let me out for this one.'

'That bad, huh?'

There was a pause on the other end of the line before Simmons answered: 'It's pretty bad. Got a pen?'

Wolf rummaged through one of the stacked boxes in the doorway and found a biro to scribble on the back of his hand with.

'OK. Go ahead.'

Out of the corner of his eye, he noticed a light flickering across his kitchen cupboard.

'Flat 108 . . .' started Simmons.

As Wolf walked into his ill-equipped kitchenette, he was dazzled by blue flashing lights strobing through the small window.

'. . . Trinity Towers—'

'Hibbard Road, Kentish Town?' Wolf interrupted, peering down over dozens of police cars, reporters, and the evacuated residents of the block opposite.

'How the hell did you know that?'

'I *am* a detective.'

'Well, you can also be our number one suspect then. Get down here.'

'Will do. I just need to . . .' Wolf trailed off, realising that Simmons had already hung up.

Between the intermittent flashes, he noticed the steady orange light coming from the washing machine and remembered that he had put his work clothes in before going to bed. He looked around at the dozens of identical cardboard boxes lining the walls:

'Bollocks.'

Five minutes later Wolf was pushing his way through the crowd of spectators that had congregated outside his building. He approached a police officer and flashed his warrant card, expecting to stroll straight through the cordon; however, the young constable snatched the card out of his hand and examined it closely, glancing up sceptically at the imposing figure dressed in swimming shorts and a faded '93 Bon Jovi: *Keep the Faith* tour T-shirt.

'Officer Layton-Fawkes?' the constable asked doubtfully.

Wolf winced at the sound of his own pretentious name:

'Detective Sergeant Fawkes, yes.'

'As in – Courtroom-Massacre Fawkes?'

'It's pronounced William . . . May I?' Wolf gestured towards the apartment building.

The young man handed Wolf's warrant card back and held the tape up for him to pass under.

'Need me to show you up?' he asked.

Wolf glanced down at his floral shorts, bare knees and work shoes.

'You know what? I think I'm doing pretty well by myself.'

The officer grinned.

'Fourth floor,' he told Wolf. 'And be careful heading up there alone; it's a shitty neighbourhood.'

Wolf sighed heavily once more, entered through the bleach-fragranced hallway, and stepped into the lift. The buttons for the second and fifth floors were missing and a brown liquid had dried over the remainder of the control panel. Using all of his detective skills to ascertain that it was either poo, rust or Coca-Cola, he used the bottom of his T-shirt, Richie Sambora's face, to push the button.

He had been in hundreds of identical lifts in his time: a seamless metal box, installed by councils all over the country. It had no floor covering, no mirrors and no protruding lights or fixtures. There was absolutely nothing for the underprivileged residents to destroy or steal from their own life-enriching piece of equipment, so they had settled for spray-painting obscenities all over the walls instead. Wolf only had time to learn that Johnny Ratcliff was both 'ere' and 'a gay' before the doors scraped open at the fourth floor.

Over a dozen people were scattered along the silent corridor. Most looked a little shaken and eyed Wolf's outfit disapprovingly, except for one scruffy man wearing a forensics badge, who nodded in approval and gave him a thumbs up as he passed. A very faint but familiar smell intensified as Wolf approached the open doorway at the end of the hallway. It was the unmistakable smell of death. People who work around such things quickly become attuned to the unique mix of stale air, shit, piss and putrefying flesh.

Wolf took a step back from the door when he heard running footsteps from inside. A young woman burst out through the open doorway, dropped to her knees and then vomited in the corridor in front of him. He waited politely for an opportune moment to ask her to move when another set of footsteps approached. He instinctively took another step back before Detective Sergeant Emily Baxter came skidding into the corridor.

'Wolf! I thought I saw you lurking out here,' she roared across the hushed hallway. 'Seriously, how cool is this?'

She glanced down at the woman retching on the floor between them.

'Could you puke somewhere else, please?'

The woman sheepishly crawled out of their way. Baxter grabbed Wolf by the arm and excitedly led him into the apartment. Nearly a decade his junior, Baxter was almost as tall as him. Her dark brown hair turned black under the gloom of the unimpressive entrance hall and, as always, she wore dark make-up that made her attractive eyes appear abnormally large. Dressed in a fitted shirt and smart trousers, she looked him up and down with a mischievous grin.

'No one told me it was a mufti day.'

Wolf refused to rise to the bait, knowing that she would quickly lose interest if he only remained quiet.

'How pissed is Chambers gonna be he's missed this?' she beamed.

'Personally I'd take the Caribbean cruise over a dead body too,' said Wolf, bored.

Baxter's huge eyes widened in surprise: 'Simmons didn't tell you?'

'Tell me what?'

She led him through the crowded apartment, which had been dimly lit in the glow of a dozen strategically placed torches. Although not overpowering, the smell grew steadily stronger. Wolf could tell that the fetid source was close by because of the number of flies zipping about feverishly above his head.

The flat had high ceilings, contained no furniture, and was considerably larger than Wolf's own, but was no more pleasant. The yellowed walls were peppered with holes through which the antiquated wiring and dusty insulation bled freely onto the bare floor. Neither the bathroom suite nor the kitchen looked to have been updated since the 1960s.

'Tell me what?' he asked her again.

'This is the *one*, Wolf,' said Baxter, ignoring the question, 'a once-in-a-career case.'

Wolf was distracted, mentally sizing up the second bedroom and wondering whether he was being overcharged for his poxy box of a flat across the road. They rounded the corner into the crowded main room and he automatically scanned the floor, between the assorted equipment and pairs of legs, for a body.

'Baxter!'

She stopped and turned to him impatiently.

'What didn't Simmons tell me?'

Behind her, a group of people, standing in front of the large floor-to-ceiling window that dominated the room, moved aside. Before she could answer, Wolf had stumbled away, his eyes fixed on a point somewhere above them: the one light source that the police had not brought with them: a spotlight on a dark stage . . .

The naked body, contorted into an unnatural pose, appeared to be floating a foot above the uneven floorboards. It had its back to the room, looking out through the enormous window. Hundreds of almost invisible threads held the figure in place, which, in turn, were anchored by two industrial metal hooks.

It took Wolf a moment to identify the most unnerving feature of the surreal scene before him: the black leg attached to the white torso. Unable to comprehend what he was seeing, he pushed his way further into the room. As he drew closer, he noticed the huge stitches binding the mismatched body parts together, the skin tented where the material punctured through: one black male leg, one white; a large male hand on one side, a tanned female counterpart on the other; tangled jet-black hair hanging unsettlingly over a pale, freckled, slender, female torso.

Baxter was back at his side, clearly relishing the look of revulsion on his face:

'He didn't tell you . . . One dead body – six victims!' she whispered gleefully in his ear.

Wolf's gaze dropped to the floor. He was standing on the shadow cast by the grotesque corpse and, in this simplified state, the proportions appeared even more jarring, gaps of light distorting the joins between the limbs and body.

'What the hell are the press doing out there already?' Wolf heard his chief shout at no one in particular. 'I swear, this department has got more leaks than the *Titanic*. If I find anyone talking to them, they'll be suspended!'

Wolf smiled, knowing full well that Simmons was only play-acting the part of the stereotypical boss. They had known one another for over a decade and, until the Khalid incident, Wolf had considered him a friend. Beneath the forced bravado, Simmons was in fact an intelligent, caring, and competent police officer.

'Fawkes!' Simmons strode over to them. He often struggled not to address his staff by their nicknames. He was almost a foot shorter than Wolf, was now in his fifties, and had developed a managerial belly. 'Nobody told me it was a mufti day.'

Wolf heard Baxter snigger. He decided to adopt the same tactic that he had used on her by ignoring the comment. After an uncomfortable silence, Simmons turned to Baxter.

'Where's Adams?' he asked.

'Who?'

'Adams. Your new protégé.'

'Edmunds?'

'Right. Edmunds.'

'How am I supposed to know?'

'Edmunds!' Simmons bellowed across the busy room.

'Work with him a lot now?' asked Wolf quietly, unable to hide the hint of jealousy in his voice, which made Baxter smile.

'Babysitting duty,' she whispered. 'He's the transfer from Fraud, only seen a few dead bodies. He might even cry later on.'

The young man bumbling through the crowd towards them was only twenty-five years old, stick-thin and immaculately presented, apart from his scruffy strawberry-blond hair. He was holding a notebook at the ready and smiled eagerly at the chief inspector.

'Where are forensics up to?' asked Simmons.

Edmunds flicked back a few pages in his book.

'Helen said that her team still haven't found a single drop of blood anywhere in the apartment. They have confirmed that all six body parts are from different victims and were roughly amputated, probably with a hacksaw.'

'Did *Helen* mention anything we didn't already know?' spat Simmons.

'Actually, yes. Due to the absence of blood and lack of constriction of the blood vessels around the amputation wounds . . .'

Simmons rolled his eyes and checked his watch.

'. . . we can be certain that the parts were removed post-mortem,' finished Edmunds, looking pleased with himself.

'That's some fantastic police work, Edmunds,' said Simmons sarcastically before shouting out: 'Could someone please cancel the milk carton ad for the man missing a head? Thank you!'

Edmunds' smile vanished. Wolf caught Simmons' eye and smirked. They had both been on the receiving end of similar putdowns in their time. It was all part of the training.

'I just meant that whoever the arms and legs belonged to are definitely dead as well. They will know more once they get the body back to the lab,' Edmunds mumbled self-consciously.

Wolf noticed the reflection of the body in the dark windows. Realising that he had not yet seen it from the front, he moved round to look.

'What have *you* got, Baxter?' asked Simmons.

'Not a lot. Slight damage to the keyhole, possibly picked. We've got officers questioning the neighbours outside, but so far no one's seen or heard a thing. Oh, and there's nothing wrong with the electrics – every bulb in the apartment's been removed except for the one above the victim . . . s, like it's on show or something.'

'What about you Fawkes, any ideas? Fawkes?'

Wolf was gazing up at the body's dark-skinned face.

'I'm sorry, are we boring you?'

'No. Sorry. Even in this heat, this thing's only just beginning to stink, which means the killer either murdered all six victims last night, which seems unlikely, or he's had the bodies on ice.'

'Agreed. We'll get someone to look into recent break-ins at cold-storage units, supermarkets, restaurants, anywhere with an industrial-sized freezer room,' said Simmons.

'And see if any of the neighbours heard drilling,' said Wolf.

'Drilling is a reasonably common sound,' blurted Edmunds, who regretted the outburst when three pairs of angry eyes turned on him.

'If this is the killer's masterpiece,' continued Wolf, 'there's no way they would risk it dropping out of the ceiling and just being a pile of bits by the time we got here. Those hooks will be drilled into load-bearing metal beams. Someone should have heard it.'

Simmons nodded: 'Baxter, get someone on it.'

'Chief, could I borrow you a moment?' asked Wolf as Baxter and Edmunds moved away. He pulled on a pair of disposable gloves and lifted a handful of knotted black hair away from the gruesome figure's face. It was male. The eyes were open, the expression unnervingly calm considering the victim's clearly violent end. 'Look familiar?'

Simmons walked round to join Wolf by the chilly window and crouched down to better examine the dark face. After a few moments, he shrugged.

'It's Khalid,' said Wolf.

'That's impossible.'

'Is it?'

Simmons looked up again at the lifeless face. Gradually his expression of scepticism transformed into one of deep concern.

'Baxter!' he shouted. 'I need you and Adams—'

'*Edmunds.*'

'. . . over at Belmarsh Prison. Ask the governor to take you directly to Naguib Khalid.'

'Khalid?' Baxter asked in shock, involuntarily glancing at Wolf.

'Yes, Khalid. Phone me the moment you've seen him alive. Go!'

Wolf looked out towards his block opposite. Many of the windows remained dark, others contained excited faces filming the spectacle below on their mobile phones, presumably hoping to capture something grisly to entertain their friends with in the morning. Apparently they were unable to see into the dimly lit murder scene that they would otherwise have had front row seats for.

Wolf was able to see into his own flat, a few windows over. In his hurry, he had left all of the lights on. He spotted a cardboard box, at the bottom of a pile, with the words 'Trousers and Shirts' scrawled across it.

'*Aha!*'

Simmons walked back over to Wolf and rubbed his tired eyes. They stood quietly, either side of the suspended body, watching the first signs of morning pollute the dark sky. Even over the noise of the room, they could hear the peaceful sound of bird-song outside.

'So, most disturbing thing you've ever seen then?' Simmons joked wearily.

'A close second,' replied Wolf without taking his eyes off the growing patch of deep blue sky.

'Second? Do I even want to know what tops this – this thing?' Simmons took another reluctant look at the hanging collection of dismemberments.

Wolf gently tapped the figure's outstretched right arm. The palm looked pale in comparison to the rest of the tanned skin and the perfectly manicured purple nails. Dozens of silk-like threads supported the outstretched hand and a dozen more held the extended index finger in place.

He checked that no one was listening in to their conversation and then leaned across to whisper to Simmons.

'It's pointing into my apartment window.'